It wasn't fear that I felt in my gut. Not trepidation, either; this was something worse.

It was excitement—polluting my thought process, strong enough that it was almost intoxicating. This was what I was made for. I steadied my pulse and concentrated on the mission at hand.

Something stirred in the ship—I felt it.

By Jamie Sawyer

THE LAZARUS WAR

ARTEFACT: BOOK ONE

Jamie Sawyer

www.orbitbooks.net

Copyright © 2015 by Jamie Sawyer
Excerpt from *The Lazarus War: Legion* copyright © 2015
by Jamie Sawyer
Excerpt from *Tracer* copyright © 2015 by Rob Boffard

Orbit
Hachette Book Group
1290 Avenue of the Americas
New York, NY 10104
www.orbitbooks.net

Printed in the United States of America

First U.S. ebook edition: March 2015
First U.S. mass-market edition: February 2016
Originally published in Great Britain by Orbit Books

10 9 8 7 6 5 4 3 2 1

Orbit is an imprint of Hachette Book Group.
The Orbit name and logo are trademarks of Little, Brown Book
Group Limited.

The Hachette Speakers Bureau provides a wide range of
authors for speaking events. To find out more, go to
www.hachettespeakersbureau.com or call (866) 376-6591.

The publisher is not responsible for websites (or their content)
that are not owned by the publisher.

ISBN: 978-0-316-38637-1

To Louise—even though I missed you with the lemonade, it all turned out for the best

ACKNOWLEDGEMENTS

I genuinely couldn't have written this book without the help of my family.

First and foremost, my wife Louise has shown monumental patience by reading the numerous drafts of this book and motivating me through the writing process. I know that it's more tiring than it looks! Thanks for putting up with me.

I'd also like to thank my brother for reading the manuscript (I know how you feel about reading, Rich!).

My agent Robert Dinsdale of Dinsdale Imber Literary Agency assisted me greatly in getting the book into shape: I promise that the second book won't be as much work…

My editor, Anna Jackson at Orbit, has also been supportive throughout and provided great feedback.

Thanks also to Yesica Coronel Scull (who provided Spanish translations for Martinez) and Stephen Deas (who kindly reviewed the science – any errors or omissions are purely my own, for the sake of telling a good story!).

CHAPTER ONE

NEW HAVEN

Radio chatter filled my ears. Different voices, speaking over one another.

Is this it? I asked myself. *Will I find her?*

"*That's a confirm on the identification: AFS* New Haven. *She went dark three years ago.*"

"*Null-shields are blown. You have a clean approach.*"

It was a friendly, at least. Nationality: Arab Freeworlds. But it wasn't her. A spike of disappointment ran through me. *What did I expect?* She was gone.

"*Arab Freeworlds Starship* New Haven, *this is Alliance FOB* Liberty Point: *do you copy? Repeat, this is FOB* Liberty Point: *do you copy?*"

"*Bird's not squawking.*"

"*That's a negative on the hail. No response to automated or manual contact.*"

I patched into the external cameras to get a better view of the target. She was a big starship, a thousand metres long. NEW HAVEN had been stencilled on the hull, but the white lettering was chipped and worn. Underneath the name was a numerical ID tag and a barcode with a corporate sponsor logo – an advert for some long-forgotten mining corporation. As an afterthought something in Arabic had been scrawled beside the logo.

New Haven was a civilian-class colony vessel; one of the mass-produced models commonly seen throughout the border systems, capable of long-range quantum-space jumps but with precious little defensive capability. Probably older than me, retrofitted by a dozen governments and corporations before she became known by her current name. The ship looked painfully vulnerable, to my military eye: with a huge globe-like bridge and command module at the nose, a slender midsection and an ugly drive propulsion unit at the aft.

She wouldn't be any good in a fight, that was for sure.

"Reading remote sensors now. I can't get a clean internal analysis from the bio-scanner."

On closer inspection, there was evidence to explain the lifeless state of the ship. Puckered rips in the hull-plating suggested that she had been fired upon by a spaceborne weapon. Nothing catastrophic, but enough to disable the main drive: as though whoever, or whatever, had attacked the ship had been toying with her. Like the hunter that only cripples its prey, but chooses not to deliver the killing blow.

"AFS New Haven, *this is* Liberty Point. *You are about to be boarded in accordance with military code alpha-zeroniner. You have trespassed into the Krell Quarantine Zone. Under military law in*

force in this sector we have authority to board your craft, in order to ensure your safety."

The ship had probably been drifting aimlessly for months, maybe even years. There was surely nothing alive within that blasted metal shell.

"*That's a continued no response to the hail. Authorising weapons-free for away team. Proceed with mission as briefed.*"

"This is Captain Harris," I said. "Reading you loud and clear. That's an affirmative on approach."

"*Copy that. Mission is good to go, good to go. Over to you, Captain. Wireless silence from here on in.*"

Then the communication-link was severed and there was a moment of silence. *Liberty Point*, and all of the protections that the station brought with it, suddenly felt a very long way away.

Our Wildcat armoured personnel shuttle rapidly advanced on the *New Haven*. The APS was an ugly, functional vessel – made to ferry us from the base of operations to the insertion point, and nothing more. It was heavily armoured but completely unarmed; the hope was that, under enemy fire, the triple-reinforced armour would prevent a hull breach before we reached the objective. Compared to the goliath civilian vessel, it was an insignificant dot.

I sat upright in the troop compartment, strapped into a safety harness. On the approach to the target, the Wildcat APS gravity drive cancelled completely: everything not strapped down drifted in free fall. There were no windows or view-screens, and so I relied on the external camera-feeds to track our progress. This was proper cattle-class, even in deep-space.

I wore a tactical combat helmet, for more than just protection. Various technical data was being relayed to the heads-up display – projected directly onto the interior of the face-plate. Swarms of glowing icons, warnings and data-reads scrolled overhead. For a rookie, the flow of information would've been overwhelming but to me this was second nature. Jacked directly into my combat-armour, with a thought I cancelled some data-streams, examined others.

Satisfied with what I saw, I yelled into the communicator: "Squad, sound off."

Five members of the unit called out in turn, their respective life-signs appearing on my HUD.

"Jenkins." The only woman on the team; small, fast and sparky. Jenkins was a gun nut, and when it came to military operations obsessive-compulsive was an understatement. She served as the corporal of the squad and I wouldn't have had it any other way.

"Blake." Youngest member of the team, barely out of basic training when he was inducted. Fresh-faced and always eager. His defining characteristics were extraordinary skill with a sniper rifle, and an incredible talent with the opposite sex.

"Martinez." He had a background in the Alliance Marine Corps. With his dark eyes and darker fuzz of hair, he was Venusian American stock. He promised that he had Hispanic blood, but I doubted that the last few generations of Martinez's family had even set foot on Earth.

"Kaminski." Quick-witted; a fast technician as well as a good shot. Kaminski had been with me from the start. Like me, he had been Alliance Special Forces. He and Jenkins rubbed each other up the wrong way, like brother and sister. Expertly printed above the face-shield of his helmet were the words BORN TO KILL.

Then, finally: "Science Officer Olsen, ah, alive."

Our guest for this mission sat to my left – the science officer attached to my squad. He shook uncontrollably, alternating between breathing hard and retching hard. Olsen's communicator was tuned to an open channel, and none of us were spared his pain. I remotely monitored his vital signs on my suit display – he was in a bad way. I was going to have to keep him close during the op.

"First contact for you, Mr Olsen?" Blake asked over the general squad comms channel.

Olsen gave an exaggerated nod.

"Yes, but I've conducted extensive laboratory studies of the enemy." He paused to retch some more, then blurted: "And I've read many mission debriefs on the subject."

"That counts for nothing out here, my friend," said Jenkins. "You need to face off against the enemy. Go toe to toe, in our space."

"That's the problem, Jenkins," Blake said. "This isn't our space, according to the Treaty."

"You mean the Treaty that was signed off before you were born, Kid?" Kaminski added, with a dry snigger. "We have company this mission – it's a special occasion. How about you tell us how old you are?"

As squad leader, I knew Blake's age but the others didn't. The mystery had become a source of amusement to the rest of the unit. I could've given Kaminski the answer easily enough, but that would have spoiled the entertainment. This was a topic to which he returned every time we were operational.

"Isn't this getting old?" said Blake.

"No, it isn't – just like you, Kid."

Blake gave him the finger – his hands chunky and oversized inside heavily armoured gauntlets.

"Cut that shit out," I growled over the communicator. "I need you all frosty and on point. I don't want things turning nasty out there. We get aboard the *Haven*, download the route data, then bail out."

I'd already briefed the team back at the *Liberty Point*, but no operation was routine where the Krell were concerned. Just the possibility of an encounter changed the game. I scanned the interior of the darkened shuttle, taking in the faces of each of my team. As I did so, my suit streamed combat statistics on each of them – enough for me to know that they were on edge, that they were ready for this.

"If we stay together and stay cool, then no one needs to get hurt," I said. "That includes you, Olsen."

The science officer gave another nod. His bio-rhythms were most worrying but there was nothing I could do about that. His inclusion on the team hadn't been my choice, after all.

"You heard the man," Jenkins echoed. "Meaning no fuck-ups."

Couldn't have put it better myself. If I bought it on the op, Jenkins would be responsible for getting the rest of the squad home.

The Wildcat shuttle selected an appropriate

docking portal on the *New Haven*. Data imported from the APS automated pilot told me that trajectory and approach vector were good. We would board the ship from the main corridor. According to our intelligence, based on schematics of similar starships, this corridor formed the spine of the ship. It would give access to all major tactical objectives – the bridge, the drive chamber, and the hypersleep suite.

A chime sounded in my helmet and the APS updated me on our progress – T-MINUS TEN SECONDS UNTIL IMPACT.

"Here we go!" I declared.

The Wildcat APS retro-thrusters kicked in, and suddenly we were decelerating rapidly. My head thumped against the padded neck-rest and my body juddered. Despite the reduced-gravity of the cabin, the sensation was gut wrenching. My heart hammered in my chest, even though I had done this hundreds of times before. My helmet informed me that a fresh batch of synthetic combat-drug – a cocktail of endorphins and adrenaline, carefully mixed to keep me at optimum combat performance – was being injected into my system to compensate. The armour carried a full medical suite, patched directly into my body, and automatically provided assistance when necessary. Distance to target rapidly decreased.

"Brace for impact."

Through the APS-mounted cameras, I saw the rough-and-ready docking procedure. The APS literally bumped against the outer hull, and unceremoniously lined up our airlock with the *Haven*'s. With an explosive roar and a wave of kinetic force, the shuttle connected with the hull. The Wildcat airlock cycled open.

We moved like a well-oiled mechanism, a well-used machine. Except for Olsen, we'd all done this before. Martinez was first up, out of his safety harness. He took up point. Jenkins and Blake were next; they would provide covering fire if we met resistance. Then Kaminski, escorting Olsen. I was always last out of the cabin.

"Boarding successful," I said. "We're on the *Haven*."

That was just a formality for my combat-suit recorder.

As I moved out into the corridor, my weapon auto-linked with my HUD and displayed targeting data. We were armed with Westington-Haslake M95 plasma battle-rifles – the favoured long-arm for hostile starship engagements. It was a large and weighty weapon, and fired phased plasma pulses, fuelled by an onboard power cell. Range was limited but it had an incredible rate of fire and the sheer stopping power of an energy weapon of this magnitude was worth the compromise. We carried other weapons as well, according to preference – Jenkins favoured an Armant-pattern incinerator unit as her primary weapon, and we all wore plasma pistol sidearms.

"Take up covering positions – overlap arcs of fire," I whispered, into the communicator. The squad obeyed. "Wide dispersal, and get me some proper light."

Bobbing shoulder-lamps illuminated, flashing over the battered interior of the starship. The suits were equipped with infrared, night-vision, and electro-magnetic sighting, but the Krell didn't emit much body heat and nothing beat good old-fashioned eyesight.

Without being ordered, Kaminski moved up on one of the wall-mounted control panels. He accessed the ship's mainframe with a portable PDU from his kit.

"Let there be light," Martinez whispered, in heavily accented Standard.

Strip lights popped on overhead, flashing in sequence, dowsing the corridor in ugly electric illumination. Some flickered erratically, other didn't light at all. Something began humming in the belly of the ship: maybe dormant life-support systems. A sinister calmness permeated the main corridor. It was utterly utilitarian, with bare metal-plated walls and floors. My suit reported that the temperature was uncomfortably low, but within acceptable tolerances.

"Gravity drive is operational," Kaminski said. "They've left the atmospherics untouched. We'll be okay here for a few hours."

"I don't plan on staying that long," Jenkins said.

Simultaneously, we all broke the seals on our helmets. The atmosphere carried twin but contradictory scents: the stink of burning plastic and fetid water. *The ship has been on fire, and a recycling tank has blown somewhere nearby.* Liquid *plink-plink-plinked* softly in the distance.

"I'll stay sealed, if you don't mind," Olsen clumsily added. "The subjects have been known to harbour cross-species contaminants."

"Christo, this guy is unbelievable," Kaminski said, shaking his head.

"Hey, watch your tongue, *mano*," Martinez said to Kaminski. He motioned to a crude white cross, painted onto the chest-plate of his combat-suit. "Don't use His name in vain."

None of us really knew what religion Martinez followed, but he did it with admirable vigour. It seemed to permit gambling, women and drinking, whereas blaspheming on a mission was always unacceptable.

"Not this shit again," Kaminski said. "It's all I ever hear from you. We get back to the *Point* without you, I'll comm God personally. You Venusians are all the same."

"I'm an American," Martinez started. Venusians were very conscious of their roots; this was an argument I'd arbitrated far too many times between the two soldiers.

"Shut the fuck up," Jenkins said. "He wants to believe, leave him to it." The others respected her word almost as much as mine, and immediately fell silent. "It's nice to have faith in something. Orders, Cap?"

"Fireteam Alpha – Jenkins, Martinez – get down to the hypersleep chamber and report on the status of these colonists. Fireteam Bravo, form up on me."

Nods of approval from the squad. This was standard operating procedure: get onboard the target ship, hit the key locations and get back out as soon as possible.

"And the quantum-drive?" Jenkins asked. She had powered up her flamethrower, and the glow from the pilot-light danced over her face. Her expression looked positively malicious.

"We'll converge on the location in fifteen minutes. Let's get some recon on the place before we check out."

"Solid copy, Captain."

The troopers began a steady jog into the gloomy aft of the starship, their heavy armour and weapons clanking noisily as they went.

It wasn't fear that I felt in my gut. Not trepidation, either; this was something worse. It was excitement – polluting my thought process, strong enough that it was almost intoxicating. This was what I was made for. I steadied my pulse and concentrated on the mission at hand.

Something stirred in the ship – I felt it.

Kaminski, Blake and I made quick time towards the bridge. Olsen struggled to keep up with us and was quiet for most of the way, but Kaminski couldn't help goading him.

"I take it you aren't used to running in combat-armour?" Kaminski asked. "Just say if you want a rest."

The tone of Kaminski's voice made clear that wasn't a statement of concern, but rather an insult.

"It's quite something," Olsen said, shaking his head. He ignored Kaminski's last remark. "A real marvel of modern technology. The suit feels like it is running me, rather than the other way around."

"You get used to it," I said. "Two and a half tonnes of machinery goes into every unit."

The Trident Class IV combat-suit was equipped

with everything a soldier needed. It had a full sensory and tactical data-suite built into the helmet, all fed into the HUD. Reinforced ablative plating protected the wearer from small-arms fire. It had full EVA-capability – atmospherically sealed, with an oxygen recycling pack for survival in deep-space. A plethora of gadgets and added extras were crammed onboard, and Research and Development supplied something new every mission. These versions were in a constantly shifting urban-camouflage pattern, to blur the wearer's outline and make us harder targets to hit. Best of all, the mechanical musculature amplified the strength of the wearer ten-fold.

"You can crush a xeno skull with one hand," Kaminski said, absently flexing a glove by way of example. "I've done it."

"Stay focused," I ordered, and Kaminski fell silent.

We were moving through a poorly lit area of the ship – Krell were friends of the dark. I flicked on my shoulder-lamp again, taking in the detail.

The starship interior was a state. It had been smashed to pieces by the invaders. We passed cabins sealed up with makeshift barricades. Walls scrawled with bloody handprints, or marked by the discharge of energy weapons. I guessed that the crew and civilian complement had put up a fight, but not much of one. They had probably been armed with basic self-defence weapons – a few slug-throwers, a shock-rifle or so to deal with the occasional unruly crewman, but nothing capable of handling a full-on boarding party. They certainly wouldn't have been prepared for what had come for them.

Something had happened here. That squirming in my gut kicked in again. Part of the mystery of the ship was solved. The Krell had been here for sure. Only one question remained: were they still onboard? Perhaps they had done their thing then bailed out.

Or they might still be lurking somewhere on the ship.

We approached the bridge. I checked the mission timeline. Six minutes had elapsed since we had boarded.

"Check out the door, Blake," I ordered, moving alongside it.

The bridge door had been poorly welded shut. I grappled with one panel, digging my gauntleted fingers into the thin metal plates. Blake did the same to another panel and we pulled it open. Behind me, Kaminski changed position to provide extra firepower in the event of a surprise from inside the room. Once the door was gone, I peered in.

"Scanner reports no movement," Blake said.

He was using a wrist-mounted bio-scanner, incorporated into his suit. It detected biological life-signs, but the range was limited. Although we all had scanners – they were the tool of choice for Krell-hunters and salvage teams up and down the Quarantine Zone – it was important not to become over-reliant on the tech. I'd learnt the hard way that it wasn't always dependable. The Krell were smart fucks; never to be underestimated.

The bridge room was in semi-darkness, with only a few of the control consoles still illuminated.

"Moving up on bridge."

I slowly and cautiously entered the chamber, scanning it with my rifle-mounted lamp. No motion at all. Kaminski followed me in. The place was cold, and it smelt of death and decay. Such familiar odours. I paused over the primary command console. The terminal was full of flashing warnings, untended.

"No survivors in bridge room," I declared.

Another formality for my suit recorder. Crewmen were sprawled at their stations. The bodies were old, decomposed to the point of desiccation. The ship's captain – probably a civilian merchant officer of some stripe – was still hunched over the command console, strapped into his seat. Something sharp and ragged had destroyed his face and upper body. Blood and bodily matter had liberally drenched the area immediately around the corpse, but had long since dried.

"What do you think happened here?" whispered Olsen.

"The ship's artificial intelligence likely awoke essential crew when the Krell boarded," I said. "They probably sealed themselves in, hoping that they would be able to repel the Krell."

I scanned the area directly above the captain's seat. The action was autonomic, as natural to me as breathing. I plotted how the scene had played out: the Krell had come in through the ceiling cavity – probably using the airshafts to get around the ship undetected – and killed the captain where he sat.

I repressed a shiver.

"Others are the same," Blake said, inspecting the remaining crewmen.

"Best we can do for them now is a decent burial at sea. Blake – cover those shafts. Kaminski – get on the primary console and start the download."

"Affirmative, Cap."

Kaminski got to work, unpacking his gear and jacking devices to the ship's mainframe. He was a good hacker; the product of a misspent youth back in Old Brooklyn.

"Let's find out why this old hulk is drifting so far inside the Quarantine Zone," he muttered.

"I'm quite curious," said Olsen. "The ship should have been well within established Alliance space. Even sponsored civilian vessels have been warned not to stray outside of the demarked area."

Shit happens, Olsen.

I paced the bridge while Kaminski worked.

The only external view-ports aboard the *Haven* were located on the bridge. The shutters had been fixed open, displaying the majesty of deep-space. *Maybe they wanted to see the void, one last time, before the inevitable*, I thought to myself. It wasn't a view that I'd have chosen – the Maelstrom dominated the ports. At this distance, light-years from the edge of the Quarantine Zone, the malevolent cluster of stars looked like an inverted bruise – against the black of space, bright and vivid. Like the Milky Way spiral in miniature: with swirling arms, each containing a myriad of Krell worlds. The display was alluringly colourful, as though to entice unwary alien travellers to their doom; to think that the occupants of those worlds and systems were a peaceful species. Occasional white flashes indicated gravimetric storms; the inexplicable phenomenon that in turn protected but also imprisoned the worlds of the Maelstrom.

"Your people ever get an answer on what those storms are?" I absently asked Olsen, as Kaminski worked. Olsen was Science Division, a specialised limb of the Alliance complex, not military.

"Now *that* is an interesting question," Olsen started, shuffling over to my position on the bridge. "Research is ongoing. The entire Maelstrom Region is still an enigma. Did you know that there are more black hole stars in that area of space than in the rest of the Orion Arm? Professor Robins, out of Maru Prime, thinks that the storms might be connected – perhaps the result of magnetic stellar tides—"

"There we go," Kaminski said, interrupting Olsen. He started to noisily unplug his gear, and the sudden sound made the science officer jump. "I've got commissioning data, notable service history and personnel records. Looks like the *Haven* was on a colony run – a settlement programme. Had orders to report to Torfis Star…" He paused, reading something from the terminal. Torfis Star was a long way from our current galactic position, and no right-minded starship captain would've deviated so far off-course without a damned good reason. "I see where things went wrong. The navigation module malfunctioned and the AI tried to compensate."

"The ship's artificial intelligence would be responsible for all automated navigational decisions," Olsen said. "But surely safety protocols would have prevented the ship from making such a catastrophic mistake?"

Kaminski continued working but shrugged

noncommittally. "It happens more often than you might think. Looks like the *Haven*'s AI developed a system fault. Caused the ship to overshoot her destination by several light-years. That explains how she ended up in the QZ."

"Just work quickly," I said. The faster we worked, the more quickly we could bail out to the APS. If the Krell were still onboard, we might be able to extract before contact. I activated my communicator: "Jenkins – you copy?"

"Jenkins here."

"We're on the bridge, downloading the black box now. What's your location?"

"We're in the hypersleep chamber."

"Give me a sitrep."

"No survivors. It isn't pretty down here. No remains in enough pieces to identify. Looks like they were caught in hypersleep, mostly. Still frozen when they bought it."

"No surprises there. Don't bother IDing them; we have the ship's manifest. Proceed to the Q-drive. Over."

"Solid copy. ETA three minutes."

The black box data took another minute to download, and the same to transmit back to the *Liberty Point*. Mission timeline: ten minutes. Then we were up again, moving down the central corridor and plotting our way to the Q-drive – into the ugly strip-lit passage. The drive chamber was right at the aft of the ship, so the entire length of the vessel. Olsen skulked closely behind me.

"Do you wish you'd brought along a gun now, Mr Olsen?" asked Blake.

"I've never fired a gun in my life," Olsen said, defensively. "I wouldn't know how to."

"I can't think of a better time to learn," Kaminski replied. "You know—"

The overhead lights went out, corridor section by corridor section, until we were plunged into total darkness. Simultaneously, the humming generated by the life-support module died. The sudden silence was thunderous, stretching out for long seconds.

"How did they do that?" Olsen started. His voice echoed off through the empty corridor like a gunshot, making me flinch. On a dead ship like the *Haven*, noise travelled. "Surely that wasn't caused by the Krell?"

Our shoulder lamps popped on. I held up a hand for silence.

Something creaked elsewhere in the ship.

"Scanners!" I whispered.

That slow, pitched beeping: a lone signal somewhere nearby…

"Contact!" Blake yelled.

In the jittery pool of light created by my shoulder-lamp, I saw *something* spring above us: just a flash of light, wet, fast—

Blake fired a volley of shots from his plasma rifle. Orange light bathed the corridor. Kaminski was up, covering the approach—

"Cease fire!" I shouted. "It's just a blown maintenance pipe."

My team froze, running on adrenaline, eyes wide. Four shoulder-lamps illuminated the shadowy ceiling, tracked the damage done by Blake's plasma shots. True enough, a bundle of ribbed plastic pipes dangled from the suspended ceiling: accompanied by the lethargic *drip-drip* of leaking water.

"You silly bastard, Kid!" Kaminski laughed. "Your trigger finger is itchier than my nuts!"

"Oh Christo!" Olsen screamed.

A Krell primary-form nimbly – far too nimbly for something so big – unwound itself from somewhere above. It landed on the deck, barely ten metres ahead of us.

A barb ran through me. Not physical, but mental – although the reaction was strong enough for my med-suite to issue another compensatory drug. I was suddenly hyperaware, in combat-mode. This was no longer a recon or salvage op.

The team immediately dispersed, taking up positions around the xeno. No prospect of a false alarm this time.

The creature paused, wriggling its six limbs. It wasn't armed, but that made it no less dangerous. There was something so immensely *wrong* about the Krell. I could still remember the first time I saw one and the sensation of complete wrongness that overcame me. Over the years, the emotion had settled to a balls-deep paralysis.

This was a primary-form, the lowest strata of the Krell Collective, but it was still bigger than any of us. Encased in the Krell equivalent of battle-armour: hardened carapace plates, fused to the xeno's grey-green skin. It was impossible to say where technology finished and biology began. The thing's back was awash with antennae – those could be used as both weapons and communicators with the rest of the Collective.

The Krell turned its head to acknowledge us. It had a vaguely fish-like face, with a pair of deep bituminous eyes, barbels drooping from its mouth. Beneath the head, a pair of gills rhythmically flexed, puffing out noxious fumes. Those sharkish features had earned them the moniker "fish heads". Two pairs of arms sprouted from the shoulders – one atrophied, with clawed hands; the other tipped with bony, serrated protrusions – raptorial forearms.

The xeno reared up, and in a split second it was stomping down the corridor.

I fired my plasma rifle. The first shot exploded the xeno's chest, but it kept coming. The second shot connected with one of the bladed forearms, blowing the limb clean off. Then Blake and Kaminski were firing too – and the corridor was alight with brilliant plasma pulses. The creature collapsed into an incandescent mess.

"You like that much, Olsen?" Kaminski asked. "They're pretty friendly for a species that we're supposed to be at peace with."

At some point during the attack, Olsen had collapsed to his knees. He sat there for a second, looking down at his gloved hands. His eyes were haunted, his jowls heavy and he was suddenly much older. He shook his head, stumbling to his feet. From the safety of a laboratory, it was easy to think of the Krell as another intelligent species, just made in the image of a different god. But seeing them up close, and witnessing their innate need to extinguish the human race, showed them for what they really were.

"This is a live situation now, troopers. Keep together and do this by the drill. *Haven* is awake."

"Solid copy," Kaminski muttered.

"We move to secondary objective. Once the generator has been tagged, we retreat down the primary corridor to the APS. Now double-time it and move out."

There was no pause to relay our contact with Jenkins and Martinez. The Krell had a unique ability to sense radio transmissions, even encrypted communications like those we used on the suits, and now that the Collective had awoken all comms were locked down.

As I started off, I activated the wrist-mounted computer incorporated into my suit. *Ah, shit.* The starship corridors brimmed with motion and bio-signs. The place became swathed in shadow and death – every pool of blackness a possible Krell nest.

Mission timeline: twelve minutes.

We reached the quantum-drive chamber. The huge reinforced doors were emblazoned with warning signs and a red emergency light flashed overhead.

The floor exploded as three more Krell appeared – all chitin shells and claws. Blake went down first, the largest of the Krell dragging him into a service tunnel. He brought his rifle up to fire, but there was too little room for him to manoeuvre in a full combat-suit, and he couldn't bring the weapon to bear.

"Hold on, Kid!" I hollered, firing at the advancing Krell, trying to get him free.

The other two xenos clambered over him in

desperation to get to me. I kicked at several of them, reaching a hand into the mass of bodies to try to grapple Blake. He lost his rifle, and let rip an agonised shout as the creatures dragged him down. It was no good – he was either dead now, or he would be soon. Even in his reinforced ablative plate, those things would take him apart. I lost the grip on his hand, just as the other Krell broke free of the tunnel mouth.

"Blake's down!" I yelled. "'Ski – grenade."

"Solid copy – on it."

Kaminski armed an incendiary grenade and tossed it into the nest. The grenade skittered down the tunnel, flashing an amber warning-strobe as it went. In the split second before it went off, as I brought my M95 up to fire, I saw that the tunnel was now filled with xenos. Many, many more than we could hope to kill with just our squad.

"Be careful – you could blow a hole in the hull with those explosives!" Olsen wailed.

Holing the hull was the least of my worries. The grenade went off, sending Krell in every direction. I turned away from the blast at the last moment, and felt hot shrapnel penetrate my combat-armour – frag lodging itself in my lower back. The suit compensated for the wall of white noise, momentarily dampening my audio.

The M95 auto-sighted prone Krell and I fired without even thinking. Pulse after pulse went into the tunnel, splitting armoured heads and tearing off clawed limbs. Blake was down there, somewhere among the tangle of bodies and debris; but it took a good few seconds before my suit informed me that his bio-signs had finally extinguished.

Good journey, Blake.

Kaminski moved behind me. His technical kit was already hooked up to the drive chamber access terminal, running code-cracking algorithms to get us in.

The rest of the team jogged into view. More Krell were now clambering out of the hole in the floor. Martinez and Jenkins added their own rifles to the volley, and assembled outside the drive chamber.

"Glad you could finally make it. Not exactly going to plan down here."

"Yeah, well, we met some friends on the way," Jenkins muttered.

"We lost the Kid. Blake's gone."

"Ah, fuck it," Jenkins said, shaking her head. She and Blake were close, but she didn't dwell on his death. *No time for grieving*, the expression on her face said, *because we might be next.*

The access doors creaked open. There was another set of double-doors inside; endorsed QUANTUM-DRIVE CHAMBER – AUTHORISED PERSONNEL ONLY.

A calm electronic voice began a looped message: "Warning. Warning. Breach doors to drive chamber are now open. This presents an extreme radiation hazard. Warning. Warning."

A second too late, my suit bio-sensors began to trill; detecting massive radiation levels. I couldn't let it concern me. Radiation on an op like this was always a danger, but being killed by the Krell was a more immediate risk. I rattled off a few shots into the shadows, and heard the impact against hard chitin. The things screamed, their voices creating a discordant racket with the alarm system.

Kaminski cracked the inner door, and he and Martinez moved inside. I laid down suppressing fire with Jenkins, falling back slowly as the things tested our defences. It was difficult to make much out in the intermittent light: flashes of a claw, an alien head, then the explosion of plasma as another went down. My suit counted ten, twenty, thirty targets.

"Into the airlock!" Kaminski shouted, and we were all suddenly inside, drenched in sweat and blood.

The drive chamber housed the most complex piece of technology on the ship – the energy core. Once, this might've been called the engine room. Now, the device contained within the chamber was so far advanced that it was no longer mechanical. The drive energy core sat in the centre of the room – an ugly-looking metal box, so big that it filled the place, adorned with even more warning signs. This was our objective.

Olsen stole a glance at the chamber, but stuck close to me as we assembled around the machine. Kaminski paused at the control terminal near the door, and sealed the inner lock. Despite the reinforced metal doors, the squealing and shrieking of the Krell was still audible. I knew that they would be through those doors in less than a minute. Then there was the scuttling and scraping overhead. The chamber was supposed to be secure, but these things had probably been on-ship for long enough to know every access corridor and every room. They had the advantage.

They'll find a way in here soon enough, I thought. A mental image of the dead merchant captain – still strapped to his seat back on the bridge – suddenly came to mind.

The possibility that I would die out here abruptly dawned on me. The thought triggered a burst of anger – not directed at the Alliance military for sending us, nor at the idiot colonists who had flown their ship into the Quarantine Zone, but at the Krell.

My suit didn't take any medical action to compensate for that emotion. *Anger is good*. It was pure and made me focused.

"Jenkins – set the charges."

"Affirmative, Captain."

Jenkins moved to the drive core and began unpacking her kit. She carried three demolition-packs. Each of the big metal discs had a separate control panel, and was packed with a low-yield nuclear charge.

"Wh-what are you doing?" Olsen stammered.

Jenkins kept working, but shook her head with a smile. "We're going to destroy the generator. You should have read the mission briefing. That was your first mistake."

"Forgetting to bring a gun was his second," Kaminski added.

"We're going to set these charges off," Jenkins muttered, "and the resulting explosion will breach the Q-drive energy core. That'll take out the main deck. The chain reaction will destroy the ship."

"In short: *gran explosión*," said Martinez.

Kaminski laughed. "There you go again. You know I hate it when you don't speak Standard.

Martinez always does this – he gets all excited and starts speaking funny."

"*El no habla la lengua*," I said. You don't grow up in the Detroit Metro without picking up some of the lingo.

"It's Spanish," Martinez replied, shooting Kaminski a sideways glance.

"I thought that you were from Venus?" Kaminski said.

Olsen whimpered again. "How can you laugh at a time like this?"

"Because Kaminski is an asshole," Martinez said, without missing a beat.

Kaminski shrugged. "It's war."

Thump. Thump.

"Give us enough time to fall back to the APS," I ordered. "Set the charges with a five-minute delay. The rest of you – *cállate y trabaja.*"

"Affirmative."

Thump! Thump! Thump!

They were nearly through now. Welts appeared in the metal door panels.

Jenkins programmed each charge in turn, using magnetic locks to hold them in place on the core outer shielding. Two of the charges were already primed, and she was working on the third. She positioned the charges very deliberately, very carefully, to ensure that each would do maximum damage to the core. If one charge didn't light, then the others would act as a failsafe. There was probably a more technical way of doing this – perhaps hacking the Q-drive directly – but that would take time, and right now that was the one thing that we didn't have.

"Precise as ever," I said to Jenkins.

"It's what I do."

"Feel free to cut some corners; we're on a tight timescale," Kaminski shouted.

"Fuck you, 'Ski."

"Is five minutes going to be enough?" Olsen asked.

I shrugged. "It will have to be. Be prepared for heavy resistance en route, people."

My suit indicated that the Krell were all over the main corridor. They would be in the APS by now, probably waiting for us to fall back.

THUMP! THUMP! THUMP!

"Once the charges are in place, I want a defensive perimeter around that door," I ordered.

"This can't be rushed."

The scraping of claws on metal, from above, was becoming intense. I wondered which defence would be the first to give: whether the Krell would come in through the ceiling or the door.

Kaminski looked back at Jenkins expectantly. Olsen just stood there, his breathing so hard that I could hear him over the communicator.

"And done!"

The third charge snapped into place. Jenkins was up, with Martinez, and Kaminski was ready at the data terminal. There was noise all around us now, signals swarming on our position. I had no time to dictate a proper strategy for our retreat.

"Jenkins – put down a barrier with your torch. Kaminski – on my mark."

I dropped my hand, and the doors started to open. The mechanism buckled and groaned in protest. Immediately, the Krell grappled with the door, slamming into the metal frame to get through.

Stinger-spines – flechette rounds, the Krell equivalent of armour-piercing ammo – showered the room. Three of them punctured my suit; a neat line of black spines protruding from my chest, weeping streamers of blood. *Krell tech is so much more fucked-up than ours.* The spines were poison-tipped and my body was immediately pumped with enough toxins to kill a bull. My suit futilely attempted to compensate by issuing a cocktail of adrenaline and anti-venom.

Martinez flipped another grenade into the horde. The nearest creatures folded over it as it landed, shielding their kin from the explosion. *Mindless fuckers.*

We advanced in formation. Shot after shot poured into the things, but they kept coming. Wave after wave – how many were there on this ship? – thundered into the drive chamber. The doors were suddenly gone. The noise was unbearable – the klaxon, the warnings, a chorus of screams, shrieks and wails. The ringing in my ears didn't stop, as more grenades exploded.

"We're not going to make this!" Jenkins yelled.

"Stay on it! The APS is just ahead!"

Maybe Jenkins was right, but I wasn't going down without a damned good fight. Somewhere in the chaos, Martinez was torn apart. His body disappeared underneath a mass of them. Jenkins poured on her flamethrower – avenging Martinez in some absurd way. Olsen was crying, his helmet now discarded just like the rest of us.

War is such an equaliser.

I grabbed the nearest Krell with one hand, and snapped its neck. I fired my plasma rifle on full-auto with the other, just eager to take down as many of them as I could. My HUD suddenly issued another warning – a counter, interminably in decline.

Ten…Nine…Eight…Seven…

Then Jenkins was gone. Her flamer was a beacon and her own blood a fountain among the alien bodies. It was difficult to focus on much except for the pain in my chest. My suit reported catastrophic damage in too many places. My heart began a slower, staccato beat.

Six…Five…Four…

My rifle bucked in protest. Even through reinforced gloves, the barrel was burning hot.

Three…Two…One…

The demo-charges activated.

Breached, the anti-matter core destabilised. The reaction was instantaneous: uncontrolled white and blue energy spilled out. A series of explosions rippled along the ship's spine. She became a white-hot smudge across the blackness of space.

Then she was gone, along with everything inside her.

The Krell did not pause.

They did not even comprehend what had happened.

CHAPTER TWO

EXTRACTION

PFC MICHAEL BLAKE: DECEASED.
PFC ELLIOT MARTINEZ: DECEASED.
PFC VINCENT KAMINSKI (ELECTRONICS
   TECH, FIRST GRADE): DECEASED.
SCIENCE OFFICER GORDEN OLSEN:
   DECEASED.
CORPORAL KEIRA JENKINS (EXPLOSIVES
   TECH, FIRST GRADE): DECEASED.

WAITING FOR RESPONSE...WAITING FOR
   RESPONSE...WAITING FOR RESPONSE...

CAPTAIN CONRAD HARRIS: DECEASED.

This was the part I disliked most.
Waking up again was always worse than dying.
I floated inside my simulator-tank – a respirator mask attached to my face – and blinked amniotic fluid from my eyes to read the screen more clearly. The soak stung like a bitch. The words scrolled across a monitor positioned above my tank.

Everything was cast a clear, brilliant blue by the liquid filling my simulator.

PURGE CYCLE COMMENCED...

The tank made a hydraulic hissing, and the fluid began to slough out. It was already cooling.

I was instantly smaller and yet heavier. Breathing was a labour. These lungs didn't have the capacity of a simulant's, and I knew that it would take a few minutes to get used to them again. I caught the reflection on the inside of the plasglass cover, and didn't immediately recognise it as *my* reflection. That was the face I had been born with, and this was the body I had lived inside for forty years. I was naked, jacked directly into the simulator. Cables were plugged into the base of the device, allowing me to control my simulant out there in the depths of space. My biorhythms, and those of the rest of my squad, appeared on the same monitor.

All alive and accounted for. Everyone made safe transition.

I had been operating a flesh-and-blood simulation of myself, manufactured from my body tissue. These were called simulants: simulated copies, genetically engineered to be stronger, bigger, faster. Based on the human genome, but accelerated and modified, the sims were the ultimate weapon – more human than human in every sense. Vat-grown, designed for purpose. Now, my simulant was dead. *It* had died on the *New Haven*. I was alive, safe aboard the *Liberty Point*.

I was a soldier in the Alliance military – more

specifically in the Simulant Operations Programme. Technically, the Programme was a special operation conducted by the Army. In truth, this was warfare on such a different level to anything that had come before, that the Programme was something separate from the other branches of the Alliance military.

I settled on the floor of the tank, unjacking myself from the control cables. The neural-link had been severed when my simulant was killed by the Krell onslaught, but pulling the jack from the back of my neck still sent a brief stab of pain through me. My arms and legs felt baby-weak, ineffectual. Hard to believe that I was going to have to adjust to this all over again. I didn't like this body much: the sim had been a much better fit.

Once the fluid had drained, the tank door slid open. I wrenched the respirator mask from my face and tossed it aside, slowly stepping out. I shook fluid from my limbs, shivering. A medic wrapped a heat-preserving aluminium blanket around me. Another reached for the biometric dog-tags from around my neck, scanning them.

"Successful extraction, Captain," he said. "Well done."

My arms and legs ached dully. There were three red abrasions across my chest – stigmatic wounds caused by the Krell assault. Inflamed welts and whip-like abrasions also marked my limbs, reminding me of the punishment my sim had suffered. I probed my chest with numb fingers – almost expecting to find stinger-spines stuck there. My ears still rang with the shrieks of the dying Krell.

All that had happened was a reality.

Just not a reality for me, at least not physically.

I was in the Simulant Operations Centre of the *Liberty Point*. As far as the eye could see, the chamber was crammed with identical bays – each housing a squad of troopers, operating simulants on missions out in the Quarantine Zone.

Around me, my squad were similarly mounted in simulator-tanks. Each trooper was undergoing the same disconnection protocol.

"Nice work, people," I managed. I spoke with the slur of a day-long drunk; like my body wasn't my own.

I took in my crew. They looked like paler imitations of their simulants, or maybe the simulants looked like improved versions of the squad. They were athletic-bodied but with determined, disciplined physiques rather than the over-muscled stature of bodybuilders.

They were all dedicated, honed troopers – mentally and physically. But we were not regular soldiers. There were important differences between a sim operator and a hardcopy soldier. Each of us was pocked with data-ports, around the base of the spine, the neck, the forearms, the thighs. Those allowed connection between the simulator and our physical bodies.

"Let's get this wrapped up," Jenkins hollered to the rest of the team. "Out of the tanks, disconnected. Double-time it."

Although she tried hard not to show it, she looked good. She had a small, trim body; dark hair bobbed for ease inside the simulators. At thirty-odd standard years, Jenkins was a ten-year Army vet and gave no hint of embarrassment at standing naked among a group of male soldiers. They barely registered her appearance.

"Yes, ma'am," Kaminski parroted.

"Fuck off, 'Ski. I'm a volunteer just like the rest of you." Jenkins shook her hair dry. "Save that 'ma'am' shit until I get the promotion."

"Yeah, Kaminski," Blake said. "How many years are you going to do as a PFC?"

"I'm not listening," Kaminski said.

He stumbled out of his tank. He ran a hand over his buzz-cut hair – he was only thirty-two standard years, but he wore it short because it was receding. He'd spent most of his military career as a private: had been busted back to the rank so many times I'd lost count.

Kaminski's torso was covered in tattoos, from a stylised phoenix to a leering Grim Reaper. Resurrection imagery: death and rebirth, something that only sim operators got to experience. Across his shoulder blades, the newest addition to this flesh tapestry read FISH FOOD in cursive text. He had acquired that particular marking after a night of hard drinking and a dare from Jenkins, which Kaminski had evidently lost. He grinned inanely, pointing out a phantom injury on his head.

"Hey, Jenkins," he said, "would it kill you to set the charges faster next time? Could've saved me a whole lot of pain from the fish heads."

"Whatever, 'Ski," Jenkins said. "At least they went for your head. There's not much in there you'd miss."

Martinez laughed. "Corporal's got your number."

The sixth member of my team hadn't taken it so well. Olsen was particularly shaken by the ordeal. The physical and mental disconnection between the simulant and operator wasn't a pleasant experience, and he hadn't been trained for it. That was why they only sent sim operators into the field: not everyone could do this. Olsen's attachment to our squad had been an expensive experiment. The data-ports on his spine and forearms had only just taken; the flesh around them an angry red, out of place against his flabby white skin.

"You'll find walking difficult at first," a medic explained to Olsen. "The simulant that you have just been operating was considerably larger than you. The difference in eye-level might be disorienting. Try to breathe slowly and deeply. Focus on this light…"

Lieutenant Dyker appeared, consulting a dataslate. He was dressed in khaki fatigues, sleeves rolled up. Dyker was our handler; responsible for directing the op from the *Point*, feeding me intel.

"Welcome back to Alliance space, Captain Harris," he said, looking up at me with a worn-out smile. Dyker never looked rested: his face was caught in a perpetual tired crumple. "Barring the sixteen million credits of military hardware that was destroyed in that explosion, I'd say that was a successful op."

Dyker was referring to the loss of the simulants and the Wildcat APS. The rules of engagement were fluid, and the sims were expendable. That made them unique in modern military terms, because sims could undertake missions that would be suicide to regular troopers. Even so, our orders were to preserve the simulants if possible – every sim had a significant credit value attached to it.

"What can I say?" I asked, rhetorically. I had time for Dyker; he gave me latitude to do what I needed to in the field. "The ship was brimming with Krell. They didn't leave us with much of a choice."

Dyker shrugged. "No matter." He threw a thumb in Olsen's direction. "I don't think that he will be trying that again."

"Best leave it to the professionals."

Dyker nodded. There was something sad in his expression. "I'll report that back to Command. The op otherwise went well. The ship has been neutralised, all human cargo taken care of. We have the black box data." He looked down at his slate. "That makes two hundred and eighteen trips out for you. You really are a stone-cold killer. Do you know what they are calling you down in the District?"

"No idea," I said, concentrating on towelling myself dry. It was a lie – of course I knew. I might not like it, but I'd heard plenty of operators call me by the name.

"They're calling you Lazarus," Dyker said. "Because you always come back. Whatever happens, you always come back." He sighed. An absent rub of the back of his neck. "Report to the medical station for psych-eval and a check-up. After that, you've earned yourselves seven days of station-leave. Enjoy it."

"I'll try to."

"I mean it, Harris."

He continued rubbing his neck, and I caught

the flash of the tattoo on his wrist – the number fifty-seven.

He left the bay, and I stood shivering and trying to forget what it was like to die. Hoping that I would never end up like Dyker: drummed out and dried up.

The medteam checked me out. I had the usual tests and the usual results.

No cerebral feedback.

The physical pain would fade.

The stigmata would eventually disappear.

Lasting brain damage was unlikely.

They went through the motions. The medtechs had stopped really bothering with the checks. They were cursory and brief; I had proven that I was a stable platform for a bio-engineered killing machine.

Of course, there were real and practical dangers to operational soldiers like me. An operator might suffer a cardiac arrest, or some extreme sensory overload while jacked into a simulant. Such an eventuality was often fatal, but it was also incredibly rare. Far more likely was a slow psychological breakdown, brought on by the inability to tell reality from a simulation. That happened more often than the Alliance military cared to admit, but such operators were usually identified early in their induction. In my case, after so many transitions, there was nothing more to be said. Unless I crashed and burnt, I would stay on the Programme.

I showered and dressed in Sim Ops shipside fatigues. I was used to the disorientation caused by transition back into my real body, and the effects faded fast. Olsen would probably find the whole experience disabling, but twenty or so minutes after I had made extraction I felt recovered.

I left medical and headed down to the inner ring of the station. Kaminski ran to catch up with me.

"Wait up, Cap," he called. "You planning on some rest and relaxation? We could head into the District, maybe hook up with some company? Blake, Jenkins and Martinez are coming."

"I'll join you for a drink. Nothing more."

Kaminski laughed. "You always get more in the District."

A siren sounded nearby. We didn't flinch – it was a familiar occurrence on-station.

"This is an emergency," said a female operator over the *Point*'s PA system. "All available military police units attend Sector Five. Terrorist attack in progress."

We casually made our way through the crowd of civilians and soldiers, heading away from Sector Five. A unit of troopers in black military police uniforms, carbines shouldered, passed back towards the affected sector.

"Looks like more trouble," Kaminski said. "If we're not fighting the Krell, we're fighting each other."

"The Directorate will never learn," I said.

The monorail station was quiet; a handful of off-duty soldiers and Navy boys milling around.

"Are you taking the monorail?" Kaminski asked. He seemed to realise his mistake immediately.

"I'll walk," I said.

Kaminski just nodded.

*   *   *

I left Kaminski at the monorail stop and took an elevator further up the hub to Sector Three. This was my ritual, after every simulant operation, and I had to do it alone.

Sector Three was virtually abandoned. Except for the occasional bereaved parent, it saw little traffic. *Mom and Pop spending their life savings on a Q-space ticket, desperate for a last chance to say goodbye to Jonny or Joanne.* The place gave me room to think.

I walked the empty corridors, heading towards the Memorial Hall. I passed view-screens showing the exterior of *Liberty Point*. It was the largest Alliance forward operating base on the boundary of the Quarantine Zone; housing several thousand troopers, and just as many Aerospace Force and Naval personnel. Not as big as the Venusian cloud habitats, but still a remarkable feat of human engineering.

Near-space bustled with combat ships and assorted shuttles embarking or disembarking the *Point*, like little flies flitting about a carcass. *More ships seem to leave than ever come back*, I thought. All manner of vessels were assembled; from small military cutters, to enormous warships, through to sleek experimental craft. This was the Alliance Navy – the combined efforts of the remainder of the United Americas, Europe, and much of the Western world.

I stopped, pressing a hand up against the cold glass of the view-port. I watched as the light cast by the Maelstrom glinted off the gathered fleet. For just a moment, I felt strangely patriotic, before I remembered where I was headed.

*　*　*

The Memorial Hall wasn't really a hall or even a chamber, but more like a wall in the station's outer ring. I reached it at about midday by the station day-cycle, and as expected it was empty.

Words scrolled along the top of the wall: TO ALL OF THOSE WHO HAVE GIVEN THEIR LIVES IN THE FURTHERANCE OF THE KRELL WAR, AND FOR THE CONTINUED EXIS-TENCE OF THE HUMAN RACE. Millions of names were laser-etched onto the wall; in chronolog-ical order, updated automatically as new casualties were reported. The list already occupied a significant portion of the outer ring for this particular deck.

Small shrines – offerings of flowers, incense burners or other little sentimental trinkets – had been left at the foot of the wall. I reverently avoided them as I found the spot, and crouched to read her name.

I needed that drink more than ever.

Liberty Point was on the very frontier of Alliance space. The nearest friendly outpost was several parsecs away and with a decent Q-drive it'd still take a good couple of weeks to reach. In any event, that was only a remote mining base. The *Point* had to be self-sufficient and, as well as housing an enormous military contingent, it was also home to a sizeable civilian population.

That was where the District came in. Sprawl-ing and ramshackle, drunken and noisy, it was an inevitable evil. Although officially designated as a civilian recreational zone, so long as you had the credits the District was open to all. A trooper could get anything he wanted down here – from illegal narcotics, to any sort of sex, through to every type of alcohol. It was like a miniature Las Vegas, before the Directorate had dropped the bomb: all neon signs, casinos, bars, strip joints.

The officers on the *Point* had a dedicated mess hall, but I preferred something rawer and always drank with my squad. Our favoured drinking-spot was a rundown, old-style bar called the Depot. It was the favourite of most sim operators – the slogan YOU MIGHT DIE ONCE, BUT TRY DOING IT EVERY DAY was painted above the entrance. But it wasn't exclusive, and also catered for regular Army, Navy, and other assorted military.

We occupied our usual table, not far from the bar. There was an unspoken rule among the regulars that this was our territory. I sat with my head hung over a half-empty pitcher of cheap beer. The table was already heavy with empty glasses. I felt comfortably fuzzy – just drunk enough to blot out the pain from my last op.

Blake and Jenkins sat with me, not far off my condition. Blake was continually eyeing a topless blonde dancer, who was obviously looking to make his pocket a little emptier. Unlike me, Blake was young enough to feel at home in his real body. He could've had any woman in the place, except for Jenkins.

She was having her own trouble; she'd already told a Navy ensign to go away several times, and was currently trying to avoid making eye contact with him from across the room.

"This always happens when I make an effort," Jenkins said. "More hassle than it's worth."

Jenkins wore a tight red dress; but no matter what she wore, she still looked like a soldier. My whole squad did – it was a state of mind, the look in the eyes.

Martinez and Kaminski were elsewhere in the crowded bar – last I had seen them, Martinez was trying to pick a fight with some off-duty Navy boys, Kaminski was adding another tattoo to his already overloaded skin canvas.

"I bailed out first," Blake said, shaking his head. "Second op in a row that I've bailed out first. I can't believe it."

"Don't worry about it, Kid," Jenkins said, placing a reassuring hand on his shoulder. Jenkins and Blake had a good relationship. She was much older, but looked out for him both during operations and when we were on downtime. He was like a little brother to her.

"And as ever, the captain was out last," Blake said, smiling at me.

"Last in, last out," I said. "There are no medals for that. Don't worry about it, Blake. You did good."

I liked Blake. He was a good soldier; showed a lot of potential as an operator. He was always like this after a mission: insistent on chewing over the details of the operation, on questioning whether he could've done things differently, eager to please. I was quite the opposite. While I wanted to get things done, I tried to seal away what had happened after each operation – to compartmentalise the detail. It was easier to forget, that way.

Jenkins sucked her teeth. "Let's have another drink. I want to keep my boys watered."

She sloppily poured us another beer from a scratched plastic pitcher, spilling some onto the grubby table. We grabbed glasses and lifted them, knocking them together noisily and spilling even more beer.

"To dying," Jenkins proclaimed.

We threw our drinks down and swallowed them in one go. The beer tasted warm and still.

The squad had a good dynamic. I'd led many, during my lengthy stint in Sim Ops, and the current configuration was the best it had ever been. Kaminski had been with me from the very start, although he hadn't accrued anything like the number of simulated deaths that I had. Most troopers liked to take downtime between operations. Jenkins and Martinez had joined my squad at about the same time – three years back. Then Blake had filled an unexpected squad vacancy, and the rest was history.

Jenkins wiped the back of her hand across her mouth, removing the overspill from her gulped beer.

"Such a lady, Jenkins," Blake said, laughing at her. "The sort of woman my mother would like to meet."

"You're always talking about your mother," Jenkins said. She slurred her words. "Do you miss your folks?"

Blake's face froze slightly. Jenkins had, inadvertently, touched a nerve. My squad's morale was a priority of mine. *Something's bugging him.* But before I could act on his change in mood, before I could question him, he was himself again – full of his usual bravado. *I'll have to watch Blake*, I decided. He was a thinker. Sometimes, for sim operators, that wasn't a good thing.

"Course not. It's just been a long time since I saw my family, is all."

Jenkins gave a sage nod. "For me? Three years and counting. You'd think those assholes would take the time to come visit me out on the wild frontier!"

Blake and Jenkins bumped fists, descending into drunken laughter.

We were all Earth-born, except for Martinez – and he liked to believe that he was only a generation away from the homeworld. Relatives, families, friends: if you had them, this far out from the Core Worlds, they were just names, pretty pictures on holo-screens.

"So, what's next for us, Captain?" Jenkins asked me. She nudged Blake's shoulder. "We should bet on it. Get Kaminski and Martinez in on the action."

"We'll get more airtime when we're good and ready," I said, trying to hide the fact that I was already yearning to be back in a simulant. "Command will make that decision. You should be enjoying the downtime." I nodded at the blonde dancer circling around our table. She was still making eyes at Blake. "I'm sure that you can find some action down here."

Something like avarice crossed Blake's face, and he seemed to sit a little prouder in his seat. At least I was getting his mind off the topic of work.

"We'll report in seven days and find out what our next mission is," I added.

"You're not curious?" Jenkins asked.

I shrugged. "Not our place to ask questions. Five years ago – that was when I decided I would just stop asking."

Jenkins looked down at her drink, her face slightly blushed. Either that, or it was the neon light.

"I know, Harris. And it must still hurt." My squad knew everything, especially Jenkins. She was the unofficial listener: someone to talk to about history, concerns, the future, when it got too much. She was a damn better listener than the psych-evals, with their cold, dispassionate eyes.

Once, you didn't mind a psych-eval so much, a voice reminded me in my head.

Jenkins leant across the table, giving me a knowing wink. "I hear that something big is happening. We're about to be *mobilised*, and I don't think it will be against the Krell. If you ask me, we're going to be deployed against the Directorate."

I barked a laugh at that. "Bullshit. If I had a credit for every time I've heard that the Sim Ops Programme would be deployed against the Directorate, I'd be a rich man."

Jenkins held up her hands, palms open. "Hey, just telling you what I heard. Seems odd to me that so many teams get extracted, and so many are sitting around the *Point* just waiting for orders. I even hear that Old Man Cole is back on the *Point*."

"I'd like nothing better than to go up against the Directorate, but it wouldn't be a fair fight.

You know they don't have a simulant programme. We'd wipe the floor with them."

Jenkins and Blake laughed again. Conspiracy theories were a constant source of chatter for Jenkins. She didn't just listen to me and my squad; she picked up scuttlebutt from all over. She could be relied upon to offer a piece of unreliable gossip. A tenacious rumour, never yet proven to be true, was that Sim Ops would be mobilised en masse against the Asiatic Directorate. Jenkins liked to recount this particular story whenever she got the chance.

Our conversation was interrupted by a persistent tapping on my shoulder. I turned to see someone hovering behind me – a short middle-aged man, wearing a distinctive blue cap and a flak jacket with MILITARY REPORTER printed across the front. He was accompanied by a news-drone – a small flying camera that flittered overhead, glaring down at us.

"Fuck off!" Blake shouted, swiping at the camera like it was an annoying insect.

"Troopers, if I might just have a few moments of your time?" he blurted. He was sweating, waving a microphone device under my nose. "I'm from *The Point Times* and newly assigned to the base. I'm compiling a piece on the Simulant Operations Programme. Your names have come up as veteran operators who can speak of the Programme."

"Didn't you hear me the first time?" Blake said.

The reporter was undeterred. He licked his lips and continued. "Just your views on the operation so far. How do you think it's going? Maybe something on the Maelstrom. Have you ever been inside?"

"We're on downtime," I said. "Go speak to someone who cares."

He shook his head, dismissing my objections. "What's it like seeing the Krell face to face – as it were – on a regular basis?"

"The man told you to go away," Jenkins said, half-standing from her seat.

"Captain Harris – you have experienced two hundred and eighteen simulated deaths. You are the most prolific simulant operator ever inducted. Some are calling you a military hero. I've heard another trooper refer to you as Lazarus – care to comment on that?" The reporter paused, waiting for me to respond. When I didn't, he pressed on, as though reading from some invisible cue card: "What are your personal views on the Treaty? You have an unusual connection with it, which must be distressing at times. Can you share your views with us?"

Martinez appeared at the reporter's shoulder, and stared down at him menacingly. Martinez was short, stocky and powerfully built: an imposing figure, especially in drink. The news-drone darted higher, detecting what the reporter seemed oblivious to.

"I think it's time you left," Martinez growled. "The captain doesn't like to talk about the Treaty, *cuate*."

He hauled the reporter by his shoulders and off his feet. The little man disappeared into the crowded bar.

"Looks like Martinez will get his fight after all," Jenkins said. "Never fuck with a Venusian."

"Go easy on him!" I called after them.

"I'd better see to this," Jenkins said, following Martinez.

That left Blake and me alone. He was watching the dancer. She'd started another lap of the bar – keen to show Blake that she was still interested.

"Captain," Blake started, eyeing the woman as she passed by, "I need to talk to you."

I smiled. "But some other time, I guess?"

"Yeah. If you don't mind."

I nodded, and Blake was gone as well.

I had promised Kaminski that I would only have a drink down in the District, but a drink after an experience like the *New Haven* was not something to be taken lightly. After the first day of drinking the rest was a blur.

On the third day I was awoken early. My room door-chime sounded repeatedly. The fact that I was in my room and not the station brig was a good start. I had a vague recollection of the *Point*'s MPs getting involved in something, but whatever had happened couldn't have been serious enough to warrant detention.

I rolled out of my cot and shook myself awake, clutching at some fatigues and stumbling into them. I punched at the door control console.

A squat yellow utility robot sat outside, with tracks and clawed arms. The bot's chest was taken up by a viewer-screen that showed an animated face. I squinted in the bright corridor lights, and the robot paused before speaking.

"Captain Conrad Harris? Serial code 93778?"

I nodded, baring my wrist. The bot extended

a scanner and swiped my serial code tattoo, confirming my ID.

"Is seven days up already?" I asked

"You have been recertified for active duty. Your station-leave is cancelled with immediate effect."

The robot jabbed one of its claws at me, and slapped an envelope against my bare chest. I slowly took it, noting the Alliance military seal. The robot's viewer shifted to display a smirking face.

"New orders. General Cole wants you to report to his office at oh-eight-hundred hours tomorrow. You have a new mission."

"Cole?" I asked, dumbly.

"That's what I said."

The robot backed away from the door. Its electronic face shifted into a frown.

"You look like shit, buddy. I'm only saying it to be kind. Clean up."

"You don't look so good yourself," I muttered.

The robot noisily rolled down the corridor. I stood in the doorway for a moment, turning over the envelope. *A new mission is a good thing*, I told myself. That ever-present urge to climb back into the simulator-tank – to make transition into my simulant – rose up inside of me.

But orders direct from General Cole? That was unusual. Cole was serious business. This had to be something big, something special.

Maybe Jenkins was right. There was a first time for everything.

The pain in my head told me that now was not the time to think about it. I fell back onto my cot and allowed my pounding headache to subside a little.

I turned, took in my room. It was a small officer's cube – nothing flash, not a larger state room.
As a captain, I would've been entitled to that, but
I didn't want it. I wasn't one for material possessions, and my cubicle reflected that: austere,
somewhere to sleep and not much more. But I kept
a random jumble of personal articles beside my cot
– just enough to remind me that I was still a member of the human race.

A preserved Krell claw, taken from a combat-
suit after a sim-op that ended with a live return to
the *Point*.

A blasted scrap of plastic, recovered from a
destroyed plasma rifle.

Some spent solid-shot shell cases.

My father's old revolver: an ancient pistol
passed down from my grandfather.

A pink-silver ring set with orange gems.

Her picture.

The photo was faded with age: a picture from
Azure. The backdrop of blue sky played to the
red gloss of her lips, the deep almond of her eyes.
Her long, dark hair; always thick with her scent. I
touched the image and it sprang to life – mimick-
ing the woman that she had been.

We had been happy, then.

I closed my eyes. I had another mission. That
was something, but it was a day away.

I needed another drink.

CHAPTER THREE

A MISSION

General Mohammed Cole was supreme officer in charge of policing the Quarantine Zone. Colonel O'Neil oversaw Sim Ops – was my real CO – but Cole was his direct superior. If I had a key operation, it was O'Neil that I'd expect to brief me, but it seemed that he had been entirely cut out of the loop. Technically an Army officer, Cole was in command of the combined military effort – not just Sim Ops, but the Alliance Army and Navy. He was answerable only to the joint chiefs-of-staff, back in the Core Systems.

I sat alone in the waiting room outside his office. It was appropriately plush, with a synthetic-leather couch and artwork on the walls. A flickering hologram of the Alliance flag filled one aspect – all stars and stripes, with a graphic representation of the worlds united under the Alliance government. Old Earth sat at the centre, although in truth that was only half ours. The rest belonged to the Asiatic Directorate – an empire incorporating the Chino Republic, Unified Korea, the Thai Confederate. The planets of the Solar System had long since been colonised and decimated, and instead the triumvirate of Alpha Centauri, Epsilon Ventris II and Proxima Alpha Prime were shown circling Earth. Those were all fittingly oversized orbs, to demonstrate their elevated importance to the Alliance. They were the Core Worlds – densely populated, industrialised, reasonable reproductions of Earth. A number of other planets were also illustrated, although I couldn't identify them all. There were over three hundred worlds in the Alliance. I sometimes felt like I'd been on too many of them.

The secretary at the reception desk looked over at me, with a polite smile. Glossy dark hair piled atop a made-up face; fingernails dancing with LED-inlays. She had been watching a newscast on a wall-viewer: something about elections for the Martian government. I returned her smile. I had been waiting for a while.

A chime sounded. The secretary straightened her back.

"The general will see you now, Captain Harris. Please come this way."

She led me through to the conference chamber. After so many years of fieldwork, my smart-uniform collar was itchy and my dress cap was uncomfortably tight. The techs had never quite managed to make the uniform fit properly: the collar of my shirt always rubbed awkwardly against the data-port at the top of my spine. I hadn't worn this uniform in years. I felt out of place here. As I followed the *click-click* of the secretary's heels, a brief sweat even broke on my brow. Security-drones flitted about us – picturing our faces, conducting body-scans and weapon checks – then darted off elsewhere into the base.

The conference room doors slid open with a low hum. Two MP guards stood either side of the entrance, armed with shock-rifles, dressed in light body-armour. More soldiers appeared, using a hand-scanner to search me. The secretary smiled politely again, enduring the same routine.

"You can't be too sure," she said. "The Directorate watches, after all."

I nodded. The secretary briskly retreated, and the doors closed behind her.

The general's room was dimly lit and cluttered. Four men sat at the end of a long dark-wood table. They studied a hologram, thrown up by a projector set into the table. I waited awkwardly as the brass bitched over something on the holo-viewer – a tri-dimensional graphic of a planet, caught in the orbit of two ugly-looking stars. After a few moments, I coughed to try to get someone's attention.

The group looked up as one.

Cole was the largest: a man-mountain, despite his years behind a desk at *Liberty Point*. His skin was light coffee colour and his hair had grown out to a curly fuzz. He was originally from Hawaii, or so they said. He wore a military smart-suit, holo-medals displayed on the chest.

Everyone on the *Point* knew who Cole was and what he did, and even before he had risen to the rank of general he had carved out quite a reputation as a decent commanding officer. Ruthless at times, but with a sound tactical mind. His nickname "Old Man Cole" had a dual meaning – a hangover of ancient military tradition, but also meant ironically. Cole wasn't particularly old for a general – that had been one of the criticisms levelled at him on his appointment to the role. He was a good enough senior officer, as far as I was concerned – but I had little respect, in general, for his sort.

I moved into a salute, standing to attention. He waved me down.

"No formalities, trooper," Cole said, voice gravelly. He gave a broad smile. "At ease. We've been expecting you. We've met before, I think – back in seventy-seven, during the evacuation of Sigma Base?"

I nodded. "Yes, sir."

Using formal military address – *sir, general* and the rest – felt stilted and unreal to me. On most sim teams formality was actively discouraged, and my unit was no exception.

"You've met Mr Olsen already, I understand."

Olsen was one of the figures seated at the table. He was a big, flabby man in real life; well into middle-age, marked by a life of lab-work. He wore a white smock, buttoned to his fat neck. His greyed hair was thinning, swept over a balding pate. Despite his age, he beamed a smile with child-like enthusiasm. While I had some regard for Cole, I had none for Olsen or the rest of the scientific contingent on the *Point*. It was others like him who had suggested the Treaty and led us to this impossible impasse.

"That was an illuminating experience out in the Quarantine Zone, Captain," Olsen gushed. "I've never felt anything like it. Disconcerting, but interesting."

I remembered his shaking body both aboard the *New Haven*, during the Krell attack, and back on the *Point*, after our extraction. Olsen certainly didn't look as though he had enjoyed the experience on either of those occasions. Maybe hindsight, or the gathered company, had altered his perceptions. His observational role on the *Haven* had been an opportunity to prove me wrong – to displace my preconceptions – but Olsen had failed dismally.

"I'm glad you found it so," I replied, and kept the rest to myself.

"You're a problem-solver, aren't you, Harris? A real problem-solver," Cole interrupted. He mulled over the words for a moment. "We've got a problem that we need solving."

The third and fourth men at the table were both civilians. One of them was scanning a data-slate.

"I'm Mr Jostin – a civilian adviser working with the current military operation. I've perused your file extensively. Well-versed in the War, aren't you, Captain? Involved in over two hundred operations out there so far, many of key tactical importance. You've been into the Maelstrom on three occasions, as I understand it."

"I can neither confirm nor deny that," I said. "If I have been involved in such operations, they would – strictly speaking – involve contravention of the Treaty. Any such operations would be classified."

He looked up over the slate and raised an eyebrow at that. "If they existed, of course."

"Would you prefer Captain Harris, or Lazarus?" said the fourth man, with a cultured but implacable accent. He didn't wait for a reply; that was enough to let me know that these people weren't just reading from my personnel file. "You're becoming something of a legend on the *Point*. Of course, we all know about your personal link to the Treaty. Your views on the same have been made known to Command on a number of occasions. In any case, Colonel O'Neil speaks very highly of you. I understand that you know each other quite well."

I hadn't spoken with or seen O'Neil in months. Maybe that was why Cole was briefing me; because O'Neil knew that there was a fair chance I'd fail to attend, notwithstanding his post as my CO. We had a history together, one that I didn't much want to share with civvies and brass.

"That's right," I said. I chose my next words deliberately, for their neutrality: "The colonel is an associate of mine."

"This is my adviser Mr Evers," Cole said, indicating to the speaker.

Evers and Jostin were identically dressed in dark business suits complete with neckties. Both were in their thirties, Earth-standard, and had the polished appearance of corporate men. Greased black hair, unnaturally tanned skin. I hadn't seen folk like this on-station in a very long time – the perils of time-dilation caused by Q-jump technology and the sheer expense of carting civilian reps this far out of the Core Systems meant that communication by other means was preferred.

"I'm sorry, I didn't catch where you two were from," I said.

"We didn't say," Evers replied. "Doesn't matter much to your operation, Captain, but we are representatives of an industrial corporation. Interested parties in the outcome of your next mission, shall we say."

Evers smiled now as well. His teeth were perfectly spaced and frighteningly white.

I immediately disliked these men, even more than Olsen. It was a sign of the times, I supposed, that corporate interests were making their presence known out here again. The Krell War wasn't hot any more; the vultures would start moving in now, eager to make their credits from the carcass before it had completely cooled.

"We're all aware of your service record," Cole said, waving his hand dismissively at Evers and Jostin. "You'll be glad to know that we're not here to talk about that, anyway. I'm satisfied that you and your team are the right people for this job."

"And what is the job?" I asked, apprehensively. I had sat through hundreds of briefings – restricted, high profile and otherwise – but none of this felt normal.

Cole pointed at the graphic on the holo-viewer.

"Welcome to Operation Keystone. This is the Helios Star System. Eleven worlds orbiting two stars, one of which is dying. Of interest to us is Helios III – the only planet within that system that harbours any form of life."

The planet was brown and white. A band of space debris lazily circled it, not quite densely packed enough to make a proper orbital ring. Through the debris, Helios was swathed in heavy cloud cover and pocked by dark rifts. It slowly turned on its axis and the display showed technical data as it went.

"A fascinating place," Olsen chipped in. "Really unique. Almost entirely desert, but supporting a complex weather system. It has extensive underground lakes and rivers. Basic insect life—"

Cole interrupted again: "Mr Olsen is correct, but none of that is why we are interested in it."

The holo-display shifted to show grainy deep-space survey images of the planet. Great weather-beaten expanses. Craggy mountains, battered by constant winds. Death Valley on a grand scale. The sort of planet that the Alliance and Krell had fought over innumerable times in the history of the War—

There's something else there.

I leant in a little, an image stirring my curiosity.

A vast angular structure jutted from the desert. It was positioned atop one of the mountains, elevated above the desert. A ruin of some sort. It was difficult to obtain any sense of scale from the image, but I got the impression that it was *big*. The feed was poor quality and low-colour, but the ruin appeared to be a matte black. *No, not black: deeper than that.* It was a yawning absence; absorbing light.

"This is from a spy-probe. We've only managed to obtain a handful of images of the site, as the weather patterns on Helios III are so unpredictable."

The image stuttered and then disappeared. *It doesn't want to be recorded*, I thought to myself. I wasn't quite sure where the thought had come from. *It doesn't want to be remembered*.

"The visuals are less interesting than the audio," Cole went on. "Whatever that thing is, it's broadcasting a signal of immense significance. The signal is repeated constantly, and does not vary."

Jostin tapped his data-slate. "We've heard it from several star systems away. A very strong signal."

"Something not Krell, you understand," Evers added. "And not human, either."

"This is a scientific find of immense consequence," Olsen said. "Something *else* in the universe. We are calling it the Artefact. From the limited evidence we have available it appears that it is constructed from non-biological materials."

"Ergo, the Krell could not have made it," Evers said.

I watched as the image played back again. The Krell were the undisputed masters of bio-technology, and had taken that art to an absurd degree. Whereas we manufactured our technology, they grew it. From a knife to a starship, they could develop a biological reproduction – a species capable of infinite development, infinite mutation. They would have no need for an enormous deep-space transmitter.

"Even more interesting is the effect that it has on the Krell," Cole said. He leant forward now, into the holo-image. His face was suddenly painted with light, with numbers and data-flows, from the projector. "Do you think of the Krell as a religious species, Captain? Do you think that they worship, that they aspire, like us?"

"Not from what I have seen," I answered, without pause.

"Perhaps this will change your mind."

The image appeared again and I watched as it looped. The desert around the structure seemed to be moving. Then I realised that it wasn't the desert moving: those were Krell xeno-types, clawing and scratching at the sand dunes to reach the ruin. Millions of them. Irregular encampments of Krell starships pocked the mountainside; twisted bio-mechanical structures littered the desert.

"This site is a pilgrimage for the Krell. They appear hopelessly drawn to the Artefact. We've never seen behaviour like this before. This could prove instrumental to the war effort."

"Imagine if that could be harnessed," Jostin muttered, absently tapping a finger on the console. "*Weaponised.*"

Maybe they had a point here. I had seen – and killed – thousands of Krell, on over a hundred worlds. I'd never seen them drawn to something like this before. *Moths to the flame.*

The military applications of such a device were obvious.

Jostin and Evers exchanged smiles; pleased that a grunt like me was impressed with their findings.

"Have we studied the site?" I asked.

Cole gave a wry smile. "Indeed we have. From a distance at first, then, five years ago, we established an on-world facility. Manned with the best personnel we could muster."

"Assisted by corporate backing, a team of researchers was inserted into the field," Evers picked up, "with the mission statement of studying the Artefact. Led by Dr Jarvis Kellerman, a renowned xeno-biologist with Alliance military approval."

A wall-screen behind Evers lit up, showing Kellerman's smiling face. Cast against the backdrop of a green forest, maybe Earth or Mars, posed as though for a press-release. Pertinent data on the man flashed alongside his image:

DR JARVIS KELLERMAN
GENDER: MALE (NATURAL)
DATE OF BIRTH: 03/01/2219
PLACE OF BIRTH: NEW CHICAGO, LUNA
NATIONALITY: UNITED AMERICAS (FULL
　　ALLIANCE CITIZENSHIP)
SECURITY CLEARANCE: ALPHA-ALPHA-NINE
PREVIOUS ASSIGNMENTS: SCIENCE
　　OFFICER ABOARD UAS BROOKLYN
　　[2259]; ATTACHED ADVISER TO ANTARES
　　EXPEDITION [2263]; ADVISER TO
　　CONGRESSIONAL COMMITTEE [2265]
LAST KNOWN LOCATION: RESTRICTED
　　[ACCESS UNLOCKED: HELIOS III, HELIOS
　　STAR SYSTEM]
NOTABLE SERVICE HISTORY: SEE FILE
　　A-987 (RESTRICTED); SEE LINKED FILES
　　A-678 (RESTRICTED) THROUGH A-787
　　(RESTRICTED)

Other relevant data flowed down the screen and I took in what I could. Kellerman looked an impressive character, an asset to the Alliance scientific mission.

"A good man," Olsen said. "I was a follower of his work, before he left for Helios. His papers were ground breaking. As you can see, he has never had so much as a smirch on his character. Perfect record."

"He was involved in some very high-level research prior to being stationed on Helios," Evers said. He gave me a deadpan look. "All classified, of course."

I realised then that Kellerman was one of *them*: a suit, a member of the brass, an element of the *intelligentsia*. Degree from Harvard. Full military clearance. Awards for his work on neutralising the Krell menace.

Evers continued, "Dr Kellerman was sent to Helios together with a small security staff and a research team. They were equipped with sufficient firepower to hold their position, but with the express intention of hiding from the Krell rather than engaging them. This all went very well for the first few years."

"They made decent progress with the site," Cole muttered. "Nothing concrete but good work nonetheless."

"You can review Kellerman's transmissions back to base, if you think it necessary," Jostin said, although the tone of his voice suggested that this would be a waste of time. "We don't need to go into detail now."

"So what happened to them, sir?" I asked.

"The station went dark six months ago," Cole

replied. "The team were ordered to broadcast a security signal every week, to update *Liberty Point* on their progress at the site."

Olsen cleared his throat nervously. "Kellerman is – was – a fastidious researcher; he wouldn't go off the grid without a damned good reason."

"Have they been overwhelmed by the Krell?" I asked. That was my first suspicion. Sending a lightly armed team of civilian contractors to study an alien archaeological site, surrounded by Krell, didn't seem a very wise idea. It was almost too obvious that they would be discovered.

Cole nodded. "That's possible, although it would be a significant shift in their behavioural patterns. From satellite obs, the Krell appear to be almost exclusively centred on the Artefact. That's a long way from the station. Helios III is too far from any established shipping lane to have fallen foul of pirates."

"How far?" I asked.

A moment of awkward silence descended over the table. Jostin and Evers exchanged guilty glances. A dark realisation dawned on me.

"It's inside the Maelstrom, Captain," Cole said, without meeting my gaze. He added, almost apologetically: "Not far in. Despite their interest in the planet, Helios hasn't been colonised by the Krell. We're not quite sure why."

"Helios System is on the edge of the Maelstrom," Evers picked up. "Barely in the Maelstrom at all, really."

"But it is across the Quarantine Zone?" I asked. There was no point in dressing it up: I was being sent to a prohibited planet, being sent into enemy territory.

"Yes, it is," Cole said. "But we've managed to conduct this operation for several years without being impeded by the Krell. We certainly can't rule it out, but there's no reason to suspect that they have suddenly changed their strategy.

"A combat team has been arranged – all experienced special operations staff. The starship UAS *Oregon* has been authorised for your use. You'll have a scientific team and a full Sim Op bay onboard. Enough simulants to see you through the operation. Science Officer Olsen will be accompanying you during the deployment."

Olsen smiled weakly. "In case you require any scientific expertise, as a result of the presence of the Artefact."

"The distance involved – across the QZ – means that localised deployment is our only option," Cole said. "If I had my way, you could operate your sims from *Liberty Point*, but I'm told that the neural-link doesn't have sufficient range to allow for that. Sending your people to Helios is the only option.

"The mission objective will be limited. Go to the facility and ascertain the reason for the failure to report. In the event that there are survivors, provide assistance. If not, do what you do best: destroy the station and retreat to orbit. Easy job."

"Your orders are to avoid the Artefact, so far as possible," Jostin said quietly. "It can be studied later. More important to us is that any research conducted by Dr Kellerman and his team does not fall into the wrong hands."

"Into *enemy* hands," Evers added.

"Journey time will be six months, objective," Jostin said. "Chances are that if the site has seen any enemy activity, it has long since finished. You and your team are ideal for the operation: no close family ties, protracted deployment history, excellent service records. The time-dilation won't be an issue for any of you."

I nodded glumly. For those with loved ones close to them, twelve months' absence might have been an issue. For my crew, it wasn't.

Cole didn't let up the pace of the briefing. The group were talking *at* me now, rather than to me: eager that I didn't ask any more awkward questions.

He went on: "You'll have the best tech we have at our disposal. The *Oregon* is a specially adapted cruiser. You'll make it back within a year, according to our calculations. And when you do, we'll talk serious shore-leave – for you and the rest of your team." He shuffled some papers in front of him, reading absently. "There will be something in this for everyone on your team. They'll all get what they want."

Jostin continued: "Naval intelligence from inside the Maelstrom suggests that there are no significant Krell fleet dispositions in the immediate area of Helios System." I winced at that: Naval intelligence was a misnomer, certainly from inside the Maelstrom, but more significant – since when did civilian reps have access to military intel? "Using a single low-profile cruiser like the *Oregon*, it is hoped that you can operate beneath the radar."

Even that was an awkward turn of phrase – the Krell had no such thing as radar. I let the error go uncorrected.

"Operation Keystone is very important to the war effort," Evers said. "We can't emphasise that enough. Your transport leaves tomorrow at twelve-hundred. Drop-bay sixteen."

He slid a mission-pack across the table. I took it and inspected the seal; biometrically locked, labelled with the words OPERATION KEYSTONE – EYES ONLY: RESTRICTED DOCUMENTS.

"You're dismissed," Cole added, just to reinforce who was in charge here.

I saluted and left.

I walked back to my quarters. Through the outer rings of the station, the longest route back, to give me some time to think.

I wasn't sure how I felt about this operation. Sure, a new mission was a good thing. In that sense, it gave me focus and motivation – set me another task.

But something felt wrong about the mission. Old Man Cole himself had given it to me. That had never happened before. Then there were the circumstances of the op: the journey into the Maelstrom, the Artefact, Dr Kellerman. The image of the Artefact, rearing up out of the desert, came into my mind's eye. The behaviour of the Krell was like nothing I had ever experienced before. It felt implacably wrong.

Maybe I should've declined the mission, I thought.

Maybe there was a choice there, a decision some-where along the way. But that was pure fantasy: I would never have refused it. The desire to make transition again, to get back into the fight, was too much to resist. *No point in lying to myself about it.* Killing Krell was all that I knew. I would've taken any opportunity to get back out there.

I sighed to myself and checked the station local time. By now, the rest of my squad would have been summoned back onto active duty, although they wouldn't know the reason. I couldn't reveal the detail until we left *Liberty Point*. I turned the scant briefing folder over in my hands.

"Looks like you get your wish, Jenkins," I said to myself.

I needed another drink. I decided that I'd stop by the station PX before going back to my quarters.

CHAPTER FOUR

INTO THE MAELSTROM

The next morning, my squad and I duly attended drop-bay sixteen. It had been cleared specially for our operation – empty, save for a transport shuttle sitting patiently on the apron. The shuttle was being refuelled for the run over to the *Oregon*.

Through the view-ports studding the drop-bay walls, I watched as the UAS *Oregon* was loaded with cargo for the op. A remote shuttle conducted a series of runs between the *Oregon* and the *Liberty Point*, working as quickly as possible.

My team anxiously milled about, eager for more information on our mission.

"This our ship, Captain?" Martinez asked me, arms crossed over his chest. "Looks all right."

"She's called the *Oregon*," I answered. "And yes, Martinez, this is our transport."

"What the fuck do you know about starships?" Kaminski asked of Martinez.

"More than you. I was Alliance Marine Corps, *mano*."

Martinez was quietest of the team but when he had something to say, I made sure to listen.

"This should be just your sort of op, then," I said. "A nice big ship and plenty of guns."

"It would help if I knew where we were going," Martinez said. He stroked his carefully groomed goatee, stared out of the view-port.

Martinez wasn't happy about being recalled back to active duty, and had already made his opinion known to me. None of the team was particularly pleased about the haste in which the operation had been assembled.

The *Oregon* did look like a worthy ship. She was the sort of vessel shown on news-feeds and vid-casts, the sort of ship that the Navy were keen to promote to the folks back home: a jack of all trades. The technical designation was "compact assault cruiser". She had a gun-like profile – all aggressive angles, nothing like the *New Haven*. The nose erupted with antennae and sensor-pods, feeling into the dark. The entire craft was polished gunmetal grey, reinforcing the impression that it was a weapon of war given form as a starship.

"She was requisitioned from the Navy fleet and retrofitted for our op," I said to my squad. I had reviewed the service history of the ship. "She's a fully manned starship, not disposable like the Wildcats."

"So we're supposed to bring this one back?" Kaminski asked with a grin.

"Most definitely," I said. "Standing crew of forty ensigns, a sizeable maintenance team, and a cadre of officers."

"What I wouldn't give for a squadron of Dragonflies in the belly of that thing," Jenkins said, nodding towards the view-port. "Or maybe even some Hornets."

"Not this time, Jenkins."

Jenkins gave a dissatisfied shrug. She was obviously probing for more detail on our operation.

The ship wasn't big enough to have a proper hangar and the belly was already loaded with a Wildcat APS for planetary insertion. Jenkins was talking about Aerospace Force support. The MG-11 Dragonfly was a multipurpose gunship, employed for close-support against either ground-based targets or enemy fighters. The MSK-60 Hornet was a highly manoeuvrable killship – used in squadrons, they could take down far larger warships, firing plasma warheads over vast distances. We'd used support from both varieties of ship in the past, but this mission called for stealth over brute force.

"It's just another operation," I said to my squad. "We've been into the Maelstrom before. Nothing new there." The group gave non-committal nods. "And we've operated sims from a starship plenty of times."

"Then why all the secrecy?" Kaminski asked. "What is the op, Captain? Our station-leave was cancelled for this. That hasn't happened before."

"Ears only, Kaminski," I said. "It's called Operation Keystone but I'll give you more detail when we get out there."

The squad grumbled to themselves. They knew the outline of the op, knew that we would be on protracted leave from the *Point*, and that our destination was the Maelstrom, but nothing more. I felt bad for not sharing the rest of the mission brief with them, but I knew that when they heard it, they wouldn't like it.

A Navy officer approached me. He was suave-looking, with a mop of blond hair and a pristine blue smart-suit like he had just come off parade. Handsome – not as good-looking as Blake, but he had youth on his side.

"Captain Conrad Harris, Simulant Operations? Commanding officer of Operation Keystone?" he asked. "I'm Captain James Atkins. The UAS *Oregon* is my ship." He puffed out his chest with pride as he declared ownership. "My crew are just confirming the manifest."

While he looked terribly young for a starship captain – barely thirty years, Earth-standard – I had already looked him up on the *Point*'s military database, and in truth he was closer to forty. He was also an experienced Naval captain, and had served as the *Oregon*'s commanding officer for five years. Even so, sailors rarely got their hands dirty – I hoped that he could hold his own out in the Maelstrom.

"That's me," I said, slinging my flight bag onto a loading pallet. "What have we got?"

Atkins gave a dry laugh. "My ship has everything. A simulant operation bay has been installed in the medical centre – you'll be able to navigate your sims from the ship. There are enough simbodies for ten missions. The armoury has everything that you boys could wish for."

"Less of the boys," Jenkins said. "And I hope we won't need that many."

"Never hurts to have spares," Martinez said.

"We'll be safe in orbit while you boys," Atkins winked at Jenkins, "and girls do the hard work. She has a decent Q-drive with good stealth characteristics. The ship has multiple stealth systems. High-end stuff – fresh out of Research and Development. We've got a complement of space-to-space particle beam accelerators, a battery of railguns and a silo of plasma torpedoes." Atkins was enjoying this; bragging about the toys on his ship. He pointed out of the view-port, tracing a line on the spine of his ship with his finger. "She's got sixteen laser batteries on the upper hull. Those can automatically track incoming enemy fire – the AI is one of the most advanced in the fleet." Atkins nodded to himself in contentment. "It's overkill, really – we've never had it so good."

"I just hope it's going to be enough," I said, bursting his bubble.

"Only the best equipment has been sanctioned for Keystone," came another voice behind me.

I turned to see Olsen, his face sweaty with exertion. He was trailing an entourage of science officers.

"We need this to go smoothly," Olsen said to me.

"We'll do our best," I muttered. "We always do."

The *Oregon* quietly simmered with activity. The Naval crew hurried with their appointed tasks, ensuring that we safely detached from the *Liberty*

Point. Space Control gave the necessary approvals for departure, and the ship navigated her way through the flotilla surrounding the *Point.*

"Safe clearance from FOB *Liberty Point* has been achieved," the ship's PA sounded.

I found my assigned quarters; a cabin about as small as that I had back on the *Point*, but a room to myself nonetheless. My squad was quartered at the aft of the ship, in a barracks usually designated for shipboard marines. The layout of the ship had taken some reconsideration, to accommodate an enlarged medical suite – a necessity given that we were to be operating the simulator-tanks from there.

Before I had a proper chance to think about exploring the rest of the ship, the PA sounded again: "Captain Harris, please report to Observation. Captain Harris, to the observation deck."

The crew politely acknowledged me as I made my way to Observation, with nods and informal salutes. My rank didn't mean much to the Naval crew – at least not officially – but I guessed that some of them had heard of me. A couple of times, whispers were exchanged behind my back. Maybe the conversations were positive, but they were just as likely to be negative. After all, who would want to travel into the Maelstrom? They probably blamed me for the operation in general.

Observation was a functional open deck, with large windows covering the outer hull wall. Already, the *Point* – with that distinctive vertical hub and multiple outer-ring formation; a giant spinning top – and the fleet were becoming more distant. Space was opening up before us: stars sprinkling the void.

Atkins stood alone at the far end of the deck, hands clasped behind his back. That seemed to be his preferred stance. He didn't turn to acknowledge me when I arrived, but gave a curt nod to my reflection in the window.

"We won't be making proper progress until the Q-drive activates," Atkins said.

"I guess we'll be in hypersleep for that. The ship's itinerary says sleep call is in an hour."

"It's standard operating procedure for ground crew to hibernate first, to be followed by the Navy staff," Atkins reeled off. He liked procedure; knowing regulation gave him a veneer of confidence. "Then the ship's AI will take over, and the Q-drive will be activated."

"I take it that you didn't call me here to talk about the itinerary?" I said. I wasn't quite sure why he had asked for my attendance; he seemed to know his stuff, and I was prepared to defer final judgement on his character.

He broke a bitter smile. "No, I didn't. It was something a bit more personal than that."

"Go on."

"The *Oregon* is a good ship," he started. Then, voice dropping in pitch a little; his confident façade seeming to crack ever so slightly: "My crew are good people. One and all."

"I know. I might be infantry, Atkins, but I'm not stupid."

"I'm asking you to look after them, is all. I'm

asking you to make wise choices while we're out *there*." He waved a hand towards the observation window, towards the Maelstrom beyond the plexiglass. It was much larger than either the territories occupied by the Alliance or the Asiatic Directorate.

"Have you ever been into the Maelstrom?" I asked.

"No, I haven't. But I've read the Operation Keystone briefing, such that I'm entitled to. The details are scant. They tell me that we're going after some sort of ghost signal – that Science Division has found an alien artefact on a backwater Krell world?"

"If you know that much, then you know almost as much as me. I'll reveal the rest as soon as I have clearance."

Atkins grew quiet for a moment.

"I understand that," he eventually continued. "Regulation and procedure must be adhered to. It's just that – well, any starship captain would be *anxious* about this sort of operation."

I rubbed my chin. "Let's agree on something. I'll depend on you to run this ship, exactly as you see fit, and you depend on me to do everything I can to bring you and your crew back in one piece."

Atkins smiled again, but this time a smile of relief. He briskly turned to me and held out his hand. We shook; his grip was surprisingly strong for a sailor. He had a wedding-band on one hand: undecorated, functional.

"You can depend on me, Captain," he said.

"And you can do the same on me. No promises – we're going into the Maelstrom, after all, but I'm not going to throw anyone away."

"Good enough."

Atkins immediately regained his composure. That was why he wanted to speak with me alone; because he didn't want his crew, or probably mine, seeing that he was disturbed by this operation. His choice to air his concerns like this made me respect him more, in some perverse way.

"Has our route been plotted?" I asked, returning to more mundane areas of conversation – a topic on which Atkins would surely want to speak.

"Very precisely," he said. He clasped his hands behind his back again, puffed up his chest: I'd read him well. "We're moving the minimum ten AU distance from *Liberty Point*, then we will be accelerating to Q-speed. We'll drop out of real-space, and the computer will take care of the navigation from there."

"How about the Great Veil?" I asked.

"We're using the most recent Naval intel, based on the Turinger Predictive Model. Highly accurate."

The Veil was another of the Maelstrom's defensive measures: a loose collection of space particulate, meteors and asteroids, amassed over the millennia in an enormous orbital cloud around the Maelstrom itself. Penetrating this cloud was the first obstacle for any traveller to the Maelstrom; given the speed that most starships to the region would be travelling, the material could cause a hull breach. The Veil was the equivalent of the Solar System's Oort Cloud, but on a vast, lethal scale.

Atkins nodded to himself. He traced an arc

with his finger, across one of the spiral arms of the Maelstrom. "Then we will be moving under the power of the Q-drive through the Ibanez Sector, directly to Helios Primary system."

"You've accounted for gravimetric storm activity in the region, I take it?"

"Of course, of course," he said. "There are predicted storms moving out of nearby systems, possibly being thrown out by a minor black hole along the Yabaris Quadrant." He again pointed to the locations of those sectors in the Maelstrom; those meant nothing to me, but I was happy to let him talk. "We *should* be safe, although nothing is a certainty."

I nodded along with him. The Maelstrom flashed and flickered in front of us, sparkling seductively off the observation window. Bright and colourful, jewel-like. The very centre of the star-swarm seemed alive with storms, pulsating with galactic energies.

"How do you feel about this?" Atkins asked. "I know it is probably classified, and I'm not asking for details. I've heard rumours that you and your team have been into the Maelstrom before."

No point in lying to the man who would shortly be responsible for all of our lives. "The rumours are true. But that isn't why I don't like this op."

"Then why is it?"

"The Maelstrom and I have a history together," I said, adopting a definitive edge to my voice: *I don't want to discuss this any more, so don't even ask*.

Atkins got the message, and our conversation

ended naturally. I stood with him for a long time, both of us silent, both of us watching the dark splendour of the Maelstrom.

At the appointed time, my squad and I reported to the hypersleep suite as required.

"Looking forward to a six-month sleep, Martinez?" Blake asked.

Martinez grunted. "Just don't keep me awake with your snoring."

We were all dressed in pale gowns, and medics attended to us. Olsen oversaw the procedure: IV drips into forearms, numerous injections to prep us for the long sleep.

The room had berths for maybe a hundred personnel, and would quarter the current starship staff easily. I smelt antiseptic and formaldehyde; a heavy odour that radiated not just from the medically pristine equipment but also my own body. The freezers were essential for a crew to travel through Q-space, to counter the demands of modern space operations. Known by many different names – cryogenic hibernation, deep-freeze, suspended animation – it all amounted to the same process: artificial, prolonged sleep.

Atkins walked the hypersleep suite, overseeing the process. Many of the non-essential starship crew – maintenance staff, comms techs and junior officers – had also started going into cold sleep. The suite was becoming jammed with personnel.

"We're going to be entering Q-space in just under three hours," he called across the room, medics tending to their subjects falling silent as he spoke. "Stealth systems will engage at this time. We will be effectively invisible to anyone who cares to look for us. Just enjoy your sleep."

"All subjects are prepped and ready to go under," the chief medical tech declared. "Permission requested to put first group in, Captain."

Atkins gave a nod. "Permission granted."

I slipped into my hypersleep capsule – a glass-and-chrome tube, already filling with preservative fluids. It was cold and unwelcoming; tomb-like on the inside. The exact opposite of the warming waters of the simulator-tanks.

"Sweet dreams," Jenkins called, as she got into her own capsule. The rest of the team followed.

"Let's hope."

The capsule canopy slid into place above me, and the sounds of the outside world became muffled and distant. Through the silvered glass, the medics hurried about the sleepers, conducting last-minute checks. Even now, their faces were becoming blurred and vague.

I've never liked the sleep and this was no different. There was nothing natural about hypersleep. *The human body isn't designed for this sort of experience.* The world around me was slowing. I was so cold – the temperature of my entire body dropping rapidly. Cryofreeze was being pumped into me, through the multitude of cables and feeders attached to my body. I turned in my capsule, watched the others going through the same procedure. I was being plunged so deep into a state of suspended animation that I was a hair's breadth from actual death.

I freaked out for just a second. Wanted to bang my fists against the glass canopy, stop the sleep. I wanted to rail against it, but my arms and legs were lead.

The shipboard lights above were hazed, adopting a star-like quality. I focused on them, as the sleep finally took me.

"Anyone who says that you don't dream in hyper-sleep is a liar." Those were the words of DI Cubbitts, my drill instructor during basic induct. That had been twenty years ago, give or take, and every time I went into the freezers I remembered those words of wisdom. *"The difference between real and artificial sleep is that you can't wake up until the AI decides that you should. If you have a bad trip, you're stuck with it."*

Cubbitts had gone full Section Eight – declared unfit for duty by reason of mental incapacity – shortly after my graduation from basic.

The *Oregon*'s corridors were empty now. The starship crew had gone to sleep as well, leaving the maintenance-bots and the AI to run the *Oregon*. With no human crew left awake, the corridors were darkened – running lights switched off to preserve power on the long journey through space.

I escaped my body, wandered the empty halls as an incorporeal entity: a restless ghost. Stole glances at the dusted, cold command stations; watched the automated security-bots patrolling the hangar bay. Observed the ship's AI plot our course through the QZ, then through the Great Veil. A mind vastly superior to mine or Atkins' or

Olsen's conducted vast mathematical calculations to ensure that we safely countered the fluctuating eddies of the Maelstrom, that we escaped the devastating effects of the solar storms.

In some ways, Jostin and Evers and the others *had* been right: we were not travelling far into the Maelstrom. To properly cross over to the most central Krell star systems would have been far more dangerous. There, the storms and pulsars and black holes were constant, and without accurate star-data and Q-jump plotting, death would be a surety.

But it has happened. It has happened before.

A thought niggled – refusing to be dismissed, irritating the edge of my consciousness. It was impossible for me to know when the event would happen but I knew that the *Oregon* would eventually cross over into the Maelstrom – into Krell-occupied space. That would be in direct violation of the Treaty.

It's already been violated. I've been here before – been into the Maelstrom.

That, and the Alliance had already sent Dr Kellerman and his staff into the Maelstrom.

But none of that meant that this operation was *right*.

This felt different – worse – in some indescribable way.

By doing this – by going into the Maelstrom – I was dishonouring her memory.

Her sacrifice.

Elena.

I didn't want to remember. It was so much

easier to forget, to just think about the next death, than to dwell on old memories. *Painful* memories.

That was why I hated the cold sleep. Because in the glass-and-steel coffin, I couldn't escape the memories – because they came to me whether I wanted to remember them or not.

CHAPTER FIVE

SOMEONE WHO ISN'T AFRAID OF DEATH, OF DYING

Ten years ago

I was a sergeant with Alliance Special Forces, serving on Torus Seigel IV, when the order came. It was a simple directive – REPORT FOR IMMEDIATE PSYCH-EVAL – together with a series of further specifics. A transport shuttle had been arranged for onward processing and I was to leave the frontline immediately.

Not even my CO knew why I was being recalled. When I boarded the off-world shuttle, the Naval crew weren't permitted to give me details of my destination, or even how long I was supposed to be away from my unit.

I was quartered on a military base, a research facility with the look and feel of an orbital station.

Time, date and location undisclosed. Six other soldiers had been retrieved from the frontline as well – all Spec Forces troopers. One of those men was a young trooper called Vincent Kaminski, a soldier under my command.

"This is some serious bullshit, eh, Sarge?" was all he could muster when we spoke on our arrival.

I couldn't have put it better myself.

The base was staffed by fully kitted MPs, dog-faced bastards who looked as though they pulled triggers first and asked questions later. The sort of staff not used to being argued with.

The guards separated us on our arrival. Alone, I was led into a room. A sign on the outer door read ASSESSMENT CHAMBER. The room itself was empty save for a metal table and a pair of chairs, bathed in clinical white light. That hurt my eyes: after a six-month tour on Seigel IV, I wasn't used to light. Seigel had been cloaked in perpetual darkness and acclimatising myself to basic human experiences wasn't easy. I'd spent six months more or less sealed inside a hostile-environment suit, on the frontline, fighting in the dark. I looked down at what I was wearing; the transport had been arranged in such a hurry, that I was still in my combat undersuit. The webbing carried the dirt and muck of the protracted Torus operation. That was a souvenir for Command, from the frontline. I still felt groggy from hypersleep, and hadn't shaved since I'd come off the shuttle.

I sat on one of the metal chairs, which was bolted to the ground. I had been waiting in the room for a few minutes, and had already tried to move the chair. *They don't even trust me with the furniture*, I thought. *Place feels like a damned prison.*

"Anyone out there going to speak to me?" I shouted, looking to the door. My voice echoed around the room, but no one answered.

This was not a regular occurrence. Grunts were supposed to take orders and die, and that was all I was. Enough of my unit had done that already. A recall to psych-eval wasn't the norm. I was angry, because in this room – on this research base, whatever it was – there was nothing that I could do to further the war effort. Out on Seigel IV, I could at least try to make a difference.

A noise from the door shook me awake. There was a sound like a mechanical lock being activated, and faces appeared at the glass window. The door eventually opened.

A woman entered the room, looking down at a data-slate, hurriedly reading from it. Immediately, this woman became the subject of my hostility. *She* had required me to leave the frontline, to leave my comrades. *She* was responsible.

The woman was slim and much shorter than me. Dressed in an intentionally dated outfit: loose white blouse, knee-length fitted pencil skirt. The combination only seemed to accentuate her tight figure. Dark hair spilled over her shoulders. Antiquated black-rimmed glasses – those were surely more an affectation than a necessity: eyesight correction was simple and cheap, widely available. Difficult to judge her age, but I guessed at barely thirty Earth-standard.

She walked with a determined gait and gave me a slight smile. Her heeled shoes pattered like hard rain on the tiled floor. Forgetting herself, she tried to move the bolted-down chair opposite me, and then frowned as she realised that it wouldn't budge. She sat.

A military guard took up position over by the door, a shock-rifle across his chest. That simply reinforced the impression that the facility was some sort of prison, making my anger even hotter.

"Those are fixed in place for a reason," he said, gruffly.

"I don't think that your presence will be required here," she said, nodding at the guard. She pushed a curl of dark hair from her face. "I'm sure that the sergeant will behave himself."

"Orders, ma'am," the guard said. "The subjects are, by their nature, prone to acts of violence."

I stood from the table, felt my face flush with irritation. "I'll bet that you enjoy your work. Fuck you, desk jockey."

The guard gave me a smug nod. "See."

The woman was completely unruffled by our macho posturing, and barely looked up from her reading.

"He is not a *subject*, guardsman. Sergeant Harris is a Special Forces soldier, and he has been selected for assessment. I think I know best here." Her voice was firm despite her small size. She was obviously used to being listened to. "And I think you are not required here."

The guard glared at me but obviously thought it

better not to argue, and stomped out of the room. I gave him the finger as he left.

The woman arranged some papers in front of her on the desk, positioning the data-slate on her lap so that she could read from it. I watched her movements; very precise, very ordered. She took an inordinate amount of time organising herself, but there was nothing uncomfortable about the silence that stretched between us.

"My name is Dr Elena Marceau, and I am a senior military psychiatrist," she said. Her voice was melodic, slightly accented – French, or at least European. If not from Earth, then one of the Core Systems. "Welcome to Jefferson Research Facility. Thank you so much for attending this evaluation, Sergeant Harris."

"I didn't have a choice."

"I understand that. But aren't you pleased to be away from the frontier of the Krell War, Sergeant? This facility has gravity, heat and air. That's more than you had on Seigel IV."

"I suppose," I answered. The truth was more complex. The absence of war was disconcerting: I had become used to explosions in the distance, used to the ground trembling with the aftershock of another artillery barrage. "You get used to war. It becomes a way of life. On Seigel IV, you learn to hate the quiet."

"And why is that?"

"The quiet comes after the bombardments. If your ears aren't ringing, then it means you're already dead."

She nodded. "I understand."

"That's just it – you don't understand. No disrespect, but what is this all about?"

She smiled. She had high cheekbones, but a rounded face, with a small, animated mouth.

"I've been asked to conduct a specialist evaluation. May I call you Conrad?"

"Call me whatever you like. Are you Sci-Div?"

"Not quite Science Division, but somewhere between Sci-Div and the military." Back on track: "Conrad – that's an unusual name, isn't it?"

"I suppose."

"Perhaps I should ask your parents about it. Are they still alive?"

"I think you already know the answer to that question."

Elena continued smiling, and momentarily looked down at the data-slate. The light of the illuminated slate reflected onto the lenses of her glasses, concealing her dark eyes.

"It says here that your mother was in the military. She served as an Alliance Navy ensign, under 301st Earth Defence Battalion. My notes indicate that she remained on a military contract even after you were born."

"Seems like you already know everything," I grunted in disdain. No one talked about my mother. "This is bullshit. You can read this without me being here. I need to get back out there – to fight the war that keeps all of this rubbish," I waved a hand at her and her data-slate, "safe and sound."

She pursed her lips. This assessment was going to go on regardless of my engagement, it seemed.

"It says here that your father was an Army man. That he reached the rank of master sergeant."

"Yeah, so what?"

Gently needling the wound. Hot bile rose inside me. Elena didn't even seem to have noticed.

"It says that he fought in the Martian War. He was also involved in the repression of the Charon Mutiny. He earned the Purple Heart for his part in the operation. You must be very proud of him, and he must be very proud of you."

"If you know so much about him, then you'll also know that he's dead. He fought for twenty-five years against the Directorate."

"His record was impressive. I meant no offence."

I sucked my teeth. I didn't want to think about my father, about Earth, about the Directorate. "Neither did I, but he died a long time ago. Look – why don't you cut to the chase? Try asking me something new – something that you don't already have the answer to."

"Do you hate the Directorate?"

"This isn't about the Directorate. It's about the Krell."

"The Directorate have indicated that they may send reinforcements to Seigel IV. How would you feel about that?"

"There's been talk of the Asiatic Director-ate sending troops to the frontline for as long as I can remember, but it's never happened." The Directorate watched, with hungry eyes, as the Alliance fought the Krell: eager to see us fall, yes, but equally conscious that the Krell might break out of the Maelstrom and present an even bigger threat. "Humanity will always be at war, whether against each other or an alien race. I'm a soldier, so more than anyone I know that. It just so happens that the Krell War is more lethal than any other – because it's a war for survival. The Krell want us dead and gone, blasted from existence.

"If we decide to wipe ourselves out, then that's our choice. It shouldn't be down to the Krell, so far as I'm concerned. I'm just a believer in self-determination."

"Very well put. But you obviously think that Alliance personnel records are more extensive than they actually are. We don't have complete data on all personnel, certainly not personnel from your parents' era. How and when did your father die, Conrad?"

I stood from the table abruptly, slammed a fist down onto it. My heart raced. I suddenly realised that I stank of days-old sweat. I could smell myself. In the race to get out here – for some dumb-shit psych-eval that could have been conducted by satellite link – I hadn't even showered.

"Have you ever seen the Krell up close?" I barked.

A face appeared at the door, bobbing about to see inside: the guard, probably eager to enter the room and use that shock-rifle on me. Elena fixed my gaze. She must have been half of my body mass but she didn't flinch. There was no fear or anxiety in those eyes. I already knew the answer to my question: of course, she had never seen a Krell. She had probably never been outside of the Core Systems, for a start.

Elena didn't even move. Her jaw muscles tightened. Not nervously, but in determination.

"I don't want to talk about my father," I said, as firmly as I could.

"Then just sit. We can discuss other things."

And like an obedient dog, I did sit. I sat and regained my composure: looked into the sympathetic eyes of a creature so different to me that she might as well have been a different species. There was me: filthy, armoured, recovering from a chemical hangover, war the only reality I knew. There was her: small, manicured, beautiful, caring.

"Let's move on then," she said. "You're thirty years old. Both parents deceased. No marriage contract. Ten years of excellent military service. Born in Detroit Metro, United Americas. Why did you join the military?"

No one had ever asked me that question before. I rubbed my chin in thought. This woman had a way of stirring something up inside me: talking about family and where I had come from wasn't an easy thing for me to do. Part of me wanted to get through this assessment – whatever it was – as quickly as possible, and get back to Seigel IV. But another part actually wanted to engage with her, to open up. Right now, both were in competition and it was unclear which would win.

I answered truthfully. "A long time ago I lost someone. They showed me that there was more to life than just the Metro. Where I grew up, you had two choices: die on the streets, or leave the Metro. Sixteen million people living in the ruins of the old world. Sounds like fun, doesn't it? I don't know that place any more. I chose to live, and joining up let me do that for at least another tour."

"And you've signed up for several additional tours. As a Special Forces trooper, you could have declined those."

"It's called re-upping."

"Of course. You've travelled widely in the defence of your government. You have an extensive record of military achievements." She looked up from the slate again. "Whatever you think of me, I value what you do. I want to assure you of that."

I sighed. "Sure. Whatever."

"You've been noted as having a remarkably stable psychological profile. Calm under fire. Good judgement. Sound tactical mind. Completely abstinent of alcoholic beverages and narcotics – legal and otherwise."

"It clouds the mind. I prefer to stay sharp."

"I can see that this assessment frustrates you, Conrad. I apologise for that, but my role here is an important one. We would not have recalled you unless we felt that there was some potential benefit. I'm going to call this session to an end."

I noticed a small spy-eye – a security camera – in one corner of the room. A blinking red light appeared inside the plastic cowling, following me as I bobbed my head.

"You got subsonics on that thing?" I asked.

Elena laughed. The sound was pleasing, genuine.

"No, Conrad. We don't use those. Maybe it just feels better to speak with someone about your experiences."

Perhaps, I realised, *she's right*. Subsonics would've

been the easy way out: sound pacification. Drench the room with the right frequencies, placate the subject. Those were used by law-enforcement agencies across Alliance space. But this was something different. For just an instant, it felt like a weight had been lifted from me.

"And in any case, we need veteran soldiers for this programme," Elena went on. "We need something unique. Someone who isn't afraid of death, of dying."

"Those are two different things," I said, without thinking. "I know death, but dying isn't as easy."

"Again, well put. I can see there is more to you that the uniform and the gun. I'm attached to a new initiative. It is currently in the trial phase, and access to the Programme is highly restricted. I think that you might be interested. My superiors have selected you as an appropriate candidate. How would you like to take the fight to the Krell?"

"I'm already doing that."

She laughed again, crossing her legs under the table. "This will be completely different. This will be something so much better."

What did I have to lose? "I'm listening."

"There will be additional training, of course, but it will be worth it. It is called the Simulant Operations Programme, and I will be responsible for your induction."

CHAPTER SIX

NOT A DRILL

"Time to wake up."

The prickle of processed air hit my skin, and with blurry vision I made out the hypersleep chamber onboard the *Oregon*. There was my squad, and the other team-members assembled for the mission. Medics were awakening us. I shook with the bone-numbing cold of hypersleep.

I dragged myself upright, and then with monumental effort got out of my capsule. The metal floor beneath me was cold against my wet feet. Better to get it over with: I yanked at the feeder cables and IV drip attached to my forearms, felt the brief lance of pain as the needles came free. Bright droplets of red blood welled from the puncture wounds.

"Morning, everyone," I managed.

My team variously groaned and grunted in response.

Another birthday lost to the freezers.

A medical drone flitted in front of me; as small

as my hand, with a medi-sensor mounted on the nose. It shone a light into my face, making me wince. I had neither the energy nor the inclination to swat the thing away.

"Identity verified," it chirped in an electronic voice. "Vitals good. Drink plenty of fluids to remain hydrated. Consume nutrient shakes to ensure swift recovery from hypersleep medication…"

The drone hovered away to inspect other sleepers.

"I hate the freezers," Kaminski said, towelling himself dry. "Always give me the aches."

"Quit complaining," Jenkins called from across the chamber. Her voice was hoarse – she hadn't spoken in six months. She stood naked, drying her bobbed black hair. "We've done this a hundred times already. You should be used to it by now."

Kaminski shrugged. "Whatever, Jenkins. Just remember how far we are from the Quarantine Zone." He scratched his head, as though thinking about that for a moment. Then, when he couldn't come up with a compelling answer to his own question: "Light-years. You get lost out here, no one is going to come help you but the 'Ski. There won't be any letters from home out here."

Blake emerged from his capsule, still dripping in preservative fluid. His blond hair was longer than the standard military cut, but on a Sim Ops unit protocol wasn't strictly enforced.

"Like Kaminski can read anyway," he said, and the rest of the squad laughed.

Blake locked eyes with a ship technician – a

young woman, pretty in a demure kind of way – who smiled, then averted her eyes. She offered him a towel to cover his muscled body, and he deliberately hesitated before taking it.

"Well, thank you very much, little lady," he said.

"I guess the hard work starts now," said Jenkins, brusquely. "We've slept for long enough."

"Damn straight," I said. A medic handed me a nutrient drink, and I swilled it down. It tasted like thick, warm piss. "Let's not forget that we were being paid for that sleep."

The group grumbled in unison. We accrued combat-pay during hypersleep, for what it was worth.

Atkins was already up and dressed, his Naval uniform dazzlingly blue to my colour-drained eyes. Martinez was next to me, flexing his arms to rid himself of the freezer aches.

"How did you get up so quickly?" he asked the captain.

"I like to set my capsule to thaw a day early," he said, grinning. "Gets me functional before the rest of you wake up. Hypersleep isn't so bad when you get used to it."

He enthusiastically clapped his hands. His handsome looks and bright-eyed nature were vaguely nauseating. Martinez rolled his eyes, said nothing: he'd probably spent more time in hypersleep than the rest of us combined, but that didn't mean that he boasted about it.

"All right, people. The Q-space drive disengaged three days ago. Ship's clock indicates we have been out of real-space for six months, exactly as planned. We're inside the Maelstrom. There have been no reported enemy contacts."

"Would we know about it if there had been?" Jenkins croaked. "I take it that the Krell would have just blown us out of space without giving a warning."

Kaminski laughed at that. "Right on, sister."

"Simmer down, people," I said. "As mission commander, I want to brief you all on the operation before we reach Helios. Assemble in the briefing room in one hour."

Briefing was tucked behind the bridge, an auditorium-style chamber that could accommodate four times the *Oregon*'s current occupants. There was my squad, the ship's officers under Atkins, and Olsen's science staff. Barely twenty personnel, all told. I had set up a tri-D viewer at the head of the room, with mission papers spread across a table in front of me.

The team gathered around and I briefed them on what I already knew about the Artefact – little as it was. Olsen must have previously prepped his people, because they showed little surprise at the revelation. They were all eager young faces, following us out into the dark in pursuit of knowledge. I'd seen their type too many times before, and the story never ended well. The Navy officers, on the other hand, were positively alarmed by the information. Save for Atkins and his closest personnel, the intelligence had been kept from the rest of the crew. This was a strictly need to know operation.

I moved on to the meat of the brief.

"The mission is codenamed Keystone, and it's an insertion operation. We'll deploy on Helios via APS. Straight down the pipe, landing virtually on top of the station. From there, we will conduct preliminary recon of the facility. Scanners are our friends, as always. We will attempt to recover any surviving station staff. We will not be attracting attention to ourselves. We will not stay and fight."

"What are the chances of finding anyone alive, Captain?" Martinez asked.

"Your guess is as good as mine."

"The station has failed to report for twelve months objective," Atkins added. He was making allowance for our journey from the *Point*. "There haven't been any fresh broadcasts while we were en route. Read into that what you will."

Jenkins took the opportunity to question the captain further. "What about engine signatures from other ships entering or leaving Helios' space? Do we know whether anyone else has been here in recent history?"

Atkins shrugged. "That's a loaded question, Corporal. If a human ship had dropped out of Q-space in the last few days, it would likely leave a tachyon spill – their trail back into real-space, as it were. But nothing. No one has been here."

"What about Krell ships?" Jenkins pushed.

"That's the complication," Atkins explained. "They rarely leave an engine signature."

"That's helpful nonetheless," I muttered, thumbing through the mission papers. "Makes it more likely that the station was overrun by a Krell Collective on the ground."

"Which is where we come in," Kaminski said, shooting an imaginary target with a pistol made from his fingers. "At least we can rule out the Directorate."

The news did little to lighten the mood though. We all knew that we were operating out here, in distant alien space, without back-up or support. The sense of anticipation was readable; an aura emanating from the gathered group. I took in their concerned faces – knew that I would have to keep morale up if this was going to work.

"Once we've established whether the station is operational," I said, "we move to stage two of the mission. If there is some genuine reason for the station failing to report – which seems less likely, based on what we've just been told – then we offer any assistance necessary. If the facility is no longer viable, then we demolish it. It runs on a standard-pattern power generator, the same as a civilian starship. A well-placed demolition charge will send the entire place into meltdown."

I activated the tri-D viewer and called up a map of Helios Station. A wireframe hologram appeared in front of me. I pointed out key locations.

"The plans show multiple hangar bays and some storage silos. A power station – which houses the generator and main power supply – sits in the middle of the outpost, alongside the Operations centre."

The power station was the lifeblood of the station, but Operations was the beating heart – a tower housing what little capacity the staff had to contact the rest of the human race.

"There are habitation modules on the perimeter of the outpost. A laboratory complex sits here."

Even in tri-D, the buildings and base looked bland. No doubt the station had been set up from orbit, and it was likely that each building had once been a module from a settler-class starship – disassembled, then dropped to Helios' surface. Given the adverse conditions in which the station was established, an orbital drop was the only safe option.

"Looks like a hundred other bases we've fought over," Blake said. "Move along. Nothing to see here."

I nodded. "Let's not get complacent. I want the ground team to study the schematics before we make transition. They will also be loaded onto the suit-computers."

"How far is Helios Station from the, uh, Artefact?" Blake asked.

"Several kilometres." I brought up another holo-map of the wider desert region, and I pointed out the locations. "But the Artefact doesn't form part of our tactical plan. If Command wants someone to babysit, then they can send the regular Army."

"What about atmospheric conditions down there?" Martinez said. "Are they human-standard? Or are we going to be buttoned up the whole time?"

"It's breathable, but not quite California," Olsen pitched in.

"Hey, since the Directorate launched that attack on San Angeles, California isn't such a picture any more," said Kaminski.

"Thanks for that, 'Ski," Jenkins said.

Jenkins' family was out of San Angeles. The city-state took over most of the western seaboard – or at least it had, until it had been nuked by the Directorate back in seventy-one. The loss of life had been immense; it was too recent an atrocity to joke about.

Olsen continued: "Meteorological data from the station satellite suggests extensive storms batter much of the planet's main continent, often appearing with little or no warning. Limited surface water, huge areas of desert. The latest weather report indicates that a storm is moving in from the west."

"The place looks like prime real estate," Kaminski said. "Maybe one of us could buy the farm down there."

Martinez and Blake sniggered, but Jenkins didn't. The California jibe had pissed her off.

"Quit screwing around, assholes," she said. "We've got a job to do."

"I know you're all running on a lot of stress right now," I said, "but there won't be room for slip-ups on this op. Olsen, you were saying?"

Olsen gave a dim smile and went on: "There is a storm moving in from the west. That will limit the window of opportunity."

"How long have we got?"

"Two days before it hits."

I indicated some printed images scattered across the viewer table. Pictures of the Artefact, angular and foreign – alien even to the Krell. I couldn't look at the warped architecture for too long without beginning to feel ill.

"Are we still picking up the Artefact?" I asked. "Is it still broadcasting?"

Atkins nodded. "The *Oregon*'s AI has been monitoring the Artefact throughout our journey to Helios. It consistently broadcasts the same signal."

"No surprises there. Have we tried hailing Helios Station?"

"Since we arrived in orbit, communications have been erratic. The signal broadcast by the Artefact is intense. It blots out most planetary comms, we think. But we have directed two short data-bursts at the station, and there has been no response."

"What technology does the station have?" Kaminski said.

"Basic survival facilities," Olsen said. "They were – are – a scientific mission. They have no extra-solar-capable transport."

"So they have no way off Helios?" Jenkins responded.

"That's right. The base has an appropriately armed security force," Olsen said. "They also have a communication and metrological satellite in orbit around Helios. No air-defence that we are aware of."

"Is their satellite still operational?" I asked.

"Appears to be," Atkins said.

That was interesting information. It seemed unlikely that a comms fault had caused the break in transmission. I rubbed my chin, considering that.

"So that's it, people," I said. "A simple job, but in difficult circumstances. Once we've investigated the station, we move back to the Wildcat APS and we evacuate off-world."

Atkins took over. "Helios has an asteroid field in

close orbit. It'll take some manoeuvring to get us into a good orbital position, but the *Oregon* will remain on standby. We'll be monitoring your progress."

"Olsen will take command in the medical bay," I said. "Captain Atkins, you have your orders on the bridge. Sixteen hours for prep and final checks, then we go into the simulators. Unless there are any questions, this briefing is over."

"There is one more thing," Olsen said, holding his hand up to halt my breaking of the meeting. "Before we left *Liberty Point*, I copied Dr Kellerman's personnel record. It includes his transmissions back to Alliance Command."

I remembered that the corporate man back at the *Point* mentioned them. His dismissive tone had made me immediately interested in them. If things on Helios did turn nasty, there might be something in them that I could use. Olsen removed a data-chip from his smock pocket, and passed it to me.

"I would suggest you study these files," he said, his expression dropping. "I have done so. Dr Kellerman was once a great man, but things might have changed."

The *Oregon* moved on through the blackness. The ship gradually slowed as she fell under the gravitational sway of Helios Star, and I knew that although I couldn't physically feel it. Moving by conventional propulsion methods now, rather than the exotic Q-drive system.

Aboard, we readied for the imminent mission. Despite her size, there was nowhere really to hide aboard the *Oregon*. There was always noise and activity somewhere. Even in the quieter hallways, or more secluded cargo holds, the constant whirring of the atmosphere scrubbers reminded me that we were in space. It wasn't the same background noise as the *Point* – I'd grown accustomed to that – and it mildly rattled me.

The vessel didn't have a dedicated gun-range, or even a simulation-booth that could emulate one. The mainframe had storage of almost all entertainment and sports programmes over the last decade, but I didn't want to fill my head with banalities before the drop.

Instead, I went to the ship's gymnasium. That was well-equipped; most Alliance starships had one. I did some cardiac exercise on the anti-grav running wheel. The physical exertion was good for overcoming the freezer aches. Sweat-drenched and mildly fatigued, I realised that it wasn't clearing my mind as well as I had hoped.

So I did the rounds.

The bridge room was crammed with view-screens, holo-displays and monitors, and despite its physical size it still managed to feel small. The blast-shutters were open, the view-ports displaying the vista of open space. The bridge sat at the very nose of the *Oregon*, allowing the best physical view of the path ahead.

Although I wasn't Navy, as mission commander I had almost complete autonomy over the ship and there was no way that the crew would interrupt my inspection. As I passed crew stations, staff officers nodded in informal recognition of rank. Captain Atkins was absent from the bridge, which I found somewhat surprising, but the rest of his command team were in attendance.

I stopped behind one of the officers, chosen more or less at random. She was a small black woman, perhaps in her mid-forties by Earth-standard, with a shaven head. She was already jacked into the *Oregon*'s control suite, and her face occasionally twitched as she received a fresh result or interpreted a new data-stream. The woman's crisp blue uniform was labelled with the name AMELIE PAKOS, the rank LIEUTEN-ANT and the speciality COMMUNICATIONS OFFICER.

"Good afternoon, Captain Harris," she said, in a perfunctory manner.

An illuminated holo-display above the command console showed the ship's time. The *Oregon*'s AI was running on universal meantime – based on an atomic clock somewhere on Earth – but that was largely irrelevant. A combat vessel, inside the Maelstrom, was always awake.

"I guess it is," I said. "The ship's chronometer won't matter soon."

Pakos nodded grimly. "I suppose that is so for the ground team. Helios' local time will become more important."

"All in hand, Lieutenant?"

"There are no issues to report."

"What are you doing?"

Pakos gave me a stern look, as though she didn't like my enquiry. Maybe she wasn't used to being questioned by a simulant operator – no doubt she thought that I should stick to my own specialism, just as she stuck to hers.

"The crew are running diagnostics," Pakos said. "The *Oregon* is breaking into a new movement cycle, and we are still slowing from the Q-space to real-space conversion. Human eyes are double-checking calculations that have already been verified by the ship's AI. There is no margin of error out here." She paused, then coldly added: "I hope that addresses your concern."

I tapped a finger on the console in front of her. "But what are *you* doing? You're a comms officer, and this is a deep-space communications terminal."

Pakos' face flushed, and she gave me a stilted nod. "That's right. Looks like you know something about starships."

"I've been in enough fleet actions in my time," I said. I was being truthful about that: I had – in my simulant body – manned Naval vessels numerous times. Simulants were sometimes even used as marine forces. "Just give me a chance to use one of your railguns, and I can show you exactly what experience I have."

Pakos' cold façade broke a little at that, and she reluctantly smiled. "I'm sorry, Captain Harris. We've seen a lot of Army men on this ship over the years. Most of them don't know how a starship works. The *Oregon* has taken some knocks from careless commanding officers."

I shrugged. "Risk comes with the territory. Now, care to show me what you are doing?"

Pakos nodded. "It'll be easier if you listen."

She unjacked herself from the console, and manipulated the controls.

A sudden analogue wail filled the room. I winced, and my instant reaction was to cover my ears. It sounded like pitched feedback; one second bordering on utter cacophony, then abruptly developing into a near melody. At first, I assumed that we were listening to the radioactive background noise caused by one of the local stars – Helios Primary or Secondary, or even one of their more distant cousins – but the noise was too regular, too cyclical. It pricked the back of my mind, beyond the rational: something darker. Piercing the veil of my subconscious.

The bridge crew paused, listening. They had been jacked-in, had all been monitoring the signal.

It sounds familiar, I realised. Not the whole sound, but an element of it. A forgotten memory; something long buried, rising to the surface—

"Turn it off," I ordered, waving a hand. I lurched forward, and used a nearby console to steady myself.

Pakos did as requested, after a momentary pause. Something like disappointment crossed her face – a shadow behind her eyes.

"We were monitoring the signal broadcast by the Artefact," she said. "It also generates a background electrical power source. As though the Artefact is not at optimal performance."

"Keep that damned thing switched off," I said. I trembled, angry not just at the effect that the signal had spontaneously had on me – but that I had shown it.

"The noise is somewhat disconcerting at first," Pakos said. "Ensign Sebas reported that she felt nauseous after the initial interception. But the sensation passes."

"I hope that it does. Why can't the AI monitor it?"

Pakos jacked herself back into her console. A spectral analysis of the sound projected in front of her, jagged peaks and random troughs. She pointed at the holo.

"The signal doesn't record well. Duplicates seem to degrade rapidly. We're not sure why. Perhaps your Mr Olsen can assist."

"Just monitor it as remotely as possible."

"As you wish, Captain," Pakos said, slightly bowing her head.

I turned and paced out of the room, the transmission ringing in my ears. The bridge doors slid shut behind me, but before they did I swear that I heard the signal again – emitting from Pakos' console, despite my order to the contrary.

It's just a noise, I told myself. *Just a signal. Get on with what you know. Keep the familiar close.*

After the bridge, I went to see each member of my squad. They had their particular methods of preparing for a combat-drop.

Kaminski was first, and I knew exactly where I would find him.

The starship had a multi-denominational chapel, which was really nothing more than a small private chamber. Tucked neatly between Medical and the hangar deck; conveniently free of view-ports or view-screens to remind the occupants that they were in deep-space.

The room was in shadow, lights dimmed to near dark, and Vinnie paced beyond the metal pews. He clutched a rosary, mouthing a prayer to himself. I watched him for a moment, lingering at the darkened door of the chapel.

"Vinnie," I eventually called.

He started, dropping the rosary beads into his pocket as though he was embarrassed to be found in this private moment.

"As you were," I said, nodding to his hand.

He smiled feebly and wrapped the beads around his palm. He might not have seemed a religious sort, and he was certainly fast to jibe Martinez about his supposed faith, but he always went through the same process before a drop: an hour or so in the chapel, on his own, praying. I'd never asked him whether he was of some formal creed, but it seemed to me that he just wanted somewhere quiet to think before the operation. Right now, I could appreciate that. I wasn't one for religion but the place had a strange calmness to it, and might be a remedy to my bizarre experience with the signal on the bridge.

"Didn't see you there, Cap."

"I'm checking up on everyone. All okay?"

"Just fine, Cap. Just fine."

"Getting some private time before the drop?"

Kaminski nodded. He didn't look so bold in that moment. Just looked like a lost kid from Old Brooklyn, whose world was a single planet. Before he had taken on this job, and had become more than a man.

"Can you do me a solid?" Kaminski asked.

"Sure."

"Don't tell Martinez that I'm down here. He doesn't know that I use the chapel."

"Consider it done."

I'd known Kaminski longer than anyone else on my team – twelve years, or thereabouts. He probably knew me better than anyone else, if the length of time we'd served together was any indicator. We'd been Spec Forces soldiers in our own skin long before I'd even heard of the Sim Ops Programme.

"Do you remember what it was like, when we had to do this in our own bodies?" I found myself asking.

Kaminski laughed, but the sound was hollow and dour. "Honestly? No, I don't remember. *This* is all I remember now." He tapped the back of his neck, indicating one of the data-ports that would allow him to make transition with his simulant. "Wouldn't want to go skinless for love nor money."

"I still think about it sometimes. Recently, even more so. I had a dream, while we were in hyper-sleep." I shook my head; thinking suddenly that this was inappropriate, sharing personal concerns with one of the team. Kaminski didn't need to be burdened with my self-doubts.

"I dreamt about *her.*"

"You can say her name," Kaminski said. "She selected me as well, don't forget. We both knew her."

I sighed. Elena had chosen him as well, weeded him out from the mass of potential recruits. 'Ski had sat through a psych-eval, been identified as a potential candidate in exactly the same way as me.

"It all started with six recruits," he went on. "Down to three of us in the end."

I nodded, wistfully. "Pioneers."

"We never really talk about our history any more."

"Too painful," I said. "It's been a long time since I dreamt about her."

Kaminski nodded awkwardly, unsure of what to say. The truth was that there was nothing he could say – nothing anyone could say – to make the pain any easier. Her memory was my load to carry, and mine alone. For Kaminski, it always seemed easier to joke and jibe than really discuss these things. For me, it just seemed easier to move on to the next transition – to get into the next simulant body.

"I'll leave you to this," I said, waving a hand at the chapel. "Whatever it is you're doing."

Kaminski pursed his lips and nodded. "Copy that."

"You know where I am. Otherwise, assemble as briefed."

"Will do."

I paced off down the corridor. Behind me, I heard Kaminski mumbling the Spacefarer's Prayer, his voice fading to a whisper as I went.

Next, I visited the squad barracks. It contained faultlessly made-up cots, with footlockers for whatever meagre personal possessions the team had brought with them. The first three cots were empty but Martinez occupied the fourth.

It was surprising that he felt it necessary to sleep, given that he had been at rest – albeit artificially – for six months. But that was his method of dealing with our situation, our mission, and I allowed all of the squad their idiosyncrasies.

Maybe it was his history as an Alliance Marine; maybe it was his Venusian blood. Either way, Martinez didn't seem fazed in the slightest by being in deep-space. I considered that he was a safe pair of hands to have on this op – that he was a fine choice for a mission like this.

I didn't wake him. I wished that I could be more like him, and that I could get some rest before the drop.

At first, I couldn't find Blake. He had tried to speak to me about something back at the *Point* – only a few days ago by my subjective body clock. I wanted my squad to have clear heads before the mission, and now seemed as good a time as any to talk privately.

I asked about him of some of the starship crew. Red-faced, a girl-ensign told me that he was in her friend's room.

"I can send a message to her if you want, Captain," the ensign said. She awkwardly added, "They won't get into any trouble, will they?"

I smiled and shook my head. "No on both counts. It isn't important."

Whatever he had wanted to talk to me about would have to wait. Sex was often Blake's way of preparing for an operation and even though we were light-years out of human space, some things apparently hadn't changed.

* * *

Jenkins was last. I knew where she would be.

The *Oregon* didn't have a standing complement of Marines, although she maintained a shipboard armoury. Under normal circumstances, it was kept locked, but Jenkins had either persuaded or bullied someone into giving her access. This was her preparation custom, and much like Blake she didn't like to vary it.

The small chamber was crowded with weapon racks. I suspected that on a usual Naval run, these would be stocked with basic armaments such as shock-rifles and shipboard-use shotguns. Now, the chamber brimmed with M95 plasma rifles, PPG-13 plasma pistols, crates of grenades and power cells – real heavy ordnance. One wall had been given over to ominous-looking and empty combat-suits – immediately before transition, the simulants would be loaded into those suits.

Jenkins was dressed in civilian clothes; a tight black jumpsuit, her hair wet from showering. Her sleeves were rolled up and her skin was slick with sweat. She grunted at me when I entered the armoury.

"I wanted to check on you. To make sure you are prepared for the drop."

"All well here, Cap."

"Is weapons prep in order?"

"That was finished hours ago. I've just rechecked the power cells on these plasma rifles."

"Is that really necessary?"

"Can't hurt to be sure," Jenkins answered, with a shrug. "Anyway, someone had to mark up the suits as well."

She raised a thumb over at the combat-suits. Sure enough, she had stencilled each suit of armour with name-tags and appropriate insignia. The suits were completely expendable, despite their credit value, but even so Jenkins had painstakingly labelled each one. Merit badges, like Blake's sniper honours or Kaminski's technical rank, had also been copied onto the armoured shoulders. The suits rarely came back, and whatever went out with the sims probably wouldn't be making a return journey.

"Good work, Jenkins."

She gave another shrug. "It was my turn. Kaminski did it last drop."

I never had a turn at marking up the suits. That was a task for my squad, but I understood in that moment why they never complained about doing it: because it gave them focus. It gave them a task on which they could concentrate, so as to avoid thinking about dying. I saw that, now, in Jenkins' haunted eyes.

I paused when I reached the rack dedicated to my combat-armour. Each suit had been marked with the captain insignia, my name, but also another tag beneath: LAZARUS.

"You didn't need to do that," I said, slightly irritated at Jenkins. She knew that I didn't like the nickname; it was something used by others on the *Point*, and not by my squad.

Jenkins continued working. "But I did, this time."

"Why?"

"Because you always come back," she said. She was making a deliberate effort not to make eye contact, I decided, by burying her head in a crate of plasma power cells. "And if you come back, then you'll bring us back with you."

It's just a name. Leave it for now, I thought to myself. Jenkins was obviously spooked.

"You all right?" I asked.

"All good here. Olsen is sending some medics down at," she paused, checking her wrist-comp, "oh-six-hundred hours. They're going to start armouring up the sims." She turned back to the nearest suit – one of her own – and continued with the stencilling. "I had better get on."

"I copy that."

I was on edge.

The Artefact's signal had been concerning, and I was irritated with Jenkins, but neither of those things were responsible for the anxiety building inside me. There was really no explanation for my condition.

It wasn't fear that was making me on edge; I'd done this far too many times to feel that. This was something worse, something deeper. I always got like this before a drop. I needed a drink badly, that was for sure. Ill-advised as it would have been, I would've liked a decent whiskey, or perhaps something even stronger, to calm my nerves. Much like Jenkins, I knew that I needed to find something to focus my mind.

So I spent the time reviewing my materials for the mission. I retired to my quarters, sat alone in my room with the lights dimmed. Images and plans soon littered the floor; I digested every scrap of material available to me.

I unpacked my few personal possessions – my collection of death-trophies, a copy of Elena's photo. I always left the original back at the *Point* – that had an increased sentimental value to me, worn and tired, touched by her hands.

My father's old pistol was the last thing out of my away-bag. The pistol was big by today's standards; a real hand cannon. Archaic, machined from a steel-plastic hybrid: worth a fortune to a collector on the gun market, although I would never even consider selling it. The weapon was suitably intimidating – with a long sleek barrel, heavy too – and it had tasted death. That made us comrades, I figured. The rotating barrel was etched with SMITH & WESSON – MODEL 913. I emptied a handful of ammo clips out onto my cot, assembled the gun holster as well.

Then I used the private terminal, equipped with a holo-viewer, to access the data-chip that Olsen had given me.

Dr Jarvis Kellerman's life story unfolded before me. He was sixty years Earth-standard, and a scientific prodigy. It seemed like every record associated with the man – educational, medical, scientific – had been stored and catalogued by the military. He had no close relations to speak of, certainly none that occupied any world or station within light-years of the Quarantine Zone. No friends or enemies of note. Many work colleagues from a variety of scientific spheres; he was highly regarded by the general community. There were hinted links to top brass in the military as well – he was obviously a well-connected individual. Like me, he spent time hopping between different planets and the effects of time-dilation meant that he had significantly outlived those close to him.

I scanned through most of the material. Some of it made me feel slightly uneasy; as though I were a spy, peering into this man's life. Infiltrating every private corner, leaving no stone unturned.

Eventually I chose one of the personnel files, and a tri-D video activated on the console in front of me.

SECURITY ACCESS UNLOCKED. EXECUTE:
   RUNFILE COMMAND.
Dr kellerman. Operational date 04/06/2263
LOCATION: ANTARES PRIME [SEE LINKED
   FILE A/9989]

A man – Kellerman – appeared in front of the camera, waving to a fellow researcher. His hair was thick, although already greying at the temples. I quickly calculated his age – forty-four Earth-standard. He wore it well, and his face was youthful, his eyes bright with passion. He stood among the ruins of a Krell starship, still smoking in places. Tattered organic material hung from alien trees above him, and he was framed by an ochre sky. He wore an Alliance Science Division smock. When he moved, the fabric grew taut over his muscled torso.

"*Quickly!*" he insisted of the camera operator. "*The retrieval team will be moving in soon. This is a primary opportunity to examine the site before they get here.*"

He crouched among the ruins, prodding a piece of carapace armour – either something torn from one of the Krell bio-ships, or the remains of a primary-form. Difficult to say: the recording was fuzzy, poor quality. Kellerman confidently babbled at the camera operator, pointing out deviations in the normal Krell development pattern. Off-screen, another science officer hastened him onwards, but he refused the request to retreat from the site.

Bravery, I considered. *Or idiocy.*

I skipped the rest of the file, then moved on through Kellerman's life story. There were several more research postings – some on worlds I'd heard of, some that I hadn't.

I found something else of interest, and activated another file.

DR KELLERMAN. OPERATIONAL DATE
    11/08/2270
LOCATION: EPSILON ULTRIS [SEE LINKED
    FILE A/9989] – ASIATIC CONFLICT – RIM
    WAR [SEE LINKED FILE A/432]

Now aged fifty-one objective years. The intervening period, since the last vid-file, had not been kind to Kellerman. He was propped up in a hospital bed and looked smaller than before; half of his body mass, perhaps. Feeder tubes erupted from his torso. A spotless white bedsheet covered his lower half, folded neatly at his stomach. Medipatches concealed some of his chest. One eye was covered by a bandage, which had already turned an off-pink colour. He was in a hospital, I realised, and his injuries were traumatic and recent.

"*Commencing psych-eval,*" an off-screen voice stated. "*Subject Dr Jarvis Kellerman.*"

"*I'm not a Christo-damned subject!*" he roared from his bed. "*I'm a man. I'm an Alliance citizen, and I don't deserve to be treated like this.*"

"*Doctor, I am here to ask you some questions. To ascertain your capacity for return to service with the Science Division. That is what you want, isn't it?*"

"*Of course it is.*" He stopped, set his jaw. Were those tears in his eyes? He sighed and shook his head. "*Of course it is.*"

"*It is unlikely that you will walk again.*"

"*I know that already.*"

"*It will take some adjustment. Your current posting is untenable given the circumstances.*"

"*I know that,*" he repeated. "*I know that already.*"

I checked the stardate again. This was before his placement on Helios, and the attached records indicated that at this time he had been permanently disabled. Loss of use of both of his legs. They had tried nano-surgery, tried every form of regenerative therapy, but none of it had worked.

I skipped the rest of that file. The eval went on for some time – hours, it seemed. Kellerman became more and more dejected. It felt wrong watching the man's obvious pain.

There were other areas of Kellerman's life that still interested me though. After he had been crippled, Kellerman had gone on to run other

Alliance scientific operations. The psych-evals noted that, notwithstanding his injury, his mind remained sharp – sharper, one report even said, than before the incident.

I finally reached the Helios files. He'd signed up to the mission because of his specialist knowledge of the Krell. Written a variety of articles on the subject.

The Krell: A scientific study of the primary-form.

Understanding communication methods within the Krell Collective.

Retrospective: A year since the Treaty.

Possible impact factors on the development of Krell subspecies.

There was a collection of vid-files broadcast from Helios, which had occasionally been attached to the regular service transmissions. Just poor-quality tri-D recordings, usually Kellerman sitting on his own in his office or lab. The transmissions started with his theories on alien evolution: he hypothesised that the Krell were an ancient predator race, perhaps having extinguished other sentient species. He theorised about the bio-technologies developed by the Krell. Latterly, he spoke of the Artefact, of how he had attempted to decipher the signal.

I began to lose interest after a few hours. I longed for the simulator-tanks; felt the pull of the simulant body.

Then the content of the files abruptly changed.

"I'm on the verge of finishing my work," Kellerman said.

There was an edge to his voice. Something more than simple passion: *obsession*.

He sat in a darkened chamber, with only a flash-light illuminating his face. Wearing a white medical smock, unbuttoned to his chest. A noise distracted him from his message, something like an explosion. Then screaming.

"This place is getting to me," he said, voice quivering. "I never sleep any more. The xenos are everywhere. The sands stir endlessly. They used to ignore us, pass us by as insignificant. Maybe they sensed our purpose here. Saw that we meant them no harm, saw that we are men of science."

He paused, looking behind himself and into shadow. I frowned. When the light caught his face, he had aged enormously. This was hardly the same man as he was on Antares Prime. He had become thin, emaciated, a wraith. The only indi-cation of a soul within his withered body were his eyes; burning bright, sky-blue. His hair was fully greyed and thinned to near elimination.

"I have isolated an algorithm in the Artefact's signal. It *interferes* with the Krell's communica-tion method. When the weather is clear here, they are almost paralysed by it."

The broadcasts became more and more troubling. Rambling now, explaining that he needed more resources. That he had sent a request to his superi-ors for more equipment. Some of the security team had vanished, or at least he couldn't hail them any longer. Suspected deserters, so Kellerman said. That was absurd; where would they go? He was always looking more and more ill, face becom-ing more contorted and distressed with each new data-file.

"It doesn't just affect *them*. Many of us here feel the Artefact's song," he continued. "The noise is driving us mad."

The last file proceeded to play, and I felt a chill run through me. It began with Kellerman in shadow, leaning back in his chair. I made out the outline of his body, clothing shredded and stained brown. He hadn't changed from that same smart-suit in weeks now.

"I'm terrified," Kellerman began. "Utterly in fear. Not myself, not myself, not myself."

The image flickered, distorted momentarily. Kellerman laughed, long and hard. The noise was sibilant, as was his voice now. As though he was having trouble speaking. I wanted to replay the audio part of the file – it was so difficult to make out what he was saying – but I felt compelled to continue watching.

He stared right into the camera, fixing me with his eyes. Looking at this man – at Kellerman – something told me that he was not a victim. Without warning, the holo lunged forwards, arms outstretched.

I flinched back, startled. Had to remind myself that it was only a recording. Quite unconsciously, I realised that I had my father's pistol in my hand: the heavy weight reassuring, some protection against Kellerman although he was still a world away.

He was an *adversary*. I didn't know why I felt like that; only that there was malevolence behind those eyes. Travelling into the Maelstrom, bringing this innocent crew out into the darkness of Krell space – this felt so wrong, so very wrong.

The image suddenly came back to life. The recording jumped onwards; probably the same day, judging from the state of the lab behind Kellerman, but at some forward point in time.

"The work goes on," he continued, shuddering in the dark. "Too well. We have made a breakthrough." He leant into the camera. His old face was tear and dirt stained. "We lost three more men today. I have so few left—"

A shrill klaxon wailed overhead, so loud that it silenced Kellerman's rambling. I jolted awake and the lights to my chamber flickered on. I jumped to my feet.

"All hands to the bridge," came Captain Atkins' voice over the ship's address system. "Repeat: all hands to the bridge. This is not a drill."

Without any rationale, I grabbed my father's old gun. I cycled the loader, clipped a fresh ammo cartridge into the feed. Solid-shot rounds; this was proper contraband, the sort of item I'd discipline my squad for bringing aboard a starship if they were stupid enough to try.

I slid the bulky pistol into a thigh holster, incorporated into my fatigues. I had the feeling I might need it.

CHAPTER SEVEN

THIS IS REAL AGAIN

The crew of the *Oregon* scrambled in response to Atkins' emergency request and the bridge was soon packed with personnel. My squad and I stood in the midst of the action, and I felt like a third wheel. The crew worked quickly and efficiently, digesting sensor-feeds and interpreting their findings. There was no denying that they were in a state of high suspense, but they still operated calmly. Most of the officers were bodily jacked into their consoles: eyes a vacant haze, concentrating on the deep of space outside. Not unlike being a simulant operator.

Captain Atkins himself sat in the centre of the bridge room, ensconced in a command throne. He had discarded his formal cap and rolled up his sleeves to connect his exposed data-ports directly to the *Oregon*.

"Why the alert, Atkins?" I asked, stepping up to his command pulpit.

Atkins gave me a nod. "We're still six hours

away from engaging high orbit with Helios, but near-space isn't as clean as we were led to believe. The asteroid belt is far more extensive. Our intelligence on the planet is either out of date, or just plain wrong."

I paced to the nose of the ship, where the blast-shutters were still open. Viewers gave a wide angle of the path ahead of the *Oregon*, affording a hundred-and-eighty-degree cone of observation.

Outside, space was immense and dark. Helios hung in the distance. Between the planet and us, a wide band of space-junk span lazily – a miscellany of rocks, either left over when the planet was formed or attracted by Helios' gravity in the millennia afterwards. Most of the debris was small and likely innocuous. That sort of material wouldn't present any difficulty to the *Oregon*, given the ablative hull plating with which the ship was equipped. But some of the larger asteroids might require a nudge off-course with a laser battery or a shot from the railgun. That was more troubling; a direct hit from one of those rocks could hull the ship, and a repair out in space would be difficult. *If not impossible*, I thought. I didn't like this at all.

The room was strangely silent for a moment, despite the number of personnel gathered, save for the gentle *ping-ping-ping* of the radar feeds. That same feeling that I had experienced back on the *Point*, when I was first briefed on the operation, arose within me.

Tell Atkins to pull out. Call off this whole operation. This is wrong. All wrong.

"We're several thousand kilometres from the optimal orbital insertion point," Atkins continued. Unlike the other officers, he seemed able to focus both on what was physically in front of him and on what he was doing in the virtual-reality realm of the starship. "Lieutenant Pakos, run amplification on the most recent lidar result, and get that patched through to my console."

"Aye, sir," Pakos replied. "You want us to go active?"

"Yes."

A holographic display unit in front of Atkins illuminated, to show near-space and the *Oregon* moving through it. There were lots of other objects in the area, moving peacefully through the nether.

"Too many hiding places..." Atkins remarked, leaving the comment unexplained.

"I don't like this at all," Jenkins said.

"I don't think that any of us do," I said.

Olsen walked the chamber, red-faced and fraught. His team huddled nearby. They did nothing to help dissipate the tension in the room. Olsen came to stand beside Atkins' command station. He tried to peer over Atkins' shoulder but then thought better of it and returned to patrolling the bridge. A young blonde medtech – the girl who had shown an interest in Blake earlier in the day – dodged out of his way as he took a wider lap of the command terminal.

"How has this happened?" Olsen queried, his voice rising in exasperation. "Why didn't you see this earlier? Surely your systems can see through some Christo-damned asteroids?"

Martinez flinched at Olsen's profanity. "Hey, *mano*, watch the language."

Olsen shot him a glare but was too spooked to argue with the trooper. "I don't understand how we've made it so far without considering this problem."

Atkins sat back in his seat. He tapped the screen of his console. "We've been watching Helios since we dropped out of Q-space, but the ship's sensors interpreted this junk as a band of small objects. As for seeing through asteroid fields, it isn't that easy."

Olsen shook his head. His flabby neck rippled unpleasantly. "I know that! Don't you think—!"

"Look, Olsen," I said, "calm down. Let the captain work."

PING-PING-PING-PING!

The pitch of the radar returns suddenly became a shrill chirping. I broke off. Every terminal on the bridge flashed with warnings. This could only be bad news. Officers started barking orders, and Atkins frowned as he read the scanner-feeds. On the holo-display, something big and angry was emerging from the asteroid belt.

But I didn't need to look at the holo.

I could already see it from the view-port. A Krell warship materialised out of the dark of space, battering aside debris as it moved into position.

"It's an ambush," I whispered.

Krell bio-ships were grown rather than built, or so Science Division insisted. Quite how a species could grow something that big, and that dangerous, was beyond my comprehension. Being formed of organic matter, the vessels were especially difficult to detect via conventional methods. Many Krell starship variants were effectively invisible to lidar and radar, and only showed up on short-range mass-spectrum scans. The hulls were of some organic compound presently well beyond the understanding of men such as Olsen. By a method we couldn't fathom, Krell ships also concealed their heat signature, which ruled out infrared as an effective detector.

All of this ran through my mind as the enormous bio-ship sailed into view. It was suddenly obvious how and why the vessel had managed to evade detection. We had fallen right into their trap. How long had this ship been watching us? No doubt manoeuvring into the best position for an assault, waiting for us to enter the field.

"She's a big one," Atkins muttered, his voice almost admiring of the enemy vessel. "Null-shields, now."

The ship looked like a mutant mollusc, with a long, sleek body and a sharp spined nose. The exterior was plated with organic armour, like that worn by the Krell primary-forms but on a massive scale. A collection of squid-like tentacles erupted from the aft. That was the engine mechanism for the ship, just about the only vulnerable spot. The flanks of the vessel were covered in what – at this distance – looked like skin pores. From experience, I knew that those pores were the Krell equivalent of hangar bays, used to either launch fighter-ships or fire spaceborne weapons. The entire vessel was black, almost impossible to distinguish against the field of space.

There was no denying that this was a warship. It was easily three times the size of the *Oregon*.

"She's a category four," an officer called to the bridge in general.

"Null-shields up," another officer confirmed.

"Has it seen us?" Olsen gasped, followed by something unintelligible. He rubbed his temples. A sheen of sweat had formed on his forehead.

"Of course she has seen us," said Atkins.

Someone from Olsen's team started crying.

"Get those people out of here!" Jenkins shouted, pointing at the medical staff. They didn't need to be told twice, and scurried out of the bridge together with Olsen.

The engine of the bio-ship fired silently, casting blue contrails across space and sending more of the asteroid field into disarray. As it moved, almost serenely, huge muscles at the aft of the vessel rippled. That put paid to any suggestion that we had evaded the ship's attention.

"Lieutenant Pakos," Atkins said, "please do tell me that she is the only one."

Pakos grimaced. "I'm detecting a further bio-signature emerging from the asteroid field, Captain." She swallowed. "It's bigger than the first."

I could see it too. Two motherships, in tandem, were assembled between the *Oregon* and Helios.

"Can you pull us out?" I demanded. "Retreat – go back into Q-space?"

Better to cut our losses – report to Command that we had met resistance.

Atkins shook his head, still intently focused on the holo. "Impossible. We'd risk damage retreating through this debris without a properly plotted course, and the Q-drive will take a minimum of six hours to calculate a return trajectory—"

"Then jump out of this star system!"

I knew that was equally unrealistic, but I wanted to try something – anything – to get us out of the threat-range of the Krell warships.

"And into a black hole or a gravimetric storm? No. We're fighting." He lifted his head, pointed to the weapons pit. "Weapons officers, be at your stations."

The weapons crew assembled around the bridge, occupying dedicated pods towards the nose of the vessel. Without ceremony, each of them jacked into their weapons systems. Reports of the railgun, laser batteries and plasma torpedo systems coming online were shouted across the chamber.

With admirable calmness, Atkins shouted: "All hands prepare to engage. The Krell have found us."

My mother was an Alliance Navy ensign. My memory of her had an age-blurred weakness to it: I could recall little about her, save that she had a kind face and was well-intentioned. She died before the Krell had even been discovered but it felt like she had given up living a long time before that. Back in her time – only a generation ago – starship crews suffered greatly from the time-dilation issue. Short Q-drive jumps cost her years in objective time. The subjective journey time to Alpha Centauri might be six months, but for the rest of the human race three years had passed. Even from a young age I remember my father seemed to age at a different rate to my mother; he growing ever older, subjected to the march of time, she remaining youthful. I think that was what eventually led my father to take on more distant tours of duty – trying, in some perverse way, to reach equilibrium with her. This woman with whom he shared two children, but with whom he increasingly had no connection.

My mother never held a starship commission and she had no dreams of being a senior officer. She wasn't a career sort; this was a job, to pay the rent on our tiny high-rise. That kind of money was hard to come by for Earthside work, and the military were always looking for fresh meat.

But she lived for her shore-leave. That was when she shone. We tried to keep in contact via FTL video-link – she would call us for birthdays or special occasions – but that wasn't the norm. I remember her in snapshots. My sister Carrie and I were passed between distant aunts and uncles as we grew up, and I treasured the time I spent with my mother.

I remember one night very well. I was an objective eight years old. My mother had been on shore-leave for two whole weeks, which was something of a novelty. My father was on operation somewhere off-world and so this leave was just for Carrie and me.

Braving the fallout and the local hood-gangs, my mother had taken us out for the day. This was before the public services had been permanently suspended and most of Detroit Metro was placed under martial law, but even then the Metro was a dark enough reality. I can't remember where she took us, but it was probably a local park or shopping mall.

Once we were back home, Carrie had flopped into bed early. My mother sat up with me in the tiny bedroom, and we watched from the tenement window as the stars came out. I hadn't ever been into space. Sometimes my mother would tell me stories about the adventures that she had experienced. It was exciting but frightening. Long after she had returned to her assignment I would lay awake at night worrying about her.

But that night was different. Although I was tired I was happy to just sit with her and watch the night sky. Downtown was busy and hot, but focusing on the emerging stars gave me some calm.

"Have you ever had to fight another starship?" I asked. "Aunt Beth lets me watch the news-feeds sometimes. They show pictures."

My mother sat silently for a long while, smiling to herself. It wasn't a joyful expression but rather a sardonic, almost bitter smile. I was about to ask her again – thinking that perhaps she hadn't heard my question – when she finally answered.

"Starship battles are the most dangerous sorts of battles, Conrad," she said, slowly. "The deep kills men. Never forget that. Space isn't your friend and will turn on you in an instant."

"But I watch the feeds," I insisted, "and the Alliance captains know what to do. I saw that the Alliance took down two Directorate ships just the other day. I'll bet you are great in a starship fight."

She continued to look out into the night sky. The smile never left her face.

"There's no honour or skill in a starship engagement. There's nothing special about it. The only trick is whoever shoots first, wins."

The tone of her voice didn't broker any further discussion, and I fell silent.

That was the last time that I ever saw my mother. My sister and I received a letter from the Department of Off-World Defence the following month, informing us that the United American government was grateful for the sacrifice that Jane Harris had made. Her ship had been destroyed during a skirmish with a Directorate vessel in orbit around Jupiter Outpost, and regrettably there were no recorded survivors.

The lead Krell warship sailed so close to the *Oregon* that I thought she was going to ram us. The prow of the ship was literally on top of the *Oregon*.

"Closing blast-shutters!" an officer yelled.

Like that's going to do us any good, I thought. *If the bitch is going to hit us, we're dead in the water.*

"Belay that order," Atkins shouted back, a hard edge to his voice. "I want to see space with my own eyes."

I searched the faces of the crew around me. All were pale with horror. If we were breached by the Krell ship, even if we made it to the escape pods, there would be no help out here. Only a slow, interminable decline as supplies ran out – light-years away from the rest of the human race.

I felt helpless. This was not my fight.

"Evasive manoeuvres," Atkins declared. "Pull us aftwards, all power."

"Aye, sir."

"Are the null-shields holding?"

Like most military vessels, the *Oregon* was equipped with null-shields: a projected energy field, capable of dispersing incoming enemy fire. It worked best on energy weapons but could be used to counter other ballistics as well. The Krell vessels had a similar technology, although it was of some biological origin.

"She's inside the null-shield," Pakos explained.

So that was the enemy strategy. To pull so close to us that our shields were useless. It was the sort of gamble that a human warship would never take, because it left the attacker open to a retaliatory strike. I watched now as the null-shields projected by both ships met; resulting in a miniature storm of evanescent blue embers.

"She's firing!" someone yelled.

The first Krell ship opened fire with a brief volley of bio-plasma shots. Inside the enemy ship were specialised, living cannons – grown to generate bio-energies every bit as lethal as the manufactured weaponry of the Alliance military. Plasma raked the hull of the *Oregon*. Somewhere port-side, not far from our position. The *Oregon*'s gravity well stuttered and the bridge shook violently as impact after impact tore into the hull. I staggered with the force of each hit, grappling the edge of a bank of monitors to stay on my feet. My gut lurched and I tasted bile at the back of my throat. Sparks exploded from a nearby terminal. An officer slumped over one of the weapons stations, dead.

I wanted to yell out for a damage report – to get answers about how badly we had been hit – but bit back on my words. This was Atkins' ship: he was in command out here.

"We have ablative plating," Atkins murmured, by way of explanation. "Lieutenant, maintain power on the shields. It'll take more than that to bring us down."

I exchanged a worried glance with Jenkins.

"But not much more," she said to me, voice barely a whisper.

"Everybody in one piece?" I asked.

Blake rubbed a bloody graze on his head, but it was only superficial. "Just about."

"Lieutenant Caitlin is dead," another officer called across the bridge. "The primary railgun is inoperative."

This was my chance to do something.

Fuck it – I'm not dying like this.

I dashed across the bridge to her post. During the preliminary bombardment, she must have hit her head hard against the console. Either that, or suffered some kind of cerebral feedback from the Krell attack. I pulled her jack-cables free, unplugging her corpse. There was no doubt she was dead: her eyes and mouth were wide, blood pooling at the ears. I hauled the body out of the chair and slid into it myself.

"Sorry, Caitlin," I said. "But I need your weapon."

Starship crew and simulant operators shared the same jacking connections – those hard-wired ports at the top of my spine, in my forearms. The jacks were still warm from the dead officer's connection; one of them slipped out of my hand, slick with her blood. The other weapons officers turned to look at me, one or two standing from their stations with concerned expressions.

"What the hell are you doing?" Pakos shouted at me across the bridge.

"What does it look like?" I replied. "I'm taking control of the railgun. I don't see anyone else doing it."

"You're not trained! The railgun requires extensive operational experience to fire—"

"And I've already told you – I've done this before." I really didn't care what she said; I wasn't going to sit there while this battle played out around me. At least I could make a difference with the railgun.

"Leave him, Lieutenant," Atkins directed. The tone of his voice suggested respect – perhaps he wasn't such a rules-man after all. What I was doing right now: this was most certainly against regulation.

There was a jag of pain as each of the cables hit home. In truth, although I *had* done this before, I wasn't experienced in the use of shipboard weaponry. The principles of connecting with the *Oregon* were roughly the same as operation of a simulant. It was the nuances that differed.

It took a moment to make the neural-link, then I was online.

I am the Oregon.

New information flooded my synapses. I was the machine. Targeting data uploaded to memory buffers in my head. For a few seconds, the flood of information was disabling – just like the initial rush of transition. Physically I was still in the bridge, but with a thought I commanded the primary railgun: a living human being inside, an enormous inert railgun outside. The holo in front of me snapped into focus.

"Primary railgun online," Pakos declared behind me.

"Fuck yeah!" Kaminski yelled.

"You might like to take safety measures," Atkins said. "This ride is about to get bumpy. Initiate defensive measures with lasers please."

The Krell warship was positioned overhead, dominating the bridge view-port. The *Oregon*'s laser batteries began shooting, meeting incoming fire. With each pulse the lasers illuminated the scarred and battered underside of the enormous ship.

"Has the fleet fought this hostile previously?" Atkins asked.

By their nature, the Krell did not give their vessels names. There was no ship title and no identification tag on the hull. To the Krell Collective, I doubt that this particular ship had any individuality or distinction beyond her size and mass. But the Navy held records, and every Naval engagement during the course of the Krell War had been catalogued in detail. Every vessel was studied, every tactic deployed considered. If a starship had a known weakness, then it would be recorded. All Navy ships were equipped with a database of known hostiles. It might give us an edge, no matter how miniscule.

This played out around me, but my focus was somewhere else entirely. I searched for targets outside with the railgun. There was something animal about the machine, something desperate. It hungered for a target and I reined it in. I commanded firepower capable of decimating an entire fleet. It was exhilarating, intoxicating.

Data flowed across my mind's eye. It was so similar to operating a simulant, yet so different.

"Database match acquired," a young officer called triumphantly across the bridge. "Primary hostile is *Death of Antares*. Category four. Last Naval engagement was seven years ago, claimed lives of nine hundred crewmen aboard battleship *Virginia Central*—"

"Keep to the essentials, please," Atkins replied. "We don't have time for the detail."

Not to mention the effect that the disclosure would probably have on the morale of the bridge staff. A battleship was four times the mass of an assault cruiser like the *Oregon* and the news that this alien vessel had taken one of those down would be understandably unwelcome.

"Known weakness on starboard port!" she blurted back. "Uploading the data to you now, Captain. It took a hit during a sighting at Proxima Yaris, as a result of a Naval bombardment—"

The *Oregon* listed again, and I swayed in my seat with the motion. Something else struck the ship, this time so hard that the entire spaceframe shook. Might've been a larger piece of local debris, or perhaps a solid-shot weapon deployed by the *Death*. Space outside was crammed with potential targets now.

"The *Death* has a weakened arterial wall at the connection point between the rear engine and the third hangar port," Atkins said. "From here, we have a clear shot at her belly."

A holo sprang to life showing the *Death of Antares* – a spinning wireframe diagram. Markers illustrated the weakened spot: the location of the previous Naval bombardment.

"Charging particle beam accelerator," a weapons officer declared. "Acquiring target."

"Permission to fire. Commence bombardment."

The view-port flashed again, and a glittering beam shot across space. Against the black, the light was so bright that it left an after-image on my retinas. The weapon scoured the underside of the *Death of Antares*, causing a rupture between two armoured plates. Fluid and assorted debris erupted from the vessel, spilling out into space. The ship continued her slow and interminable manoeuvre overhead, but I could tell that she was hurt.

Damn it. I felt a pang of annoyance that I was not the operator to take first blood. The railgun swivelled angrily outside.

"Did we kill it?" Blake asked, excitedly.

The weapons officer's impact had caused some minor structural damage – a report filtered through to my station.

"Not quite," I growled. "But we're close. This is my kill."

The ship sailed overhead, and I saw my chance.

I didn't wait for an order. I opened up with the railgun. It was nothing more than a dumb killshot weapon – slow and unguided, but absolutely lethal at this range. It could punch a hole through hull plating and open the enemy ship to vacuum. That was the goal: make the enemy ship bleed to death. I fired a short volley of super-accelerated shots into the underside of the *Death*.

To me, immersed in the operating system of the *Oregon*, each shot seemed to take an eternity to reach its target, all the while the *Death* firing barrages of bio-plasma into the *Oregon*. The reality was that it took microseconds for the rounds to impact.

I knew that the *Antares* was dead before she did.

First one, then two, railgun shots pierced the lower hull. Assisted by the *Oregon*'s AI, my aim was good, and each shot hit the same weakened seam on the underside. In slow motion, the rounds punched right through the armour plating. More debris poured from the puncture wound, more fluid spilled out into space – freezing before it had even left the vicinity of the vessel. The ship seemed to wobble, the engine-light flickering. The bio-plasma pores stopped firing.

"Confirmed hit," I declared. "She's moving beyond our shield perimeter."

A cheer went up across the bridge. This was better than I had expected. I felt a surge of hope run through me. The weapon still hungered, and

I felt the enormous barrels cooling, but if nothing else I had bought us some time.

There is still another one out there, a voice sounded in my head. That was either me, or the railgun AI – now reloaded, eager for another target.

"Any database match on the secondary hostile?" Atkins yelled.

"The *Great White*, sir," the same officer from earlier replied. "Responsible for the scuttling of three Alliance Navy ships at the Battle for Gavis Prime." What was it with this officer and bad news? "Category six. No known weaknesses, sir."

"What's a category six?" Kaminski called.

No one bothered to answer him. Krell starships were categorised according to their threat level – based on intel held on specific vessels, cross-referenced with size. A category six ship was *big*.

"What category are we?" Kaminski followed up.

"We're a three," I called back.

"Ah, shit."

The *Great White* made ponderous progress through the asteroid field, firing brilliant lance-weapons as she went. She was further away than the *Death* and well outside our null-shield. Each shot fizzled against the shield, now holding firm and protecting us. The enemy ship was still partially concealed by the asteroid field and as she moved the loose debris was sent scattering.

I'll take you down just as easily, I promised. The railgun was getting the better of me. I *had* to fire.

"I'm continuing fire on the *Death*," I declared.

It was as though the *Oregon* was possessed by

some feral, bloodthirsty spirit – and therefore I was too. The railgun fired. There was no recoil, no aftershock from each shot. Around me, other weapons officers followed suit. All weapons converged on the crippled enemy ship. Torpedoes launched, and as soon as the particle beamer had recharged it fired again as well. There was a strange detachment from the battle itself; save for the occasional, and probably quite significant, creak and groan of the *Oregon*'s chassis, the battle was fought silently. This was the difference between firing starship-bound weaponry and fighting in a simulant: there was no pain, no immediate consequence of my actions. *I fire, something out in space dies.* Inside my sim, everything was visceral: the simulated became real. I felt the ache to get back into my simulator-tank, though the sims would be no use against warships.

Even as the *Death*'s fuel tanks ruptured, exploding in a magnificent and short-lived flash, there was no sound. Pieces of the *Death* scattered across the view-port, striking the reinforced windows with percussive thuds. Smaller bits of debris sparked against the null-shield outside. Although a significant portion of the vessel still lingered in space, the ship was finished. Most of her interior was now open to vacuum, and the Krell crew would die to the void just as quickly as us.

"Primary threat neutralised."

I was dripping in sweat, I realised. Despite the circumstances, I was enjoying the carnage, enjoying doing this. Perhaps *because* of the circumstances I was enjoying it. I fired the railgun with a reckless abandon. The ammunition counter eventually began to deplete, and a warning flashed – informing me that I was reaching a critically low projectile count.

"That's a confirm on the non-operational status of the *Death of Antares*," Atkins bellowed behind me. "Cease all fire on the vessel."

Was that directed at me? I wondered. In any event, I pulled back in my seat and stopped firing the railgun.

"Now we only have to deal with the *Great White*," he said.

The battle was far from over. The *Great White* fired a constant stream of energy beams into the *Oregon*. The null-shield wouldn't hold for ever. We would have to take some offensive action, to bring down the other ship.

Atkins reeled off orders to his crew. The *Oregon* shuddered momentarily, and I felt myself drifting upwards. The gravity well was malfunctioning.

"Secondary hostile is about to take further action," Pakos said.

The *Great White* had stopped moving, and the pores lining her flank started to flex rhythmically. Smaller flying vessels were being ejected from the ship and forming up as tight attack wings.

"I told you we needed Hornets," Jenkins said to me. During the bombardment, she and my team had assembled around my weapon station.

"Identifying multiple inbound hostiles," Pakos called out. "Less than twenty seconds until they reach optimal firing distance. They're trying to get inside the shield."

The disembarking fighters were sleek and needle-like. While obviously of the same mould as the bigger Krell warships, these were much faster and more manoeuvrable. Engines ignited to close the distance between them and us, leaving bright tails of plasma across space.

I scanned the area for targets. The railgun automatically tracked the incoming fighters, but didn't fire. The railgun rounds were slow; the weapon would be no use against these new threats.

"Damn it!" I yelled.

But the *Oregon* responded in force. I felt the tug of torpedoes firing from bays somewhere beneath us, and watched on the holo as they met the oncoming fighter wing. Multiple ships exploded before they had even reached our position, disappearing from the scanner. There were a series of vivid flashes – each marking the death of a fighter. Each was extinguished almost instantly in the cold of space.

Returning fire raked the *Oregon* though. Energy beams impacted our null-shield, and it was inevitable with this volume of enemy fire that some shots would get through. Something popped deep within our ship, and this time I felt and heard the explosion.

This is real again.

The battle in deep-space had been computer-controlled, sanitised. Silent explosions, fighting through machines, dispatching targets many kilometres away. The explosions sounding around me, as the *Oregon* fell under heavy enemy fire: they were *real*.

I pulled at the jack-cables, immediately breaking the connection with the *Oregon*'s weapon systems. The other dimension of awareness was suddenly gone. That same wave of uncertainty washed over me and I shook my head; concentrating on reality.

"Stay bolted down!" Kaminski yelled. "More incoming!"

The deck shook uncontrollably, then gravity cancelled altogether. This time, I took immediate evasive action, and grabbed onto the armrests of the weapon station. My squad did the same with anything fixed to the deck. It felt like all of my internal organs were suddenly loose inside me. For the first time in a long time, I was glad that I hadn't drunk recently. Nausea overcame me, and I just managed to hold down the contents of my stomach.

The comms blurted with traffic, as maintenance reported damage across the ship. A crewman was screaming about a fire on the lower deck. It was impossible to ignore the smell of smoke in the air.

No getting away from this.

"Permission to vent decks three and five," Lieutenant Pakos called out.

She was a damned comms officer – not responsible for maintenance or any other aspect of the ship's running. From the corner of my eye, I spied another dead officer – spinning across the room in the failing gravity. *Looks like Pakos just got a promotion, whether she wants it or not.*

"Not unless absolutely necessary!" Atkins roared.

Gravity shifted again. I grabbed for the chair,

missed it, and sailed towards the ceiling. At the last moment, I managed to put out my arms to soften my landing. Around me, the other occupants of the bridge were in the same condition.

"It really is," Pakos shouted back to Atkins. Her voice broke. "It really is the only way."

"So be it."

I caught sight of Atkins' face as I drifted above him. He scowled angrily. While opening decks to deep-space would certainly solve the fire hazard, it also meant that anyone who had not taken protective measures would be sucked into space. Pakos was taking the hard choice – expending whoever was left on those decks for the good of the rest of us. It wasn't a decision I would've wanted to make.

"Where is the worst damage?" Atkins queried.

"Life support has taken a hit," someone answered.

We're finished, I thought to myself. Life support was the most heavily shielded area of the ship. If we were taking hits there, then our oxygen and heat supply would be next.

Then, as suddenly as the gravity lapse had started, it finished. I thumped down to the ground hard. Kaminski landed next to me, groaning to himself.

Atkins bobbed his head, considering something in the *Oregon*'s operating system. For the first time since the battle had begun, he appeared to consider that we might actually lose: that we might actually die out here.

"We're haemorrhaging cryogen from one of the rear supplies," he declared morosely.

"Which means?" Jenkins asked, steadying herself as another impact hit the *Oregon*.

"That we can expect to lose our atmosphere in approximately twenty-five minutes."

"We must be able to do something!" I shouted, scanning the faces of my crew and looking to Atkins.

"The damage is external," Atkins said. "Unless you can get outside, under that fire," he pointed at the view-port, "then there isn't anything that can be done."

I smiled at Jenkins but she was already staggering towards the bridge door.

"Keep firing on that bitch," I ordered, "and we'll take care of the damage. Comm Olsen and tell him to power up the tanks."

CHAPTER EIGHT

FIVE-MAN ARMY

We took the shortest route to Medical. The ship's gravity generator was working only intermittently, and as a result we were deprived of the simple act of forward motion. The dash through open corridors became a three-dimensional affair. The deck swayed and shuddered constantly, and it felt as though we were being attacked from every direction. One moment we were dashing along on the ground, the next we were forced to crawl along the ceiling. I lurched forwards, using ladder rungs as handholds and propelling myself through closing bulkheads. The lighting flickered and flashed, then briefly we were plunged into absolute darkness. I passed a maintenance team feverishly spraying a chamber with fire extinguishers. The air tasted smoky but paradoxically the temperature was dropping rapidly. Panic hung like a miasma; about as breathable as the vacuum outside.

The *Oregon* was dying and only we could save it.

"Next junction," Martinez shouted, taking point, pushing himself off a wall to generate some onward momentum.

The ship PA hissed with static.

"This is Captain Atkins," came a voice. "Science Officer Olsen says your tanks are a go. Get moving!"

Medical was a hive of activity. Wall-mounted monitors showed the *Oregon*'s continued assault on the *Great White*, but now we were firing less often and less successfully.

The simulator-tanks were primed and ready. Olsen's medical techs had been whipped into shape by the threat of the failing life-support system, and reacted with commendable speed.

"Get me into that tank *now*!" I bellowed. I didn't care who I offended, didn't care what procedure was cut short.

"I – I'm hurrying!" a medtech replied, checking me over.

"Leave me – I'll do it myself," I said. I pushed the tech aside. "Help Blake."

I slid my father's pistol from its holster on my leg, and hung it beside my tank. A medic frowned at me, went to examine the gun, but I waved him away.

"Leave it and do your job."

Each of us was attached to the simulators. Olsen oversaw the procedure. Jacked cables to the spinal ports, into the limbs, the same as the procedure on the bridge. Respirator masks in place.

I was lowered into the amniotic fluid of the

simulator. An operational tank would be full of steaming hot, conducive amnio-fluid; now the stuff was tepid, but increasing in temperature. The respirator mask pumped my lungs with cold oxygen. My pulse raced: I wanted the connection so badly. The simulators were delicate pieces of equipment, not made for manhandling in zero-gravity or under fire, but we had no other choice. There was no time for formality.

The jacks ached in my arms. *Like a drug addict, taking the needle.* But in much the same way, I knew that it was a good pain. *It means you're alive*, I told myself. That ache also meant that the ultimate euphoria wasn't far off: that soon I would have the exhilaration of transition.

Come on! Come on! Do this already!

I had a bead in my ear, allowing me to communicate with Medical and the rest of my team.

"Fuck yeah!" Kaminski roared from inside his mask. "Let's do this shit."

Jenkins, Blake and Martinez howled like dogs. Some of the medics flinched back from the sim-tanks.

"Are the sims ready?" I asked of Olsen.

Everything outside the tank was a blue haze. Olsen stood in front of me, clutching a clipboard or data-slate, and nodded his head.

"Yes, Captain Harris," he mumbled. "After transition, you will need to follow the path pre-set by Captain Atkins. Your suits have been loaded with tactical maps of the interior and exterior of the *Oregon*."

Olsen stood back and indicated the far wall of Medical. There, opposite my tank, were five gods of war. Five statues, cast from grey flesh; wrapped in the best Alliance military tech. Five hungry, empty vessels: eyes lightly shut behind semi-mirrored face-plates. Hung on hooks like joints of meat. Plasma rifles magnetically locked to the back-plates of each suit. *It's close. Soon – it'll happen soon*.

Another enormous boom sounded somewhere deep in the *Oregon*, echoing through the empty metal corridors. Red emergency lighting illuminated Medical. A tech scrambled over to my tank and sealed me in.

"This sector of the ship has access to the emergency power reserve," Olsen said. "Unless the ship goes down, we'll have power in Medical until the end."

"Good to hear," I said. "Now get on with it, and get us out there."

The same tech double-checked the other simulator-tanks.

"Good luck," Blake yelled. "See you all on the other side."

The words were repeated by each of us like a chant.

"Establishing remote link with the simulant bodies," a tech called out. "Link is good, repeat link is good."

"Are the sim operators ready for transition?" Olsen asked.

One by one, we motioned from our tanks that we were ready. Olsen watched each of us in turn, then raised a hand and spoke into his communicator.

"All operators confirm readiness. We are good to go, repeat good to go. Commence transition."

It couldn't come soon enough.

This was like my connection with the *Oregon*, but it was also different. *So much better.*

I looked out of my tank, watching Olsen and the scurrying medics. For a split second, two realities were superimposed on one another. I was in two places. Two biological entities vied for dominance, commanded by a single mind. My real heartbeat and that of the simulant fell in step; slowing down.

Strength sapped from my limbs. I tried to move them, to lift an arm in the syrupy blue fluid.

I am in control of every aspect of my body. I lift both arms, but must be careful not to over-react: my strength is amplified by my suit and knows no bounds.

I was forty years old, Earth-standard.

I am just born.

My every sense was sharpened, hyper-alert. It was so disorienting that it was almost painful.

But not for me. I am alive again.

I wasn't inside the simulant. I *was* the simulant.

The hooks holding the previously inert body in place gave way and I stood for the first time. The body was newborn but I felt no shakiness, no uncertainty.

My real body was curled inside the tank in front of me. *Weak, human and fallible.* So easily destroyed. It had been replaced by something else, something better. I flexed my arms and legs.

I rolled my head, felt taut muscles in my neck. I breathed deep. Everything worked exactly as it should.

"Transition confirmed," I said.

My tactical combat helmet activated. The interior of my face-plate flushed with systems diagnostics for a second, then it was flooded with real-time battle data from the *Oregon*. The rest of my combat-armour came online.

"Everyone ready?" I roared into the comm.

"Finally!" Kaminski yelled. "We are a five-man army."

There was a round of "affirmatives" from the others.

"Let's do this."

Olsen and the rest of the science team parted before us and we stormed off through the *Oregon*.

The nearest primary airlock was through Medical, past Storage, then back through Communications. In our real bodies this would've been an arduous journey. Now we handled it easily. Gravity continued to fluctuate: we had magnetic locks integrated into the soles of our boots for that. The atmosphere was fouled by smoke and other pollutants: we had internal atmosphere supplies for that.

We occasionally passed crew and other staff. Despite the panic, despite the danger of immediate extinction, they stopped to stare at us. The Simulant Operations Programme was no secret but even the Alliance Navy rarely got to see a simulant up close like this. From the expressions on the faces of the Naval staff, I doubted that this was something they'd want to see again.

Ahead, a handful of crewmen wearing emergency respirators were fumbling with a bulkhead door. Two slabs of six-inch-thick metal were being held open by a fire extinguisher; the door motor was whining in protest. A warning light set in the ceiling bathed the area in yellow light. The crew were shouting to one another. As we approached, the bulkhead sounded again – that nerve-jangling screech of metal on metal – and the extinguisher hissed as it ruptured.

"Get out of the way, *now*!" I bellowed over my combat-suit external speakers. My voice was a deep, ribcage-rumble – amplified now.

Six men were flagged on my HUD; glowing icons, broadcasting bio-signs. Elevated heart-beats, dangerous levels of carbon dioxide consumption.

I led my squad, and the crew turned to respond to me as one. Their faces were masks of pure dread; horror that someone in the Alliance could've devised something so precisely honed for the art of war. The crew were like mites to me – had I wished, they could be so easily extinguished. I waded through them all. The only thing that mattered was reaching the airlock.

I am doom, a voice in my head said. *And I like it.*

"Y-yes, sir!" one of the maintenance crew managed, stumbling back from the door.

I bolted forward and caught the bulkhead as it was about to close. I prised open the two metal slabs with my fingers. The metal squealed again but gave way. The hissing extinguisher fell to the floor, still pumping foam. I forced the door panels into the wall, leaving the access clear.

"The airlock is that way," I indicated to the others. "Double-time it."

"Affirmative, Cap," Jenkins said over the comms channel, with a snigger, as she jogged on past the terrified crew.

I didn't bother reprimanding Jenkins. That was the worst part of all this: glancing down at those men, I enjoyed their reaction.

I wasn't like them any more.

I was something better.

CHAPTER NINE

SPACE WALK

We finally made it to the *Oregon*'s primary air-lock. I opened a communication channel to Olsen back in Medical.

"This is Harris. We've reached the lock."

"Receiving," Olsen said, his voice fluctuating with static. "Captain Atkins reports continued bombardment from the enemy vessel. Godspeed."

"Solid copy. Harris out."

The airlock was a sterile white chamber, with one end leading into the belly of the *Oregon* and the other directly into space. An armoured bulk-head, replete with warnings as to the dangers of exposure to hard vacuum, sat at that end of the chamber. That was our destination. A porthole offered a view into the black outside.

The combat-suits allowed for operation in deep-space just as easily as in an atmosphere. Indicators on the inside of my helmet illuminated: my suit was powered up and atmospherically sealed.

"Right, people. Confirm suits are sealed and weapons are primed."

Shouts of agreement.

I braced my body against the airlock door, clasping the manual locking handle. Without pausing, I twisted the release valve. The door gave way easily, exposing the chamber to vacuum. There was a rush of atmosphere escaping, then absolute calm.

"Initiating EVA," I said.

A timeline appeared on my HUD: seventeen minutes until life support failed.

Space opened before me. I plodded out of the airlock. The soles of each boot immediately magnetised, attaching me to the ship's hull. The others followed suit.

The gravity well generated by the *Oregon* did not extend past the inner decks, and as soon as we were outside the ship proper, there was no gravity at all. My plane of balance shifted: where once down had been dictated by the artificial gravity field, now my only point of reference was the activated mag-locks on my boots. The sudden change in gravitational pull brought with it a bout of nausea, but the medical suite on my combat-suit instantly corrected that. Space sickness was a petty concern, of no issue to a simulant.

The *Oregon*'s hull was a vast, barren plain. Bare metal reached for hundreds of metres in every direction, punctuated only occasionally by a communications mast or weapon array. Running lights flickered in the distance, studding the ship's flank. The airlock was roughly amidships, on the starboard side. As soon as I left the confines of the airlock, my HUD lit up with a tactical map showing me the most direct route to the damage site. I ignored that for a moment, though, and focused on the enormity of the view.

The *Oregon* was positioned in the midst of the asteroid field and rocks drifted by. Beyond, space opened to infinity: a tapestry of brilliant white pinpricks against a silky blackness. Each of those lights represented a star, each circled by a plethora of Krell-occupied planets. We were *inside* the Maelstrom. The idea took my breath away for a second and I felt my suit responding with an injection of sedative. It would be easy to get lost out here, to feel dwarfed by the vastness of space. The thought was intrusive and persistent; not my own.

Below, beyond the curve of the *Oregon*'s polished hull, Helios beckoned. I imagined myself, for just a moment, releasing my mag-locks and drifting off into space – to be sucked down to Helios, by the pull of planetary gravity. Helios itself was an ugly mess of a planet. It was a brown, dusty orb; swathed by yellow cloud cover and angry storm-swirls. No oceans or large bodies of water, the monotonous brown broken only by infrequent mountain ranges. Perhaps there was some grandeur to the planet, but I couldn't see it. This place held no beauty for me. The Artefact was visible even from space. It was so big that it rose up through the clouds, like an angry finger pointing to God.

But that wasn't the worst of the view.

"Christo," Kaminski said over the communicator. Martinez didn't bother to rebuke him this time. "Just look out there."

He indicated the *Great White*. From the bridge, viewed via the holo and even the view-port, the *White* looked singularly black. Up close, she was a variety of shades of dark. Her hull had been repaired innumerable times, with new armour plating grown over damaged portions. Ugly welts and scars lined the visible flank of the ship, like this was some huge living beast rather than a constructed starship. The thing looked as though it was *hurting*, and the scarring gave the impression that it had been hurting for a very long time. Even so, she continued to fire bright bio-plasma streams into our ship, igniting lance-beams through the asteroid field. Every impact caused the null-shield to light brightly, and my suit face-plate to polarise. Near-space was like an Alliance Day fireworks display.

"This is really something, *compadre*," Martinez said, as we went. "If just one of those beams hits us, we're dust."

"I think that the Krell have more to worry about than us," Blake said. "Or at least I hope so."

They were both right. The alien ship probably couldn't detect us at this range, but if somehow we were caught in the crossfire then death was inevitable.

"Move out. Tight formation," I said, as we began the spacewalk proper. "Keep together."

"You heard the man," Jenkins said. "Stay on it."

The squad deployed smoothly out, rifles panning

the geography. In zero-gravity, every footstep was a struggle. If I overstepped, I knew that I could be propelled out into space, but time was also of the essence. Our combat-suits automatically adapted to the starfield, and the outlines of each trooper appeared to shift. My HUD notified me that active camo was operational. Each squad-member was tagged, aura-codes flagged even though I could hardly see their outlines with the naked eye.

There was a prickle of anxiety at the back of my mind, so deep that no drug could touch it. I'd spacewalked a hundred times before but it had never been an experience I'd enjoyed. The post-transition psych-evals had diagnosed me with borderline agoraphobia, reasoning that my upbringing in the cluttered tenements of Detroit Metro made me more comfortable with confined spaces. I thought that it was deeper than that. I didn't like being in space simply because death could come so quickly and without warning. Considering my profession revolved around dying, that was saying something. War might sometimes depend on luck but surviving a fight in a vacuum was entirely random. In space, we were robbed of so many advantages of our combat-suits and simulants. That confidence that I had felt back aboard the *Oregon*, when we had made transition, was rapidly ebbing away. We were as vulnerable out here as our fleshy bodies were inside the *Oregon*. A stray piece of debris, a misconnected hose, a fractured face-plate: all of those things spelled death in hard vacuum.

I'd seen men driven wild with panic, out in

space, in lesser circumstances than this. The human race was becoming domesticated, more familiar with the darkened interiors of a starship or a space station than wide-open exteriors. There was something to do with the sense of openness, the sense of desolation – of lost hope – that was almost overwhelming.

The universe doesn't care, a voice whispered in my ear. *Everything you do is irrelevant.*

"We now have exactly sixteen minutes to reach the damage site," I said, shaking myself out of it. "I don't want anything holding us up. Scanner sweeps set for a hundred metres."

"You expecting some trouble?" Jenkins asked, as she plodded alongside me.

"We're not taking any chances out here," I said. "But I sincerely hope not."

"Scanner isn't worth shit," Kaminski said. "The debris is creating ghosts."

Just then, something drifted past us, and I paused to watch it go. A corpse – a crewman, still dressed in Alliance Navy shipboard fatigues. The body was frozen solid, face held in an eternal rictus of horror. The hands were outstretched, fingers clawing for purchase. In contradiction to the terrible expression on the corpse's face, the body calmly floated away from us, and into the asteroid field. I realised that much of the debris in our vicinity was actually parts of the *Oregon*, ranging from damaged armour plating through to the bodies of crew.

"Eyes on the prize, people," I muttered, waving ahead. "The damage site is three hundred metres in that direction."

*   *   *

The walk seemed to take for ever, and it was difficult not to be distracted by the firefight taking place overhead and around us. I had a prime view of the action. Brilliant rays of energy discharged across the void, tearing into both ships. The primary railgun – enormous, built to level cities – sat a few metres away. Hard to imagine that the gun had been slaved to my will just minutes earlier; as I passed it I felt an unconscious niggle in my spinal-port, in recognition of our pairing. The gun was cold and still now, without an operator.

Above us, dimensionally-speaking, a battery of lasers fired incessantly. The *Great White* had obviously expended her reserve of fightership ships but her other ordnance appeared unlimited. She constantly fired bio-plasma from organic guns, sending multi-coloured energy discharge into space, leaving behind beautiful rainbow streamers.

It was awe-inspiring, in a way. Here were two species, so very unlike one another in many ways but so very similar in many others, expending literally every ounce of their being in an effort to exterminate each other. *Reflections in a dark mirror.* Even more irrationally, in that very instant, I hated the Krell more than ever.

We had broken into a measured bounding motion – *one foot up, one foot down*: sure to always have at least one mag-lock in contact with the *Oregon*'s hull at all times. Kaminski and Martinez at the rear. They carried the repair gear, proofed for use in space, and so needed to be protected. Kaminski was the most technically minded, and he would repair the breach once we reached it.

"Closing in a hundred metres," Blake declared, on point.

"Cover the objective."

The metal landscape ahead was broken by a rupture in the armour plating – a gouge, metres wide and deep. Fluid drained from inside, immediately freezing into dirty white snow, and messy cabling was exposed beneath. My HUD informed me that this was the location of the hull breach, even indicating the necessary steps to fix it.

"Wide dispersal around the site."

My squad responded.

"Twelve minutes until our life support expires."

Deep within the *Oregon*, our real bodies waited. If the ship went down, so did we. There had never been a more personal motivation to achieve our mission objective.

"Get working, Kaminski."

"Affirmative, Captain," he replied, already unshouldering the repair equipment. "Martinez, give me a hand with this shit."

The pair continued unloading the gear, mag-locking items to the exposed hull. Kaminski clambered down into the breach and started poking the damaged innards.

"You think you can fix it?" I asked.

"I have to," Kaminski called back. "Don't worry. I've never found a machine that I can't handle. Someone pass me that sealant spray."

Except that Kaminski isn't a starship engineer,

and never has been. He was a specialist-grade sim operator, and the best chance we had at this.

I crouched on the hull, scanning the immediate area. The apparent openness of the artificial terrain was misleading, I decided. If I looked for them, there were hiding places everywhere. The grooves between armour plates were like trenches. The shadows cast by antennae and gun-turrets could've concealed an army. Each spinning asteroid, just beyond the overhead glare of the null-shield, might harbour a Krell horde. I breathed hard, activating the auto-targeting feature on my M95 rifle. The only sounds were my own clipped breathing – short, controlled inhalations, as I had been trained to do – and the low hum of the oxygen pack on my back.

Kaminski and Martinez still worked away in the hull breach. I tasted something acid at the back of my throat, like the tang of burning plastic. *Is this the taste of the* Oregon, I wondered, *burning up?* I shook myself out of it again. It was impossible; while I occupied the simulant, there was no way I could experience transference from my real body.

Get a damned grip.

"Ten minutes," I said. "You need any more help down there, Kaminski?"

Kaminski appeared at the lip of the breach, reaching for another can of sealant spray. He shook his head.

"Nearly done. Give me another minute."

"Stay frosty, people," I muttered, to keep myself talking.

"Hard not to," Jenkins replied. "It's damned cold out here."

"I hear that, Jenkins."

Even inside the suits it was uncomfortably cold. Partly physical, partly something else: the chill was hard to shake, born out of an aversion that man has to being in space. It was a natural reaction, hard-wired as the need to breathe. I wondered whether the Krell felt the same way. Blake shifted beside me, panning his rifle over a moving shadow. He was edgy, getting too nervous. His biorhythms appeared on my HUD and I noticed his increased heartbeat.

"Blake, activate your medical suite," I ordered.

I caught a glimpse of his young face behind his face-plate. He looked uneasy, even in his sim. I'd never seen him like that before. Then his face-plate polarised, as the reflection of a far-off energy beam caught the mirrored surface. His rhythms calmed a second later.

"I'm all right," he said. "I'm with it."

"Stay that way. Nine minutes!"

"Another minute," Kaminski muttered. "Martinez, can you pass me that wrench?"

The coolant had stopped escaping from whatever was damaged inside the ship, so that was something. Kaminski tossed away an empty sealant can and it lazily drifted out into space.

I activated my communicator and tried to establish a link to the *Oregon*.

"*Oregon* Medical, this is Captain Harris – do you copy?"

"This is Olsen," came a distorted voice in response. "The firefight is interfering with communications. How goes the repair?"

"Well enough. Are we holding out against the enemy ship?"

"So far as I can tell. Captain Atkins has things in hand."

"Good enough for me." I turned to Kaminski, switching comms channels again. "How long, Kaminski?"

"Another minute."

Do you really know what you are doing down there? I was starting to wonder whether Kaminski was telling me the truth. But there was nobody else to turn to.

Then back to Olsen: "We'll be done in another minute. Keep me posted of any developments."

"Copy that. Olsen out."

Another long, cold minute passed. EIGHT MINUTES REMAINING, my HUD flashed. Then something else appeared – a further warning marker.

"You done yet?" I barked at Kaminski. "My suit tells me that another fault is developing in life support. What are you doing down there?"

Kaminski grappled with the edge of the ruptured armour plate, and ungraciously pulled himself out of the hole. He gave an exaggerated nod.

"Nearly," he said. "Another minute. It isn't my best work, but it will have to do. I just need to reset the outer heat exchange." He swallowed anxiously. "That's the other fault. Rerouting the cryogen flow through the outer exchange has caused—"

"Just tell me what you need done."

"It's further down the hull, under an external

maintenance plate. Someone will have to go down there and manually open the release valve."

I sighed. "I'll go. The rest of you, cover Kaminski. Blake, watch me as I go."

"Affirmative, Cap."

My HUD lit up with the location of the release valve: fifty metres aftward of our position. It was painfully slow going. I presented an easy target for any watching snipers. I bounded on, each step a leap through the unknown. I immediately wished that we had been better equipped for this. We hadn't figured on any EVA; the newer Class V combat-suits carried specialist thrusters for use in deep-space, but as we hadn't figured on this part of the operation these Class IV suits didn't have them.

A small city of sensor-masts erupted from the hull, housing local comms gear and other life-support apparatus. My HUD suggested the location of the release valve, hidden behind a bolted metal plate on the hull.

Seven minutes.

Helios' primary star cut a crescent behind the arc of the planet below, big and yellow. Beyond, barely visible, was Helios Secondary. That star was pale and distant, having long ago lapsed into decline. The combination of both light sources threw bizarre and awkward shadows over the surface of the hull; as a result, this area of the ship was in almost total darkness.

"I'm at the release valve now. Moving to activate."

There was no time to safely remove the metal

plate, so I grappled with my fingertips and tore it free. Bolts and secreted dust floated off into space. Beneath, there was a nest of electronic components and wires.

Kaminski's voice broke into my comm: "You need to reset the valve intake. Should be a button."

Six minutes.

I hurriedly scanned the maintenance duct. A label proclaimed WARNING! COOLANT RELEASE VALVE. DO NOT OPERATE UNLESS OUTER EXCHANGE IS CLEAR! There was a flashing red button beneath.

"You sure about this, Kaminski? There are warnings on this panel."

"Ah, I think so. I hope so. It'll work. It should work."

"I'm activating now," I said, and thumbed the button. "For all our sakes, I hope that it does."

"Copy that."

I paused over the maintenance plate, watching for any immediate response to my actions. My HUD hadn't updated: the warning continued to flash. That didn't look good.

"Kaminski, did it work?"

"I think so. Give me another minute to confirm."

"You keep saying that! My HUD is still reporting a problem."

I looked back at my squad. They were assembled around Kaminski and the hull breach, rifles panning back and forth. The hull itself reverberated underfoot as the *Oregon* took another hit.

Five minutes.

I turned to take in the vast, empty landscape of the hull, and plodded over to the nearest comms mast to evaluate the shadowed area. Just then, an enormous explosion flared overhead. The *Great White* had taken a serious hit to the bow. She seemed to teeter, briefly, turning away from the *Oregon* to prevent a further shot at the damaged area. Pieces of the *Great White* were thrown out into space, blazing as they hit the *Oregon's* null-shield. The *Oregon* certainly seemed to be putting up some resistance.

"You know, Jenkins, we just might make this," I said, more to myself than to her. "That was a good shot. I don't think that the Krell ship will take much more—"

I saw them before my suit bio-scanner did.

Oh shit.

A horde of Krell primary-forms.

In an effort to stay attached to the *Oregon's* hull, they were anchored to every possible surface feature. Some had crawled into gaps between armoured plates, using them as cover from the battle above. Six or seven hung on the shadowed underside of the comms mast. These were specialised Krell forms, bred for ship-to-ship combat. Protected from vacuum inside their bio-suits, with enormous globed helmets and clawed gauntlets to attach themselves instead of mag-locks – up-armoured like lobsters. Among the horde, there were also secondary-forms – gun-grafts – evolved for ranged combat. One clung to a piece of piping, much bigger than the others, directing them on. My HUD identified the xeno-type immediately, flagging the bastard as an alpha-level threat.

A leader-form.

The Krell equivalent of an officer for the massed primary- and secondary-forms. It was a nasty fucker; armour weathered from exposure to space, back-plate erupting with quivering antennae.

The Collective moved along the hull, and for just a second they didn't seem to see me. *They're creeping – moving slowly to avoid bio-scanner sweeps.*

"Contact," I whispered into the communicator.

I knew full well that even the briefest radio communication would alert the mass of aliens to my presence. At this range – virtually on top of them – their delicate sensors would be preternaturally responsive.

Four minutes, my HUD told me. I cancelled the warning. *Let me deal with one problem at a time.*

The Krell didn't disappoint.

The Collective looked up, as one. The leader-form evaluated me with alien eyes under the globed helmet: perhaps wondering why a lone human would be out here in the dark. Its communication spines bristled angrily.

Need to see how many of you there are out here, I thought. *Better to know exactly what I'm up against.* Any advantage of surprise that I might have achieved was already lost and I needed proper intel.

I activated my rifle and fired a starburst flare overhead. Brilliant red light flooded the area, glinting off armoured bodies, and the flare floated off into space.

Finally my suit caught up and relayed a brief

tactical analysis: there were at least a hundred Krell. A terrifying picture developed. Slowly, surely, signals began to build all around me.

"Contact on my three o'clock," I yelled, firing my rifle – this time, a volley of plasma pulses. "Weapons free."

I turned to take in my team, but the Krell had cut me off. They were suddenly everywhere, streaming along the hull towards the squad.

"I see you," Jenkins shouted. "They're moving in fast from your direction."

"Take down all confirmed targets," I ordered.

Three minutes. I kicked off my mag-locks and pushed my body back towards my team. Unhindered by gravity, I sailed backwards and away from the massed Krell. I fired a volley of unaimed shots. Thankfully, the M95 had no recoil, and I could fire on the move even though my aim was shit. As the pulses penetrated their protective bio-suits, Krell bodies exploded and drifted into space. My suit confirmed three hits.

I landed hard on the hull, and my mag-locks activated again. The force of the impact shook my legs and my whole body absorbed the landing.

The leader-form waved the swarm onwards. They moved relentlessly under my fire, ignoring casualties. It didn't matter to them: so long as one of them survived, then their mission would be accomplished. They were moving in literally every direction, and now that the pretence of stealth had been lost they were engaged in a frontal assault.

Was this a sabotage operation? Had the Krell been tasked with damaging vital shipboard technology?

Or had they been sent as a boarding party, intending to breach the *Oregon* and take the fight to us while we were still on the ship? Whatever their objective, the Krell were *here*.

I stole a glimpse at the positional relay projected onto my HUD. It showed that the squad were formed up on Kaminski, firing in controlled bursts into the mass of Krell. Still thirty or so metres between me and the rest of my squad. The annoying, ever-present countdown overrode other warnings on my HUD.

"Two minutes left, Kaminski. Please tell me that you are done."

Kaminski didn't answer.

"They really do *not* want us landing on Helios," Jenkins remarked, crouching to aim at the incoming mass of xenos.

"Just makes me want to get down there all the more," I replied. "Must've landed on the *Oregon* during the battle – they were probably outflanking us all along."

The gun-grafts were armed with boomers – a long-barrelled organic weapon, capable of firing ranged energy blasts. One of them fired in my direction, sending a bright multi-coloured pulse across my flank. I returned fire into the horde, then steadied myself – ready to take up a better position to fire on the aliens below.

The nearby sensor-masts were like miniature towers, topped by aerials as thick as my neck. I quickly decided that those posts would give me some range over the battlefield. The tallest had the best vantage point. I had to get up there.

There was no time to properly prep myself for the jump. I just leapt onwards.

Fuck it!

I sailed over the Krell, too focused on landing to return their fire now. I realised that I had overstepped – I was going to hit the mast hard and fast. The Krell responded immediately: like a volley of arrows, stinger-spines filled the area. *Am I hit?* I asked myself. SUIT INTEGRITY MAINTAINED, the AI responded. I reached an arm out to snag the sensor-mast and managed to hold on to it. Again, the landing was bone-jarringly hard. I awkwardly repositioned myself, firing at the group below. More stingers sailed past, some slashing into the hull, others impacting the mast.

"Kaminski!" I shouted. *"Tell me you are done!"*

I looked down at a sea of Krell, from my position on the mast. They were everywhere. When one was cut down, two more appeared. Out of frustration more than any strategic initiative, I activated the underslung grenade launcher on my M95 and fired an incendiary round. It exploded, sending a ripple of xenos off into space and charring the hull armour. I pumped the launcher; fired again and again.

One minute. My HUD was still flashing the secondary life-support warning – whatever I had done to the exchanger hadn't resolved the problem.

The tac sit was quickly dissolving into absolute chaos.

More Krell fire flew past my head. My suit continually warned of potential impacts. I returned fire again, ducking back behind the sensor-mast for some cover. Not that there was any of that; the Krell swarmed around the base of the mast, some starting the slow and interminable climb to my position. Another grenade: another handful of dead Krell.

"Kaminski! Update *now!*"

Then my AI auto-targeting programme crashed – reporting too many viable targets to operate effectively.

But I wasn't a spent force yet. As I gazed out into the sea of xeno-forms, an idea formed – an irrational, impossible suggestion, but the only thing with any chance of success. *Cut off the command chain. Only way to do this. There are too many of them out there to kill individually.*

Now or never.

I leapt out into the horde, plasma rifle pulsing continuously. A primal sense of purpose drove me on. This foreign body, this simulant built only for war, did what it had been made to do. I selected an impact point in the midst of the mass of bodies – targeting the enormous Krell leader-form crouched there. It was easily twice my size and dripping with bio-tech.

The force of my landing among the Krell sent a wave of invaders off into space, scrabbling to regain purchase. I fired wildly, again and again, at anything nearby. It was impossible to miss at such close proximity. There, ahead of me, was the leader-form. The Krell closed ranks around the vital battlefield link—

My suit warned me of the tactical implications of engagement with the leader, especially in zero-G. Data scrolled across my HUD. The message was clear: retreat was essential for survival. This beast was the very pinnacle of evolution. A dose of combat-drugs hit my bloodstream, calming my pulse.

The leader-form roared behind its bio-helmet, scattering lesser-forms out of the way.

I immediately understood what it was doing: the leader was issuing a challenge.

"Nearly done, nearly done, nearly done," Kaminski suddenly broke in over the comms, panting as he worked.

I had to tie the xeno up, give Kaminski and the others some precious time.

My rifle was up, firing—

The leader-form launched forward, head lowered. Leaping over bodies to reach me, smashing primary-forms aside. It closed on me in a heartbeat; slammed an enormous claw against my rifle. The weapon slid from my hands.

The leader-form hit me like a battering ram, full on in the chest-plate. Something cracked either inside me or in my armour; I had no time to check what. The force was immense. I flung an arm, grabbing the xeno's body to make sure that I didn't sail off into space. Joined, the xeno and I spiralled out between two sensor-masts.

There was no method to the fight. Combat discipline was gone. My body became a weapon.

I crashed down onto the *Oregon*'s hull, still holding the xeno. A warning icon on my HUD illuminated: mag-locks activated. Impossibly, I managed to remain upright.

Soundlessly, we grappled with each other. The monster's shell felt slick and wet, even in this extreme cold. Its maw was open and slavering inside its helmet.

I balled a fist with one hand and continually pounded against the thing's body. Its armour carapace busted in so many places. Still hanging on – *got to stay in one place* – I tore away a piece of bio-armour; felt pulpy organic material beneath—

The xeno persistently stabbed at me with its raptorial talons, using the smaller forearms to hold me down. Each blow sent crippling pain through my chest and torso. My suit responded with dose after dose of pain-suppressing meds, but there was only so much that the simulant could take.

"Fuck you!" I yelled, even though the bastard couldn't hear me. "And the rest of them!"

A noisy alarm sounded in my head. My HUD began to warn me of impending atmospheric loss. Suit viability was failing. I prayed for another dose of combat-drugs, another hit of analgesics.

Keep going!

I prised something free from behind the alien's head.

Although we fought in silence, the thing's face contorted in agony. More plating came free: more alien flesh. I dug my fingers in, twisted.

The xeno butted its head against my face-plate, jabbed at me again with the talons.

Every heartbeat was a war. Being this close to one of them, face to face, filled me with revulsion. The reek of the thing was intense, not in my nose or my mouth: in my mind, in every molecule of my artificial body. I didn't feel like a god any more. *Whatever the Alliance has given me – this tech, this new body – it isn't enough.*

The alien rose over me. I saw my own whitening reflection in its sight-orbs. Blood flecked my lips, sprayed across the inside of my face-plate.

The communicator was suddenly awash with voices. Jenkins, Kaminski, panicking. *"Life support is online!"*

My HUD flashed with an updated message, indicating that the fault was fixed, with only seconds to spare. I couldn't respond to my team, could barely focus on my HUD. I grunted, landing another open-handed blow on the leader-form's carapace. My mag-locks gave way. The thing gained on me again and I slid backwards.

Another flash of an energy beam above – more alien gargoyles clambering over the hull, looming out of the dark.

Muscle fibre burst in my arms. I ground my teeth, ripping off a piece of the leader's carapace—

The bastard abruptly stopped.

I felt a shift in the thing's weight. I slammed another fist into its head, tore at the plating again and again. More armour came free. I realised that it was clawing at its own shoulder, clutching at a rent in the bio-armour. A fine white mist was spraying from the punctured armour, crystallising as the creature began to drift away from me. Its mouth moved silently behind the fractured helmet, shrieking a cry that no one would ever hear. The xeno thrashed futilely, floating off the ship. It began to cartwheel, spilling more and more frozen liquid from its suit. Had to be some sort of suit malfunction.

There was no time to dwell on my victory. I controlled my breathing, rapidly scanning the area around me. Leaderless, the Krell would be momentarily stunned – probably retreat from the position. I unholstered my PPG-13 plasma pistol, got ready to continue the fight—

There was a spike of activity around me. The primary-forms scuttled back into their hiding places.

They all looked up, past me, at space above.

Wait. Something is wrong here.

They understood what was coming. The *Oregon* was doomed.

"Captain, providing covering fire for your retreat," Jenkins insisted over the comms. "Get moving back to our position."

I ignored Jenkins' request and looked up, saw what the Krell concentrated on. I swallowed hard.

"Don't bother, Jenkins. Stand by for updated orders."

My comms bead whined with feedback, and I wasn't sure whether Jenkins could even hear me. Maybe my communications rig had taken damage during the fight.

Helios Primary was just breaking from behind Helios, casting a crescent of pure white light across near-space. *Something* was moving beyond the arc of Helios, crossing the terminator. Just a silhouette, but perfectly illuminated from behind by Primary it was unmistakable.

A third Krell warship.

Great White had simply been stalling, delaying for the arrival of the real threat.

The massive ship was still a distance from our position, but she was moving fast. Even at this range, she bristled with hostility. She wasn't alone either: a locust-like plague of fighter-ships poured from the warship's flanks, and she was escorted by an armada of smaller attack vessels. Like an angry shoal, the great swarm of ships moved on through the black.

That has to be a category ten, I decided.

"Jenkins!" I hollered. "Retreat back to the airlock – get inside the damned ship right now!"

There was no response over squad comms. I looked down at my wrist-comp – shattered and dead.

No one can hear me. This is it.

I was powerless.

All of this – fending off the ambush, repairing the *Oregon*, fighting the Krell – had been for nothing. The Navy intel had been plain wrong. I knew in that instant that we had been fools to think that we could do this. This had been a terrible and precise trap. This was Krell space, and they had the numbers. The Collective had won.

My position on the outer hull suddenly felt like a very lonely place indeed. I stood there, watching the incoming enemy fleet. This was the moment of perfect calm before the storm.

I ran through my options: I was surrounded, and my suit viability was failing. I tried to open a channel back to Medical but that didn't work either. My comms were completely down. I was cut off from my squad.

Even without this new attacker, I probably had a minute or so of operational time left inside my simulant. I was never going to make it back to the airlock. In any case, if I made it back inside the *Oregon*, I needed to get to Medical and properly extract. That was never going to happen.

There was only one logical choice that I could make, and there was no point in delaying it any longer.

After all, suicide runs in the family.

The tip of the Krell spear was already poised to strike. A clutch of fighter-ships impacted the null-shield, breaching it and strafing the *Oregon*'s hull with bio-plasma. Several larger vessels were seconds away from engaging. The warship's organic engines were firing.

"Captain, I can't read you," Jenkins said. "The Krell have fallen back—"

I didn't know whether the squad could see the new attacker from their position, because of the curve of the *Oregon*'s hull. But more important than warning them, I had to warn the rest of the ship.

If you are going to die, then at least die a good death.

I tossed my pistol away and grappled with my helmet, probing the external locking mechanisms with my fingers. Without pausing – not even to steady myself for the pain I was about to experience – I blew the safety catches on each side of the helmet. My suit streamed warning markers across the HUD and the shrill chirping of an alert siren sounded in my ears, until that too fell silent—

No time.

I tore off my helmet and threw it, watching it spin away from me through already boiling eyes. Then I kicked off my mag-locks and bowled into the Krell.

It's a myth that exposure to vacuum makes the human body explode – it only feels that way.

Intense cold filled me. I knew what came next: instant depressurisation. I screamed, but there was no noise and my vocal cords were already destroyed. My lungs ruptured. The pain in my ears and eyes was incredible – so much pressure building up so quickly. Not even a simulant could survive that.

But I didn't want to survive.

I wanted to *extract*.

Death two hundred and nineteen: by vacuum.

The blackness was momentary.

For what it is worth, Sci-Div is divided over whether the speed of extraction is faster than light or instantaneous. For me, it couldn't happen fast enough.

As soon as the simulant body deceased, the neural-link was severed.

One second I was screaming silently in the void.

The next I was screaming audibly in the simulator-tank.

It was the same process of transference in reverse. Except that now I was extracting back into a fallible, weak and human vessel. All of the pain that my simulant had experienced in death was poured into my real skin.

Pain is good, I insisted to myself. *It means I'm alive.*

There was that same disorienting sense of two realities, that same sickening sense of unreality.

I was between worlds. The cold of space in my head, in my lungs; the ringing of sirens, the screaming of panicked crew, in my ears.

"His biorhythms have flatlined!"

"Emergency extraction on squad leader."

"Cap, report. We're taking heavy enemy fire again. The Krell are swarming our location. What's happening?"

"This is Captain Atkins of the UAS Oregon. *All hands – prepare to abandon ship. Initialising emergency evacuation procedure."*

CHAPTER TEN

EVACUATION

The dream ended.
Reality commenced.

EXTRACTION PROTOCOL INITIATED...
CAPTAIN CONRAD HARRIS: DECEASED.

I was back in the *Oregon*.

I thrashed in the simulator-tank. Pain like no other seared through my head and for precious seconds I rode it. The tank began sloughing out, but far too slowly for me. *There's no time for this.* I smashed a hand against the emergency release button inside the tank and the simulator door burst open. Like afterbirth, the blue fluid sloshed onto the floor of Medical. With hands still aching from simulated exposure to the cold of space, I fumbled with the cables connecting me to the simulator and unjacked myself.

"What's happening?" Olsen shouted. "Where is the rest of your squad? What the hell is going on?"

The *Oregon* deck shook violently and I tumbled out of the tank, dripping wet. I moved like I was unfamiliar with my own body – legs too weak, body too small. Panicked techs came to assist me but I threw them off. Grabbing some fatigues, I dashed to the wall-mounted communicator – the quickest and most direct way of contacting Atkins on the bridge. Olsen and his team were still harassing me, questioning me, as another explosion sounded inside the *Oregon*.

"Atkins!" I yelled into the comm. It was an emergency audio-only link. "This is Harris. I've extracted, but my team is still outside. Another warship is approaching from the asteroid belt."

"We've detected her," Atkins replied, resignation sounding in his voice. "We're experiencing serious incoming fire." He was silent for a second and I imagined him evaluating the holo-feeds and the damage already done to his ship. "For what it's worth, you fixed that coolant leak, but the null-shield can't take this sort of punishment. We're going down, Harris. The *Oregon* is finished."

I breathed deep and nodded. "Understood."

"Just get your team out. The med-bay will detach – use it as an escape vessel and get down to Helios."

"What about you?"

Atkins laughed, humourlessly. "I'm staying put and going down with my ship. I've sounded the evacuation and it's every man for himself."

"So be it."

"Your promise – back at the *Point*," Atkins said, solemnly. "I want you to know that you made good on it. There's nothing else that could be done. Good hunting, Captain Harris."

"Good journey, Atkins."

I cut the link, and I knew that Atkins had signed his own death warrant. I had been wrong about him. I pounded a fist into the terminal. He was a good man after all. How many of his crew – all decent, all dedicated – were going to die on this damned mission?

Act now or it's over for real. The question suddenly wasn't whether the *Oregon*'s crew was going to die but whether I wanted to join them. I looked to the simulator-tanks – still occupied by my squad. I had a duty to them.

"We're leaving," I declared.

I bashed my fist onto the big red button labelled EMERGENCY EVACUATION. The *Oregon* trembled and creaked. Metal was shrieking somewhere, followed by the boom of an explosion. My teeth chattered in my head and I tasted iron blood in my mouth.

Not simulant blood: my blood.

"Strap in, Olsen!" I shouted over the cacophony. "The ship is going down."

Olsen realised what was happening; he had bumbled into a safety harness, screaming commands at his techs to do the same. Through shuddering vision, I saw that the other simulators were still operational. View-screens above each tank displayed the vital signs of the occupants. The simulators would be losing power, imminently, and the connection between the simulants and operators would be broken.

"Prepare for emergency evacuation," came the ship's computer, in a calm female voice. The machine had no right to sound so relaxed. "Medical bay will detach from the main vessel. All personnel to take appropriate safety measures."

It happened so quickly, automated by the remains of the ship's AI. The structure of the *Oregon* yawned. The main body of the starship was modular, made so that more important sections were detachable in an emergency. This clearly qualified. Dull metallic detonations sounded nearby. Explosive bolts holding the ship together activated, parting the major crew modules.

Then there was a sudden tug of acceleration as the bay was thrown clear of the main ship – built-in thrusters propelling us away from the battered vessel, to achieve safe distance. I staggered to a safety harness attached to the wall, grappling with anything nearby to remain upright. Medical equipment was thrown across the room; glass smashed against the walls. A technician sailed past me, hitting one of the tanks. Blood splashed the white walls. Anything not bolted down was in free fall. Consoles were smoking, sparking, on fire. It felt as though my world was shaking apart. My ears popped again, as the atmosphere equalised. I ground my teeth, riding out the artificial quake. Above it all, emergency sirens wailed and wailed.

"Christo – someone – help me!" a tech screamed.

"Get buckled in!" I shouted back.

I stared over at the view-port, looking out into space. The *Great White* and the new warship both concentrated fire on the *Oregon* – crossing plasma beams, disgorging more fighter-ships. Atkins was right: the *Oregon* was finished. The null-shield flared one last time, then its oily shimmer vanished. The shield had collapsed.

Something heavy hit my leg and a sharp – *real* – pain erupted in my right thigh. Blood gushed up from the wound, droplets spraying in zero-G. Disengaged from the *Oregon*, Medical had no gravity of its own any more.

"Umbilical with *Oregon* is disconnecting," the computer voice came again, only now it pitch-shifted and warbled as though the main computer was developing a fault. Finally, the machine was feeling the pain along with the rest of us.

Something struck the medical bay and the techs around me shouted out in terror. Our vehicle suddenly skewed, shifting angle so that I could see part of space beyond Helios. Perhaps whatever was left of the navigational AI had decided that this approach vector was too dangerous.

I looked back at the *Oregon*. Brilliant plasma and laser beams tore into the ravaged hull – without the null-shield, every impact causing an explosion. Although I saw other parts of the ship breaking away, so much was caught by enemy fire and I held no hope that there would be survivors. Evacuation pods flew past us, streaming their contents to the void. I saw some of those being chased by fighter-ships, yielding short-lived explosions as they were torn open.

If one of the fighters chose to pursue us, then we would be equally defenceless. The medical bay was inelegant and unguided – spinning end over end towards the surface. It wasn't a ship in and of itself; it had simply detached and started accelerating towards Helios' surface. We were lucky, I guess, but it didn't feel that way from where I was sitting.

As the view spun again, away from the *Oregon*, I saw my squad – still clinging to the hull, surrounded by Krell. The once-proud Naval vessel had been knocked from her orbit; was being pulled down to Helios as well, striking asteroids as she performed an uncontrolled descent to the planet's surface.

I yelled until my voice was hoarse. I was so incredibly angry: with the world, with the universe, with any deity that cared to listen.

We've lost.

The *Oregon* grazed Helios' atmosphere. Her back broke. A tremendous explosion bloomed from the bridge, filling the view-port with white light. Then it just caved in on itself, breaking apart. Several components offered their own detonations. The Krell ships gave no quarter and relentlessly fired on whatever was left of the ship.

I had been in fleet actions before, but never anything like this. It was a massacre; pure and simple. There was a reason that troopers didn't experience such battles: because no one ever lived through them.

Inside their simulator-tanks, Kaminski, Jenkins, Martinez and Blake began to thrash, eyes wide open. Hands pressed against the insides of the glass shells. In their own bodies, they were as panicked as everyone else.

I tried to raise a hand, to signal that we were

evacuating – to tell them something, anything – but the med-bay shifted again and I was forced back into my harness. We were moving at a gut-wrenching speed. Up and down held no meaning. My body ached with the immense gravitational force. I wanted more than anything to tell my people that we were going to get through this, that we were going to survive—

Conscious thought became so hard to undertake, so difficult to achieve. There was no time to fear death. We were at the mercy of chance; nothing more. There was no preordained, divine plan for our survival.

And what was one more death, anyway? I'd lived through enough of those. This felt unreal, impossible. Surely I wasn't really going to die out here, orbiting some Christo-forsaken dust-ball on the fringes of the Krell Empire—

Then the view through the view-port changed. Helios spiralled, so enormous that it filled the entire portal. The planet was rapidly approaching, the cloud cover coming up to meet us. We were breaching Helios' atmosphere, drawn to Helios' gravity and plummeting comet-like through the sky.

And just for a moment, everything was still.

Nothing mattered.

On Helios' surface, the storm clouds eddied and churned around a single point of focus: the Artefact. So black that it absorbed the light from its surroundings. A perfect anchor to this madness.

I heard its malevolent, dark signal; piercing the shroud of white noise that existed aboard the med-bay.

You're imagining it, I promised myself. *There's no way that you can hear it from here.*

Then the moment was gone, and all I could hear was the screaming of the dying and the howling atmospherics against the med-bay hull.

"Emergency warning. Brace for impact," trilled the Medical AI. "All hands: brace for impact."

I closed my eyes. Someone nearby was sick, then with a wet crunching sound abruptly went silent.

Fade to black.

CHAPTER ELEVEN

THIS WAR WON'T LAST FOR EVER

Eight years ago

Elena and I had been together for two years, while we both worked on the Sim Ops Programme. I was eventually transferred from Jefferson Research Facility to Azure. Astronomical designation Tau Centauri IV, Azure was home to Fort Rockwell – an Alliance Army facility, and the biggest extra-solar military base. It was to become the launching point for the Sim Ops Programme.

Elena had persistently petitioned for a transfer, to follow me out here. Finally, that request had been granted. She had been on Azure for a week but was quarantined to Arrivals the whole time, acclimatising to the gravity and lower atmospheric pressure.

I met her on the day of her release. Arrivals was something like a spaceport terminal – a sterile, ugly building; six storeys high, with tiny cubicles to house immigrants. I waited inside the terminal, in

Post-Quarantine Citizen Processing. That was just as bland and pale as the rest of the facility – the only dashes of colour the Arab Freeworlds flag draped on one wall and the Alliance badge opposite. Other soldiers, of assorted military stripe, milled about the room – no doubt awaiting the arrival of loved ones.

Those came and went. People hugged around me. A bored-looking military clerk called names as each citizen was processed. I waited anxiously, eager for my turn. Awkward in my own skin. This wasn't me.

"Marceau, Elena," the clerk finally declared. "French citizen of the Alliance, indefinite leave to remain."

She wandered through the plate-glass doors.

I paused for a moment, overwhelmed. It was difficult for me to process just how happy I was to see her.

Then Elena ran forward and flung her arms around me. Neither of us said anything: just embraced. I buried my head in her hair. Took her in: the warmth of her body, the smell of her. It had been three long months since we had last seen each other.

"Are you hungry?" I finally asked.

Elena nodded. "Very."

"They have a refectory on base. We could go there now—"

"This place has no character," Elena said, with a shrug. "It's unpleasant. Could we go off-base for a while?"

It didn't matter to me where we ate or what we did; Elena was here. That was enough for me.

"I know somewhere."

* * *

We left the base, crossed the military checkpoints and the perimeter. Passing Rockwell security; irritated troopers in flak-jackets, wearing tactical helmets, red-faced in the persistent heat.

"Passes, people," the guard said as we approached. "Biometrics or papers, doesn't matter to me."

He scanned the serial code on my inner wrist. Nodded to himself.

"What I wouldn't give for a combat-suit and some proper air-con, eh?" he said, reading his scanner. It was clear that the comment wasn't meant for us, and that this was a regular topic of conversation for security.

"Heck yeah," the guard's partner muttered.

The first guard waved us through. "Cleared for off-base interaction. Interpreters are available at the kiosk. Just make sure you're back before twenty-two-hundred hours, and watch out for the base-rats. They bite."

"Copy that," I said.

Elena watched on in bemusement at the exchange, but I hurried her on through the checkpoint. Security-drones skimmed overhead, collecting on a group of children outside the perimeter fence: those were the base-rats the guard had been referring to.

We made our way through the bustling streets of downtown Azure City, through the civilian districts. Elena's small hand held mine firmly as we pushed through the crowds. Walking at a slower pace so that Elena was comfortable. The shopping districts were packed.

We were hassled by traders at every turn. I confidently waved them off, but Elena was a little less certain. She paused to look at a gaudy trinket or listen to the banter of a wizened seller.

"They can tell that you have come straight out of quarantine," I said. "You're an easy target. How long do you have to wear that suit for?"

Elena wore a black bodysuit, tight to her slender figure, with a hydraulic frame on the arms and legs. She walked with a halting gait, not quite natural. The callipers allowed her body to adjust to the lower local gravity.

"This old thing?" Elena said, lifting an arm. She sighed and shook her head. "Hardly high fashion, is it? The medtechs advised two weeks. But we'll see."

"You mean that the medtechs *instructed* two weeks?"

Elena laughed and shrugged. "Like I said, we'll see."

"Tell me if you need a rest," I said, gently squeezing her hand.

"I could perhaps sit for a while," Elena replied, blushing. "The heat is a little oppressive."

I knew Elena well enough that if she admitted she was in a little discomfort, it probably meant that she was in a lot. She was tough – tougher than me – and didn't like to admit that she needed help or a break.

"We'll be there soon. We need to get out of the midday heat – it's sapping. You'll learn to avoid the boulevard when the sun is at its peak. This is different to Earth. The Azure heat will knock you out if you don't take cover."

Elena looked up at the sky. It was a bright blue, cloudless in every direction; a heavy orange sun high overhead.

* * *

The café didn't have a name – very few of them did, in this district – but I'd eaten there before and knew that the food was good. There were tables and chairs arranged outside a sandstone building, and we sat. I chose a spot in the shade of a woven awning, tattered and faded from constant exposure to sunlight. The café was quiet, occupied by a mixture of military personnel and a couple of local families.

I called over a waiter and ordered for us both. He disappeared into the shadowed interior of the café.

"This place is amazing," Elena said. "It wasn't what I was expecting."

"What do you mean?"

"I thought that it would be more sterile. I didn't think that it would be so much like *Earth*."

I sometimes forgot that she hadn't travelled like me. She had a cultured naivety, a candour that fascinated me.

"It isn't like the Earth that I recognise," I said, shaking my head. "But I know what you mean."

The boulevard was lined with primitive buildings, cast from locally produced sandstone bricks and plaster. Across the street from us – nothing more than a beaten dirt track, worn by the tyres of heavy ground vehicles – dark-skinned men lounged in shaded open doorways. Some rocked on rusty metal chair-frames. Ancient two-D television sets blared from inside empty-windowed domiciles, volume turned up too high so that the audio became an angry crackle of static. Mothers chased down errant children – shouting rebukes in their mother-tongue.

"The first colonists here were Arabs," I muttered.

I wasn't really interested in the background of the place, but I'd picked up some of the history during my posting. "The Freeworlds claimed it, back before they joined the Alliance, during the Second Space Race. Then the war with the Directorate started and it didn't matter who owned it."

"Who would think that such military might dwells in such beautiful surroundings?" Elena said, glancing about at the ancient buildings. "We might have squandered Earth but the cosmos still holds surprises for us."

She smiled. Her perfect white teeth were cast brilliant in the sunlight. My gaze lingered on her face – oval, warm.

The waiter arrived at our table, sidling up with two bottles of beer and two plates of ersatz spiced-rice. He bowed, then disappeared back inside.

Elena hungrily devoured the food, spooning down mouthfuls. I did the same. It was hot and plentiful – brown rice, mixed with real spices and a repro-meat of some sort.

"I read that Azure is on a rationing system," Elena said. "Will I need a chip?"

"The military are exempt. One of the perks of being Alliance Army."

"Good," Elena said. She tapped one of the bottles with a finger, and raised her eyebrow in surprise. "But a lager? Is it alcoholic?"

"Only weak. Why? Do you want me to order you something else?" I asked. I swigged back a mouthful of beer; the bottle was warm, and had been relabelled. Probably substituted for a cheaper brand, maybe locally produced. The indigenous population

– indigs – certainly didn't drink, but the military machine on Azure kept the alcohol trade alive.

Elena went to say something, but just then a squadron of Dragonfly gunships screamed overhead. Six ships in formation. Gun-pods stowed, missiles racked under each wing. Like their namesakes; fast and deadly. Their engines were loud and they flew low over the city; leaving white engine trails in the sky. Elena involuntarily flinched as they went.

"It's okay," I said. "Just running drills. They happen daily, several times sometimes. You'll get used to them."

I'd already grown accustomed to the constant air traffic. There was no fighting on Azure but there were regular manoeuvres.

"If the Sim Ops Programme takes off, then we might not need this martial force."

"It will take off. I'm sure of it. You would not believe the things that I've seen. The things that I can do in one of those simulant bodies." I shook my head. It was true: the early days of populating a simulant were like being born again. Such incredible feats of agility, of strength, of stamina.

"This is going to change everything. The next generation might find that there is no need for the regular foot soldier," Elena went on. "Actually dying at war might become a thing of the past."

"Let's hope."

"We're part of something out here, Conrad. Part of something big." She stopped eating, glanced out into the dusty street. She was smiling to herself. "We're pioneers. If the Programme expands – there is no telling where it could go."

"I'm just a soldier. I do what I'm told, go where I'm told."

She nudged me in the arm. "You're more than that. What about the promotion? Has Command approved you for full commissioned officer status?"

I chewed over a mouthful of rice, swilled it down with another swig of the warm beer. "I'm not sure about that. It'd mean commanding my own team."

"You're more than capable. I know you are."

"Maybe. But let's not talk military. You're here, and we're together. That's enough for me."

A gaggle of small children ran past us. Barefoot, dusky-skinned; wearing oversized frayed denim shorts and T-shirts emblazoned with logos for American corporations. They kicked a ball into the café, and I knocked it back out into the street.

"What do you say about making a contribution to the next generation?" I asked, pointing to the street children.

"What could you possibly mean?" Elena said, coyly. Her mouth seemed to shrink when she looked at me like that; a look that she only ever gave me. "You've got to make an honest woman of me yet."

"So you want a marriage contract, is that it?"

"Maybe. Or maybe I want *you* to want a marriage contract."

"But if I ask you, how do I know that you'll say yes?"

"That's for you to find out. A girl has to keep some of her secrets."

"Last time we talked about this, you told me that it was too soon. And as I recall, we've talked about this a *lot*."

"When you asked me before, we were on Jefferson Research Facility. Now you're asking me on Azure. It makes a big difference." She shrugged her small shoulders, as though her explanation made perfect sense and I was a fool for not understanding it.

"I don't recall actually ever *asking* you – at least not directly."

She pursed her lips, tutted to herself. It was all play-acting, of course, all part of her show. That was Elena. Theatrical, full of life.

"In any case, there would be things to do before you asked me. You'd need my father's permission for a start." She shook her head. "Christo bless him, he has never even left Earth."

I winced, also light-heartedly. "So, let me get this straight: I have to travel back to Earth – cross however many light-years – go to France, and ask an old man for your hand in marriage? Your father is old, right?"

"Of course," Elena replied. "He's ninety-three objective years. And did I forget to mention that he doesn't speak a word of Standard?"

"So I have to learn French as well. Then I ask you, and you may or may not accept. Then we get to have a hundred beautiful kids and settle down with a farm of our own on Azure?" I said, puffing out the last few words like I was out of breath.

Elena nodded knowingly. "That is exactly right. Surely you would cross light-years of time and space to be with me?"

"I'd cross the universe to be with you," I said. "Truthfully."

Elena leant into me, and we kissed. This was

something deeper than the heart-flutter of a new relationship. I had never felt like this before. In that instant, staring into Elena's eyes, I knew that I would never feel like this again. Her eyes were so wide, so deep. I was lost in them.

"Pretty lady! Pretty lady!" came a voice beside us. "You speak American Standard? You American tourist?"

A shadow fell across the table. A doubled-over old man, with skin like worn leather, stood over Elena and implored her to try some jewellery. He was dressed in colourful but stonewashed robes, and wore a cloth mask, his eyes peering out from a darkened face. He carried an oxygen tank on one shoulder and a water-cooler on the other. Over a knotted claw of a hand, the old man held out some necklaces and rings. He waved his hand and the jewellery clattered noisily.

"You buy pretty wife a necklace, Mr Soldier?" the old man asked, turning to me. He spoke broken American Standard, with a Middle Eastern lilt that could have been Egyptian or Iranian.

Elena inspected the jewellery. "Such beautiful handmade things."

"They can tell you're straight off the boat, Elena. You stop to talk to them."

Elena was fascinated by the rings and reached in to touch one of them. It was an iridescent pink-silver, lined with tiny burnt orange gems. The hawker quickly took it from his hand and encouraged Elena to hold it.

"Finest Azure jewellery, only best for pretty lady. Made with original metals recovered from local area."

Elena toyed with the jewellery.

"And, of course," she said to me, drawing out the words melodramatically, "if you *were* to ask me for a marriage contract, you would definitely need a ring. This would be a very nice start, even if only as a stand-in."

"Only best jewellery for pretty lady – good price for soldier," the hawker added excitedly, ignorant of the conversation between us.

I reached for some paper cash – my unicard was no good here, on the grey market – and produced a handful of notes. The hawker became even more animated at the suggestion of money.

"Can take UA dollar or Alliance credits," he said, gesturing to the ring. "Put it on, please do. Only one hundred credits."

I paid the hawker, and he left us.

"It is a beautiful thing," Elena said, nodding towards me. "If you would do the decent thing, Conrad."

I slid the ring onto her finger. It was predictably too big – Elena had such slender fingers – but the sentiment was there. I focused on her face. She was beaming, happy. Her hand held mine more firmly.

"I would," she said. There was a bright glint in her eyes, like unshed tears. "If you asked. I think I would. But for now, thank you for bringing me here, for getting me stationed on Azure." She pushed her plate across the table, now empty. "What do you say about making a start to that contribution? The next generation, I mean."

I left some crumpled Alliance credit notes on the table, and we swiftly departed the café.

* * *

Indig boys watched us from shadowed alleyways, eyeing Elena's fair skin and my military uniform, as we walked through the city. Not quite children but not yet men; gangly-limbed, upper lips topped with thin moustaches. They observed us suspiciously and carefully: their intentions never quite clear. Something like jealousy, not yet bordering on anger, lurked behind their dark eyes. There was an element of menace to Azure City, at times, that I had only really noticed now that Elena was here with me.

The outside walls of the sandstone buildings were plastered with propaganda posters, loud and tri-D: advertising the Alliance military operation. On some buildings, enormous murals had been painted – faded, just like the rest of the planet. BRINGING PEACE TO THE EASTERN SECTOR, one said, with a picture of a soldier in full combat-armour standing over a dead Krell. A smart-ass had corrected the pastel-coloured wording with bright red paint, so that the words now read BRINGING WAR TO THE EASTERN SECTOR. There were other Alliance propaganda pictures displaying food rationing for local citizens, water supply monitoring.

There were towers, here and there, among the tightly packed residential buildings. Those were always lit; either by cheap electric lights or old-fashioned burning sconces. The azan – the call to prayer – droned from the minarets. The noise was still alien to me; seemingly broadcast night and day. It reminded me that I was a visitor to this world, that whatever Alliance Command thought, we came to Azure as occupiers not guests.

There were several hotels on Azure, but for that night we chose the most expensive – the Weskler-Trump International, right in the middle of the financial district. It was a luxury hotel, much plusher than I was used to, and catered for political visitors and the rich. I felt enormously out of place even checking in, but Elena was as self-assured and confident as ever.

We lay together among the tangle of bedsheets, dwarfed by the enormous hotel bed. It was late now and darkness had fallen hours ago. The suite windows were open wide, allowing a soft breeze into the room. My skin was clammy and sweaty from our lovemaking, frenzied and desperate as it had been. I dozed, Elena under one arm, a shot glass of whiskey in my other hand.

"Will we get in trouble?" she whispered.

"Why?" I asked. My eyes were closed and I drifted into that twilight between sleep and waking.

"It's nearly twenty-three-hundred hours. That guard – he said we had to return by twenty-two-hundred."

"What are they going to do, fire me?"

"Won't you be AWOL or something?" Elena said, fumbling over the unfamiliar acronym. It reminded me that she was not real military.

We laughed together, harmoniously.

"I'm confident that it will slide."

I felt Elena sit up in bed, propping herself with

some of the pillows. She took the shot glass from my hand and noisily sipped the whiskey.

"It's good stuff," she said, a throaty edge to her voice. "Must be imported."

"It's American, single malt. This hotel has a nice range."

She paused. I opened an eye. I could tell that there was something else that she wanted to say, that she was hesitant to voice to me.

"And what else?"

"Since when did you start drinking?" she asked me.

"Since I have things I need to forget," I said, the truth unconsciously slipping out. Inwardly I cringed; this was too much to share. Not a topic for here, for now.

"What sort of things?"

I turned over in bed, facing her, and smiled. "Just things. Nothing."

"Be careful, *mon cher*," Elena whispered. The odour of whiskey carried on her breath as she leant in to me. "Don't take on too much. How many transitions have you made now?"

I quickly calculated in my head. "Sixteen, I think. Three at Jefferson, the others since."

"That's more than anyone else on the Programme. Please, promise me you will be careful."

I had died sixteen times. Even lying in that bed, in the most expensive hotel on Azure, if I closed my eyes I could mentally recall all sixteen deaths. Without even thinking, I took the glass from Elena and knocked back the remainder of the whiskey. The liquid felt hot and churlish in my stomach:

reminded me immediately of the burn of Krell bio-acid on my skin, the look on Kaminski's face as we had been surrounded by primary-forms—

Then I reached over to the bedside cabinet and poured myself another. It was an autonomic response – no thought involved.

Elena's smooth hands reached onto my torso as I lay back on the bed. I was growing hard again. Her naked breast pushed against me. Her body was soft and exciting; still new to me. A real woman, not fabricated and augmented and modified like those I was used to. Her imperfections were part of her beauty.

We folded in to each other, but instead of realising my hunger, she touched the data-port on my left forearm. Circled the cold steel connector.

"Is this connection sore?" she asked me.

"Perhaps a little," I said. I really didn't want to talk about this here, now, but Elena obviously wanted to.

"The skin looks raw."

I sipped down more of the whiskey. The skin looked raw because I'd had the ports drilled in quite recently. Under general anaesthetic, the military surgeons had gone through muscle, bone and bodily tissue to put the seven connections into me. They were eternal reminders of my new profession.

"Sometimes pain is good," Elena murmured into my ear. "When you stop feeling it, you are dead. You said something like that to me, a long time ago. It means that you are *alive*."

Elena stroked each of the data-ports in turn, slowly, curiously: one on each arm, at the top of my spine, on each thigh, two on my chest.

"What is it like, to make the transition?" she

asked me. Her voice had dropped again to a husky whisper, and her French accent – usually masked, barely detectable – seemed thicker. "What is it like to be so intimately connected to the simulant? Is it the connection of lovers?"

I laughed softly. "It's not like that. The simulant is just a machine."

"But a flesh-and-blood machine."

"Let's not talk about it now. It's work."

Elena sighed. "You don't like to open up, Conrad." She sat up, pulling back the sheets, and clambered out of bed.

"I thought the medic's orders were two weeks in the suit?"

Elena gave a dry chuckle. "And I said I'd see. Stop changing the subject. We were talking about you opening up."

"Where are you going?"

She pulled on her underwear and padded to the pile of her clothing, retrieving a packet of cigarettes from inside.

"To the balcony. I need to smoke."

She gave me a disappointed pout when I didn't immediately follow her. I unashamedly watched her go: appreciating the gentle swing of her buttocks.

Eventually I followed her through the gossamer drapes of the balcony. The breeze outside felt good against my sweaty skin. Although it was night, Azure was very much awake. Three small bright moons hung on the horizon, casting a light strong enough to read by. Our suite was on one of the upper floors, and allowed a wide view of the city below. That too was a source of light: from the markets drizzled with multi-coloured street lamps, to the flicker of aircraft warning beacons on some of the larger buildings. Then, in the distance, Fort Rockwell itself. The base never slept; starships landed and took off from there throughout the day and night.

Elena leant on the gilded-metal balcony handrail, supporting herself while she gently dragged on the cigarette. She looked unreal, I decided. We had been apart so long that having her here, on Azure, felt incredible.

She caught me watching her, and gave me a small smile. "What? Why are you looking at me like that?"

"I didn't mean to upset you."

She pursed her lips. "It's all right. I understand."

"I do want to open up to you. I mean it."

"Then tell me something about yourself, Conrad. Tell me something that matters. Something that you have never told anyone else."

I sighed. For a long while we just stood and watched the city below. It wasn't that I didn't want to tell her something. It was that there was so much I could say.

"When we first met," I started, haltingly, "you asked me lots about my family. About my upbringing, where I was from."

Elena nodded patiently.

"And you asked me about my father. About what had happened to him. I didn't tell you. It isn't in the records, isn't logged by the military so far as I know. I told you all about my mother, about how she was in the Alliance Navy. She died back when I was a kid."

Elena listened solemnly now. She could tell that this was difficult for me. I fixed on a point on the horizon, on the flicker and flash of incoming air traffic.

"My father was in the military as well. You know about his record. Both of my parents were away for most of my childhood. Busy enough keeping ration-packs on the table, keeping Carrie and me fed. When my mother died, my father lost it."

"Did he leave the Army?" Elena asked. Her tone was unobtrusive. She was a psych, after all.

"Nothing so easy. He loved my mother, I think, although near the end of her life they barely saw each other. When they were on shore-leave together, all we ever heard of them was the shouting from their bedroom. The tenements – they had thin walls. She would cry lots, my mother.

"So, my mother died fighting the Directorate. A while afterwards, father came home on shore-leave. Carrie and I had already moved in with an aunt and uncle. They tried to do good by us, but they had children of their own and there wasn't much space or money to go around. There were lots of aunts and uncles in those days; and if you asked me now, I probably couldn't name most of them.

"When my father came home for shore-leave, he stayed in a basement room in Aunt Beth's tenement. We couldn't afford to pay the rent on another apartment, and even the cubes were out of our price range. So he rented this tiny, dismal chamber from the caretaker. Aunt Beth tried to encourage him to see us, to spend time with us, but it was no good. I think that he was lost, then."

Elena gently gripped my arm. Gave me a reassuring smile.

"One day I went down to the basement to see him. The door was locked, but I knew he was inside: the tri-D television was blaring away on full volume." I gave a long sigh. "So Carrie and I knocked the door in."

"It's okay," Elena said. "You don't need to tell me any more if you don't want to."

"You've opened the gates now," I whispered. "I do want to tell you. I want to. My father was in the room, lying over the caretaker's workbench. He still had his gun in his hand. The viewer had cloaked the shot, I suppose, and no one above him had even heard it. The medics reckoned that he had killed himself the night before: taken the gun and placed it under his chin, fired it. Both hands on the trigger – he must've been pretty determined."

Elena's eyes were wet with tears, and she gripped my arm more firmly now. I grimaced, waved her off. Nothing more to be said; his death hadn't been recorded in his military record as a gift to Carrie and me.

"Death follows me, Elena," I said. Suddenly eager to move on from the memory: to avoid recalling my father's cold body, that pool of black blood around his head. "See, doesn't matter where I run – it follows me. Always has, always will. That's why I don't have anything to fear from this job: I already know death."

Elena clasped her body against mine.

"This war won't last for ever," she said. "And when it's over, when the Krell are done, you won't need to fear anything."

CHAPTER TWELVE

SEVEN SHADES OF HADES

Pain.

Real, unsimulated pain.

I tried to move. My right leg erupted in agony, and I cried out. There was pain all along my right side, concentrated on my ribcage. I'd felt the sensation before: *broken ribs*. Multiple. My fatigues were stuck to me, wet in places. *Blood*.

Worst of all was the intense ache that dwelt behind my eyes, deep in my head. Rolling thunder; a pressure headache like a tactical nuke firing in my skull.

For a long while I just lay there.

I wanted to sleep so badly.

Get up, I told myself. *This is real. Fuck this up, and you won't wake in the simulators.*

Vision came back to me in snapshots of the outside world. I was in the wreckage of the medical bay, still strapped in by the safety harness. Fabric straps bit into my shoulders. I struggled to move an arm. Fumbled with a release buckle, but it was too much for me to get myself free of the webbing.

Need to sleep.

Don't. Stay awake!

I was awake for a few seconds, then unconscious again.

I breathed deeply, feeling the tang of alien atmosphere in my mouth. Gravity and atmosphere felt wrong. Medical was at the wrong angle. The floor was slanted, and parts of the external structure had punched through the walls of the module. An emergency lamp set in the ceiling flashed red. Dirty light streamed in from holes in the outer hull. Every window, every view-port, had been shattered during the crash. Parts of the bay had come away during the evacuation, and the entire structure yawed and creaked with the motion of the wind outside.

If I sleep now, Death comes later.

Good enough.

I was on Helios.

I awoke again to a sharp, urgent pain.

"Get away from me!" I yelled, twisting my arm in the safety harness.

Jenkins' face came into focus above me. She held my left arm, and I realised that the pain was from my outer forearm. My fatigue shirt was rolled up and Jenkins held a hypodermic to the skin. A small well of blood told me that she had just injected me with something.

"It's me, Cap."

I rubbed my arm, groaning to myself.

"Just some painkillers and a stimulant cocktail," Jenkins said. "It'll help with the pain and keep you awake for a while."

I pulled myself into a more comfortable position. The chemical rush hit my bloodstream very quickly and the fog of pain dispersed. I felt mildly more alive – I could operate, at least.

"Take it easy," Jenkins said. The concern in her face was enough to make me pause. I looked down at my right leg and grasped the ripped fatigues. They were caked in hot, sticky blood. Something metallic and sharp had penetrated my fatigues. It had pierced tissue and muscle, part of it still protruding from my leg above the knee. I looked in disbelief at the injury.

Why hasn't it started healing yet? I asked myself.

Then a sick realisation hit me. I was in a real, fallible human body: not an improved simulant. I would bleed and I would die – maybe for good.

"Are you all right?" Blake asked, standing beside me.

He was dressed in shipboard fatigues but his hair was still slick with amniotic fluid from the simulator-tanks.

"I'll live, I think. Have I been out for long?"

"Couple of hours," Blake said, noncommittally. "Give or take."

I could tell that he was lying.

"How does that leg feel?" Jenkins said. "We need to get it bandaged. I tried while you were out, but you kept moving around." She frowned at me. "You were talking while you were unconscious – something about Elena."

"Just help me out of here," I said, struggling free of the remainder of the safety-webbing.

Jenkins and Blake assisted me. I ground my teeth against the pain. My entire body hurt; I felt bruised and battered on every level. Standing from the harness was a mission. I could see Martinez and Kaminski getting their bearings. All four of my team had made it, at least.

"I feel about as bad as you look," Jenkins said, wiping a cut on her head. "But it could be worse."

She motioned towards the back of the medical bay. In the dim light, I made out bodies pierced by support struts and squashed beneath heavy equipment. A couple of the techs were no more than smears on the walls, thrown about so viciously during the landing.

"Welcome to Helios." Kaminski spread out his arms, encompassing the med-bay. "Hot towels and drinks will be served at your seats. If you require any assistance disembarking please await a hostess. As our regular attendants are either dead or about to be eaten by fish heads, you will have to make do with Jenkins – she scrubs up okay if you don't look too hard. This is totally FUBAR."

"Leave it, tech boy," Jenkins said, punching Kaminski in the arm. "This isn't the time or place."

"I guess being inside the simulators during the crash saved us," Martinez said. "Acted as a cushion, or something. We got lucky. *La gracia de Dios.*"

"Olsen was the only other survivor," Jenkins said. "He took a bad knock to the head, but he'll live."

She jerked a thumb towards Olsen's body, hanging in one of the wall-mounted safety harnesses.

His smock was shredded at the front and a huge egg-shaped lump had already formed on his temple. His skin was an ashen grey colour but his chest was just perceptibly moving.

"Jenkins sedated him," said Blake. "He was becoming hysterical. The others... Well you don't need to be a medic to realise what has happened to them. I guess that some might've escaped from the *Oregon*, like us, in evac modules."

In my mind's eye, I remembered the fleeing evac-pods. There was no way that anyone else had made it down to Helios: the Krell had mercilessly dispatched everything that had left our ship. I closed my eyes. Nightmare images of the evac were painted inside my eye-lids as well. I wouldn't be able to escape those memories easily; the experience would be one I would relive again and again.

"I saw what happened," I said, "on the way down. There won't be anyone left. No point in setting a distress beacon, at least not yet. There was another Krell warship. The asteroid field – I think it was a trap."

I swallowed, recalling the cold of space as it claimed my body. That had felt significantly worse than I did now, but I'd known that pain was fleeting. I wouldn't be able to get away from *this* pain anywhere so swiftly.

"We saw it too," Jenkins said. "The *Oregon* didn't stand a chance. We've been awake for a while, and I ordered a stocktake of our supplies. Most of the spare simulants made it."

"*Most?*" I questioned. Jenkins was holding something back.

"Just rest," she said, holding my shoulder. "No need to worry about that now."

"I need to know everything," I said.

Jenkins bit her lip, and I pushed past her: scanned the destroyed interior of the module.

Sweet Christo.

At the back of the med-bay, among shattered storage tubes and twisted metal, sprawled parodies of my real body. What little strength I still had seemed to ebb from me. Most of the simulants were a sickly, fish-belly white colour. Several of them had bled out. Although they were incredibly resilient, the bodies had been thrown about like trash. The inactive simulants hadn't stood a chance.

Snuffed out as easily as the medical team.

I gingerly picked my way through the wreckage to investigate. It was like looking at myself, in a variety of different poses: each corpse killed in a different way. One had been pierced by a support strut through the gut, leaving an eruption of intestines and other internal organs. I involuntarily touched my own stomach; felt my own intestines twist in psychosomatic sympathy. Another had been cleanly decapitated. Then another had been caught up in electrical cabling that had come loose from the ceiling, lighting it and leaving it blackened and burnt.

I grappled with an upturned console, steadying myself. It was sickening. I was trapped inside this damaged, imperfect body: trapped on Helios, surrounded by Krell. Even if we had the right equipment with which to do it, I was quite sure that none of the bodies were salvageable. The idea of being on Helios, without a simulant to hide inside, filled me with dread. I felt physically drained.

No point in going on any more. If you can't use your simulants, what sort of a soldier are you?

"I told you not to look," Jenkins whispered.

Blake sighed. "At least the others made it, although the tanks are in a bad way."

The simulants for the rest of the squad sat in their pristine glass storage capsules. They were still clad in combat-suits, dull-eyed and ready for activation. The simulator-tanks themselves weren't so well-preserved; spider-web fractures marked the outside of each tank. Several of the delicate connection-cables had been torn from their moorings.

"Looks like those tanks will need work before they're operational again," I said. Needed to concentrate, for the good of my squad if nothing else. "I want to get this place secure, and scout the immediate—"

Thump. Thump. A series of percussive booms echoed through the abandoned module.

"What the hell was that?" Jenkins asked.

Something was on the roof outside, and had hit the hull hard. *Thump. Thump.*

"A survivor?" offered Blake.

"More likely Krell," I said. This had suddenly stepped things up; we had to act fast. There was no prospect of staying in the crashed module if we were about to be swarmed by Krell. "Have we got weapons? Are they useable?"

"Yeah, they made it down fine," Jenkins said with an empty laugh. "Proper Alliance-issue, made to last. Or something like that."

Jenkins opened the metal crates of unused M95 plasma rifles and grenades. She quickly distributed the weapons, and we each took a rifle and a pistol.

I held a rifle in both hands, felt the weight of it. *We won't stand a chance out there*, I thought to myself. I loaded the power cell into the stock – even that looked ridiculously oversized in human hands. Like the rifles were made for adults, and we were only children, playing at being soldiers. I lifted the M95 and fumbled, could barely operate the heavy weapon. There was no way that I would be able to carry the gun for any protracted period of time, let alone operate it.

"Isn't there anything more appropriate?"

"The armoury went down with the *Oregon*," Jenkins said. "This gear was an overstock. Just happened to be in the med-bay during the attack."

Then I saw my pistol, hanging from the holster beside the crushed remains of my simulator. Perfect condition, the burnished metal grip gleaning, ammo clips still loaded into the webbing. Taunting me. I hobbled over to it, strapped the gun and ammo to my leg.

No time to argue. There was more thumping outside, only now it sounded like it was coming from all around the module – as though there were attackers all around us. I considered our choices. The module was unpowered and there was no way we could set up the simulator-tanks without Olsen. In any event, they'd been badly damaged – I didn't know what sort of repair work was necessary to get them running again. Olsen still lay comatose in his harness, eyes tightly shut; he was out of action for now. Whatever was outside, we would have to confront it. I swallowed back fear and staggered over to the exit door.

"You might say you feel okay," Blake said, frowning at me, "but you sure don't look it. Maybe you should stay inside, while we go investigate."

More pounding on the hull. The screeching of metal on metal somewhere outside.

I waved Blake away. "I'll be fine. Form up on me; I'll pop that hatch and then we move out together."

The main entrance door to the med-bay acted as a bulkhead but had become deformed by the force of the impact, and broken free of its frame. I kicked it with my good leg and it came open easily. The squad deployed smoothly out of the ship, rifles aimed into the unknown.

A storm seethed. The wind was a roaring inferno, carrying with it sharp, angry sand. The landscape was a blurred orange-red, almost burnt. Huge sand dunes shifted and lapped like waves, topped by a deep red-brown sky. Through the intense wind, it was impossible to gain any sense of geography or scale: Helios just looked like endless, unforgiving desert. Bulbous, low-lying clouds filled the sky. Barely visible were two huge suns. They sat bloated on the horizon, just beginning to rise from their slumber. Dawn was coming.

"I thought that Olsen wasn't expecting the storm yet," Blake shouted, over the wind.

"I don't think that the storm has hit," I said. "This is Helios on a good day."

"Ah, shit," Blake replied.

Just then, there was an enormous thunderclap and a brilliant flare lit the sky. Lightning streaked down from the pregnant clouds in angry red forks. The ground shook violently as each clap sounded. The sky flashed again and again. In those brief seconds of illumination, I made out shapes all around me. I backed down into the door.

There were figures out in the storm and they were rapidly moving towards the wreckage. Kaminski fired once, twice, three times with his rifle. Every shot missed, but the nearest figure dropped into a prone position. Another took its place, turning glowering red-and-green eyes towards us.

"This is all we need!" Kaminski shouted, sending more bright plasma shots into the miasma.

His aim was off; outside of a simulant, such heavy ordnance was very difficult to operate. I wasn't doing any better with my rifle. I fired several times, every shot going wide. The rifle was meant to slave with a combat-suit, not to be fired manually. I jammed my finger on the firing stud, aware that warning lights illuminated on the rifle control panel. Without a tactical helmet, I couldn't even tell what the warnings were. I dropped the rifle to fire it from the hip, but the dimensions were all wrong, and the ugly metal stock jarred against my broken ribs.

Damn it! I tossed the rifle away. *This isn't going to work*. The muzzle was red-hot, smoking.

I unholstered my pistol. I fired into the storm, my eyes stinging with the sand in the air. The Smith & Wesson was a slug-thrower – firing basic manstopper rounds. Those would shred a man at close range, but I didn't know whether they could stop a primary-form. It occurred to me that I'd never actually fired the gun in combat; that I didn't know whether it had been fired in anger before. I'd fired it on a range, back at the *Point*, but the last person to properly use it had been my father. I repressed the memory: instead, fired until I'd spent all ten rounds. I couldn't tell whether I was hitting anything with such restricted vision, and equally I couldn't tell whether we were being hit. The rest of my squad were just vague blurs in the midst of the storm, only properly visible when their rifles illuminated with plasma discharge. I prayed for a combat-suit and a tactical helmet.

The figures continued their advance.

"Fall back to the medical bay," I called out.

I looked back at the tortured remains of the module. The hull was still smoking in places, and it had settled in a blackened crater, surrounded by torched rocks and superheated sand. Dark shapes clung to the outside of the wreck.

My squad fluidly fell back, firing as they went. My injured leg briefly gave out beneath me. I stumbled. Blake caught me and dragged me back into the wreckage.

"Jenkins, prep explosive grenades for clearance inside this bay," I ordered. "Take out as many of them as we can."

She nodded and knelt beside me, fumbling with a satchel of grenades. She scattered a handful of them in front of her, clasping her rifle over her chest. Martinez and Kaminski took up positions near the shattered door, while Blake crouched over me protectively.

A figure appeared at one of the view-ports, peering inside the module. Then another. Then finally, a silhouetted outline materialised at the door.

The wind eased for just a moment, allowing me a clear, unhindered view of the attackers. The alien eyes turned, and I saw them for what they were. Lowlight goggles of some design, worn over a primitive and battered black helmet. Human tech. The figure – a man – paused and raised his rifle. He waved a hand.

"I am Security Officer Deacon of Helios Station," he growled, using an archaic speaker-unit that distorted his voice into an angry buzz. "I'm ordering you to cease fire!"

I raised my hand.

"Weapons cease, repeat weapons cease," I shouted.

Immediately, the squad stopped their assault. We froze as the man entered. He was dressed in a black bodysuit, carrying a tank of oxygen on his back and wearing a respirator mask over his face. As if to reinforce the point that he was no xeno, he yanked it free. Underneath he was rugged and scar-faced. Middle-aged, I'd guess – his dark hair was peppered with grey, and he had a full beard. He was a big, well-set man; taller than me, broader-shouldered. He eyed us wearily and advanced into the bay, equivocally covering us with an ancient solid-shot carbine.

A handful of similarly dressed figures filtered in behind him. Still more appeared at the shattered view-ports. Most did not reveal their faces and only some lowered their weapons. All armed with rifles and shotguns. None of them looked even remotely like Krell.

Deacon looked over the interior of the crashed module, setting his chin. He took a breath from his respirator before speaking.

"Care to tell me what in the seven shades of Hades is happening out here?" he asked. He had a strong Texan drawl, real Old Earth. "Y'all could start a fight in an empty house. Someone could've been killed out there. You Directorate or something?"

"We're Alliance military," I said flatly. "We're conducting a rescue operation."

"So you're here for us?" Deacon said.

He pointed to an embroidered badge on the shoulder of his bodysuit. It showed a yellow planet, circled by two stars. Under the emblem, it read HELIOS EXPEDITION. Beneath that was sown a small United Americas flag.

"Looks to me like you're the ones who need rescuing," he said. "We saw you come down. Must've been a hell of a firefight, but I guess you already know that." He jerked a thumb at the destroyed bank of computers. "I'd strongly suggest that y'all turn that shit off. You're calling every Christo-damned fish head on this continent to your position."

He laughed, then made a high-pitched *beep-beep-beep* sound, mocking a radio beacon. It was about as humourless as the rest of his presentation.

"I'd have thought you military types would know that already."

Another man tugged at Deacon's arm, and Deacon paused to speak into his communicator. The expression on his face indicated that he wasn't happy with whatever news he had just received.

"Your arrival has stirred up the natives," he said. "They get all tetchy whenever something makes planetfall. Choice is yours, but I'd strongly suggest that you come with us. If you stay out here, you'll die. Simple as that."

Then he turned back to his rag-tag security team, and began giving orders. The men, still buttoned up, started dismantling the medical bay – stripping out everything that wasn't bolted down, and much of it that was. They presented as experienced scavengers, systematic and fast. It was almost impressive.

"Are we just going to let them take our stuff?" Jenkins asked me, indignantly.

"It's not like we have much of a choice," I said. "Everyone stay collected and with it, until we know what's going on down here."

There were grumbles of acceptance from my squad, but they sounded about as convinced as I was.

"So are we going with them?" Blake asked.

"We don't have a better option," I said. We needed shelter and medical aid, and I reasoned that it was better to hold fire for now. The blazing storm outside made that decision for us.

Deacon turned back to me, looking me up and down. Black dust lined his already weathered face, and there was a deep suspicion in his eyes. *He doesn't want us here. Why is that?* His team was cut off on Helios, without any support from the rest of the Alliance, and yet this was our welcome? It didn't make sense.

"Y'all waiting for a formal invitation? I said,

move it. We have a sand-crawler outside. Maybe ten minutes until the Krell get here."

"I take it we're going to Helios Station?" I said.

"That's right. The Doc wants to see you."

"Kellerman is alive?"

Deacon grunted a laugh. "Alive, but not quite kicking. You'll see soon enough."

Wearing respirators and stuffed into whatever hostile-weather gear we could find onboard the medical module, we struggled out into the storm. Visibility was reducing and the weather was becoming more intense. Grit stung my eyes, chafed every inch of exposed skin. My leg burnt deeply as I placed my weight on it, and the pain in my ribs was constant, but there was no time to dwell on any of that.

Not far from the crashed module, maybe fifty metres, were two large land vehicles. Both were half concealed by a sand dune, and whether that was some deliberate camouflage to fool the Krell or an unintended consequence of the storm I couldn't say. Even with running lights on, they were barely visible until we were on top of them. The lead sand-crawler had a massive weathered chassis and three pairs of enormous wheels, set on an adapted suspension bed for cross-country use. They were strictly civilian-issue models. The vehicle engines were still running; sending out thick black plumes of smoke from chemical-burner engines.

These were the sort of vehicles used on colonial outposts throughout Alliance space – ubiquitous, sometimes dependable, always cheap. But the tech was nothing like what we were used to: these were not only civilian transports, but they were old and badly maintained.

Jenkins nodded at me. "Looks like our rescuers have recently had a run-in with the Krell."

I saw that the flanks were pocked with boomer-fire and the rear vehicle had been struck by stinger-spines.

"Too recently for my liking. I just hope that they know what they're doing."

"I thought we were the rescuers?" Kaminski added.

Deacon was at my shoulder, barking orders to get supplies into the crawlers. He waved his carbine in my direction.

"The storm does something to block out the signal broadcast by the Artefact," he said. "Gives them back a little of their self-control, or something like that. The Doc has studied it. They often move in this direction when the storms come in, and sometimes batter up against our defences. Hurry up and get inside."

The sand-crawlers were manned by another security crew. They wore a variety of mismatched uniforms and hostile-environment suits; none of it new, most of it re-patched many times over. They looked like an Old Earth hood-gang; faces concealed by headscarves and respirator masks. Their uniforms carried a bizarre array of badges and iconography, suggesting tours of duty on many planets and outposts. All of them were emblazoned with the Helios Expedition badge, but they were obviously a seasoned crew. These were civilian contractors, not proper military.

"Nothing more than damned mercenaries," Jenkins muttered under her breath.

"Just keep quiet for now," I ordered.

We were hustled aboard the lead crawler, into the passenger cabin. Seats lined the flanks of the cabin, big enough to accommodate maybe twenty personnel. A separate driver cab was upfront and more guards manned that.

"Get the fat one in there as well," Deacon snarled in his Texan burr. Two men appeared dragging Olsen's still body out of the wreck. They brusquely dumped him into a passenger seat aboard the transport. "Leave the bodies behind – no point in fussing over the dead."

Good men and women who died for no reason, I thought. *Who died trying to get us down here, and save your asses*. Martinez and I exchanged a look.

"This isn't right, *cuate*," he whispered.

I didn't say anything to him. He eventually glared down at the floor, boring a hole into the deck plating. Leaving bodies behind wasn't the military way, and it wasn't Martinez's way either. I bitterly wanted to confront the security officers, to argue with them; I just didn't have the energy.

The security team ventured onto the module to take surgical equipment and simulator-tanks, but they seemed most interested in shipping the boxed foodstuffs and ship rations. When that was done, they unloaded the armoury. Watching them from the open hatch of the crawler, I realised how few of them there actually were. They appeared capable of carrying and dragging much more than their number and worked at a determined rate. *They're frightened*, I concluded. *Frightened of being left out here, or running into a Krell patrol.*

"They're taking everything," Kaminski said, glumly.

"Even the heavier shit," Jenkins said. "They must have the whole medical bay on that other crawler. Good job I kept this handy." She patted a plasma rifle on her lap.

"Keep the safety on until we know what's going on out here," I ordered, glaring at her. I had kept my pistol, still strapped to my leg, but I didn't think that it would do me any good.

"They're even taking the sims," Blake added.

Sure enough, the group were wheeling and levering the remaining sims out of the wreckage. Deacon didn't seem in the slightest phased by the deactivated bodies but some of his crew stopped to tap on the glass. The bodies inside didn't respond, and the security men quickly lost interest. Each capsule was loaded up onto the crawlers.

Soon everything was aboard. Deacon sent most of his guards to the other transport, then took up a seat in the driver cabin of our crawler. He ordered another man to act as driver, and set a guard in the back with us.

"It's not far," Deacon called back into the cabin. "Just sit tight."

The crawlers moved off in unison, and trudged cross-country away from the crash site.

CHAPTER THIRTEEN

THIS IS ALL THAT IS LEFT

The drive to Helios Station was rough on me. The broken terrain made for a bumpy ride, constantly provoking pain in my head, my leg and my side. It definitely wasn't the way I'd have preferred to travel, given my condition.

"I think Martinez has the right idea," I said.

He was slouched back in his seat, eyes closed and mouth open, fast asleep. A sheen of spittle had formed on his open lips.

"He'll sleep anywhere," Jenkins said, rolling her eyes. "How's the damage?"

"The painkiller is wearing off fast," I said. I rearranged myself in the seat. "My leg hurts pretty bad."

"Maybe when we reach the station, a real doctor can have a look at it for you."

"Deacon mentioned Kellerman. Sounds like he's still alive."

The guard manning the passenger cabin sat several seats away from us, his battered ballistic helmet pulled down over his face. He wore a basic flak-vest, that didn't seem to match his headgear, and beaten greaves over his boots. When I mentioned Kellerman's name, he suddenly came to life. He grappled the carbine to his chest, pulling at the canvas strap over his shoulder, and frowned at me.

"Don't talk about the Doc."

"Why?"

"Because I said so, asshole."

And you're the one with the rifle, I answered to myself.

"Message received."

We sat in silence for a while. I could see the outside world through the view-screen upfront. The sky was an ochre colour, swirling with clouds and a constant sandstorm. Deacon and the other security man in the driver section were having a conversation, and I listened in because I had nothing else to do.

"How much further?" the driver asked Deacon, his voice juddering in time with the crawler engine. "Everything out here looks the same to me."

Deacon shook his head. "Quit stressing. We'll be there soon. You know the route well enough."

"This is why I don't like leaving the station. Never know what will happen. Our fuel could run out, we might hit something, get ambushed. Like Keres – you hear about her? She was out in a crawler and the drive axle snagged on a rock or something. Got stuck outside and toasted, by all accounts. Tyler says she could only be identified by a smudge left on some rocks."

Deacon seemed to be doing his best to ignore his colleague, and was focused on the landscape outside.

"Would you fuck Tyler?" the driver suddenly asked Deacon.

"Christo, now that is a question. Would I fuck the only piece of ass this side of the Maelstrom? Tough call."

The driver grunted. "She's a bitch. Not sure I would even give her the time."

"Since when does that make a difference?" Deacon said, shaking his head. "I didn't realise that you were so Christo-damned sensitive. She might be a bitch, but I got a thing for blondes. And like I say, not a lot of selection out here. Although maybe one of these new arrivals could change that." Deacon turned and glared back into the passenger cabin, hungrily eyeing Jenkins. "You all right back there, California girl?"

He smiled maliciously and continued staring for long enough to make his intentions clear. She stared him down.

"Like I say," he repeated, "not a whole lot of selection out here."

Don't even try it, Deacon, I thought to myself. *She'll rip you to pieces.*

The driver hunkered down over the control console and the conversation ended. We travelled on for a few minutes, and began to climb uphill. Huge mountains appeared in the distance. The crawler engine changed pitch as we went.

"Approaching destination," the driver announced. Helios Station loomed ahead. It had been concealed by the dust-storm, cast about the site like a shroud, but for just a second the wind seemed to cease altogether and I got an unimpeded view.

A ragged prospect of blackened buildings, mostly low and dust-stained. Many leant at absurd angles, like old tombstones in a graveyard. Some structures had disappeared altogether, but those remaining looked semi-derelict: tortured by the extreme elements. Very few running lights gave any indication of human occupation. I'd studied the schematics, and I expected more of the outpost than this. It was as though the planet was attempting to suck the structures in, remove any trace of the human settlers. The twin suns – Helios Primary and Secondary – hung behind the station, cutting a pointed and eerie outline.

The station itself was crammed inside a low security wall, battered but solid. A flag post was positioned atop that, and I could just about make out the Helios Expedition flag, and beneath that the Alliance colours. Both flags were tattered and worn, reduced to little more than rags. As a finishing touch, the name HELIOS STATION had been stencilled onto the perimeter wall; the letters I, O and S painted over, so that the name now read HEL STATION. The description was strangely apt.

"We've travelled across light-years of space for *this*," Jenkins whispered to me. "We lost the *Oregon*, nearly got killed for real…"

"Looks that way," I answered, but I shared her sentiment.

What the hell is this place? Would Command really have sent us all this way for what was left? That feeling I'd had back aboard the *Oregon* – that Kellerman wasn't someone to be rescued, but that he was an adversary – surfaced again. Only now I was injured, I needed urgent medical help, and we were without the support of our starship.

On the approach, a pair of laser batteries mounted on the perimeter jumped to life, tracking the crawler. I had no faith that the machines would be an effective deterrent to the Krell; they looked so old and weathered that I questioned whether they even functioned.

Deacon activated a communicator on the control console.

"Tyler, this is Security One inbound," he said. "We're coming into range. Deactivate the lasers and open up."

The console crackled, whining with background static. A woman spoke: "I hear you, Chief."

The battered security doors peeled open, with the angry whine and crunch of damaged gears.

"Security Two inbound," the communicator hissed.

The crawlers trundled through the gate.

"Everybody out!" Deacon ordered.

The crawler came to a stop inside an enormous hangar bay, crammed with work vehicles of every kind – fusion-borers, more crawlers, drilling machines. Real functional shit; the sort of heavy earth-moving equipment and transport vehicles that couldn't be reproduced on-world.

I stiffly climbed down from the crawler, groaning at the pain in my leg.

"Who's in charge here?" I barked, my voice echoing across the hangar. "I have a science officer in need of medical attention, and I want to speak with Dr Kellerman."

My squad formed up beside me. The security team suddenly stopped, looking to Deacon for further orders. Out of the corner of my eye, I noticed some of them reaching for their weapons. Jenkins must've seen it too.

"I think the man asked you a question, and my friend here," she shouted, as she patted the metal stock of her plasma rifle, "deserves an answer."

Deacon turned a venomous glare on Jenkins but she didn't flinch. Her M95 powered up with a high-pitched whine: a just-audible sound. I drew my pistol, pulling back the hammer. I tried to conceal the pain that flared in my ribcage; I didn't want to show any weakness to these bastards. The hangar grew quiet for a moment, save for the background howling of the wind. No one immediately went to attack but no one made any effort to answer me either. Stand-off.

"I need access to the Operations centre and your communications equipment," I said, waving my pistol.

Again, no response from the gathered group. Jenkins sucked her teeth beside me – raring for a fight.

A woman jostled through the security officers, waving her open hands towards us. She was dressed in a black tank-top and worn combat trousers. Blonde hair pulled back under a bandana, maybe late-twenties. Her bare arms were thin and grease-stained.

"Looks like we got a live one here," she said, laughing. When she moved, a tool-belt at her waist clattered with various devices. "You go, girl. Deacon, try not to be such an asshole to the new arrivals."

"Show some damned respect," he growled. "I'm chief of security."

"Yeah, you're both."

"I was a sergeant in the Army."

"Well you're not any more."

A couple of Deacon's group laughed nervously; enjoying the play between Deacon and the woman.

"Any casualties?" she asked.

"None from us," Deacon said. "Although our guests here had plenty."

The woman gave me a brittle smile.

"I'm Jenna Tyler. I run Operations out here. Alliance grade three systems technician," she said, holding out her hand. "Been a long time – a *very long time* – since we last had visitors. Did you enjoy the trip down? Quite a ride out in that storm, I should imagine. Helios has a way of making things hard on people."

I shook Tyler's hand, but kept my pistol unholstered. At least it was a better greeting than I'd received from Deacon and his men.

"Captain Conrad Harris, Alliance Simulant Operations Programme. Where is Kellerman?"

"I am Doctor Jarvis Kellerman," came a voice from the back of the hangar. "Welcome to Helios Station."

A small, wizened figure glided into view.

So here is the man himself, I thought. That same itch of anxiety; something in the back of my mind telling me that this man was not to be trusted. The group around him parted, stood back in respect – or fear.

Kellerman was lean and chiselled and every bit as downtrodden as the rest of the outpost. Balding, head and face pocked by dark patches – probably radiation-spots, caused by long-term exposure to Helios. He wore a deep cobalt jump-suit, with his identification badge and the Helios Station logo embroidered on the shoulders. *He looks even worse than he did on the tri-D recordings*, I thought. His eyes held me: brilliant blue-steel, full of determination. *The eyes of a fanatic*.

The hover-chair in which he was encapsulated emitted an electric hum as it went, and he sat in it awkwardly – leaning forward as though urging the device onwards. He came to a standstill in front of me, Deacon flanking him with his carbine over his chest.

"I really would prefer that weapons are not discharged within the station walls," Kellerman said, with an irritated frown.

Jenkins remained steadfast. She was about as frustrated as I was; probably would've liked nothing better than to open up with the plasma rifle. That would be pointless bloodshed, though, and right now I had to focus on keeping us all alive.

"Stand down, Corporal," I muttered under my breath.

The pitched whine from the plasma rifle gradually

diminished and Jenkins' posture relaxed. Tyler whistled, long and high. Deacon did his best to keep up his stony façade, but even he seemed to settle a little. His men visibly relaxed.

"That's better," Kellerman said. He spoke with an indeterminate American accent; Midwest, maybe, refined by an upbringing on the Chicago Lunar Colony. "Captain Conrad Harris, is it? Am I to believe that you are in charge of this operation?"

I nodded. "What's left of it."

"We tracked your ship on the way down, and were unsure of your allegiance. We heard your transmissions. You were trying to contact us."

I waved the pistol in Kellerman's direction. "Then why were you unsure of our allegiance?"

"The mind can play tricks," Kellerman said. "In any event, even if we had wanted to, we are currently unable to make orbital communication. We have had certain technical difficulties. Given our remote location, these were insurmountable."

"We were sent to establish why this outpost has broken contact with *Liberty Point*. We already know that the deep-space array is working – our ship analysed it before we were ambushed."

"No matter – you are here now," said Kellerman, dismissively. He swivelled his chair, looking to the supply-laden sand-crawler. "Security Chief Deacon, please ensure that all supplies retrieved from the escape vehicle are stored appropriately. They will be most useful."

Another security man stepped to the task, dragging crates out of the crawler. Without his headgear, the man looked decidedly unwell. Alien starlight, processed air, and ration-packs do not make for a healthy life.

"What a terrible shame," Kellerman said, scowling as one of the guards wheeled a simulator-tank past him. "Some of the equipment appears to be damaged. Are those simulators? They will need work before they are operational again." He addressed the guard directly: "Was it spoiled during the crash, or the retrieval?"

"Er, the crash," the guard said. "Definitely the crash."

There was fear in his voice; fear of Kellerman.

"Very well," Kellerman said. He waved the man on.

"Thanks for the supplies," Tyler interjected, stepping between Kellerman and me. "We can always use more foodstuffs and medicine. We've got no fast-response or air support out here, no starship capabilities and nothing else you would want in a hostile environment. We haven't got shit."

"That's hardly the attitude," Kellerman said. His face was caught in a permanent grimace – it was difficult to see him working well with anyone, let alone Tyler. "As I always say, a positive state of mind is essential to survival on Helios." He turned back to me. "And you will get whatever answers you need in due course. Until then, I think that you will find our facilities sufficient for your needs. We have heat, water and food – the essentials of human life. Your squad can take one of the vacant habitation units. There are plenty to go around."

Kellerman started to reverse his hover-chair, moving back into the recesses of the hangar bay.

"How many of you are there left?" I called after him. I was angry that he was dismissing us so easily – my unit had just suffered an enormous loss of life, and yet Kellerman showed no signs of urgency or concern.

He paused, half-turning to face me as though his response really wasn't important.

"This is all that is left. Maybe a couple of my research staff hanging around the place somewhere, but everyone else is gone. Like Miss Tyler says – Helios is hard on people. Now, I must get back to my research. Mr Deacon – arrange a stretcher for the injured science officer. Perhaps, Captain Harris, when you are cleaned up, you might like to visit me to discuss my findings."

I watched as he disappeared into the darkness, and took in the twenty or so survivors of Helios Station – all that was left of the two thousand staff that had been shipped here.

CHAPTER FOURTEEN

STRANDED

As Kellerman had directed, security escorted us to an abandoned habitation module. A hover-stretcher was organised for Olsen, and Martinez and Blake dragged his sagging frame onto the levitating bed. The machine dipped erratically to take his weight; he was still out cold. We were led through a series of covered walkways – the wind battering against cheap polytunnel walls.

"Doc says that someone will come over and check out your leg when they have time," the lead guard said as he left, grinning a black-toothed smile.

I'm not going to hold my breath on that.

Without any further explanation, the guards sealed us into the unit and left.

We explored our confined quarters. The module had originally housed fifty or sixty personnel, in double-berth cubicles. Some of the rooms had been stripped down to the bare essentials – empty walls and cots – but many others looked as though they had recently been abandoned. The place had a mournful, ghost-town feel to it. Shift rotas were still displayed on notice boards. Photos of home were tacked to the walls. Coffee cups and empty plates lined consoles. Some wise-ass had pinned holo-pictures of legendary Earthside landmarks to a computer monitor: the Antarctic City, the half-submerged Sydney Opera House, the canals of London Central. It was inviting to imagine that the former occupants of the hab would return anytime soon, exhausted from the morning shift. In the centre of the unit, abandoned as abruptly as the rest of the place, was a mess hall, replete with dust-lined tables and cooking pots full of mouldy foodstuffs. A large display board sat at one end of the hall, proudly declaring DAYS WITHOUT RAIN: 398. Storm-shutters covered every window, simultaneously protecting us from outside influences and trapping us inside.

"And I thought that the living quarters on the *Point* were bad..." muttered Blake.

"There are beds, *cuate*," Martinez said, wandering out of one of the empty rooms. "That's a start. And we got power and food."

"You sound like you don't mind it here," I said.

Martinez shrugged. "So long as we can sleep, Cap. Answers later, I guess."

"The window shutters are locked down," Kaminski said. "This place is like a prison."

"Kaminski has a point," Jenkins yelled, from further down the corridor. "Those bastards have locked us in. The doors are electronically keyed."

I followed her to the only exit from the unit, and she pointed out the locked door.

* * *

I called for a briefing in the mess hall.

Blake sat on an upturned food crate. His chin was speckled with stubble and his uniform was dust-stained. When I entered the room, he started slightly as if to regain some military composure, but I muttered for him not to bother. None of that was necessary out here: protocol had pretty much gone to shit.

Kaminski drifted past. He ate from a self-heating MRE – a "meal-ready-to-eat" – shovelling the rations into his mouth with a metal spoon. He barely registered me.

"Food any good?" I asked.

"It'll do," Kaminski said. "Potatoes and steak."

The food smelt stodgy and bitter-sweet, as though maybe the meat had gone off, but Kaminski continued eating.

Jenkins sat at a table in the corner of the room, with the innards of a disassembled plasma rifle around her. She was engrossed in cleaning every component, reassembling the rifle then going through the same procedure all over again. Martinez watched her, muttering to himself in Spanish. I pulled up a chair and sat down with Jenkins.

"All right there, Cap?" she asked, still focused on her rifle.

"Not really."

Jenkins continued working on her gun. *Scope goes here. Lens connects to power feed. Chamber must be clear to allow maximum polarisation of charge. Pulse pin enters there. Charger connects to stock.* She never missed a single part. This time was no exception.

Olsen was semi-collapsed on an old mattress someone had dragged into the corner of the room, with his head in his hands. He had awoken shortly after our arrival in the hab. Science staff, working on ships and stations and the sterile end of the Alliance military effort – they didn't get to see and feel the Krell menace up close. He'd tasted it once, aboard the *New Haven*, but being down here in his own skin was a nightmare become real. I had already explained to him how the med-bay had been gutted, about Kellerman's bizarre presentation in the hangar. He looked like shit and sounded worse.

"We're stranded out here!" he said, suddenly becoming animated. An ugly black-and-blue lump had formed on his left temple, so big that it made his head look deformed. "Dr Kellerman is our only avenue of escape and from what the captain says he is a madman. No one is all right, Corporal."

Jenkins snapped the power cell into her M95 with cold precision, then looked down the scope towards the science officer. She gave a sharkish grin.

"Hey, Olsen," she called across the room, "you wish you'd brought a gun with you now?"

"Maybe the little man has a point," Kaminski offered. He looked to Martinez and Blake for approval, but neither of them backed him up. "We're trapped on this rock, at the ass-end of the galaxy."

"Hold it together, Olsen, and you too, 'Ski," I said, as sternly as I could. "Wallowing in this shit isn't going to solve anything. Just hold it together. We're soldiers, and we need to plan around what we know. It's a fact that the *Oregon* is gone. Any distress beacon onboard is either wasted, or it would attract the Krell to our position. The crash has changed our mission parameters. It was never the plan to be here in our own bodies – to be down here skinless. Immediate objective: we need to find a way off Helios."

My squad exchanged glances. The team grew more intent on what I was saying. It felt good to have some focus, I guess. We were still military and having an objective suddenly helped bring the group together again.

"Yeah, man," Kaminski said. His mood had swiftly shifted. "Fuck Kellerman. Fuck them all. They're welcome to stay on Helios, with the fish heads."

Getting my squad off Helios was my priority, and now my *only* priority. Enough good people had already died.

"From what Kellerman said in the hangar – about watching us in orbit – the station communications satellite must be functional. Before the *Oregon* was attacked, Captain Atkins said that the satellite had power."

I left out that Atkins, along with the rest of the *Oregon* crew, was now consigned to a cold grave in deep-space.

"And if the satellite has power, it can send a communication off-world," Kaminski said, between mouthfuls of food. "But we'd need to get access to the Operations centre."

I nodded. "Which means we will need the Ops manager on our side. That woman – Tyler – might be able to help us."

"She seemed a little less *neurotic*," Jenkins said, pausing from her rifle assembly.

"That sounds like a plan," Kaminski said. He nodded enthusiastically. "We can get back-up, get a ship, and bug out!"

He fist-bumped Martinez and Blake.

"What if we can't get access to the Operations centre – to the comms satellite?" Olsen asked nervously, blinking red-rimmed eyes. "How long before we're declared overdue?"

I rubbed my chin, contemplating whether to tell him.

"I'm not sure whether you'll want to hear this."

"Tell me," Olsen said.

"It'll be a minimum of six months objective before we're declared overdue. Then another six months for a ship to reach us – provided that the Navy can spare a fast starship. But the reality is that Alliance Command may never send assistance."

"That surely can't be right!" Olsen whined.

"That's the situation. We're inside the Maelstrom. There are just too many risk factors to consider."

The group quietly reflected on that. Rescue and retrieval protocols were suspended for this sort of operation. The *Oregon* probably hadn't even sent a mayday signal. For all Command knew, we might have encountered a technical problem aboard the *Oregon* en route to Helios. What with the history of Kellerman's failure to report to the *Point*, it was hopelessly optimistic to think that anyone would be coming after us.

"Not to mention the cost of sending a further

rescue op," Jenkins said, bitterly. "Always that to consider, before they send someone else."

I shrugged. "Those are the facts."

"All right," Blake said, standing to pace the room. "Then how do we do it? How do we get to Tyler and Operations?"

Olsen roused again. "Maybe we should shoot our way out. The corporal has a rifle."

"No point," Martinez muttered. "Those security men are armed. There are more of them than there are of us. The captain is injured." He nodded over in my direction. "We've only got one rifle and the captain's pistol."

"I could take them," Kaminski said. "Just give me the rifle."

"All ten of them? In your real body? The simulators are wasted," Jenkins said. "Those security men are jumpy. They'll shoot at the first opportunity. A round from one of those shotguns is going to kill you just as easy as a pulse from a plasma rifle. Stupid asshole."

Kaminski shrugged. "Just saying what I see. I could take them."

"Real helpful, Kaminski, real helpful. As always, the brains behind the operation," Jenkins said, shaking her head.

"I mostly just kill stuff, mostly," Kaminski said. He returned to his food can.

"Cut it out, you two," I said. "No one is going to get killed out here. We're not taking any chances."

"I'll settle for just surviving," Olsen chipped in.

"Yeah, well, you're not like us," Jenkins said.

Olsen put his head in his hands again.

"Jenkins, leave him alone. We have to bide our time. No one is going to blast their way out of here. We sit tight until the opportunity arises. Nothing else to it. Kellerman wants to speak with me, apparently. I'll listen to what he has to say and then we'll plot our next move."

I stood up, and involuntarily cringed as I put weight on my leg. I tried to hide it, but Blake noticed my facial expression.

"Maybe Olsen can take a look at that leg," he said, nodding over at the science officer.

"I'd like to make myself useful," Olsen said. "If we have some medical supplies, I'll gladly help."

"I saw some dressings and other first-aid gear in one of the empty rooms," Blake said. "Come with me, Olsen, and I'll show you. Captain, I think you should rest."

I reluctantly nodded and sat back on the seat. "The rest of you should do the same. Get some shut-eye. When the opportunity to move on Kellerman arises, we need to be prepped and ready. Meanwhile, I want a watch on this hab at all times."

Day passed into night. To give them something to do, I ordered my squad to stockpile MREs and water-packs. They searched their quarters for anything useful, but this was a civilian hab and there was nothing of offensive value. Martinez and Kaminski tried to lever open one of the storm-shutters, attempting to get outside. That didn't work. Eventually, the squad dispersed and found safe rooms to occupy for the night.

We agreed on a watch rota but in the end I couldn't sleep anyway, and so I took the duty alone. If the others could find some rest, then they were welcome to it.

I paced the empty corridors of the hab module. Although the storm had broken at some point earlier in the day, the wind was still incessant. It shrieked like the cries of dying xenos through the structures around us. Sometimes it was so strong that the module itself seemed to shake. That had to be my imagination, working overtime.

Hours after sundown, I sat alone in the mess hall. Save for my old handgun, Jenkins' plasma rifle was our only weapon, and so we shared ownership. I checked the power cell for the hundredth time. The wind and situation in general was getting to me. I propped my injured leg on a metal chair, and rested back on another. The pain in my ribs had settled into a dull ache, and no matter how I lay, sat or stood, the pain was always near.

There was a creak behind me. I immediately grabbed the rifle, and half-stood, aiming into the gloom. *Damn, this rifle is heavy.* I probably couldn't hit anything with it anyway.

Blake stood in the mess hall entrance, hands up defensively, showing his palms. "It's only me."

I nodded, and slung the rifle onto the table in front of me. It clattered noisily. "Sorry, Blake."

Blake wandered over to the storm-shutters, peering between the battered metal slats.

"I couldn't sleep either," he stated baldly. "The wind is too loud. How do you think that the staff put up with it?"

"They adapt, I suppose. Same as us."

"You want some coffee?" he asked, fetching a couple of cups of self-heating java from the corner of the room.

"If you're buying."

Blake sat opposite me in the dark. We popped open the cheap plastic cups – long-lasting rations – and the drinks instantly warmed. The smell of coffee bean substitute filled the mess hall.

"What's with the lack of light?" he asked. "Isn't it bad enough that we're in the back end of the galaxy, surrounded by hostiles? Someone has to go turn off the lights."

Blake was referring to the blackout. At some point after the suns had gone down – without access to any computer tech, we could only estimate planetary time by the movement of the suns – the power to the module had been cut. This seemed a deliberate decision, because the electronic locks on the doors still functioned.

"Kellerman is likely preserving power. Probably directing it to whatever he thinks is essential. In this case, that's not us."

Blake nodded. But this discussion wasn't about power or lights: he was talking because he wanted company. Because this situation made him nervy, and it was easier to focus on trivialities than the bigger picture.

A long moment passed. I sipped at the boiling hot java, felt the thick liquid sit at the back of my throat. It represented some semblance of normality.

"Something on your mind?" I asked, as gently as I could.

"What the fuck are we going to do, Cap?" Blake whispered. "I didn't want to act up in front of the others, but we're trapped down here. No sims, no hope. Skinless."

Your simulants are fine, I thought. *It's only mine that were killed in the crash.* But voicing my concerns wouldn't help my squad's morale, and I needed them on form if we were going to move on Kellerman. Blake didn't need to hear my doubts right now; he needed encouragement. Sometimes I forgot that about Blake.

"The tanks can probably be fixed," I said. I hoped that was the case, but I didn't know whether it was true. "We'll get out of this just fine."

"How do you do all of *this*?" he asked me. "I mean dying, living – over and over again."

So this is what he really wants to talk about, I thought to myself.

"You think that I have a choice?"

"I dream about death every damned night. Every time I close my eyes, I see myself dying." He lifted a hand, held it horizontal. He visibly shook. "You know, if I concentrate, I can imagine what it felt like to be blown off the *Oregon*'s hull. I can *feel* every atom of my body – every last iota – being pulverised."

"Don't dwell on it – move on. We do this because we have to."

Unperturbed, unpersuaded by my answer, Blake continued: "And it's not just that death. It's *every* death."

"Have you spoken to the psych-techs about it?"

Blake raised his eyebrows, pulling an unconvinced

face. "Like they help. How could they? They don't know what it's like. No one does, unless they've been through it. Take Olsen; he accompanies us on a single operation, and I'll bet it will never leave him."

"I'm sure he won't forget it. Look, I'll put in a request for psychosurgery when we get back to the *Point*."

"I reckon if a head-doctor examined Olsen right now, while he's asleep, he'd be dreaming about the *New Haven*. Not what he's just been through, but dying."

I had the sudden feeling that I was out of my depth with this conversation – that maybe it was Blake who needed the psychosurgery more than Olsen. He shivered, seemed to shrink in front of me, nervously rubbed his eyes with his forefinger and thumb.

"It's just this fucking place," Blake added, an almost diffident tone to his voice. "Sorry. I shouldn't be saying any of this."

"How long have we known each other, Blake?"

"Three years, objective. Thirty-seven ops."

"Every time I've taken you out into space, I've gotten you home in one piece. This op is no different from the other thirty-seven."

"I know," he said, waving a hand as though he really did know all of this already.

"You might be the youngest member of my team, but I know that I can rely on you. I chose you. I've never told you that. I *chose* you."

Blake fell silent, but his face illuminated a little at that. I had recruited Blake directly from basic infantry training, from the Alliance Army camp at Olympus Mons, Mars. He hadn't elected service on a Sim Ops team but his psychological profile had been ideal for the placement.

"There were a lot of candidates for your role on the squad. As team leader, I had to review them all. Did you know that some of the brass thought you were too young for this posting?"

Blake shook his head. "No, Cap."

"But I didn't. I saw your potential. Your basic training reports were exceptional. I knew that you'd make a perfect simulant operator. Over the last three years, you've proved yourself. You've never let me down."

"Thanks," Blake said. "But there's something that I want to tell you."

"I remember now – back at the *Point*. Go on."

Again, just a few days ago for us – drinking in the District. That felt like a lifetime past now: gone were the safe, comfortable corridors of the *Point*. I had forgotten about the conversation.

Blake paused awkwardly, then said, "I've made a decision. All of this – it's changed me."

As soon as Blake uttered those words, I knew what was coming. *Damn it*. I should've seen the signs. I had been here before, with other simulant operators. *I was a fool for not recognising this.* Blake was burning out.

"Don't make a decision yet," I said. "We'll talk about it when this is over, back at *Liberty Point*."

"I filled out the papers before we left base. Command will take a while to release me from service, but it will happen."

His decision had been made. He wanted to unburden himself, to tell me now so that I knew it was final. I grimaced. *Cole had known.* He had known in my mission briefing, on the *Point.* He had damn well known what Blake wanted, what was going to happen, and he'd still sent him out here. *"There will be something in this for everyone on your team. They'll all get what they want."* This was to be Blake's way out of the Programme. I suddenly felt very angry, and very disappointed. Not with Blake, but with the whole military machine: the whole damned system.

Blake shook his head. "I'm tired of this. I can't do what you do. I can't go on dying like this."

"We'll talk about it later."

"Once we get back to the *Point,* I'm off the force," Blake said. He set his jaw, and looked as determined as I had ever seen him. "I want to settle down. Have a proper life. My ma and pa want me back." He shrugged, as if embarrassed. "I miss Earth."

I wished that I understood that: missing Earth.

"How long has it been since you went back?" he asked me.

"Not long enough. Earth doesn't have anything for me but bad memories. I wasn't much younger than you when I signed up with the Alliance Army, and I haven't been back since. I can't understand why you would ever want to, but that's your choice."

"I want to see my family before they're taken from me."

That was something that I could understand,

albeit not my family. There *was* someone I missed, but she was already gone – had already been taken from me.

For a moment, I wondered whether maybe Blake had the right idea. Maybe this was all bullshit. Maybe it didn't mean anything. Except – *except!* – that every dead Krell was a step closer to her. To Elena. And I couldn't ever give up that dream.

"I know that things haven't been easy for you, either," Blake said, as though realising my train of thought. "But I'm still young."

"Just give it some time. Don't tell the others about your decision. When we're back at the *Point*, we'll talk some more."

"None of the others know, and I won't tell them unless you think that I should," Blake agreed. "How's the leg?"

"Olsen has taken out some metal, but he says there are still fragments in the muscle. He doesn't have the equipment he needs to remove them."

I pulled back the shredded fatigue to show the bloody wound. It was a nasty gash, even cleaned and dressed with medi-gel. The bleeding had stopped, thankfully, but the tissue looked an unpleasant grey colour. Strange to think that I had seen far worse injuries, on my own body – my simulated body – over the years of my service. Those had caused no emotional response whatsoever, but this was entirely different. It wasn't so much the constant pain – although that was bad enough – but the reminder of my own mortality. None of the team was first-aid trained, not like regular Army, and we had no proper medic on the squad. In the normal course of events, we just wouldn't need one.

Blake frowned at me. "Looks infected."

"Christo, Kid, talk about positivity!" I said, laughing. "Remind me not to ask you for good news."

"But it really does. Hopefully Kellerman will help you."

"I'm not sure that Kellerman is going to help with much at all. We're going to have to watch him, very carefully." I stood from the table, using it as a support. "Now, go and get some rack time. That's an order. The wind has let up a little. I need you to be frosty tomorrow."

Blake nodded. "Thanks for the pep talk."

"No problem, trooper. I'll owe you for the coffee."

The conversation with Blake had set me on edge. There had been a time when I'd dwelt on every transition. For most sim operators, it was a hump to get over. It had been for me, during my earlier years stationed on Azure. For Blake, I thought it was something deeper. I wasn't sure at all that he'd be able to get over it.

I wandered the corridors like a ghost, like the only awakened member of a starship crew when all others had gone into hypersleep. Unlike my experience on the *Oregon*, this was real – not imagined.

Helios had such long nights. Dark, cold, noisy.

But it wasn't the wind keeping me awake. I was

lying to myself about that. Something else lurked in my head.

The ache in my skull was worse than that in my ribs or leg. Hours after Blake had finally gone for some rest, I looted the medicine cabinets in the hab module – searching for some painkillers.

I found an empty washroom. The walls were dusty and dirty, and the shower cubicles long dried up. The place stank of shit and piss; hadn't been cleaned a long time before it was abandoned. Using the rifle as a prop, I hobbled over to one of the black-stained sinks. Overhead, an electric light flickered on. Evidently not all power to the hab had been cut. My fractured reflection appeared in a broken mirror in front of me. A hundred tiny images of me looked back: stooped, shaking, tired.

Forty-one years old now, thanks to the freezers. Far too old for this shit.

My headache was piercing, almost incapacitating. For a moment, I thought that I might throw up. No point in shouting to the others, no point in waking them for a stupid headache. *It's probably just the after-effects of the crash*, I reasoned. *Or maybe the lingering side-effects of hypersleep.* I hadn't been awake from cold sleep for long.

I need a drink so bad. That was probably it: I needed a drink. I hadn't drunk anything in days, not since I was back on the *Point*.

I opened one of the plastic bottles, half-full of painkillers, and tipped the contents into my palm. I rabidly gobbled them up, swallowed them without water. That didn't matter. Ancient pain-relief tabs, not smart-meds like I was used to.

For a long while, I looked at my reflection in the mirror. I kept telling myself that the ache in my head would go, that it was nothing more than a migraine.

But you know exactly what it is.

When I closed my eyes, I heard the Artefact. A squalling, repeating static loop. There was something behind the noise, something agonisingly familiar that I just couldn't place. Like the remnants of a dream, gnawing away inside my head.

A tone, a melody—

That was what was causing the aching inside of me, not some explainable biological process. This was something deeper, something that no painkiller could displace.

It's not just a noise. It's a transmission, a signal. Language.

I opened my eyes and stared into the mirror again. It was an insect's eye; throwing back tiny images of everyone who had died back on the *Oregon*. Atkins, Pakos, Olsen's science staff, the bridge and maintenance crews.

And in the middle of the mirror, caught by the concave silvered plates, were my simulants. Miniature reflections of me, caught in ten different death poses.

Sometimes I felt that dying was the only thing I was actually good at. It was the parts in between, the *living*, that I couldn't cope with. All Blake's talk of family had made me think of Elena again.

In the very centre of the mirror, so tiny that I had to strain my eyes to see it – was her image.

A memory – a bad memory – suddenly welled within me.

CHAPTER FIFTEEN

A CURFEW IS IN EFFECT

Six years ago

I wasn't used to full dress uniform, but Elena had insisted. That, and the commanding officer of the entire Sim Ops Programme had required formal dress for the event. Even so, I begrudged it: the starched collar, the pressed trousers. I hardly ever wore full blues.

Elena and I stood on the platform edge, getting ready to leave Fort Rockwell. It was approaching dusk and the monorail station bustled with a horde of personnel. Fort Rockwell was now nearly two million Army and Naval personnel, together with associated support staff. The camp had a dedicated transport network, reaching out into the civvie districts.

"Are you excited?" Elena asked, clutching my arm.

She wore a short black dress, something I had insisted she wear. If I was going in dress uniform, then she had to look the part. It was made of shimmering spider-silk, imported from off-world, and fitted closely to her every curve. Over that she wore a long black velvet coat. She was timeless; a classic beauty among the false smiles and augmented body-sculpts.

"What's to be excited about?" I said. "I don't need a title. I've never been one for medals or badges. You know that."

"But a promotion is really something, isn't it?"

"I'm not sure. Maybe I won't accept it."

"You'll be a captain," Elena said, drawing out the words. She gave a hoarse chuckle: her dirty laugh. "That means something."

Tonight was to be my award ceremony, a dinner to mark my promotion. Hosted by Major O'Neil – noting not just my performance, but the success of the entire Sim Ops Programme.

Elena was right, though: the promotion *was* something. It was more than honorary. I was being promoted to full commissioned officer status, way beyond my pay grade. It was well outside the standard military career structure: a recognised exception to the regulations, as a result of my performance as a sim operator.

"There are going to be other promotions as well," I said, deflecting some of the attention away from me.

"I know, I know. Will Vincent Kaminski be there?"

I shook my head. "Got busted bringing company back to his quarters again."

Elena raised a thin eyebrow. "So another six

months before he can be considered for promotion?"

"*Another* six months. This is his third – ah, indiscretion."

"But it doesn't detract from your achievement. Forty-three transitions…" She shook her head. "And over a hundred inductees on the Programme. It'll be exponential now."

I shrugged. The truth was that I enjoyed Elena making a deal of my promotion. I didn't have anybody else. She was my world. We had moved in together, occupied a decent-size domicile in the Army district – a two-bed apartment, usually reserved for those on marriage contracts.

Another exception to the regulations, that was one of the benefits of being on Sim Ops. Over the last few years, it had become the military's favourite new project. Money and resources were being poured into the Programme, faster than new recruits could be found.

"I wonder what the venue will be like," said Elena. It was she who was excited: her face was radiant. "I hope it isn't anything like that restaurant that you took me to when I first arrived here."

"You didn't like that? You should've said."

"I expected you to read my signs. Don't you know me well enough by now?"

"I don't think that I know you anywhere near as well as I would like."

Just then, the monorail silently glided into the platform, slowing to a stop. Sleek, white; almost new. A considerable crowd had gathered by now, and passengers jostled each other as they boarded.

Arms linked, we chose one of the emptier carriages at the rear.

Elena sat, tutted at the NO SMOKING ABOARD TRAIN sign. She smoothed down the iridescent fabric of her dress, crossed her legs. Leant in to me, against my shoulder.

"This dress makes me look fat," she whispered.

I turned to look at her. She had discarded her glasses, just for tonight. Her make-up and jewellery were understated, naturalistic. She gave me an inscrutable half-smile. Cheeks suddenly flushed. I squeezed her hand.

"I don't think that I have ever seen you look more beautiful. And I don't think that you look fat at all."

The train started up, and sped out of Rockwell Central station.

The carriages began to get busy as we picked up several more passengers at the next few stops, all still within the perimeter of Fort Rockwell. A variety of different military staff both boarded and left, but I was engrossed in conversation with Elena and took little notice.

"Isn't the sunset stunning?" Elena asked.

She looked over my shoulder to appreciate the view. Tau Centauri was low on the horizon, throwing dazzling sunrays over the ragged skyline. The vista was a luscious orange – unpolluted, welcoming.

"It's something about the composition of the upper atmosphere. But it's nice, I guess."

"Don't take the fun out of it, Conrad!" Elena chided. "Just enjoy it for what it is. We're here, together, on this planet. We have to be grateful for the small things in life, and then everything else will fall into place."

The city lights flew past us, as the train moved at high speed, and crossed the perimeter into the surrounding metropolis. Only the distinct lit towers of the skyline remained constant. One of those was the Weskler-Trump International.

"Do you remember when we stayed at that hotel?" she asked. "When I first arrived here?"

The train drew into the next platform. Another tranche of military personnel, a handful of down-trodden civilian workers. Vacant faces, weathered hands, dust-stained overalls – workers from the local spaceport. Two small children scurrying around an old man's legs. A woman wearing a hijab, a tiny mewling child in her arms.

"I remember. We should go back there someday."

A tall man boarded the train, dressed in a military uniform. He scanned the carriage, made brief eye contact with me: then turned, and walked to the end of the carriage.

Close-cropped grey hair, but he wasn't old. Tall and lean. Piercing steely eyes; he flinched slightly when we made eye contact again. His face was anonymous – forgettable even – and I didn't recognise him. He sat, deliberately facing away from me, a silvered attaché case on his lap. Hands clasped atop it, protectively. Over his head, like a guardian angel, an Alliance Army recruitment poster loomed: RECRUITING ON YOUR WORLD, IN YOUR CITY, IN YOUR NEIGH-BOURHOOD it threatened.

What's inside the case?

Elena was still talking but I had stopped listening now. The train was moving off, fast, gathering speed as it moved through the city proper.

Although I didn't recognise the face, I recognised the uniform. *Simulant Operations.* Something didn't seem right here. Wearing duty fatigues, not dress uniform.

I know Sim Ops, I thought, *and I don't know you.*

Elena kept talking, oblivious. I stood, grabbing a handrail to steady myself. I pushed aside some indigs. Needed to get a better look at the man.

"Conrad!" Elena called. She tried to stand to see what was happening. "What's wrong?"

The man swallowed hard – ten, fifteen metres away from me – across the carriage. He twisted to look in my direction, maybe alerted by Elena's voice—

I noticed his fatigue sleeve rucked up, just a little—

A tattoo on the arm. A tattoo of a hydra—

"Elena – get down!" I managed to shout, through the throng of passengers, half-turning to look in her direction. I already knew that it might be the last thing that I ever said.

"For the Directorate!" another voice yelled behind me.

Then there was screaming, for just a split second, as the train descended into madness—

The attaché case exploded.

I lay in the wreckage.

I had no sensory perception save for the constant ringing in my ears. The sensation was excruciating: a demonic sine wave enveloping everything, becoming my only reality.

Is this what real death feels like?

An endless nothing – dark, shrouding, all-encompassing. But the noise told me that I wasn't dead. So I held on to it, rode it.

I wanted to panic, to cry out – not for me: for Elena – but I couldn't.

While I lay in the twisted remains of the train carriage, I considered what had just happened. What was the real target of this attack? Had this train been the target, or something or someone else? I discarded any notion that *I* had been the target: I was just a soldier, no matter how good I was becoming at operating a sim. There was no way that the Directorate would dedicate resources to eliminate me. But was it an attack on Sim Ops?

Murky, flashing lights appeared overhead. Red, blue: the shrieking of a police siren. Then brilliant white light, flickering somewhere far above me.

People were crying for help all around me. Nearby, someone was praying – mumbling words in a language that I didn't understand, over and over again. Something or somebody was on fire nearby. The scent of smoking flesh was thick in the air.

"Elena!" I yelled.

No response.

It was impossible to orient myself. Something had pinned me down – a piece of metal. I scrabbled to get free of it, to pull my body out of the wreckage. Glass fragments had penetrated my chest. My shirt was blood-stained, the ridiculous dress jacket torn. I couldn't feel any pain, yet – couldn't see or feel how bad the damage was. I didn't *want* to know.

There were twisted metal spars above me. Blackened by the intensity of the explosion. Difficult to discern what those were; whether they had once been part of the window structure or whether the diamond-tread pattern meant that they had been part of the floor.

More light coalesced above me. Bright beams penetrated the gloom, slowly panning back and forth. Searching.

A voice rang out, loud and clear, from somewhere outside of the wreckage: "*A curfew is in effect. Please return to your homes. A curfew is in effect. Alliance Army soldiers are inbound for your protection.*"

It came from a military drone, I realised. Hovering low, probing the wreckage. The searchlight slowed, panned again. Someone nearby shouted something in Arabic. The drone's light focused on our position and I held up my hand to cover my eyes.

"*A curfew is in effect. Please return to your homes. A curfew is in effect. Alliance Army soldiers are inbound for your protection.*"

"Survivors!" I shouted. "Survivors in here!"

Faces appeared above me. Dark-skinned, wearing peaked law-enforcement caps.

"We've got live ones down here," one of them muttered. "Get med-evac ready for casualties!"

They took me out of the rubble, along with fifteen other survivors recovered from the same carriage. I don't remember much about that, except that a police utility robot managed to clear the heavier pieces of wreckage away while medics removed the bodies and survivors.

I was immediately taken, by a med-evac transport, to Rockwell Infirmary.

The hospital accident and emergency wing was seriously taxed by the immediate influx of new cases. The sterile white hallways were filled with the walking wounded. As more casualties were recovered from the wreckage, those with less serious injuries were placed in the waiting rooms and lobbies. Not just soldiers, not just Alliance military: women, children, the young and old. All around, people were crying, clutching injured loved ones. A woman was screaming uncontrollably as she grasped a tattered bundle of bloody rags. An old man with one eye, gore already streaming from a freshly applied bandage. And everywhere, Alliance Army troops patrolling the corridors – carbines slung over shoulders, watching on with an air of detached suspicion.

I sat in a padded chair in a corridor, still wearing the remains of my uniform. Shell-shocked was an understatement.

Later, I was told that three hundred and twenty-five people were seriously injured on the monorail train. There were ninety-eight killed. Of those, sixteen were minors, twenty-three female.

Elena was just a statistic.

A rogue terrorist, acting on his own agenda. Whatever I had heard or seen, it wasn't sufficient to prove otherwise. The Asiatic Directorate officially denied responsibility. The agent had self-terminated. He was never traced. There was no evidence left to identify him. In the scheme of things, the terrorist attack on the train was a minor incident.

The attack was catalogued as one in a series of Alliance-Directorate hostilities. It didn't trigger any formal declaration of war. It was easily forgotten, in a universe consumed by constant conflict. Just another day.

Most forgot about it.

But I didn't.

"Sergeant Conrad Harris?" a medic called, reading from a data-slate.

"Yes, that's me."

The medic was only a young girl. Short blonde hair pulled back from a painfully thin face. Wearing blue scrubs, the name-tag on her chest askew: KASHA, A. (INTERN GRADE).

Not even a real doctor.

"I'm not qualified yet," she said. Must've seen me looking at her tag. "The doctors and medtechs have their hands full with the more serious cases – those with life-threatening injuries." She raised an eyebrow. "Is it a problem for me to treat you?"

I shook my head, mute.

"You've suffered minor lacerations to the chest. We've removed the glass and dressed the cuts.

Some bruising to the legs. The X-ray doesn't show any breaks. You'll make a full recovery."

"My ears – I can still hear the explosion."

Kasha nodded. "That will disappear. You'll probably have some permanent hearing loss at those frequencies though." She tapped my chest with a pen, through the wad of dressings that had been applied there. "Your data-ports are undamaged. I expect you'll be able to make transition."

"That doesn't matter," I mumbled.

Kasha gave me a disbelieving look. "Of course it matters. I know what you sim operators are like. You'll be back out there before you know it. Didn't do you any good this time though, did it?"

"I was on the train with a woman – she was sitting near me—"

"Name?"

"Marceau, Elena."

Kasha glanced down at the data-slate, clucking her tongue as she read. "We have her here. DNA confirmed her ID."

I felt a burst of relief.

"Is she alive? Is she injured?"

"She's in theatre right now."

All energy drained from me. I collapsed back into the chair, my head in my hands. I couldn't think. That ringing in my ears, in my head, was overwhelming. If Elena was dead, if she was really gone—

"Wait here," Kasha said, backing into the emergency room again, reading from her data-slate. "Congrats on your promotion, by the way. Your personnel file just updated."

And so I sat and waited, a captain now.
None of that mattered to me.
Not unless I had Elena.

Hours passed.

The same faces stared back at me. Military advisers visited some family members. I heard wails through the corridors, from adjoining family liaison rooms. "Sympathy suites", they called them.

An enormous electronic board in the lobby listed the names of patients currently receiving medical attention. The list changed constantly, with updates such as IN THEATRE – AWAIT NEWS. Some posts were of a more final nature: SEE MORTICIAN.

Through tired, blurred vision I made out her name:

MARCEAU, ELENA
IN THEATRE: RECEIVING TREATMENT
AWAIT NEWS

Other wall-mounted monitors broadcast the degree of devastation. Vid-feeds from drones, flown high over the explosion. The entire monorail train had derailed, and the force of the detonation had collapsed some adjoining buildings. Emergency services were on site. Police air-cars, ambulance ships. Military dropships, soldiers streaming the adjoining streets. All transport shut down. The sky was closed: orbital access suspended for the next twenty-four hours.

"Captain Conrad Harris?"

A small, elderly man stood in front of me. Weathered skin, a bright white drooping moustache. He was a doctor: white coat, liberally stained and splashed by iodine and blood. A veteran of the long war. He dug his hands into his pockets. Awkward, uncomfortable.

"Yes," I said. I had the feeling that I was speaking too loud, that I was adjusting for the noise in my head. "Is she—?"

The doctor grimaced uneasily.

Please no—

"There was nothing that we could do. She suffered a significant blow to the abdomen."

"I need to see her."

The doctor fished something from his pocket: a cigarette. He flipped the lighter.

"Of course. Do you mind?"

"I need to see her – *now*."

He bobbed his head, sucked on his cigarette.

Fuck no, fuck no, fucknofucknofuckno!

My blood ran cold as hypersleep cryogen, but my data-ports burnt red-hot. For all of my military prowess, there had been nothing I could do. Nothing I could actually do to stop that bomb going off.

"She suffered significant internal bleeding. We've tried nanite surgery, but the impact," he shook his head, "was major. She won't be released for at least a couple of days. We'll have to keep her in for observation."

My vision suddenly cleared, the whining in my head diminishing for just a second. I swallowed.

"She's not dead?"

The doctor frowned. "No, Captain. But I'm afraid that the baby is."

Elena wasn't even on a proper bed. I supposed that those had been reserved for more serious cases. Instead, she was curled up, semi-foetal, on an examination couch – an inert medical scanner on a metal arm still propped overhead. They had put her in a private chamber, just off one of the ER corridors. The strip-lamp above flickered, waxing and waning.

I stood at the entrance to the room, gently pulled back the plastic curtain dividing the enclave from the rest of the ER. Such emotion ran through me, such depth of feeling that I could not process it all at once. My head throbbed, but my heart broke for her – for both of us.

Elena was drowning in a pale green hospital gown, far too big for her. Her hair was tussled, unkempt; make-up in streamers down her cheeks. She'd been crying – was still crying, as I watched her – but the noise had settled into regular sobs. The sort of noise that a person makes when they have no energy left to cry, when they cannot muster the strength to continue the physically draining action of producing tears. Her feet were bare – dirty, stained by blood and soot.

I went to her, and held her. She cried some more – now deeper, more heart-felt moans. I had never heard her cry like this and every noise that escaped her body fuelled the growing fire in my chest.

"Why didn't you tell me?" I asked. My voice sounded stilted, formal: choked with grief.

"I did not know. I didn't even know."

We held each other for a long time, until Elena had cried herself to sleep, and the hospital staff told me that I had to leave the ER.

CHAPTER SIXTEEN

WHAT MATTERS

A new day dawned on Helios.

A contingent of security men collected me early. My squad reluctantly stayed at base camp – I was in this alone. Under armed guard, I was trooped across the compound.

The weather had improved significantly, and both Helios Primary and Secondary shone brightly on the horizon. It was hot and still outside; so different from the storm the day before. Difficult to imagine that I was on the same world.

Kellerman's quarters were probably the largest on Helios Station, and could easily have been on any of the Core Worlds. An old oak desk dominated one wall, surrounded by upholstered leather chairs. *Real wood on an outpost this far from Alliance space:* the cost implications were shocking. Antique electric lamps were sunk into the walls and ceiling. Alcoves around the room were loaded with stacks of paperwork and data-slates. The walls were pinned with holographic plates and aerial photography of Helios' surface. Many of the pictures were of the Artefact, but the images were always slightly skewed or out of focus.

The rest of the chamber continued in the same vintage theme. A series of photo frames hung behind the desk. Each of those held bleached, ancient pictures of the current and former presidents of the Alliance; even a hopelessly dated photo of President Francis. He looked far more youthful than the last time I had seen him. That bizarre little detail gave me a sudden pang of homesickness – inadvertently reminding me of how far from *Liberty Point* we had come.

Deacon met me at the entrance to the room, and pulled up a chair in front of Kellerman's desk. He kept his firearm across his chest and acknowledged me with a curt nod. Then he took up a post by the door, stock-still. With his worn features and sand-mat skin, he looked like a golem thrown up by the desert.

I sat down and the leather of the chair crunched. The room had three large, vaulted windows that gave a panoramic view over the desert. Right now, the sky looked a murky pink-red.

Kellerman trundled into the chamber, hovering over to his desk. He awkwardly reversed himself into position behind it.

"Damned chair," he muttered. "Always getting in the way. My apologies for keeping you waiting, Captain. There is so much to do and so little time in which to do it. My body is not what it was. I trust that your leg has received some attention?"

"My science officer assisted," I said bluntly. I added silently: *No thanks to you.*

Kellerman frowned and tilted his head. "Very well. As you can see, the manpower available to me on-station is significantly depleted. Medical and scientific personnel, in particular, are at a premium. So, let us start at the beginning – why are you here?"

"You failed to report to Alliance Command," I said: the facts spilling out of me like an indictment before a court of law. "Your orders were to send a broadcast every week and you have failed to do so for the past twelve months. Command believed that a rescue operation had become necessary."

Something in the response angered Kellerman and his frown deepened. "I already know that. You can stop wasting my time with information I already know. What do you *want* here?"

"Now? Just to get off this damned rock," I said, meeting his gaze across the desk. "My crew will be reporting to Command as soon as we are able. I'll need access to your communications satellite in order to send a broadcast to *Liberty Point.*"

Kellerman nodded absently – like his mind was elsewhere.

"I suppose that Command doesn't want to lose sight of a significant investment." I wasn't sure whether he was referring to Helios Station, or my team. "There is, after all, still a war going on. It might not be the hot war that our ancestors fought, but it is just as important. Even with the Treaty."

There was something knowing in his eyes, for just a second, then it was gone.

"You will have access to Operations," he said. He paused, considering his next response. "I'm a man of my word, Captain. I suppose that you deserve some sort of explanation. I am committed to my mission here. As you heard yesterday, Helios is a harsh mistress. The Krell are everywhere. The station has suffered a series of debilitating attacks and I have lost many personnel. I take the responsibility for the care of my staff very seriously."

"Where is the rest of your staff, then?" I asked. *Over two thousand men and women, all gone. That isn't taking responsibility seriously. It's madness.*

"That isn't important."

"They're all dead?" There was no point indulging in niceties with this man; he immediately struck me as senseless.

Kellerman shook his head. "None of that is important. The site – the Artefact – that is what matters now. It really must be seen to be believed. I can explain my failure to report to Command."

"It doesn't matter any more. I just want to protect my people."

"I think it's best that I tell you anyway. If I don't, then Command will only send another team to investigate. There may be additional unnecessary casualties." He sighed. "The Krell have developed an interest in our radio communications. By sending a regular broadcast, we were almost *beckoning* them to our position. We found that when we refrained from broadcasting, the frequency of Krell raiding parties decreased significantly. Mr Deacon, bring me that data-slate."

Deacon retrieved a battered data-slate from a nearby table. Kellerman called up some biological diagrams and slid it across the desk to me. The slate showed intensive and comprehensive examinations of Krell specimens, complete with annotations. Brain wave patterns, frontal lobe concentrations, dissections, examinations of the communicator antennae and spines found on the primary-forms.

"Certain radio waves – certain broadcast spectrums – actively *interfere* with the brain functions of the Krell. This is likely how the leader-forms exert their will over the lesser xeno-forms, the so-called primary-forms and secondary-forms."

He was excited now, in full-flow: gone was the emotionless veneer. *Which is the real man?* I wondered. He motioned to Deacon again, who retrieved a stack of papers. The security chief looked decidedly unimpressed at being used as Kellerman's assistant, but Kellerman didn't seem to notice. He splayed the papers across his desk, searching for individual sheets and sliding them across to me. Soon, a stack of papers, slates and files was assembled in front of me.

"As I said, they are attracted to certain wavebands. These are interpreted by areas of the alien brain," he pointed to a schematic showing parts of a primary xeno-form skull cavity, "and then obeyed as though they are a direct brain impulse from the actual organism."

"How did you discover this?"

"As a result of the Artefact," he said, drawing his words out. "By just listening to the broadcast, and observing how the Artefact affects the Krell population of Helios."

I pulled back from the desk, and scanned over the documents, sighing heavily. For my own part, the documents didn't seem to prove anything like what Kellerman was proposing. I was no scientist, but much of his evidence looked like the jumbled rantings of a madman rather than reasoned conclusions.

"If any of this is correct, then this site could break the Alliance or make the Directorate," I said. "It cannot fall into the wrong hands. You were ordered to remain in contact with Command."

Kellerman tutted in exasperation. The old Kellerman returned immediately.

"This is the most significant find in human history. It is more important that petty political squabbling and bureaucracy. I'm quite sure that the Directorate knows nothing of the Artefact."

I baulked at that. To describe the Directorate–Alliance hostilities as squabbling was a step too far. Unexpectedly, I felt a twinge of grief for my mother, and for a life that had been denied. Kellerman's facial expression didn't reveal whether he had seen the shift in my presentation.

"The Artefact is what matters," he repeated. "It is *glorious*, Captain. Simply glorious. Understanding the Artefact's signal is more important than remaining in contact with Command." Kellerman's mood changed again, and his face positively glowed. "We have ascertained exactly what it does and why it was left here. But that is hardly the same as *understanding* the signal. The Artefact is something ancient, something so alien that even the Krell do not understand it."

"I've heard enough of this," I said quietly but sternly. "I need access to Operations. *Now*."

"And as I have said, you shall have it. But there is time for that. Our satellite will not be in optimum position for communication with *Liberty Point* until tomorrow afternoon, at the earliest. It takes an inordinate amount of power to activate Helios Station's radio antenna. I would prefer that you do so when the chances of making contact with the satellite are best. I am sure that you understand."

"So long as we can send a broadcast to Command."

"You have my word," Kellerman said, nodding readily. "But that leaves us some time to fill. I don't want this to be a wasted opportunity. There is something that I would like to show you – so that you can take an aspect of my findings back to Command, so that you can tell them how important my research really is."

I predicted where this was going, and tried to head Kellerman off: "The Artefact? Our mission parameters specifically excluded visitation of the site." I was happy for it to stay that way.

"No, most certainly not the Artefact. It would be almost impossible to reach the Artefact itself, such is the concentration of Krell in the surrounding sectors. This is something else."

"What?" I asked angrily. I was fed up with Kellerman's games.

"It will be easier to show you, rather than try to

explain," Kellerman said. "But it is quite a discovery. Tomorrow morning, we are going to go on an expedition into the desert."

Behind me, I heard Deacon groan. Kellerman scowled at him.

"We'll take a crawler. There will be room for some of your squad, if you wish. Bring along a couple of soldiers. Those of a more martial disposition will undoubtedly appreciate the find."

"So long as I have access to Operations," I said, as I stood to leave the room.

Kellerman's face remained fixed, but something flashed in his eyes. "Tomorrow, Captain. You will have access tomorrow. Until then, you are free to move about the station as you please. You're not a prisoner here, but I will bid you farewell until tomorrow morning."

Back at the hab, I hastily convened another meeting.

I was dubious of Kellerman's explanations, of his staged performance. He was hiding something, of that I was sure. But equally, he was the authority on Helios, and only he could sanction use of the deep-space communications array. For now, at least, we had to play ball.

I relayed everything that Kellerman had said to my team. This was my decision, how to work the situation, but I'd never been one to take decisions without exploring them with my squad. They were a tempering counsel.

"So, if we go through with this, we can use the Ops centre?" Kaminski asked.

"That's what Kellerman says."

"Do you trust this crazy old bastard?"

"Not at all. But he knows the planet better than us, and I don't think that he's lying about the satellite. If our best chance of sending a signal off Helios is to go out into the desert and see whatever it is he wants to show us, then so be it."

Kaminski nodded. "I suppose so."

"It just doesn't feel right," Jenkins added, without any further explanation. "Did he tell you what he wants to show you?"

"He kept that part under wraps. But I suppose he is right about a report back to Command. If we organise an evac without making any effort to investigate Kellerman's research, then questions are going to be asked."

"I guess," Jenkins said, clucking her tongue.

"I'm going to need a couple of volunteers to join me tomorrow," I said. I could order my troops to join the expedition, but I'd much rather have two willing volunteers.

"I can't say I want to go," Blake said, "but it beats sitting around the hab all day."

"I'll go," Kaminski added.

That selection suited me: I wanted to keep Blake close, after his disclosure the previous night, and I wanted to keep an eye on Kaminski just because. He'd made it plain that he'd rather shoot his way out of the situation than reason with Kellerman, and I didn't want to come back to the station to find that he'd implemented that plan.

"I just wish that we could climb into the simulator-tanks and sim-up," Blake said. "Would make sense."

"Fuck, yeah," Kaminski said. "We're on a hostile planet, surrounded by fish heads. Maybe we should wait until the simulators are repaired."

"Simmer down. You both know that the tanks are out of action." I frowned, looked over the group. "Where is Olsen, anyway?"

Jenkins sighed and shook her head. "He's already taken a look at the simulators, and he isn't sure whether they can be repaired. Reckons it will take a few days, minimum. He went with some of Kellerman's research staff. Said he'd be back later."

"That sees to 'Ski's idea, at least for now," Martinez said.

"Doesn't mean we have to like it," Kaminski grunted.

Of course, I couldn't use my sims even if I wanted to. My data-ports unconsciously throbbed for a moment and I rubbed the back of my neck.

"It's decided then. Kaminski, Blake – be ready for pick-up at sunrise tomorrow. Martinez, Jenkins – stay on-station and keep an eye on the hab."

"What do we do until tomorrow?" Martinez asked.

"We wait," I said. "I like this even less then you, but if we can get out of this situation without any more bloodshed, then that has to be worth something."

I couldn't sleep that night, either, so I took watch duty again. My ribs felt considerably better, or at least sufficiently numb for me to operate, but my leg still ached.

I was just passing time until dawn, until Kellerman's expedition. Then I would have access to Operations, and could at least update Command.

Whenever I closed my eyes, I saw Elena's face. If I stayed awake, I thought that I could hear voices in the corridors: Atkins and Pakos, yelling commands to the bridge staff.

"All hands – prepare to abandon ship. Initialising emergency evacuation procedure."

Just the wind.

I didn't want to revisit any more painful memories, didn't want to remember, but I really wanted – needed – to get some sleep. So I used the remainder of the painkillers. They felt chalky and dry in my mouth. Took enough so that my consciousness would be sufficiently blunted to avoid dreaming.

Eventually, I collapsed into a dead man's bunk.

Dead woman's bunk, I corrected myself.

There was a wrinkled two-D photograph tacked to one of the walls, beside the unmade bed. It showed two women embracing – not the clinch of lovers, but a tender moment between friends or sisters – against a blue-and-green backdrop. The two looked alike; one younger than the other, both blonde-haired and blue-eyed. The older was familiar. The tech from the hangar bay, I realised. Tyler, that was her name.

I hoped that her sister wouldn't mind me taking the bed. She was dead, probably, and undoubtedly didn't need it any more. The two smiling women looked down at me as I tried to sleep, their eyes full of promise and hope.

Helios didn't have either of those properties.

When it was quiet, when everyone else was

gone, that was when I felt the Artefact's signal most. Kellerman hadn't told me anything about the effects on the human mind, not in his chamber today, but I remembered that his broadcasts back to Command had noted it.

I had chosen not to mention it to the others. They would surely think that I was mad, that I was going down the same path as Kellerman.

Maybe he hears it too.

Maybe I should ask him about it, when I get the chance. Or maybe I should hide it away, keep it buried inside.

Perhaps I am going mad, I reasoned. *There's already so much buried away. There's hardly room for anything else.*

Two pairs of eyes watched me as I lay in the dark. The smiles were mocking me, I decided.

I need a drink. I really need a drink.

No you don't. This is something different.

Finally, I slept a drug-induced sleep.

CHAPTER SEVENTEEN

THE SHARD

We met in the hangar bay, the next morning. I'd managed a few hours' sleep – desperate, fitful – but I felt better for it. The ache in my ribs had reduced and my head felt almost normal.

Kellerman assembled Deacon, a driver called Ray, a meteorologist who introduced himself as Farrell, and a couple of his researchers. Kaminski and Blake accompanied me.

A sand-crawler was packed with supplies; enough to last us a few days on the outside, I reckoned, but Kellerman insisted that we would be back by late afternoon. The researchers appeared enthused by the idea of going off-station, but Deacon was the opposite. He grunted a greeting at me, then went about running operational checks on the crawler.

"Be more careful, Christo-damn it!" Kellerman shouted from across the hangar. "I'm a man, not an animal. You people treat me worse than the Krell!"

We watched the scene playing out. Two of Kellerman's researchers had lifted him out of his hover-chair, and were holding him by the arms to support his weight. They were trying – unsuccessfully – to guide his legs into the lower half of a hostile-environment suit.

"I'm sorry, Doctor," one of the researchers mumbled.

The suit exterior had been grafted with a complex arrangement of attenuators and pistons. The design looked archaic and barely serviceable, an exo-suit cobbled together from a variety of different sources. As Kellerman was finally lowered into the suit and interfaced with it, his legs began to twitch. He stood up on his own. He swore at another of his researchers, who fussed about him to ensure he was properly connected. The exo-suit gave an angry hiss as Kellerman flexed each leg. Researchers continued plugging wires into dataports on Kellerman's neck, while he struggled into the upper half of the exo-suit. His people bolted a Y-rack onto his back, between the shoulder blades, then added other components to his arms. He rotated each arm, shrugged his shoulders.

Whenever a researcher touched him, or went to assist in some way, he angrily threw them off. His face grew red with something approaching rage, as he stomped around the hangar bay. His pace was awkward and irregular. It was not a combat-suit by any stretch, but the exo was capable of interpreting whatever spinal capacity Kellerman retained.

"I apologise that you had to see that," he shouted

over to me. "My idiot researchers do not appear to recognise that my condition causes me gross humiliation."

Nothing that I had seen suggested that Kellerman's people were treating him with disrespect, but that wasn't what his comment was really about. He was angry that he had to depend on others, that his legs had been taken from him. I recalled the images I'd seen back on the *Oregon* – of Kellerman lying in that hospital bed, undergoing psych-eval post whatever incident it was that had claimed the use of his legs. That anger hadn't dissipated much, despite the passage of years.

"Impressive kit," was all I said.

"It was custom-made for me after my accident. It enables me to continue field studies in a way that the hover-chair would not. It is based, in fact, on the same technology as the combat-armour that your simulants wear."

Was that just a throwaway comment, or does he really know about the simulants? It shouldn't have come as a surprise to me, really – Kellerman was a member of the Alliance scientific community – but even so, I was mildly disturbed by it. I didn't want Kellerman to know the strategic value of the simulant bodies, for some reason that I couldn't really justify.

"Everyone get suited up," said Deacon. "Although the atmosphere outside is breathable, there's a lot of airborne particulate. Better to be safe than sorry."

We were issued with mismatched environmental wear – real old tech. I struggled into an oversized H-suit; completely unpowered, lined with protective padding. Something like the EVA suits worn by starship maintenance personnel – like an ancient astronaut's vac-suit. It had once been white but was now stained a dirty beige.

"I wouldn't want to use this in real vacuum," I muttered, as I suited up. The H-suit was patched with emergency taping at the wrists, holes amateurishly stitched at the knees.

"Looking good there, Captain," Blake said.

"Like you're any better, Kid?"

Both of my team wore similar ill-fitting protective suits, and grinned sheepishly as they got dressed.

"We have to make do with what we have out here," Kellerman called over.

Each suit carried a personal oxygen tank and breathing kit, enough for hours of extra-vehicular activity in the event that the atmosphere turned hostile. Kaminski, Blake and I were equipped with backpack-mounted kits, very large and bulky. The weight of the pack was immediately demanding; I didn't relish the idea of carrying it on a protracted op.

"You okay with that?" Blake asked me. "Do you want some help?"

I wriggled into the harness, drawing the straps tight over my chest and shoulders. I made an effort to avoid pulling my ribs. I didn't want help, didn't want to admit that I was struggling. *Just like Kellerman*, I thought with annoyance.

"I'll manage."

"Watch the packs," Deacon warned. "These are strictly civilian models. The oxygen tanks are not shielded. You breach the tank – it goes up."

He tapped the exposed oxygen tank on my pack – chipped and battered, a hazardous materials warning sticker so faded that it was barely visible.

"We're military. We've done this before."

Deacon gave a dour nod.

"You have communicators," Kellerman added, pointing to wrist-mounted computer devices, "but the range is very limited. They are isolated to reduce the danger of Krell interception, and they are strictly suit-to-suit. Keep communications to a minimum. Although it is highly unlikely that we will encounter the Krell, use caution."

"Do we have weapons?" Blake asked.

"There will be no need for heavy weaponry on this expedition," Kellerman said, frowning. He spoke slowly, deliberately. "It is no more than an exploratory survey. I assure you, we will be quite safe. Deacon and Ray are carrying enough firepower to protect us all."

"More important than guns," Farrell said, "is water. Outside, you'll need to keep hydrated. The suits carry enough water for several hours, but watch your supply."

Farrell was an older man; hunched over, with burst blood vessels across his big nose. I made a mental note: perhaps alcohol wasn't banned on the station. Maybe I should see whether Farrell could get me some.

"Where exactly are we going?" I asked.

"We will be examining an archaeological site of great interest," Kellerman said. "There is virtually no possibility of encountering a Krell patrol when the weather is this clear."

"Doc is right," Farrell chipped in. "Clear weather allows the Artefact to broadcast over most of this continent. With the signal obtaining such clarity, the xenos will be congregating around the Artefact."

"And I have weapons," Deacon said, flashing a rare smile. "We won't be going anywhere near the Artefact."

"I don't trust this at all," Blake murmured softly.

"We don't have much of a choice," I said. "Any sign of trouble, and we'll bail out to the crawler. Simple as that."

Eventually, all safety protocols recognised, we mounted the sand-crawler. Kellerman and Deacon sat in the passenger cabin with my men and me. Ray drove, and Farrell acted as navigator.

With an ominous engine rumble, the crawler rolled out of Helios Station and into the darkness of Helios' dawn. Helios Primary provided a guiding light, just breaking the cloud cover. With practised ease, Ray drove the vehicle out into the desert. We went through the same procedure to sign out as we had on our arrival, with Tyler approving our departure. The ancient laser batteries traced our progress.

Kellerman stood and peered into the driver cabin, his legs whirring and clicking as he went. He was unsteady on his feet.

"Is the radio mast muted?" he asked.

"All radio contact is suspended per protocol, Doctor," Farrell said, absently.

"Have you checked for any signal leakage? Please do so. We can't afford to be traced out here."

"All checked, no bleed," Farrell said.

Obviously happy with that response, Kellerman sat down and buckled himself into the crawler safety harness.

We travelled for hours.

Through ravines and gullies, brutal architecture created by a world of endless dry seasons and baked by two alien suns. We were well out of the reach of Helios Station, which was a psychological burden as much as a geographical one. There would be no help for us out here. Thankfully, the route was largely deserted: the world outside still and quiet.

"I've done this run lots of times," Ray bragged from the driver section. "Too many to count."

I wasn't sure whether Ray was a researcher or a station maintenance tech. He was swarthy, with mousy-coloured and unkempt hair. A sagging paunch of a belly stretched at his jumpsuit, but he didn't seem mean or vindictive like most of Deacon's people. If anything, he appeared eager to impress us with his knowledge of Helios' topography.

"Watch him," I quietly said to Kaminski, indicating to the driver cab. I was wary of his apparent self-assurance.

Both Kaminski and Blake nodded.

I sat back in the passenger cabin, and took the opportunity to question Deacon and Kellerman.

"So where exactly is this site?" I asked Kellerman.

"It isn't far from the station. You will find it most interesting."

"We've been driving for hours."

"The terrain is not conducive to land travel."

"Is the site linked to the Artefact?"

"Just be patient," Kellerman said. Then, in an obvious attempt to change the subject, "I am most intrigued by your simulant technology. I have inspected the simulant bodies that we recovered from your landing craft. The technology was developed, as I understand it, to specifically counter the Krell threat. Let me make sure I have this right: you are able to enter a state of suspended... ah, consciousness... in the simulators, and thereby interface with the simbodies?"

"That's about the size of it," I said – again, keen not to give away too much.

"The goal being that the operator is exposed to limited risk. The sim-body dies, but the operator is unharmed. These simulants, what mental capacity do they have?"

"None. They are grown for the job. They have an adapted neural interface that allows us to inhabit the body. No higher brain function."

"Advanced bio-technology and gene-engineering, coupled with mechanics. So you intended to remain on your starship, and conduct the rescue operation remotely?"

"That's right. It didn't work out."

"Where the Krell are involved, it rarely does. Could you make transition to another simulant body – perhaps one of those grown for use by another squad-member?"

I shook my head. "The bodies are individually encoded for use by a specific trooper. I couldn't make transition to a sim grown for use by Kaminski or Blake, or any of the others."

Kellerman frowned. "It appears that some of the simulants were damaged, Captain."

"That's right. My sims were destroyed during the landing."

"The simulator-tanks were also damaged. While we are away, I have asked my researchers to attempt to repair them. Your Mr Olsen is assisting."

"We don't need the tanks. My squad and I – we're still soldiers, even without the simulators."

"Of course. I simply felt that it might be prudent to repair them as a contingency." Kellerman shrugged. The exo-suit shoulders buzzed when he moved. "It may be some time before the Alliance sends assistance. We have such limited security personnel on-station; the extra manpower of an operational simulant would be much appreciated."

"I don't think that even Olsen can repair those tanks," I said, lying as best I could. "The technology is very advanced, very specialised."

I didn't want Kellerman to have use of the simulators. Hunched in the safety harness as he was, wrapped in the exo-suit, he appeared to be a spent force – old, weak, harmless. And his words were always sensible, reasoned. But his eyes revealed the real spirit of the man: and when he caught me in his glare, I knew the truth. Here was a man capable of potential depravity for his cause. *Two thousand staff disappeared, with no explanation*.

Then there was the fact that my simulants were all dead. Even with the tanks fixed, I couldn't make transition. I suddenly felt the nagging ache in my injured leg. I felt vulnerable. I had not been to war in my own body for many years and right now it felt incredibly fallible. Physically, I was about as much use as Kellerman.

"Anyone who fights the Krell is okay by me," Deacon interjected. "Y'all just don't do it the old-fashioned way. Up close and personal, that's what I'm all about. Fucking hate those fish heads."

"I hear that, brother," Kaminski chanted, knocking fists with Blake.

"I apologise for Mr Deacon's crudity," Kellerman said. "Mr Deacon, please check on our progress."

Deacon reluctantly unbuckled and stalked into the driver cabin, using overhead handholds to steady himself as he went. He had stripped to the waist, out of his H-suit, and had a series of messy scars over his shoulder blades and neck. He had a tattoo on his back: "Death from the stars – XXth Division."

"He is a Rim War veteran," Kellerman said, looking after Deacon as he went. "He fought the Asiatic Directorate on Epsilon Ultris. Honourably discharged. This placement was a reward, if you will, and he acts in a civilian capacity. Difficult to believe that such resources were consumed by a war between two human factions. But then these are harder times."

"Weren't you on Ultris?" I asked. The personnel records, I remembered, stated that he received the spinal injury on Epsilon Ultris.

Kellerman paused and frowned. "Why yes, I think that I was. So many planets, so many postings – difficult to remember them all."

Is he seriously having trouble remembering? I wondered. I didn't believe that someone like Kellerman would forget the location of such a pivotal event. He gave no other reaction to my question, and I decided not to press it any further, but his response struck me as strange.

Deacon clambered back into the passenger cabin. He must have heard us talking, because he pointed to a hideous scar on his chest. I winced even as he showed me; the result of a Krell boomer, I guessed.

"I made sergeant in the Alliance Army," he said, with something approaching self-satisfaction in his voice. "Did two tours on Ultris. Eleven confirmed Korean kills. Three years, objective, of military service. And I never got a scratch on me, not a single one. Then I was stationed on Helios – four weeks in, I got *this*. There was a really bad storm, and a leader-form got into the station. Took out sixteen of my men, before we could bring it down."

"You were lucky to get away with only the scar," I said. "I've seen what that stuff can do. Strip a man of muscle in under an hour."

"You've seen what it can do to a sim," Deacon scoffed. He had no way of knowing of my background in the Alliance Special Forces, and I wasn't about to correct him. "You can't imagine the pain when it happens to your own body. The bastard wasn't particularly big, just a mean son of a bitch. Carried one of those cannons. Fired at me as it was dying. Churned right through my H-suit."

Deacon's smile became fixed, his eyes glassy as he recalled the memory.

"If there is one thing that I hate more than the Directorate, it's the damned Krell," he said.

We reached the site somewhere approaching late morning, local time.

"Stop over there," Kellerman directed. "By the crater. Not too close to the edge."

Ray obeyed and manoeuvred the crawler. Then the vehicle stopped, and Kellerman's people began to unpack a gun-bot. It was a small quadruped model – multi-legged to traverse broken terrain. About as intelligent as a dog, armoured with metal-plating and equipped with a heavy-calibre solid-shot assault cannon. The main body was taken up by a variety of sensory apparatus, used to scan for viable targets. Simple security issue, although similar units were deployed by the Army. Someone had scrawled SCRAPPY on the bot's body.

"Mr Deacon – get outside and scout the immediate vicinity," Kellerman barked. "I don't want to take any risks."

Deacon cracked the hatch to the crawler. Immediately, a wall of hot, still air hit me. He jumped down from the cabin and disappeared for a few moments. The crew continued prepping the gun-bot.

"Best to be safe," Kellerman said to me, without explaining himself.

"Of course."

Deacon reappeared at the hatch, his carbine cocked on his hip.

"Safe," he announced.

Kellerman nodded sagely. "Your efforts are

appreciated, Mr Deacon. Everyone can disembark now."

His people deployed the bot – carrying it outside, then placing it on the ground. The bot activated and began to ponderously patrol the sand-crawler. Its metal legs whined and pumped as it went, multi-coloured eye lenses scanning the desert.

The rest of us cautiously dismounted the crawler. Before I had even got out of the vehicle, I felt the prickle of sweat breaking on my brow. The H-suit didn't have an atmosphere control unit, and moving about was hard work.

"As I explained, personal communication outside of the crawler is permissible," Kellerman said. "But try to stay together so far as possible. The Artefact is approximately twenty kilometres west of here. And so, as you can see, the Krell leave this region well alone."

"Let's hope," I said.

I took in the detail of the location. A crater, maybe a kilometre across, set between two enormous mountains. The area was pocked with rock structures, twisted into bizarre shapes by the elements. The two suns threw out long shadows, providing precious shade. Here and there, bloated insect-things flitted in the cool. Stunted and warped coral-like formations – barely recognisable as some sort of plant-life – ringed the basin but did not invade it. The horizon was heat-blurred, and the whole place – protected from the worst of the wind by the mountain range – was blisteringly hot.

The away team spread out from the crawler. I paced – stretching my legs and testing the capabilities of my H-suit. It was equipped with a basic respirator mask. The churning of my individual oxygen-processing tank was a constant companion. I remembered my last sim op – clutching the cold hide of the *Oregon* in orbit around Helios. Then I had been in a sim, able to withstand the extremes of war. Not now.

Kaminski and Blake stood with me, scanning the horizon.

"So why exactly are we out here?" Blake muttered, his voice hazed by the hum of his own oxygen supply. "All I see is sand."

Kaminski nodded. "I hear that."

Kellerman clumsily came down the slope, the crawler behind him. Walking through sand was even more difficult for him; his exo-suit leg motors protested noisily.

"Beautiful site, isn't it?" he said, indicating to the desert basin.

"What's to see?" I asked.

Kellerman pointed with a gloved hand towards the bottom of the basin. "There."

From a distance, it looked like just another rock-structure – a series of serrated spires, erupting from the crater floor. Caked in sand and stained the same colour as the surrounding desert, they looked innocuous enough. But Kellerman thrust a pair of battered electronic binoculars into my hands. In reconstructed monochrome I realised that this was an artificial edifice – reaching thirty or forty metres out of the ground.

I started off down the basin slope and the rest of the group followed. I broke into a jog, despite my leg. Kellerman fell back behind me, doing his best on his new legs. Deacon ran ahead, two rifles strapped across his back. As I got nearer, I saw that a small tent had been set up alongside the structure. The entrance door flapped lazily in the wind, slapping against the sagging fabric walls.

A half-buried construction rose out of the sand. Like the ribcage of some titanic alien creature, the skeletal structure had been pierced in places. The spars were of some metallic substance, unmistakably. Most of the thing appeared to be submerged.

"What is it?" I managed. I even felt a spark of excitement at the discovery.

Kellerman wandered towards the entrance to the tent. It covered the largest opening. The interior was dark, shadowy; leading directly into the alien derelict.

"We believe that it is a starship," he proclaimed.

The spires were covered in intricate, swirling hieroglyphics. I stood back, to better take in the big structure. Every exposed surface was covered in the markings. I couldn't focus on the language; it made my head spin. But the architecture was inimitable: this was surely made by the same engineers as the Artefact.

"So they didn't just leave the Artefact behind..." I muttered.

"Fucking A," Kaminski replied. "This is some serious shit."

"They left so much more," Kellerman said. "But the trajectory of the ship suggests that it was heading for the Artefact. Perhaps as a result of enemy fire, it crashed here. Please, do come inside. Mr Farrell, Mr Ray – you will stand guard duty. I want you to watch for intruders and monitor security of the sand-crawler."

Ray and Farrell peeled off from the group. The rest of the team carefully picked their way into the craft.

Inside, the ship was labyrinthine. The corridors were wide and empty; the walls cast of some iridescent black material – cold to the touch, even through gloves.

"We still don't know what the structure is made of," Kellerman said. "Certainly not an alloy known to the Alliance."

The going was slow and sporadic, with Deacon leading the way and Kellerman giving directions. The tunnels were ovular, making them difficult to walk through, and mostly indistinguishable from one another. Some ended abruptly in walls of sand or stone. There were very few chambers or control rooms, but we passed through several spaces full of long-dead computer banks. Cuneiform patterns had been etched onto every possible surface – walls, floors, ceilings. Intricate, tight script: pressed as though it had been stamped by a machine, like ancient circuitry. Occasionally, when I touched a wall with my hand, the scripture seemed to illuminate – but I dismissed that as a trick of the light.

There was no crew to be found at all, not even dead bodies. Nor any space for a crew; no seating, no stations. The layout of the craft didn't seem to favour a manual crew at all. Maybe, I considered, the ship had been automated: a huge artificial intelligence, manned by a robotic crew.

The place was insulated from the wind outside and in the lower levels it was intensely silent. When an echo did sound through the empty halls, it sounded to me like a reproduction of the Artefact's signal. No one else seemed to notice that, and I thought better of mentioning it. Probably just my imagination; the squealing in my head had died, and I was sure that this sound would too.

I followed Kellerman deeper into the hulk. We used flashlights and glow-globes embedded in the walls for guidance. Kellerman regularly consulted a hand-held data-slate that he manipulated clumsily in his protective gloves. Sometimes, when the terrain became especially rough, one of his people helped him – even though they were well-meaning, Kellerman would invariably bark his disapproval.

"How long has it been here?" I asked him, as we went.

"Likely many thousands of years. We've attempted carbon-dating techniques, but the materials used in the construction of the ship are highly advanced. If our premise is correct, just think about that for a moment. This vessel, as sophisticated as it is, was the product of a starfaring civilisation." He shook his head. "It probably crashed when we were still monkeys in the trees."

"Not too much further," Deacon cautioned. "We should be getting back to the crawler soon."

"Why?" I asked.

"Some of the lower corridors are crushed,"

Kellerman answered. "The original starship must have been vast. I believe that it crashed in some tremendous catastrophe, and many parts of it were shorn off. During the long sleep, those elements have been claimed by the desert. Only a tiny proportion of the ship has been mapped."

"Does the engine still work?" Kaminski asked. "We could use it to jump this planet."

Kellerman scowled. "No, it does not. While we have met with some limited success in activating the control systems, repairing the main engine is beyond our capabilities."

"Unsurprising, really," Deacon pitched in, "when you consider what this thing must have gone through."

"It did better than the *Oregon* when it came down," Blake added.

"That it did," Kellerman said. "But even so, I was concerned that the structural integrity of the lower decks had been compromised. That is where the engine is located. As a result, I have prohibited excavations past a certain depth. Some of the rooms have been cleared of debris and atmospherically sealed, to enable proper cataloguing of finds, but most have fallen into a state of complete disrepair."

"We need to get moving again," Deacon reminded Kellerman.

"I want to show the captain some of our discoveries before we leave," Kellerman said. "It seems an awfully long way to come without showing the military expedition what we've found."

Deacon just grunted.

We eventually emerged into a huge chamber,

with a vaulted ceiling far above us. It was perhaps twenty metres tall and fifty or so across; easily the largest chamber I had seen inside the alien ship. It was also more ornate than most of the others. Huge, obsidian-black consoles rose out of the walls. The ground was pitted by larger hieroglyphs and scripted markings. Although everything was coated in dust, this room had clearly seen some recent attention from Kellerman's people. Tracks and footprints marked the floor, criss-crossing at times. Kellerman followed one footprint path across the room, illuminating glow-globes in the ceiling. There was a jury-rigged lighting system above us: lamps trailed from cables, connected to a battered power generator.

Kellerman stopped. "Mr Peters, Miss Dolan – come here."

The two researchers obediently obeyed – beaming, so pleased to be on an away-day from the station. In the middle of the room, assembled on a tattered plastic sheet, was a series of mechanical and electronic components, and Kellerman's group assembled around it. The items had been reverently cleaned and labelled.

"Mr Peters," Kellerman said with a wave of his hand, "you have the honour of showing the captain what we discovered in this room."

"Of course, Doctor," Peters enthused.

Peters placed a metal case down on the floor – something that he had brought with him from the crawler. He slowly opened the catches on the box, grinning as he peered inside. He lifted the contents in both hands, standing slowly, careful not to drop the item. He delicately tilted it. It was a bladed metal instrument, as long as my forearm. Cast from the same matte-black material as the rest of the starship – obviously conscientiously cleaned. It was covered in tiny, barely visible alien scripture.

Just an old relic, I told myself. But the thing radiated a malevolence beyond its physical presence: something that I couldn't explain to myself, something that wasn't logical. In contradiction, Peters just grinned and grinned; ignorant of my inexplicable reaction.

"We believe that this was part of the ship's control unit."

Peters was a young man but with a tired and wrinkled face. His hair was grown out, framing his dark eyes. He wandered over to one of the consoles and inserted the device. The lights overhead dipped, throwing the room into darkness. Kaminski and Blake started immediately but Kellerman held up a hand for calm.

"Please, don't be startled," he insisted.

A low keening sounded in the background. Then the chamber suddenly became illuminated again. The overhead glow-globes activated, but also the glyphs set into the walls and floor. The alien consoles around the perimeter of the chamber initiated. Soon the entire chamber was full of humming, operational machines and glowing iconography. The place was *alive*: I could almost sense the data-streams around me, as the machines communicated. That image of a ship navigated by a huge AI came to mind again.

I inspected the nearest console, watching as the machines powered up. Kellerman and his crew were in wonder at the living chamber, but I was less pleased. This felt wrong: as though we were messing with something that we didn't understand, awakening something ancient and unknown. Blake and Kaminski seemed to share my sense of unease.

"This place safe?" Kaminski asked of no one in particular.

"We call the creators of this ship the Shard," said Kellerman, "because that is all that is left of them – shards of their civilisation. Shards of a technically brilliant alien race. You have nothing to fear from them. Miss Dolan – please initiate the main console."

"Yes, Doctor," the other researcher replied.

"Kellerman – are you sure about this? Do you understand—?" I started.

"Just watch. Look at the walls."

The walls were covered in the same insanity-inducing alien script that I had seen throughout the ship.

"Looks like a load of old chicken-scratch to me," Kaminski piped up. "Same as every other…"

Kaminski's words trailed off.

A bright, mercurial substance was flowing into the recessed patterns. Instead of beading on a flat surface, as real mercury did, the fluid poured into every groove and crenellation. Like a living, voracious thing – seeping, crawling up the wall, to the ceiling above, into the patterns on the floor.

"Don't touch anything!" I shouted, my voice

echoing through the chamber. I jumped aside, away from the grid as it moved beneath me.

Kaminski and Blake leapt back as well, but there was nowhere safe to move. It was everywhere now.

"It's all right," Kellerman said. "It isn't harmful."

It was like a tree, planting roots deep underfoot, throwing branches far overhead. A precisely detailed image covered every wall, the floor, the ceiling – filled the chamber. It glowed brightly, and I picked out thousands of tiny icons, each annotated in alien script. Every individual item swirled and shifted, moving with a life of its own.

"It's a map," I said.

Kellerman smiled fanatically. "It's a map of the Maelstrom. Welcome to the planetarium."

Soon I came to recognise the various stars and formations that made up the Maelstrom. They were cast indelibly into my memory, but standing in the midst of the flowing and swirling display I had momentarily been disoriented. I spent long moments just pacing the planetarium.

"The Shard knew the Maelstrom very well," said Kellerman. "We've been able to recover map data of the entire region – better than any astrocartography I've ever seen. Even better, the Shard once knew of a number of stable Q-jump routes through, and into, the region."

Flickering silver strands – like a spider's web – sprang from some worlds, linking to others. I traced some, and my touch caused the mercurial matter to flow red like capillaries. Each seemed, impossibly, to avoid the morass of black holes and gravimetric storms that blighted the region.

Is this finally it? I asked myself. An incredible prospect dawned on me. I turned to grab Blake by the shoulders, shaking him. My heart skipped a beat. The implications made me dizzy.

"Do you hear that, Blake? This thing can give us maps of the Maelstrom!"

Kellerman strode into the middle of the planetarium. Caressed some of the planets; the silver substance briefly changing colour in response to his touch. Blake just looked on in confusion, unable to understand my sudden enthusiasm.

"In theory," Kellerman said, "it would be possible to use Q-space jump points – mapped out by the Shard – to travel right into the *heart* of the Krell Empire."

"There's the Quarantine Zone," I said, pointing out the great rift at the edge of the chamber. "What is this star, in the middle?"

There sat a huge, pulsing star system – a sun surrounded by numerous bloated planets. A beating heart of mercury: actually shivering as though it was a living thing.

"I believe that is the Krell home system."

I swallowed, trying to digest Kellerman's words. My mouth was dry. I suddenly had a new purpose. *This is a second chance – a new beginning.* I let go of Blake. For the military, for the Alliance, the place had even greater implications. A fleet could strike at the home world – take the war to the Krell.

"Mr Peters, if you will," Kellerman said with a wave of his hand. "Explain the rest."

"I ran a code-breaker algorithm on one of the minor starship control units," he said. I was only half-listening, still heady from what had just been revealed. "Then Dr Kellerman – the real mastermind here – was able to show that the scripture of this device matched one of the consoles over there." He waved to a covered machine embedded in a nearby wall. "We really came across these by chance. We discovered that each acted as a key to activate certain functions of the ship." He let out a long sigh. "There is still so much to be done here. Large portions of the vessel remain unknown to us. We've only managed to explore a tiny fraction of it."

"Where are *they*?" Blake asked of Kellerman. "Whatever xenos built this ship?"

Kellerman scowled at the interruption. He didn't seem to like it when my team addressed him directly.

"They are long gone. Dust, all dust."

"But how do you know that?" Blake persisted.

"Because, as I say, the ship crashed thousands of years ago."

"You said that it was carbon-dated as being thousands of years old," Blake said. "That's different."

"The distinction is, at best, fine," Kellerman replied. "I believe that the crew died in the crash. The conclusion is supported by all available scientific evidence."

"You better hope that the Shard don't come back, looking for their ship," Kaminski added. "Because I'll bet they will be mighty pissed to find that primitives like us have been poking around in the wreckage."

"I'm quite sure that will not happen," Kellerman said, with an edge of finality.

Blake and Kaminski exchanged loaded glances. I shared their concerns, but right now I didn't care. I continued pacing the room, trying to take in everything that I was seeing.

"I think that you should tell the captain the best part," Peters said with a boyish grin, indicating to Kellerman.

"We found the Key in one of the lowest chambers of the ship," Kellerman resumed. "We've been able to decipher some of the alien language – some of the scripture on the walls. This was certainly a battleship, and I suspect that the Shard were once at war with the Krell. The device – the Key – has quite specific instructions."

"What did you discover?" I asked.

"It has the same markings as those found on the Artefact, on some of the more minor alien relics surrounding the site." His arms moved as he spoke, motors whining. "We have examined the Artefact from space. We have even run unmanned drones over the region that it occupies. I can show you the proof. Those markings are exactly the same. We can do it – we can activate the Artefact."

Kellerman's revelation perhaps didn't have the effect on me that he had planned. I wasn't interested in activating the Artefact – only using the starmaps. I couldn't draw my eyes away from the walls.

"Just imagine, Captain," Kellerman went on, trying to engage me, "*harnessing* the Artefact, understanding the signal and the influence it holds over the Krell. The Key will activate the Artefact."

"Even more reason that Command should be made aware of your findings."

"Haven't you worked this out yet, Captain? With what little scientific apparatus I have here, don't you think it fairly impossible that I could have reached the conclusions that I have?" He searched the faces of my squad. "Command hasn't told you the whole truth about your mission. They have known about the Shard for a long time. My research has been built on the shoulders of giants."

I frowned, continuing to inspect the alien display. I wished that I could memorise the Q-jump routes – an insane navigational network, spreading throughout Krell space—

"Helios is one of several sites of significant scientific interest," Kellerman declared, frustration in his voice. "It is but one of several locations left behind by the Shard."

And there it is, I finally realised.

Worst of all, for all of his insanity, I knew that it had to be true. There *was* no way that Kellerman could have done this on his own, no matter what other scientific support he had behind him. Alien devices, star-data intelligence, the discovery of the Krell home star system: it was too much. *Too many questions. Maybe not even Kellerman can answer these.*

"I'm telling you everything," he went on. "All that I know. Ask yourselves this: would Command really have risked a Sim Ops team – really have sent you out here – if the site was of purely theoretical interest?"

Kaminski sighed. Blake just looked shell-shocked. *You're young, Kid.*

I knew that I couldn't trust Kellerman, but my intel on this planet had plainly been wrong. The Alliance knew of the worth of the Artefact. Knew of the worth of the station's findings. Jostin's words haunted me: "*Imagine if that could be harnessed. Weaponised.*" They had known, and they had sent us out here to bring Kellerman back. This was why he was so important. I was quite sure, then, that Command didn't care at all about the two thousand staff, about the security team, about the credit value of Helios Station. They wanted Kellerman, and what he held in his head. My squad and I were just cogs in the machine, nothing more.

Deacon suddenly intruded on our conversation, tugging on Kellerman's arm. His face was pale, respirator hanging round his neck, beard streaked with sand.

"I've lost communication with Farrell and Ray. We should get moving back to the surface."

"It will likely be interference from the ship," Kellerman said. "Don't be unduly concerned. But you are right that we should be going."

"We're not going anywhere without the stardata," I said, holding up a hand for calm. "Whatever Command has or hasn't done, I need this."

"We already have it, decoded and ready for onward transmission," Kellerman said with a nod.

And with that, Peters deactivated the device. The humming sound ceased and the chamber darkened. The silver substance gradually drained from the cuneiform: shrinking rather than expanding. First the ceiling, then the floor, then finally the walls – retreating like a living organism, disappearing as quickly and as mysteriously as it had appeared. The intricate patterns were gone – the star-map impossible to divine from the random collection of marks on the wall.

But I couldn't get it out of my head. It was a thing of beauty, but so much more. It had been such a long time since I'd felt it, that I barely recognised the emotion it stirred in me.

Hope.

Deacon led the way, and we eventually ascended to the surface levels again.

"Ray!" he barked, into his communicator. "This is Chief Deacon! Respond!"

When that didn't work, he tried the same with Farrell. Both channels were empty static.

"Probably just a transmission problem," Kellerman insisted. He was panting, taking tortured and clumsy steps in his exo-suit. Still, he refused any help from his researchers.

The exit came into view ahead, and I picked my way through the broken terrain. Slashes of bright light fell through the breach in the starship hull. Inside the vessel, it had been so dark that it took a moment for my naked eyesight to adjust to the new conditions. The temperature gradually increased as we went: outside, it was approaching high noon now. The desert was deathly still – whatever life Helios harboured, as basic as it was, knew to avoid the extreme midday heat.

Ray and Farrell stood together, heads bobbed as though in conversation. Ray was consulting a data-slate. Farrell manipulated the device and pointed to something. We were virtually on top of them before either of them even noticed. They stood just outside the hole in the starship hull, within the shade of the tent. The enclosure outside was still open, and the overhead suns so bright that they shone right through the fabric.

Thank Christo for that, I thought. *No Krell.*

"Hey, assholes!" Deacon yelled. "How about one of you answer the damned comm?"

Ray turned to face us, his back to the alien desert. He gave a weak grin.

"No problem, Chief. Just chewing the fat with Farrell."

"Catching up on station news," Farrell said in support.

"Anything to report?" Deacon barked. "At least tell me you've been on watch."

"All fine out here," Farrell said. "The gun-bot is guarding the crawler."

Ray backed him up again: "Yeah, nothing to report whatsoever. Quiet as a tomb, in fact—"

Shree!

Ray's head suddenly exploded in a mass of blood and bone and gore.

Then the world descended into confusion, shouting and fire.

CHAPTER EIGHTEEN

IS THIS HOW IT ENDS, THIS TIME?

Instinct took over.

I was on the ground, on my belly in the dirt. Moving fast, taking cover. Savage pain exploded in my leg and ribcage, but I had to ignore it. There was a sand ridge ahead, just beyond the entrance to the ruined starship and the tent. In the seconds it took me to reach the ridge, I worked out that the attack was coming from the general direction of the sand-crawler.

"Blake, Kaminski!" I yelled. "Sound off!"

I frantically looked back in the direction of the ship. Kaminski had followed me, and Blake wasn't far behind.

"Affirmative," they both chorused.

"What's happening?" someone shouted.

I twisted to see Kellerman and Deacon further down the slope, still in the shadow of the starship. Both men were ashen faced. Deacon clung to the ground and panic dominated his eyes.

Stinger-spines volleyed overhead. Percussive roars sounded the discharge of Krell boomers. Fire impacted the hull of the alien ship, punching holes in the outer shell.

"Stay down and stay quiet!" I ordered. "We're under attack."

"Gun-grafts," Kaminski added. "Must be a couple of hundred metres out from the wreck, give or take."

"At least it isn't the crew coming back for their ship," Blake said. I knew that the comment wasn't meant glibly. "We know the Krell."

More shots came in overhead. I heard Peters moaning, complaining about the damage being caused to the Shard ship. We were using the open suit-to-suit comms network; I imagined our transmissions giving us away to the Krell like a bad smell, data-streams rising up from our position. The Krell couldn't understand what we were saying, but they would detect the actual transmissions.

"Get over here and take cover," I ordered Kellerman and the others in the group. "Keep the radio traffic down. They're listening."

With obvious trepidation, Kellerman, Deacon and the others slowly crawled away from the alien ship and settled against the sand ridge I was using as cover. Kellerman's progress was especially slow, and his legs whirred angrily as he moved. The suit wasn't made for this sort of mobility. Deacon cradled a rifle, with another long-arm strapped to his back. His beard was smeared with Ray's blood.

"Ray's dead!" Farrell said, shuffling along last

in line. "He just *died*! He's gone! Like that: completely snuffed out."

Farrell's voice was wracked with sobs and his words trailed off to a whimper. I motioned with a hand to stay low to the floor. *Got to stay hidden.*

From the corner of my eye, I glimpsed Ray's tortured body. He lay like some bizarre marionette, caught in the metal bones of the ruptured Shard hull. His suit was slashed with bloody holes, stained black by boomer-fire.

"Don't look back the way we came," I ordered. "Just focus on getting out of here alive. Stay behind this ridge. We need to find how many of them there are and work on a plan to get back to the crawler."

Farrell snivelled in response, but froze where he was, still several metres from the ridge. More boomers sounded overhead. Flecks of bio-matter pitted the ground nearby. Kellerman signalled for Farrell to follow him.

"You said that you checked the radio mast, Farrell!" he hissed. "You're an idiot! You led them right to us!"

"I did check it! I checked it. I – I'm sure I checked it, on last rotation of that crawler. I ran diagnostics on the mast unit last time it went out."

"Not last time it went out – *this* time!" Kellerman spat the words. "Last rotation was two weeks ago. That crawler should have been checked today."

"It doesn't need checking that often," Farrell said. His voice was weak: he was having trouble convincing himself of the force of his argument, let alone Kellerman.

"You promised me that you had checked it!"

"Well I didn't!" he wailed back.

"Leave it!" I ordered. "This isn't the time for accusations."

More shots hissed overhead. The boomer-fire left red and green trails of colour as it ignited the atmosphere. Kellerman riled beside me; he simply could not leave the issue.

"Christo-damn it!" he ranted, through clenched teeth. He was talking to Farrell. "You *deserve* to die out here. I lost my legs on Ultris due to the incompetence of people like you!"

No time for your shit now, Kellerman, I thought. But there it was: he knew that he'd been on Epsilon Ultris. Why the contrived memory loss earlier in the day? It didn't make sense, but this wasn't the time to deal with that either. I glanced sideways at Kellerman's prone, old body; his face flushed with barely contained rage, lips wet with spittle. He caught my eye, and looked away. *He knows that he has said too much already.*

"How many shooters we got, 'Ski?" I asked.

"Six shooters, tops," Kaminski said.

"Maybe more primary xeno-forms," Blake whispered.

I knew exactly what the Krell would do: pin us down here, outside the starship, where we had nowhere to run. They'd suppress us until they could call in reinforcements, and circle round our position. Outflank us, then take our small group apart.

"I'm not staying here!" Farrell suddenly declared. He clambered up the sand ridge before I had a chance to react. His boots dug into the ground clumsily and he fumbled once, twice, as he attempted to climb the bank. I reached up to grab his boot.

"Get back here, Farrell!" I bellowed. "Never mind what caused this. Just get back here and stay down."

Farrell half turned to face me but continued to pull himself up the bank.

"What, and stay out here in this heat? We'll all boil to death faster than you can kill those things. I'm making a run for the crawler."

With an unexpected burst of strength, he twisted his ankle free from my grip. I tried to grab him again, but he was already up the side of the crest. He hauled himself over the edge and grunted with exertion. Then his legs disappeared as he reached the top.

"Get back here!" I yelled, trying to follow him up.

I only saw the region over the bank for a split second.

Farrell was up on his feet, and took a step out of cover. He was panting hard, hauling his old environment suit. The extra weight made him slow and vulnerable. He turned to face the crawler – so distant, still so far from where we were trapped – and took another step, head lowered in determination.

"*Get the fuck down!*" I shouted.

Stinger fire came from the area behind the crawler – an elevated position that overlooked the entire crater. There were at least six – Kaminski had been right. Three or four shots tore into Farrell.

I'd studied Krell weapons in detail. Seen all manner of bio-weaponry; from flamers grown on limbs to living ammunition designed to hollow a man out from the inside. The stinger was the most common Krell weapon – a simple biological projectile thrower, loaded with hollow flechette rounds. Those stinger-spines carried an explosive charge, but were also poison-filled. Designed to disable, to debilitate.

The first stinger pierced his abdomen; the others were aimed at his legs. He collapsed, managing a stifled cry. His suit burst open and spilled precious blood. He spun sideways, away from the ridge, and tumbled to a stop several metres from our position: cleanly pinned to the floor by stinger-spines.

The other shooters aimed for us. Boomer-fire whistled past me, and I ducked back. Kaminski and Blake did the same, hugging the ridge.

But Farrell wasn't dead. He screamed, clearly enough that I could understand he was in excruciating pain. He literally wailed. The sound was barely human, but it was just possible to make out words.

"Christo – please no! I – have – had a *son*! Please – not like this. S-someone, please – s-s-s-someone help me. F-fuck! So – hurt – so bad."

I didn't know Farrell, but as a fellow member of the human race, it was impossible not to be affected by his pleading. He might well have doomed the whole expedition, but it didn't mean that he deserved to die like this. *No one* deserved to die like this.

"We – didn't mean to…" He choked. "Sh-shouldn't have – please, help m-m-me!"

I felt the sand against my gloves: hot, unforgiving.

"Should we help him?" Kellerman asked.

I wanted to. I really wanted to – even if only to put a round in his head, to stop his pain. That would be a mercy. But the crater was covered by Krell snipers, and to get into range would expose the rest of the expedition to the same fate.

I shook my head. "He's finished."

We waited for a few minutes. The Krell sounded one or two warning shots, to keep us down. After what had happened to Farrell none of Kellerman's men tried to move from the position.

Farrell's screaming went on and began to sound wet. The pleading became more desperate. He was shouting a name, I think, but I couldn't hear him properly any more. I set my jaw, tried to filter out the noise.

"They didn't want to kill him," Deacon said, to no one in particular. "They wanted to hurt him."

I nodded.

I didn't know what biological atrocity was loaded into the stinger ammunition. I never knew: it always seemed to be something different. Sometimes the stingers burnt – corrosives, acid in the blood. Other times they carried slowing agents, complex venomous compounds. Always painful, rarely fast acting. I'd felt that same sensation in my own body, too many times. *My simulated body*, I reminded myself. Farrell eventually gasped for breath. The stinger poison was spreading all over his body now. Organs, skin, heart. I forced my eyes shut, felt a cold sweat forming on my brow. His screams were horrifying.

"Farrell was right about one thing," I said. "We need to get back to the crawler. It will get hot out here. Then when dusk falls, it'll be cold – real cold. When those suns set, the temperature is going to plummet."

"If we're exposed for more than a couple of hours after sunset, hypothermia is inevitable," Kellerman said.

"Then how long until sunset?" I asked.

"Six hours," Deacon said. "Give or take."

"That'll be plenty of time. Give me the rifles."

Deacon unquestioningly shuffled across to where I lay and offered me the rifle from his back. I took the gun and turned it over in my gloved hands. The environment suit I wore was not for combat – the gloves were old and heavily padded – and neither was the gun modified for use in a suit. I was going to be clumsy and slow. *And even slower in your own body*, a voice persisted in my head. I checked the digital display – one hundred rounds. *This gun will jam in a pinch – I would've under-filled the clip*, I thought. It was an older civilian security model, a carbine made for defence forces. I briefly inspected the weapon mechanism and satisfied myself that the rifle worked. Heavy-duty tape was wrapped around the stock, and the trigger unit was worn.

"You carrying ammo?"

Deacon paused. "There's a whole box of clips back at the crawler."

That isn't going to do us any good out here.

"And the other rifle?"

Deacon passed the second rifle to me. I checked that one as well. It was an ancient Alliance ground-infantry pattern, much older than the first, but in better condition. An antiquated sniper rifle; with a scope and a range-finder device attached to the stock. Longer barrelled than the first rifle, likely better range. Both were solid-shot projectile weapons – inferior to energy weapons like our plasma rifles – but they would have to do.

I looked to Blake and Kaminski. They were both good, fast shots, but this was not a firefight we were trained to undertake. Blake had the marksman award: he'd be the better sniper. I waved him nearer to me and passed him the rifle with the scope.

"I can do this, Cap," he volunteered. "This is a good old rifle. Ruversco 950. A real family heirloom."

He took the gun and ran his hands along the barrel, then looked down the scope back towards the alien ship. I felt a moment of indecision – had Blake actually ever fired a weapon in anger, inside his own body? I swallowed. He had never been to war for real.

"Nice for such an old gun," he said. "Reasonable scope, decent range."

"Make every shot count, Kid. I know that I can trust you." No point in voicing my doubts; I needed Blake to know that I believed in him. I turned to Deacon: "Any grenades, other weapons?"

He shook his head mutely.

"We didn't think we would need any," Kellerman said.

"We'll talk about that later. Blake, suppress the shooters. Flush them out. I'll cover the ridge, then we'll take them out one at a time. They are beyond the crawler, elevated above the crater rim."

Blake nodded. "I can do this, Cap."

He gave me a brittle smile: he was scared shitless. I just nodded. He was a good kid.

I slipped my elbows onto the edge of the sand bank and used a piece of rock as further cover. I propped the rifle in place, just over the lip of the bank. Scanning the crater edges, I took in as much detail as I could. Blake found a post and did the same. Kaminski took up a position between us, acting as spotter.

"We see it, we kill it," I whispered.

"Fuck yeah," Kaminski said.

"The xenos are going to move fast," I continued. "And don't expect them to stop if you hit one." The rifles weren't anti-Krell tech – I hadn't checked the ammo type, but I doubted that it was armour-piercing. I'd have preferred proper AP rounds, explosive-tipped; with the suns creating heat hazing. Even some tracer ammunition. "They might rush us. If they do that, take out as many of them as you can."

"Affirmative," Blake said.

"And when I say they'll move fast, I really *mean* it. Inside the sims, we're evenly matched. Out here, they have the edge."

Nothing stirred across the endless desert. I flagged available cover. Rock formations provided low and hard concealment for the xenos; there was plenty of shadow for any raiding party to move—

"Left flank, three hundred metres!" Kaminski shouted.

I swivelled left, carbine muzzle aimed into the desert. Just a flash of carapace – camouflaged against the alien sand – moving fast between one rocky outcropping and another. It was a primary xeno-form, long-legged and spindly, tail swinging for balance. It built up speed as it covered the distance between the two areas of cover. Became a blur, legs moving so fast.

"Contact!"

The carbine bucked as I fired a volley. At range, the weapon was highly inaccurate. Every shot went wide but the loud report of the weapon caused the alien confusion. The sound bounced off the surrounding structures – a harsh bark – and the creature responded by turning to face us. The eyes were emotionless, scanning for our position. It wore a wetware bio-suit with organic piping covering its back and mouth. Before I could take in any more detail the xeno was moving again.

Blake fired. His rifle muzzle flashed. The shot caught the xeno in the leg. The creature spun backwards. Blake fired again. This time the shot hit home: a single round impacted the alien's head. Punching right through the xeno's armour, exploding its skull. There was a brief blossom of black blood, then the body collapsed out of view.

Threat neutralised.

"Target down," Blake muttered. He licked his lips noisily. "One all."

"Two one, actually. But good job, Kid."

Damn better than I had expected.

Success was short lived. Another xeno broke cover.

"Gun-graft making the same run," Kaminski said.

Head down, the xeno carried a grafted black stinger-rifle. I fired a volley, and it flinched back into cover. *Self-preservation – an unusual reaction from a primary-form.* Maybe they knew that they were as endangered out here as us, and were reluctant to senselessly throw away their number. The xeno's head panned right, looking directly at us.

Blake fired again. The shot clipped a nearby rock. The creature leapt back into cover.

"Down!" I yelled.

Reflexively, Blake and Kaminski obeyed. A concerted barrage of boomer-fire rained overhead. The sand bank absorbed the brunt of the assault. The ground trembled softly with each impact.

A fish head shrieked in the distance. The undulating sound carried in the thin atmosphere and made me cringe. They would be coming for us soon.

Time passed.

Same manoeuvre several times over.

No casualties on either side. My read-out showed twenty-six rounds.

Blake looked tired but he didn't complain. I forced the group to switch off the communicators, tried to remain as low-profile as possible.

"You remember Proxima IV?" I whispered to Blake.

"How could I forget? It was my first mission with the team, my first simulant operation."

"This is just the same. Only colder."

Blake laughed but remained poised, covering the desert from his vantage point. Proxima IV was a jungle world – blisteringly hot both day and night. The memory was burning bright, through the miasma of other sim ops.

"Gavantis Prime," he whispered back to me.

"Yabaris Main," Kaminski said, his voice also low.

"Quebec Station," I added.

"Kavaris Star," said Blake.

We went on for a long time, listing those missions. Listing operations, remembering easier times.

They all had one thing in common: they had ended with death.

The civilians ran out of water first.

Mine was exhausted next.

Then Blake's ran out shortly after.

"Someone could go back into the ship and get Ray's bottle," Kaminski suggested. His voice cracked, throat sounded dry. "Or maybe you could lay down some fire with the rifle, and Deacon and I could drag Farrell's body back."

"I'm not losing either of you out here. That's a negative."

"Let me share out what I have left," Kaminski said.

"See to the civvies first."

Dusk was fast approaching. Helios Primary dipped on the horizon, and Secondary had also begun to set. Three hazy and undersized moons rose overhead, casting a sickly yellow light across the desert. The pain in my injured leg had developed into a deep, plaguing ache. *Maybe Blake is right*, I thought, *and it is infected*. Then I remembered Farrell's tortured body, and I immediately put my own injury to the back of my mind. Couldn't dwell on what wasn't immediate, what wasn't happening in the here and now.

But a thought nagged. Why were the Krell out here? There hadn't been a storm. Intel suggested that the area was clear of a Krell presence. They were supposed to be influenced by the Artefact. Something had gone desperately wrong.

Out in the dark of the alien desert, there was time to ask only one question: *Is this how it ends, this time?*

I couldn't answer that.

My head was throbbing again, and the signal was back.

The ground under me grew increasingly cold. The stifling, dry heat of midday seemed like a distant dream. My wrist-comp indicated, as if I didn't know it already, that night had fallen. The temperature gauge dropped at an alarming rate: negative five degrees Celsius, then negative ten. I began to shake inside the suit.

Civilian piece of shit.

My stomach churned with a real, deep hunger.

I kept the carbine in both hands – poised, ready. I'd been holding the same position for so long that even my arms ached. Except for the occasional warning shot, the Krell hadn't shown themselves or moved on us.

What are they doing? I wondered. *Waiting for*

reinforcements? Waiting for the cold to wear us down? Or hoping to kill us with the occasional burst of stingers and boomers?

It didn't really matter. Whether it was the environment or the Krell that got us, we were dead either way.

After a long wait, Deacon shuffled up beside me. The sand underneath him crunched quietly as he moved.

"We don't have long out here," he said.

I repositioned myself on the bank, watching for movement. The area beyond the ridge was empty and silent. I answered Deacon without taking my eyes off the Krell position.

"I know."

"It's getting too damned cold. If we're going to do this, we should do it now."

He was right. We were running out of time. The cold was growing in my bones, making my muscles ache. I stole a glance down at my wristcomp. *Negative fifteen degrees Celsius.* I needed to rethink the strategy.

"Change of plan," I announced, sliding down the bank.

The rest of the group huddled nearer, shuffling on bellies or crawling on knees. Only Blake held his post.

"These fish heads are playing the long game. They want to flush us out. They know we have limited resources. They know we can only survive out here for so long."

"This isn't usual Krell behaviour," Peters responded. "When we have seen them before – they've rushed us. Sent waves of primary-forms to meet our security forces."

Peters looked like he had been drained of all fluid. His skin was cast matte by the dust and sand. His voice had developed an unpleasant rustle. Just listening to him speak reminded me of how thirsty I was.

Kellerman nodded. "Perhaps these xenos are wary of the Shard craft. They don't want to get too close to it. It's interesting behaviour, to say the least: maybe on some instinctual level, the wreckage repels them."

Can't you just leave it, Kellerman? We're dying out here and all you can think about is your next hypothesis!

Instead, I said: "Whatever their reasons, it doesn't matter. They're a small group, as Kaminski says – there are six of them. We took down one. That leaves five. I'm going to fire another volley into the crater. Blake, you watch my fire and when the Krell react, take down any exposed targets. When they start to return fire, then we move."

There were some vague nods and mutters of agreement.

"I want all of you to limber up. Unlock limbs, shake out the frost. When we start firing, go round the side of the Shard craft. Don't look back. Kaminski, you go with Kellerman and Deacon."

He nodded.

"Blake and I will follow once the return fire starts. Keep to the edge of the ship, then head south across the basin."

"That seems an awfully long way," one of the

researchers said. "Can't someone make the run and bring the crawler back?"

I sighed. This was not a plan, and I knew it: this was a suicide run. I remembered my last suicide run. The *New Haven* felt like a different life. *That's because it was; and don't forget that you died on that last run.* I didn't want to explain to the woman that the distance between the crater edge and the sand-crawler was going to be too far for all of us to make it. Or worst of all, that by having multiple targets running for the crawler, we were at least increasing the chances that one of us would get away. No, all of that would be too morale-destroying to reveal, and I needed the group to stay focused.

And so, I said: "It will be easier if we all move together. If the Krell try to swarm our position, we can use the rifles."

She nodded, at least superficially content with my answer.

"What about the doctor?" Peters asked.

"One of you will have to help him."

Kellerman's face immediately reddened. Even now, facing death, he was still obstinate and belligerent.

"I have adequate mobility," he murmured.

"No, you don't. Just this once, let your people help. It's a long way back, and I'm not going to leave anyone out here. If you don't want your researchers or Deacon to help, then Kaminski can do it."

Kellerman glared at me with slitted eyes – glints of white in the darkness. *I'm trying to get us out of here alive, you asshole!* There was such intense resentment in his face. But he didn't say anything, and as far as I was concerned the matter was resolved.

"Communicators on," I said. "Just in case." Then, as an afterthought – almost forgotten among the chaos of the ambush: "Who has the Key?"

Dolan, the female researcher, bobbed her head. "I do. It's safe."

"Keep it that way."

I moved back up the bank, using some rocks for purchase, and readied myself. The rifle ammo counter displayed a warning sign, indicating low ammo. Beside me, Blake got comfortable and cycled the loader of his rifle. Kaminski scurried further down the bank and remained in cover. The rest of the civilians, with Deacon and Kellerman, had taken my instruction and were flexing arms and legs.

"You ready for this?" I asked Blake.

He gave a slight smile. "Always ready. I didn't get that badge for nothing."

"You pull this off, and I'll see to it that you get another one."

"I'm not so sure badges and medals matter to me any more."

"Whoever said anything about a medal?"

We laughed, low and meaningless. The laughter of men who know that their time could be up. I closed my eyes for a second, felt my pulse racing. Deacon was right: it was now or never.

"Do it!"

Then we were up. I fired my carbine into the

desert. Short, controlled bursts. Two, three, flashes of black, as Krell exposed themselves to take shots back at us. Blake was at my flank and fired his rifle smoothly. There was a flash and a target vanished.

"Go, go!" I yelled.

Kaminski moved, shouting orders of his own. I concentrated on my fire, and only half registered the progress of the group.

"Left rock, on the crater edge!" I shouted.

Blake swivelled his rifle. He spat rounds into the position. Another Krell went down, sprayed across a rock. Then two more popped out of cover, their shimmering eyes just visible.

"Got one!" Blake declared.

My carbine shook. The barrel heated with overuse, steam rising into the air. That might have been my imagination, or maybe my pathological need for some heat. I paused, eager not to expend more ammo than necessary. Blake fired again and again—

Boomer-fire shrieked past our position, setting the atmosphere alight. Rounds impacted all around us.

"Down, down!"

Blake went to sink beneath the ridge—

A Krell stinger span past his head, and he ducked sideways. Too slow. Another, probably accounting for his response to the first, impacted with his shoulder.

For a long moment, Blake didn't react. He was frozen in disbelief.

Then he slipped backwards down the bank. I

lowered my rifle and caught him. He started to scream.

"It's okay!" I mumbled. "It's okay!"

I knew that it wasn't.

Blake had taken a sound stinger impact to his right shoulder. An ammo-splinter of black bone, coated in caustic gel, poked out from his body. The round had pierced right through his suit; and through the tear in the suit, I saw blood and human bone. He abruptly stopped screaming and started to hyperventilate.

His face was deadly pale. I knew that his pain management would kick in soon. After all, he had been here before: only in another body. He'd been trained to deal with this sort of agony, trained how to ride it to stay operational. He ground his teeth against it, his eyes bulging. He shuddered in my arms.

"Man down!" I shouted, although not quite sure at who or even why I was shouting it. There was no one to help us out here, not now or ever. *Shit – this can't be happening! Not Blake. Not the Kid.*

"They got me," he muttered. His voice was already distant and there were flecks of blood on his lips.

"It'll be okay," I said. Again, the lie came easily.

It was only then that I realised Kaminski was trying to reach me – his voice becoming increasingly demanding over the communicator. I must've phased him out, so focused on Blake, because suddenly he was yelling. I fumbled with the bead, positioning it in my ear. I looked down the ridge, towards Kaminski and the rest of the group. They had reached the far end of the sand bank, and were about to break cover to make the last dash towards the crawler. Kaminski was at the head of the group, keeping low, indicating to the rest to copy him.

"What's happening?" he insisted.

"Blake's down," I answered. The words were final, irrevocable. "Kaminski, I need you to get to the crawler. Break out the medical kit. Sweep back down towards the ship. Get Deacon to lay down suppressing fire with whatever gear he has aboard the transport."

Blake grunted and tried to prop himself up, still holding the rifle. He shook his head.

"That's a negative," he said. He coughed hard, spitting up blood. "Just follow them. I'll hold the fort while you're gone."

"I'm not going without you, Blake. Kaminski, execute those orders and move now."

Kaminski nodded – visible only as a tiny figure at the far end of the ruined Shard ship. But Blake held up his hand.

"Belay that order, Kaminski," he said, using his communicator and a good deal of his available strength. "Don't bring the crawler back. Just move. Cap – please go with him."

"I'm not leaving you out here!"

"It's okay," Blake said. "It's okay. None of it's real. We'll wake up in the tanks. I promise you that."

"I'm not leaving you! We'll go back to the crawler and—"

"*Just go*," Blake said, a powerful edge developing

to his voice. He coughed again and righted himself a little more. "I'll use whatever I have left in this rifle to give you some covering fire."

He struggled with something around his neck, then passed it to me. His biometric dog-tags. With monumental effort, Blake pulled his forearm up and checked his wrist-computer. The model was old and worn out, and blood-stained now. The display blinked erratically.

"My oxygen tank is half-full. Remember what Deacon told us? If it breaches, it'll go up. Help me to put it on my chest."

"No – just sit tight. That's an *order*!"

"I'll only do it on my own if you don't… help…me."

He tried to disconnect the tank hose, his fingers fumbling with the release mechanism. He really couldn't do it on his own. Ephemeral wisps of smoke were starting to rise from Blake's wound.

"You don't have to do this."

"My choice, Captain. Now, please…help…me."

Reluctantly, I unstrapped the oxygen processor from his back. Unclipped the hosing.

"That's it," he said.

He clutched the tank to his chest and repositioned the rifle. It was awkward and difficult, but I realised what Blake was going to do.

"If they get near to me, I'll blow the tank," Blake said. "Take out…as…many of them as I can. Rookie mistake to get shot…in…the first place."

I nodded, utterly numbed.

"I'll see you on the other side," he said to me. Those words: they had a different, more poignant meaning now. "Give my t-t-tags to my folks."

"Anything you want, Blake."

"Now, just go."

He got ready to aim his rifle, but nodded back towards Kaminski. He waited at the very edge of the bank, the civilians in an orderly line behind him.

"Take care of Jenkins for me, Kaminski," Blake said, over the communicator. His voice was wet and gravelly. "Make sure she stays in check. And one more thing: I'm…tw-tw-tw-twenty-three standard years."

Kaminski nodded. "Be seeing you, Blake."

Then Blake was up on the ridge again, hunting for targets.

I had watched Michael Blake die thirty-seven times. I had been with Kaminski, Jenkins, the rest of my squad, and seen and heard all of them die. But this was different. This was real; not simulated. This was happening to Blake, not some distant flesh copy. I hated myself for not being able to help him. This would be his last death. As I took one final look at Blake's dying body – the only one that he had left – something perceptibly died inside of me as well.

I was empty. So cold inside and out, that I had nothing left to give.

I stooped, moving as fast as I could towards Kaminski. My legs screamed with the effort and I yelled to Kaminski to just move.

* * *

Ahead of me, Kaminski leapt between broken areas of terrain. He herded on the civvies. Deacon had his arm around Kellerman, kept the old man moving. The researchers did their best to keep up.

My progress was slower. Every injury that I'd experienced over the last couple of days descended on me, with a vengeance. I ground my teeth as I took another step, pain exploding in my leg.

Through the swirling, dust-ridden wind, I made out the hulking black shape of the crawler. The Krell nest was to my right, up on the crater edge. They had camped behind a collection of boulders and were using the hard cover to move as quickly as possible into the crater.

Blake continued firing somewhere behind me, although far less often. In contrast, the return fire from the Krell was becoming more ferocious, more concerted. Whenever Blake rested, I glimpsed the Krell descending another level into the crater. The fish heads were absolutely focused on Blake.

I paused for a second, gasping to catch my breath, and checked by wrist-comp. By now, I was well out of communicator range with Blake, so instead I babbled commands at the rest of the group.

"Keep going!" I shouted at Kaminski.

He never paused, never questioned me.

The sand-crawler was ahead. The gun-bot was in pieces nearby, blackened with corrosive Krell ammo.

"Kaminski – get everyone onboard and power up the engine!"

We were suddenly at the crawler entrance hatch, and I drove the others inside. The sky behind us was alight with blues and reds: boomer-fire rained down on Blake.

"Start this thing up. We're going back for Blake."

"Affirmative, Cap," Kaminski shouted. He was in the driver cab, powering up dormant systems.

Deacon slammed shut the hatch, sealing us in. The transport hummed to life. Kellerman grappled with ammo crates and scattered clips across the cabin floor.

"Take us right down into the crater. Deacon, get armed and keep the hatch covered. When we reach Blake, cover me. I'll go outside and retrieve him."

I stumbled into the driver cab, activating the secondary systems. *Too slow, too slow – got to get down there.* The crawler started to move off, jerkily at first as Kaminski tested the controls. The vehicle had a basic sensor-suite, and I activated that too. Hot signals appeared all around us.

"We got Krell on the six," I muttered, looking out of the view-screen ahead. "Let's make this fast and—"

"Christo," Kaminski whispered. "Oh Christo."

There was a momentary flash outside, from Blake's position. Inside the crawler, I couldn't hear the explosion, but I knew that it was considerable.

Kaminski brought the crawler to a stop. He just stared ahead, into the swirling darkness outside.

The sensor began a steadier, more hostile chiming. *They're coming for us.* My head swam, and I lurched up and out of the cab.

"I do hope that the explosion has not damaged the Shard starship," one of the researchers said.

It took some serious self-restraint not to react to that. I held myself in check, fixed my eyes on the view-screen. Kellerman had no such qualms.

"Have some respect for Christo's sake!" he shouted.

Kellerman reeled across the crawler cabin, with indomitable force. The exo-suit servos screamed as he pulled back his hand, and landed a single back-handed blow across the researcher's face. The woman flew backwards, hand to her cheek, but made no sound. A streak of blood landed on the cabin floor; pure red.

No one came to help the female researcher. She was wide-eyed, staring up at Kellerman. He flexed his machine-assisted hand, the hand that he had used to strike the woman, and just stood there: furious, fuming, lips peeled.

"Have some damned respect," he repeated, now in a breathy whisper.

"I – I'm sorry," the woman stammered.

"Leave it, Kellerman," I said, pulling his arm.

I couldn't deal with this now. Blake was gone! This wasn't the time to mediate these fanatics.

Something struck the outside of the crawler. The same tech who had been the subject of Kellerman's anger began to whimper. The sensor was trilling.

"Cap – we've got to pull out," Kaminski said. "Unless – unless we want to end up the same way."

Something screamed outside.

Fuck it!

"Do it, Kaminski. Get us out of here."

* * *

The return journey passed in silence. The dark outside was thick and impenetrable, and Deacon assisted Kaminski in plotting the route back. Kellerman's people sat in a dazed stupor – in equal parts awed and horrified. Horrified by the idea of being ambushed by the Krell, awed by their leader's earlier outburst.

Someone suggested that we might sit out the night, buckle down in the crawler until sunrise, but that idea was quickly dismissed. No one wanted to be stuck out in the dark with the Krell.

I didn't have the strength – mental or physical – to do anything to help. I broke out a water flask and drank from it, but the lukewarm fluid did nothing to satisfy my thirst.

Everything feels wrong.

Blake had become an irreplaceable member of my team. His loss would be felt by all of us. He had died because of me, because I'd led us out into the Maelstrom.

"Just add his name to the butcher's bill," I said to myself.

Everything had been taken from me. I wanted to stir my anger, my hatred of the Krell, but I couldn't even muster that. It was simply too much for my crude senses to properly comprehend. That emptiness I had experienced after Blake went down threatened to overwhelm me, engulf me.

Kellerman sat across from me in the passenger cabin, slumped in one of the seats. It had taken hours for his demeanour to soften, for that wrath to dissipate. Maybe he was angry with me for suggesting he accept some help, back in the crater, or maybe because I had intervened to stop him striking his researcher. She sat alone in one corner of the cabin, cradling her jaw. It had already swollen and turned a pained black-blue. For a long while Kellerman and I sat in silence; I wasn't eager for conversation. I didn't really care what he thought of me, whether he was angry with me or not.

"I don't know my own strength sometimes, in this suit," Kellerman finally said. His voice was barely more than a murmur. "I didn't mean for you to see that."

I didn't reply. Too much to think about, too many ghosts. *Would he have killed her?* I wondered. He certainly looked like he might've hit her again. The exo was clumsy and ungainly, but he had vastly increased strength inside the thing. Maybe that was something to note. There was an expectant air between us; as though Kellerman suddenly wanted to talk, to get something off his chest.

"I lost my legs on Epsilon Ultris," he said. "The memory is so painful. I try to forget about what happened. It's not easy. Sometimes it's easier to pretend that I was never there."

"Whatever," I said. I didn't care any more.

Kellerman added, abruptly: "I'm sure that your colleague was a worthy soldier, and that he will not be forgotten."

"You didn't know him."

We sat in semi-darkness and I could just make out the pale moon of Kellerman's face. He gave me a curt nod.

"You were very interested in the planetarium, back on the Shard ship. Why was that?"

"Something that happened to me, a long time ago."

I'd felt hope for the first time in too long. I could follow her. I could find her. Her face, her voice, just *her*: it was impossible to put her out of my mind.

But hope was also a terrible thing. It had cost me Blake. I felt such a mixture of emotions that it literally exhausted me. With intense guilt, I looked over at the crate housing the Key. It sat undamaged, innocuous, on one of the empty passenger seats. Power emanated from that sealed crate. I couldn't allow myself to feel excitement, to feel pleasure at this discovery. Those emotions were alien to me. I didn't *deserve* to feel those things.

"When we get back to the station, I want that star-data," I said. If it wasn't given freely, then I would take it.

Kellerman nodded. "And you shall have it."

"You know what the Artefact is, don't you, Kellerman?"

Now it was Kellerman's turn to sit in silence. He rubbed a gloved hand across his chin, pulled a face as though he was in deep thought.

"I do," he slowly proclaimed. "I've known for a long time."

"Then tell me. I lost a good man out there today, and I deserve to know."

"It's a beacon," he said. Still so reluctant to reveal what he knew, still the guardian of secret knowledge. The man disgusted me. "The mechanics remain unclear, but I'm learning. A deep-space beacon, capable of sending a signal across the Maelstrom."

"A neutrino signal?"

"Probably not. This is something different. It's far more advanced. It can be detected in the same way, but the signal is something else. Something that we don't yet understand. There's something hidden inside the signal, another broadcast method that the Shard relied upon. Our science is fallible – it can't explain everything."

"Command told me that it had been heard from several star systems away, not the whole Maelstrom."

"That is where the Key comes in. The Artefact is not fully operational. There is a power source, somewhere inside or beneath the structure. We have detected it via our comms satellite. The Key will activate the Artefact – broadcast the signal across the entire region. Enable other ships – Shard, maybe human – to use the Artefact's transmission as a Q-jump point. Imagine a lantern, visible to those who care to look for it."

His face illuminated again, and I saw that instantaneous change of mood that seemed to have become the man's defining feature. He flashed me a rare smile.

"What about the Krell?" I asked.

"What of them? The Artefact's signal is strong enough to draw them here when it is not even at full power. It is already nearly disabling for them. Now imagine what the Artefact would do to them at full power."

I found myself – involuntarily – nodding along

with Kellerman. It would surely destroy them – override the Collective, send them over the edge into madness. A whole world of Krell, destroyed in one fell blow. Maybe more than a world, maybe a star system—

Like all deadly viruses, his fervour was infectious.

"I know that you hear it as well," Kellerman suddenly said, leaning across the cabin. His face looked especially gaunt.

I wanted to deny it, to lie to Kellerman, but my response came unwillingly: "Sometimes."

"I hear it too. Not everyone is so receptive. My research suggests that the sound is different for each subject. I don't quite understand why. Be warned: it is a mixed blessing. There are *consequences* for those who hear it."

Eventually, Kellerman drifted into a sleep, still propped up in his seat. The exo wasn't made for sitting or resting. Peters carefully placed a blanket over his lower body, breaking open a crate of emergency supplies. The cabin grew quiet.

Everyone has their demons, I considered.

I tried to stay awake. I didn't want to remember any more. But I was so tired, so completely exhausted, that I knew sleep was inevitable. Hours into the journey, I couldn't resist it any longer.

CHAPTER NINETEEN

NOT AN ECHO OF YOU, NOT A SIMULATION OF YOU

Five years ago

We'd been on Azure for three years.

I remember the day too well, with a clarity that I wished dimmed with age, but has instead grown.

Our last day.

I had been operational for three weeks running. By now the Sim Ops Programme had been an unrivalled success and my record of effective missions was unsurpassed. I'd spearheaded a large simulant op out on the Rim; disabled a Krell battleship; rescued the marooned crew of an Alliance space station. The border with the Maelstrom was all-out war, but slowly, so slowly, the Sim Ops Programme was making a difference.

It was a short route between the officers' habs

and the Simulant Operations Centre, but I walked through Fort Rockwell in a sort of daze. My own skin felt uncooperative and unforgiving. The sky overhead was brightening now – pre-dawn light filtering in from the east. Inside the compound, the streets were like a grid, with expected military precision.

I went straight to the base PX. It was open all hours, and I was sure that I would have broken in if it hadn't been. A young-faced Army clerk served me two bottles of Earth-imported Scotch – raising an eyebrow at me as he rang up the total cost.

"Hard night?" the clerk asked, as he wrapped the Scotch bottles and placed them into a brown paper bag. He had a smug look to him, the blush of fresh acne on his forehead.

I nodded. "Something like that. Let me ask; you ever seen real combat?"

"No, sir," he said. His expression froze, eyes dropping to the Sim Ops badge on my lapel.

"So you've never looked down the barrel of a Krell bio-gun, seen the look in a fish head's eyes as it takes you apart?"

The kid swallowed. "No, sir. Not sure I'd want to either."

"Thought so," I said. "Assumption isn't good for you. I've been working. Bet you supposed I was drunk?"

The clerk looked down nervously. "Apologies, sir. I – I didn't realise that you were Sim Ops."

I swiped my unicard and left the store.

Of course, the clerk was right.

* * *

Elena was waiting for me when I got back to the hab.

Our domicile was split over two levels, set into a block with twenty other officer suites. Facing the sunrise: affording a decent view as Tau Centauri rose every day. Elena had chosen it because it was quiet – the opposite end of the base to the main spaceport. Two bedrooms. Although one of those had never been used, logistics hadn't asked us to consider moving.

"Welcome home, Captain Harris," the household AI chirped, as I stumbled inside. "You have sixteen new messages for approval. I can route those to your wrist-comp if you would—"

"Shh!" I hissed. "Keep it down. And I told you to call me Conrad."

"As you wish, Captain," the AI said, voice pitching a little lower but still too loud for this hour of the morning.

"I'm already up, or still up, depending on how you want to look at it," Elena called from the bedroom. Her voice sounded brittle: accusative. "Are you drunk?"

I didn't answer but I stopped by the front door, looked at a mirror set into the wall. I'd asked Elena to take this away plenty of times, and looking into it I remembered exactly why. I was tired, with rings under both eyes, but that wasn't the reason I didn't like the mirror there. It was because I didn't recognise the face looking back at me. Because I didn't *want* to recognise that face any more.

I stalked through the apartment, fetched a glass

tumbler from the galley. Elena had gone silent, hadn't followed me. I didn't immediately know whether that was a good or a bad thing. Had to face the music. I paced into our bedroom.

The window shutters were open, and the room was filled with pale strands of morning light. Individual shafts fell across the chamber, illuminating drifting dust-motes.

"You couldn't sleep?" I asked, vaguely registering that the bed was still made, that Elena was sitting on it rather than in it.

"No," she said, firmly. "I didn't sleep. I waited up for you." She wrung her hands on her lap. That was another of her habits, another of her tells. "You said that you were coming off-duty at twenty-hundred hours. I asked you a question: are you drunk?"

"I've had a drink."

"Where have you been? It's nearly five in the morning."

"So what? I haven't been anywhere." I hoped that this wouldn't be another argument. We had been having too many of those lately, and always over the same things. "Just venting some energy. I'm due shore-leave in two days. Only one more op to go."

Elena wouldn't meet my gaze. She knew that shore-leave meant nothing to me, and I think that it had started to mean less than that to Elena. She sat so rigidly, upright. Dressed in a formal smart-suit, her hair clipped back from her face.

"And what will you do with your shore-leave?" she asked.

"You mean what will *we* do. Look, we'll talk about this later. I'm tired. It's late, or early, or whatever."

I sat the Scotch bottle down on the bedside cabinet, unwrapped it. The cap seal clicked off, and I poured a finger into the glass.

"Are you listening to me?" Elena said. "What's the point of shore-leave? When you're not working, all you ever want to do is work. You'll be consumed by running checks, thinking about your next operational period."

I knocked back the Scotch. Focused on the tri-D caricature on the side of the bottle: a black-and-white dancing cowboy, the words YANKEE MALT. An ashtray on the bedside cabinet literally brimmed with cigarette butts: Elena must have been smoking all night.

"You only ever take minimum downtime between transitions," Elena went on. "And don't think that I haven't seen your psych-evals."

"Those are confidential. Between me and whatever tech—"

"I'm on the Programme, Conrad! I can see whatever I want. And I've accessed your files. I'm not a fool, so please don't take me for one. Your most recent report recommends a year to eighteen months' shore-leave, and a rehabilitation and adjustment course."

Elena had, I suddenly realised, lost weight in the last few weeks. It pained me not to have seen that before now. She had been crying. Her pale skin – always pale, despite the heat – was streaked red. Even then, I didn't want to talk about this – didn't want to do anything except think about that next transition, think about skinning up.

"It's too light in here," I decided. "Those shutters should be closed."

As I passed Elena, I noticed that she was rubbing the ring on her finger. She slid it off smoothly, covering the motion – almost apologetically – with her other hand. That was the ring that I had bought her when she had first followed me out to Azure. I hadn't seen it in months, but the memory of her arrival came flooding back. I stifled it, buried it away. The window shutters adjusted, casting light like energy beams across Elena's legs.

"There is something that I need to tell you," she muttered.

"Can't it wait? I'll have some proper downtime after the next op. Oh-eight-hundred tomorrow. Another battleship raid. Command thinks that this will break the back on the second advance—"

"It *can't* wait," she hissed. "It can't."

I poured another drink and downed it. The warmth in my gullet, spreading to my stomach, from the Scotch, was in stark contrast to the chill growing in my heart. A paralysing realisation hit me: *this isn't just another argument. This is a different and more serious beast.*

Elena sighed and looked away from me – fixing her glassy eyes on a particular spot on the empty wall opposite where she sat. Our hab had taken on a strangely anonymous feel; there were no ornamentations or personal objects left here. *How long has it been this way?* Had I just noticed the change, or had Elena removed them months ago? Even Elena's holo-pictures of home, of Normandy, had been taken off the walls.

"I'm not happy here. I gave up everything to come out here with you. Whatever happened to getting married, settling down, having children?"

"What difference would a marriage contract make to our relationship? You know that we wouldn't get a licence for a child, let alone children. It was just talk. Maybe one day."

"*One day* will be too late!"

"It was all easy talk. You never wanted any of those things, anyway."

"How the hell would you know that? I *did* want those things. And there was a time when you did too." Elena abruptly threw up her hands, becoming animated again. "When did things change?"

I traced the edge of the glass with my index finger. Said nothing. Maybe I could get out of this by just letting her blow off some steam; maybe leave the hab, come back tomorrow—

"We both know when things changed," I said. "And we both know why things changed."

"How many times do I have to tell you?" she continued. Her voice was raised to a shrill pitch and her face had reddened. "Let me spell it out: I did not know. You think I would have hidden that from you?"

We hadn't learnt much from the medics after the terrorist attack. Elena had been two months' pregnant, still in the early stages. Did I blame Elena for our loss? I didn't want to blame her, I really didn't. But I needed *someone* to blame.

"Doesn't matter if you did, because she's gone

now anyway," I blurted, before thinking about the hurt my response would cause.

"What? And you blame me for that?" Elena roared, standing from the bed. "I did not know I was pregnant. There, I've said it. There was nothing that I could do that night."

I slammed the tumbler onto the cabinet top, producing a loud crash. The glass immediately broke with the force of the impact. A shard slit my thumb. *Concentrate on the pain. Pain is good.*

"And there was nothing I could do either. Nothing I could do to save you or her. Do you know how that felt, Elena?"

"Don't you dare use her against me! What would have been different about that night if you had known about it?"

"The bomb – the monorail," I stumbled. "We would never have been on that train. We'd have caught an autocab, sat out the ceremony."

"Bullshit."

"I wanted to make a difference. I wanted to make this place safe for you—"

"You're a war junky," Elena proclaimed, stabbing a finger into my chest. "And if you can't get over what happened that night, then how will I? I've given up everything for you. For what? Check your personnel file: over the last twelve months, you've spent more time in a Christo-damned simulant than your real body. You're never here. Always out there – in the Maelstrom – fighting a war we'll never win. At least, not like this."

She was shaking.

Just let her vent, I repeated to myself. *She'll get over it. We'll sort this out tomorrow—*

"When you're here, all you want is to be back out *there*! And when you are *there*, you are alive! I've lost you to the war. I can't face that any more. I'm leaving."

I was silent. There was no intelligent answer that I could give. The voice in my head, telling me that this could be resolved, had suddenly and irrevocably silenced.

"I've decided to take up a long-term placement on a new project," Elena said. Her words tumbled out as though she was reading from a script: I could tell that she had practised this, had worked on it, for some time. "I'm going to be a shipboard psychiatrist for a new Alliance initiative."

"All right. Do that if you need to, and then come back—"

"It isn't that straightforward."

"If it's local space, even with the dilation you can be back in a few months. Take the job – it might be good for you."

Of course, I didn't want her to take any such placement. But I was too damned tired to argue, and if it would placate her then maybe it was best.

"You won't like it," Elena said, "but I have to do this."

The firmness in her voice told me that this was not a standard placement at all, that this was something different. Elena sat back on the bed, exactly as she had done before, and fidgeted awkwardly. There was something that she didn't want to tell me.

"The UAS *Endeavour* is going outside of registered space. I'll be gone for a long time."

"Tell me. *Now.*" Panic gripped me.

"I can't. It's classified."

I slammed a fist into the wall; the pain in my knuckles suddenly felt good.

"Tell me. You owe me that much."

She swallowed, ran her tongue over her teeth. "The Alliance is seeking a truce with the Krell. A Treaty. There has been communication between Command and senior members of the Krell Collective—"

"You want to make peace with those monstrosities?" I shouted.

"I'm sorry that I ever drafted you into this. The Programme has destroyed you!" Elena shouted back. "You're never happy unless you are in a sim. I need you. I *needed* you. I need to be with you. Not an echo of you, not a simulation of you!"

I slammed the same fist into the wall. Where it struck, I left a bloody knuckle print.

Elena continued on autopilot, desperate to tell me the details of the scheme. "It's highly classified. A delegation of human staff will be meeting with the Krell in an effort to establish a Quarantine Zone – between the Maelstrom and us. The team will require a long-term psychiatrist to evaluate performance while away from the Core Systems. I applied for the job and got it."

The words wounded me like knives. Every syllable a gut-punch, every sentence a gunshot. Anger overrode any logical thought process, obliterated neural pathways.

"It's a promotion for me," she said, tears streaming down her face. "I'll be in the Maelstrom for a year, objective, but possibly much longer. Then the team will return to the Core Systems. The project will be unveiled publicly very soon. It will be a huge step for all of us."

"We will never have peace with the Krell. Mark my words. You walk out that door, it will be the last time I see you. I can promise you that."

Elena hung her head, but her decision had already been made. I watched, seething with anger and hurt and pain, as she clutched a carry-all. She brushed past me, and I smelt her scent, felt the touch of her hair against my face. She slowly and deliberately dropped the ring onto the bedside cabinet.

She looked back at me once, then she was gone.

I took both bottles of Scotch and went straight to the Simulant Operations Centre. I got in easily, and found it deserted. Still several hours until the morning shift commenced, and I had the place to myself.

The ops room was dark and cold. I deliberately seated myself, facing the empty simulator-tanks. The inert sims were behind me, watching on with hooded eyes.

Then I drank straight from the Scotch bottle. Lapped up the harsh, smoky liquid. Swigged it down, voraciously. Spilled spirit over my hand, winced as the alcohol hit the broken skin.

I screamed as loud as I could. I flung the bottle against my simulator-tank. Watched as it shattered, spraying liquid and glass fragments across the floor. I took off my boots, felt the glass biting into the soles of my feet. It was so good to *feel* something.

I was in agony, inside and out. The woman I loved had been taken from me, and there hadn't been a damned thing that I could do to stop it. Not a Christo-damned thing.

How can you miss something that you never even knew that you had? I asked myself, as I swilled down the second bottle of Scotch.

The child. *My child.* Gone, taken from Elena and me by a bomb probably not meant for us. I raged again, throwing myself against the simulators, bouncing harmlessly off the plastic.

Filled with alcohol and hate, I stripped off my fatigue shirt. It was already stained with blood, useless. I tore back the fabric, tossed it away. Circled the data-ports in my forearms, in my neck, on my chest.

CHAPTER TWENTY

HE'S GONE

We made it back to Helios Station just as the two suns were beginning to rise. For all the expectant anxiety of the research team, there hadn't been any Krell ambush. Just a long, uneventful journey through the desert, with only my memories to occupy me.

I gathered Jenkins, Kaminski and Martinez in the mess hall. I had to do something that I had always dreaded, that I had hoped I would never have to do. This was something I hadn't done since joining Sim Ops. But I was commanding officer and it was my duty to inform them of what had happened. I knew that I would have to do the explaining all over again when we got back to *Liberty Point*.

Jenkins and Martinez were silent as I gave the account. Kaminski quietly paced behind me, neither adding nor detracting from the report.

"Where is his body?" Jenkins said. I knew that she would take it the worst. "He can't be left out there."

I shook my head and avoided making eye contact with Jenkins. It was too painful to look at her. She was usually so strong – the cornerstone of my squad – but now she was broken. I'd never seen her like this, in the entire time I'd known her.

"We had to retreat. The Krell swarmed his position."

Jenkins' eyes flared with mad, impossible hope.

"Then he might still be out there!" she said. Her voice broke with emotion. "We have to go back. We have to. We never leave anyone behind."

Kaminski banged an open palm down on the table, sighing.

"You weren't there, Jenkins. The Kid is gone. Gone."

"Fuck you, 'Ski!" she roared, standing to face off against him.

"There was nothing we could do. He's gone. He saved the rest of us – took out the Krell with him so that we could get away. As soon as we got back to the crawler, they were all over us. If we had stayed, they would have taken us as well."

"So, you bugged out and left the Kid to deal with it?"

"It wasn't like that at all!" I said, staggering to my feet. I could see where this was going, and I didn't like it one bit.

Jenkins frowned at Kaminski. "Like losing the Kid means anything to you, anyway. You were always messing with him. Are you glad he's gone?"

"This is madness," I said. "Both of you – cut this shit out. Martinez, help me here." I grabbed

Jenkins' arm, pulled her away from the table, but she struggled against me. Martinez jumped to it and placed an arm across Kaminski's chest.

"How can you say that?" Kaminski bellowed. He pushed Martinez away, hard. "I always looked out for the Kid."

"By jibing him about his age? I don't call that looking out for him." Now Jenkins lurched away from me and I wasn't fast enough to catch her. She turned her scathing glare on me, pointed a finger into my face. "And you're no better. You took him out there! No simulant, no guns. What were you thinking?"

"Leave it!" I barked. "I don't want you to say something that you'll regret later. I'm commanding officer of this expedition—"

"What expedition?" Jenkins sneered. "We're trapped on this rock, a simulant team without any simulants, surrounded by fish heads, with a madman in charge. I don't see you doing anything to get us out of this cluster-fuck!"

"What the hell is with you?" I shouted. "There was nothing that we could do. Do you think anything you say can make me feel any worse? I haven't got anything left. I'm done. I don't have anything else to give."

"Fuck you," Jenkins said, through gritted teeth. She set her jaw. The muscles all around her jowl twitched with tension.

"Don't speak to the captain like that," Kaminski said, pushing past Martinez, now moving right into Jenkins' space. "You weren't there, and you don't know what happened—"

"I know *exactly* what Blake went through," Jenkins said, very slowly, very carefully. "I know *exactly* how it would feel to die out there." She looked around the group. "We've all died simulated deaths by boomers, by stingers. Felt that shit in our blood, seen what it can do. Only Blake went through it for real, and he was only a kid. That's on your heads."

Kaminski puffed up his chest and looked from me to Jenkins, then back again. For a terrible moment, I thought that one might hit the other, so high were tensions. I couldn't have that, not on my team.

"Both of you just leave it," I shouted, pushing them apart bodily.

"Whatever," Jenkins replied.

She gave way and backed off from the table. Her eyes were anger-filled, red-hot. She sucked her teeth, then stormed out of the room.

"Fuck you, Jenkins," Kaminski called after her as she went, his words echoing through the empty mess hall.

Just like that, our unit had been torn apart, and would never be the same again.

The following day, we held an informal ceremony in one of the hangar bays. In between time, none of my squad had spoken – right then, I wasn't sure whether the rift between Jenkins and Kaminski was ever going to heal. I was just too damned tired with all of this shit to make an effort myself – thinking beyond our current situation was impossible.

But I ordered everyone to attend, and out of

respect for Blake they did so. Kellerman, Deacon and a handful of other station personnel also appeared, although they made sure to keep a respectful distance.

All this took place in a dingy and utilitarian storage hangar, the building in which we had arrived when Deacon first brought us to the station. Still crammed with exploration and excavation equipment: sand-crawlers, diggers, a couple of enormous fusion-borer machines. Hardly the kind of place for a funeral.

I sealed Blake's combat-armour in a military-grade crate, and Kaminski welded it shut with a hand-held tool. The armour was custom-made for his simulants, and wouldn't do anyone else any good.

Olsen had, of his own initiative, retrieved the sim-bodies that Blake would have used on future operations. They were equally useless to any other operator, only capable of activation by his genetic signature. Taking each tube in turn, Olsen deactivated the life-support systems that kept the sim-bodies in suspension. He triggered the purge cycle on each capsule. We watched silently as the tubes filled with caustic black fluids, anathema to the blue amniotic liquid in which the sims were preserved. For all their military might, the sims did not fight back, did not even squirm, as they died.

Fifteen or so cold faces stared down at the caskets. I knew that I should say something. I barely had the strength for a public speech, so I just said what I felt.

"Let's take a moment. Private First Class Michael

Blake was a respected member of the Simulant Operations Programme. But more than that, he was a good friend. He's irreplaceable. I had the pleasure of knowing him for three years. I wish it could have been longer."

Martinez came to stand beside me, placing a hand on the nearest tank. He put the other up to his chest, over his heart. The gathered copied him.

"Christo Almighty," he started, "watch over my *compadre* as he makes his final journey. And watch over us, too, during these dangerous times. Watch over all of those who would give their lives to the cause, to the continued protection of the Alliance. Remind us not only of the passing of Michael Blake, but of the deceased aboard the UAS *Oregon*: of Captain Atkins, of his officers and crew, of the science team. Allow us to uphold the values of the Constitution of the Alliance. Make us righteous in our indignation against the Krell, against all of Your enemies. Guide us in our bleakest hour so that we might do the right thing, so that we might see the right choice. *La gracia de Dios*. Amen."

"Amen," echoed around the hangar bay.

It wasn't any sort of prayer that I'd ever heard, but it was good enough. Martinez fell silent and bowed his head, paying his final respects to the departed. Jenkins held a salute, tears welling in her eyes but remaining stony-faced.

There was nothing I could say to her to limit her loss. There was nothing I could say to any of them.

"There should be a flag and shit," Martinez eventually added. "You know, over a coffin."

"If we had his body, we could take it back to the *Point*," Jenkins said, accusatively. "There would be a proper ceremony. His folks would want that."

Jenkins didn't know that Blake had wanted out of the Programme. It would do no good to tell her now. *Some things are better left unsaid*, I decided. I closed my eyes and imagined Blake's name on the Memorial Hall wall: just another name eternally etched onto the cold steel. Would his parents visit that spot every year, to commemorate the loss of their son?

"A body doesn't matter," I finally said to Jenkins. "It doesn't matter at all."

Jenkins went to say something, but then decided that it was better not to. The glare that she shot me was enough.

I knew that my words were a lie. I had to grieve Elena, and I had no body to say goodbye to. Was that why I couldn't let go?

Not only that, but *my* body did matter. I hurt all over. My leg seared with pain every step that I took. The activity out in the desert had aggravated my injuries, reinforced the already-present pain from the crash-landing only days ago. I felt old and tired; too tired to watch young men dying under alien suns, too tired to explain to colleagues and friends that their comrades weren't coming home.

Then there was the Artefact's signal. Surely it was just lack of sleep, but the alien whine felt like it was echoing in my head during the day now, as well. *Is it getting worse?* I wondered. There was no one to talk to about it, no one to confide in.

There was no service or ceremony for Ray or Farrell. That I heard, no one even commented on their deaths. It seemed an unspoken conclusion that they had been at fault for what happened. I did wonder if they had partners or family else-where – whether they would be missed – but anger quickly derailed that train of thought.

I considered Deacon's reaction to the ceremony, his head bowed and eyes sullen. He certainly did not seek to detract from the loss of Blake. There was no gloating comparison over the loss of so many of his own officers, as opposed to a single trooper from my team. His security detail, by any reckoning, had been reduced to barely a handful of men. I supposed that when the crew became too few to operate properly, Deacon would ask for staff to assist him from other departments. Even-tually, ground down to an absolute skeleton crew, the station would cease to operate at all. Then Kellerman would have no option but to leave the accursed planet behind; there wouldn't be enough researchers or scientists or technicians to keep him here.

Someone coughed behind me, and I turned to see Tyler standing in the hangar door. She looked almost as discomfited as Deacon: her hair escap-ing from beneath her faded bandana, thin muscled arms crossed over her chest. She gave an embar-rassed smile. We were now on our own in the han-gar bay, I realised. Everyone else had filed out of the room and I had been lost in thought. My hand was still resting on the casket of Blake's dead sim.

"I guess you want to say sorry as well?"

"Not quite. Your squad is out of *Liberty Point*, isn't it?" she asked. "I guess that you are more up to date with current affairs than we are out here."

"I don't feel like talking right now."

But she held her ground, nervous energy prickling around her like an aura. She stood in the shadow of a giant fusion-borer – a tracked vehicle, not unlike a crawler, with a nose terminating in a huge drill-piece. The drill was capped with a thick layer of Helios' sand, but the heating elements – industrial lasers that would burn through even dense rock – had been cleaned.

"I'm a speedball fan," Tyler said, pointing to a faded emblem on her headscarf: SAN-ANG SENTINELS. "I wondered whether you – or maybe one of your team – could let me know how the Sentinels are doing this season? We don't get news updates."

She made me very angry. *A damned speedball team, at a time like this?* I wasn't in any mood to talk with her about sport.

"I know they played in the twenty-two-hundred series – which was, what, three years ago?" she persisted.

"Get your sports updates from someone else."

"You'll miss him, huh?" she suddenly asked.

"Of course I will."

"Happens a lot out here, on Helios. People die. It's what this place does to you. Gets every one of us, in the end."

Her reaction should have made me even angrier – she was a civvie and didn't have any idea what losing someone like Blake meant – but something caused me to pause before responding. Looking into her eyes, my venom seemed to slowly dissipate. Then suddenly the moment – whatever it was – was gone, and Tyler was smiling again.

"Kellerman said to speak with you about using Operations to contact *Liberty Point*," I said. "We want off this rock. He's welcome to whatever he finds down here."

Tyler moved a finger to her lips, so briefly that I barely saw it. Her eyes remained locked on mine.

"Listen, if you want a warmer area of the base, feel free to drop by and see me sometime," she said. "We can talk more sports."

She fidgeted with the toe of her boot on the floor, then shrugged and left. I watched her go, frowning uncertainly at her behaviour. Maybe she was interested in me. I wasn't interested in her, but it had been too long since I'd felt wanted. She was a pretty girl, and I was flattered.

There was something on the floor, written in the dust. Tyler had drawn something.

M11.

Module Eleven. She wanted a meeting. I slid my own foot over the characters, blurring them, and looked about cautiously. The bay was still empty. Tyler had chosen now to approach me and whatever she wanted to say she couldn't say it in front of the rest of the crew. She'd been speaking in code: there was no twenty-two-hundred series for speedball. She was referring to a time.

I stood silently, turning Blake's dog-tags over in my hands, feeling the pressed metal and the embossed biometric chips. I slipped the neck chain over my head, and tucked them inside my fatigues.

There had been so much activity over the last day or so, I'd almost forgotten about using the comms rig in Operations. This was my opportunity to make contact with *Liberty Point* – to get the rest of my squad to safety. I was going to make sure that no one else died on Helios, not on my watch.

My squad languished back at the hab. I didn't explain to the others that Tyler wanted a meeting, and as darkness fell I slipped out. With everyone wrapped in their own private sorrow it was easy enough to get away unnoticed.

Dressed in fatigues and a makeshift facemask, I braved the swirling winds and dropping temperatures. It was approaching twenty-two-hundred hours by the station sleep-cycle. A mixture of fear and excitement lurked in my gut. It finally felt like I was doing something right – for the first time since we had arrived on Helios.

The rest of the station was dark and deserted. I remembered the location of Module Eleven from my reconnaissance aboard the *Oregon*, and I headed straight there. The module security doors were open. *Is this part of Tyler's plan, to get me through the station undetected?* I felt as though I was being guided. Or perhaps *lured*.

Just in case, my Smith & Wesson sidearm was strapped to my leg. The holster was reassuring, and I had already cycled off the safety. No chances out here. I trusted Tyler about as much as I trusted Kellerman.

Glow-globes installed in the walls led the way through a junction. Cabling and pipes lay strewn across the corridor, and the nearest bulkhead security panel had been torn open. It sparked violently for a few seconds, then went dark. I edged past the damaged unit but jumped with a start as it hissed to life again.

The temporary flash of light was enough to illuminate a corridor wall: LIFE-SUPPORT SECTION – T5 TO T8.

There was a muffled step behind me, and I twisted to face the attacker. I reacted as quickly as I could. Someone was on me. My ribs exploded with renewed pain. Rough hands from a second assailant grabbed my jaw. I smelt grease and oil. I brought up my right elbow and smashed it into something hard behind me. There was an encouraging crack as the blow connected with a ribcage or sternum, followed by a pained grunt. The attacker fell backwards. I arched my back, struggling with the second assailant. They fought to hold on, but seemed to pause as the first went down, as though shaken by my reaction.

I took immediate advantage of that. With a single motion, I grabbed the attacker by one arm with both hands. I reached over my right shoulder and pulled hard. The figure sailed over my shoulder – then slipped and crumpled in front of me.

I instantly went for my pistol, unholstering it and bringing it up to fire.

"Harris! Harris! Stop – it's us!"

I looked down at the groaning figure on the floor, and realised that it was a male tech. He was sprawled across a pile of debris, at an entirely uncomfortable angle. He half-rose, rubbing his side with both hands. I turned to look behind me to find Tyler. She had her hands up, defensively, backed against a wall.

"Hell of a welcome. Don't you people know how to just say hello?" I muttered, looking back to the tech.

The man was about the same age as Tyler, with a crop of sandy hair, dressed in a Helios Expedition jumpsuit. The name R FLYNN was printed on his lapel. He winced as he sat up. I reached out my hand to help him, and he slowly took it. Tyler seemed to relax, but only momentarily. She ran back the way that I'd come, and looked down the corridor.

"We're clear," she said, her tone hushed.

"I was trying to stop you from calling out," Flynn said, still rubbing his ribs in an exaggerated fashion. "Tyler, will you be all right down here on your own? I should get back up to Operations."

Tyler nodded. "I think I'll be fine with this old tiger. A little late for introductions, but this is Flynn. He's in on this – we can trust him."

"Less of the old," I said, but the nagging pain in my leg caused by the sudden bout of exertion told otherwise. "And what exactly is *this*? For the record, I'm not in on anything until I say so, and I don't trust either of you."

"I don't blame you," Tyler said. Then, to Flynn: "Go back up to Ops. You can do more for us there anyway. My shift doesn't start for another few hours – cover for me."

Flynn nodded and followed Tyler back up the corridor. She waved him off, then immediately came back.

"Follow me," she said.

Tyler led me into an unlit corridor. It looked like it had either been abandoned or otherwise was in a state of construction. She unholstered a torch from the tool harness around her waist, and periodically shone it into the gloom. We passed darkened, empty chambers, moved through rooms filled with noisy life-support facilities. The background hum of the complicated machinery was deafening at times and the place was unbearably hot. Sticky sweat formed on the back of my neck, made my fatigues cling to my chest.

Just as I felt that I couldn't follow Tyler any longer without some sort of explanation, she stopped. Leaning against a wall, she eyed the section of corridor. Some emergency glow-globes had been installed in the walls and the ceiling was dominated by a series of air-recycling fans. As the enormous blades of each fan lazily turned, they caused the light from the globes to strobe. Tyler's sweaty face glistened in the flashes of light. She looked out of breath and exhausted.

"This is the place," she said. "He won't be able to hear us in here."

"Who won't? Kellerman?"

"Of course – who else? He has the entire station wired. He watches and hears everything. I need to tell someone – to tell you – what has been happening here."

"I'm listening."

"There's no one else I can turn to. Kellerman is a damned maniac."

"All right – then tell me. Start at the beginning: why did the station stop reporting?"

"Kellerman just decided one day that we had

to stop transmitting. It was entirely his decision. I run Ops, for Christo's sake, and he's never explained to me why we stopped. Whatever this planet is, whatever the Artefact and that Shard ship are here for: we're messing with something that none of us understands, him least of all."

"Take your time," I said. I could tell that Tyler was finding this difficult, that she had a lot to tell me and couldn't really decide how to do so.

"I was one of the two thousand and thirty-two original station staff."

"What happened to the others? I asked Kellerman, but he wouldn't give me an answer."

"He threw them away. Spent them. Just like he spent Sara."

She began to pace nervously, occasionally stealing a glance in my direction as if to evaluate my response. I listened to everything she was saying, considering whether I believed her.

"Kellerman is obsessed with the Artefact. He doesn't know what he's doing."

"He told me that it was a beacon, that it can transmit a signal across the Maelstrom. The Shard ship might be a genuine breakthrough. I saw what the researchers uncovered."

"*Everything* and *everyone* could use that beacon for a Q-space jump – Krell, human, maybe even the Shard if they are still out there. Do you want our first contact with another alien species to be fronted by Dr Kellerman? Not only that, but if the effect on the Krell is as Kellerman predicts, then whoever controls the Artefact will have a planet-killer: an instant red-button."

I sighed to myself. Kellerman had shown me some of his research, sure, and his remit on Helios had been to study the Artefact. But his intention to take control of it, for his own purposes, wasn't part of the plan. The idea of a single man, wielding power over the Krell species, terrified me.

"Tell me about the missing personnel," I insisted.

"Kellerman is preoccupied with activating the Artefact. He ordered Sara and the rest of this damned outpost to their deaths."

"Who's Sara?"

"My sister," Tyler said. Her voice was fraught, emotional. "We came to Helios together, when we were kids. Can you imagine? Sara was twenty-one years old and I was twenty-three. We both had degrees in Colonial Tech, and we were invited to apply for the posts by Alliance Command. This was going to be some big adventure – something to tell our children about. We signed official secrets declarations, the whole deal. This thing – the Artefact – was going to be the next big discovery." Tyler let her words hang. "Sara died the year after our arrival."

"I – I think I saw her picture," I said, rubbing my temples. My head was throbbing so badly. "Back in the hab module. It was above one of the bunks."

"That'd be right. Your squad is holed up in her old unit. The whole hab is gone now."

Am I this person? Am I Tyler's saviour? I wasn't sure. All I knew was that I wanted off Helios, and my team off too. Of course, I felt for Tyler – I'd lost Blake out here, just as she had lost Sara – but she wasn't my problem. The tactical situation on Helios had changed dramatically with the crash of the *Oregon*, then again with Blake's death. I had to focus on my own people. Could I leave Tyler out here though? She was in opposition to Kellerman. Maybe that was enough to make her an ally.

"How did it happen?" I asked. I was sure that she was going to tell me anyway.

"Dr Kellerman started to conduct sand-crawler runs right into the Artefact. They began as automated ops – just gun-bots or security-eyes on crawlers. None of them got anywhere near the Artefact. If you've seen it from space, you'll know that it's surrounded by fish heads."

Tyler bit her lip, eyes growing distant. As if she was remembering something too painful to properly focus on.

"You've never seen so many of them. They stretch the desert floor like particles of sand. Primary- secondary- and tertiary-forms. Leaders, gun-grafts and everything in between – all of them driven insane by the Artefact.

"He began to use manned sand-crawlers. Wanted to see how close he could get to the Artefact. Every time a team went out, they would be ordered to get a little closer. Every time they got closer, they would have to fight more and more Krell."

"Why did they agree to go out there, if it was so dangerous? It's obvious that anyone travelling through the desert is going to meet with severe resistance."

"The Artefact doesn't just send the Krell mad.

Staff started losing it. Have you slept well since you came to Helios? I didn't think so."

Fuck. It's happening to me. I swallowed hard. *Don't admit anything. Easier to bury it, pretend it isn't happening.*

"Not everyone is affected. Some get hit by the signal worse than others. For many, it starts and stops with insomnia. For others, the signal means madness. There have been over a hundred suicides on this station. Probably more. Add to that the accidents, and the unexplained disappearances."

This confirmed what Kellerman had told me. It explained why the rest of my team weren't reporting the same symptoms as me. Through some misfortune, I was the only one touched by the madness. *Is this going to get worse? Am I going to descend into insanity, like Kellerman?* If his mania was fuelled by an alien transmission, what were the depths of his ambition? I'd recognised him as dangerous, but this was so much worse.

"Your sister died out in the desert?" I asked. "Like Blake?"

"No," Tyler said, shaking her head. "Under the Artefact, the planet is a honeycomb of tunnels. Maybe natural, maybe created by the Shard. Does it even matter? The tunnels are big enough to drive a sand-crawler through, and they gave Kellerman an idea. He ordered teams into the tunnels, to approach the Artefact from underneath. Sara was on one of the teams. She went into the tunnels willingly. She *wanted* to go; wanted to do this thing for him."

"What did she find?"

"Nothing. The nearer you get to the Artefact, the more powerful its song becomes. We traced her progress via a beacon on the sand-crawler, but we lost radio contact with her unit before they actually made it to the Artefact. By then, everyone on her team had gone mad. I – I stopped listening to their transmission—"

Tyler shook with rage and grief. She wouldn't let herself cry. She just stood, looking at me with big, red-rimmed eyes. I awkwardly put an arm around her shoulder.

"Eventually, the sand-crawler ops stopped because Kellerman ran out of bodies," she concluded.

"All I want is to take my squad back to *Liberty Point*. You can come with us. I just need access to the Operations centre, to send a message back to Command—"

"You think Kellerman will let you do that? He'll never let you leave. Deacon is with him on this."

"So what do you want me to do about it?"

"You and your squad could overthrow him."

I mulled over the suggestion. Tyler stared intently at me as she waited for a response. I had the dread feeling that this would be another decision that I would have to justify back at the *Point*. It wasn't to be taken lightly. Command would need more than the say of the Ops manager. I needed something concrete.

"Please, you have to help me," she whispered. "The Artefact isn't safe in Kellerman's hands. I can give you proof. Kellerman keeps everything in Operations under constant surveillance. He will be watching for me. I don't think he trusts me anyway, but at the moment he doesn't suspect what we are trying to do. Flynn can fool him for a few hours."

"All right," I said. "Let's go."

Tyler was up and waving me to follow her. In the strobing, stop-start light effect created by the fans above, it looked as though she was making jumps in and out of reality. I felt as if I was out of synch with reality as well, but I followed her.

"We have to move quickly. This sector isn't bugged, and I've asked Flynn to knock out surveillance for the silo as well. If we move now, I can show you all the proof you need."

CHAPTER TWENTY-ONE

A SECOND CHANCE

Bent-double against the cold, dusty wind, we dashed across the compound. Tyler appeared to act at random, moving between buildings and taking cover behind battered vehicles. She crouched by a wall, poking only her head around the corner of a junction to evaluate the road ahead. Satisfied with whatever she saw, she waved me on. We stalked to the next intersection and repeated the procedure.

"He has security-eyes on some of the buildings," Tyler said, pointing to the corner of a module ahead. A glossy-black globe dangled from a cable above. "Flynn's temporarily deactivated them, just until we reach the lab."

Tyler led me to an enormous silo. A single gunbot was sprawled like a sleeping dog in front of a double bulkhead. The door was ajar just enough for us to squeeze through.

"Flynn again," Tyler said.

Cautiously, we moved past the bot. I kept my

eyes on it – the machine had more than enough firepower to kill us both – but it remained inert. I paused at the door, and had the sudden and very real feeling that this was the point of no return: that to step across the threshold into the room beyond would change everything. Tyler turned back to look at me, and gave a weak smile.

"This is what I wanted to show you."

There was a huge laboratory inside. I tried to take in as much detail as I could, conscious that at a later time someone would want my account of this moment. Isolation booths, with robotic manipulators, patiently waited for new users. I walked the narrow space between benches dedicated to monitors and holographic displays. The interior of the silo was darkened, lit only by computer screens and sleeping machine terminals. Tyler manually slid the doors shut behind us.

"This is Kellerman's main research facility."

"What's he doing here?"

"See for yourself."

She hit the lights, and one corner of the lab was illuminated by a bank of overhead bulbs. I drifted over in that direction.

The smell hit me like a wall: musky, fishy, rotten. Unmistakable.

There were Krell carcasses everywhere. Pinned to tables, nailed to walls. Tyler moved to the back of the room, into an area filled by enormous Krell skeletons. These specimens had grown huge, with ridged, thorny skulls. Although dead, and even though I'd faced a legion of them in my lifetime, I felt an uncomfortable shiver down my spine.

Tyler activated a metal shutter on one of the lab walls. It smoothly lifted, revealing another chamber beyond. I peered into the shadowy depths.

Oh, fuck!

A Krell sprang from the dark. The creature was an evolved primary-form – body a sleek black, sprinkled with barbed protrusions. Its eyes fixed on me, and it swung its raptorial forearms. I involuntarily recoiled, wincing at the high-pitched squeal the creature made as it attacked.

"Easy, tiger," Tyler said, catching me with an arm around my shoulder. "It'll stop in a moment."

"A little bit of warning next time," I said, composing myself.

The xeno was held in a small plasglass cubicle, barely big enough to contain it, and it harmlessly slammed against the observation window. There were a series of caged cubicles beyond the shutter. Each was filled with a different Krell specimen.

Tyler punched buttons on a nearby control panel. Spotlights, one by one, fell on the cubicles. Several of them were empty.

"The room is shielded," Tyler said. "They won't attract any attention."

"What is he doing with them?" I said, shaking my head. "This is a huge security threat. It's insane."

Kellerman must have risked the lives of his security men to capture these xeno-forms – and was risking the lives of the rest of the station staff by keeping them here.

"I'm honestly not sure," Tyler said, shrugging. "He encrypts his research files. Initially, I think that he was running standard biological response tests. But I haven't been able to get into his research for months, and now I don't know what he is doing with them."

The Krell thrashed in their cages. Most had been tethered with primitive chains. The things were in a killing rage: spitting, slathering, squealing masses of hate. Many had reacted angrily to the spotlights and were swiping ineffectually at the lights overhead.

I drew back from the wall of cages, and took in the rest of the lab. This part of the room was dedicated to a different sort of research. The dirty walls were plastered with images of the Shard starship. Relics lay disassembled on workbenches. When Kellerman – I had no doubt that he was responsible – had exhausted his supply of data-slates and paper, he had taken to scrawling his workings on the wall.

"These are star-maps," I realised, examining the drawings. The more I looked at them, the more familiar they became. "I've seen these before. These are drawings of the planetarium – of the star-data from the Key."

Tyler just shrugged. "I don't know where it came from, but he has lots of data on the Maelstrom—"

"Can you copy the data?"

"I guess so."

That impossible hope filled me again.

"I need you to download Kellerman's research for me – *everything*. I *need* that star-data." I smiled at Tyler, broadly. "I can follow her!"

This is a second chance.

Tyler scowled at me, reminding me of Blake's reaction back in the Shard starship. She didn't know the reason for my excitement, but I would tell her when I could. Maybe she was questioning whether she should trust me – whether I was just as mad as Kellerman.

"Slow down. Downloading Kellerman's research will have to wait. As soon as I start the process, he'll know that we're moving against him. That'll blow everything. Like I said, he has Deacon and security on his side. And anyway, I haven't shown you everything yet."

"It has to be now – I can't wait. I'll explain everything when I can, but that star-data is crucial—"

Ignoring me, Tyler walked over to one of the consoles and hit another button. More lights flashed on, illuminating the rest of the darkened silo. I was still giddy from the prospect of finding Elena—

There was a starship at the back of the silo.

I circled the craft, inspecting it. The ship was small and squat, sitting on landing supports like an insect waiting to take flight. Just the outline of the craft implied menace. She was a highly advanced model and looked to be in almost pristine condition – she certainly hadn't been operated on the surface of Helios for long, if at all, and the metalwork gleamed under the silo lighting.

"Fucking Directorate..." I whispered.

The name *Pride of Ultris* was stencilled in American Standard on the nose, beneath the bridge module, along with some Chinese characters. Those were so fresh that it looked as though the paint might still be wet. An icon had been printed beneath the ship's name; a multi-headed hydra, coiled around a sword.

My blood ran cold. I'd seen it on the train on Azure. The memory was indelible. I'd seen it many times since. Now the Directorate were here, following me across time and space.

"Directorate Special Operations," I muttered. "Deacon told me that he fought on Epsilon Ultris. Kellerman was there as well – that was where he lost his legs."

What's the relevance there? I wondered. *Is that where the Directorate got to Kellerman? Or did he turn because of what happened on Ultris?*

And in that instant, I found myself again. I wasn't empty any more: I was driven, motivated, flooded with anger. I hated Kellerman more than ever. I wanted to destroy him, not just kill him. The memory of Elena sobbing in pain, in the Rockwell Infirmary, threatened to overwhelm me for a moment, and I bit my knuckles to hold back my wrath. I felt, briefly, the Artefact's signal in my head – that pitched whining.

Everything fell into place.

That was the sound I heard, wrapped in the alien static. A sound within a sound – the ringing in my ears after the terrorist attack on the train. That was the sound I heard when the Artefact called to me. The signal was taunting me; reminding me of my failure.

Tyler followed me around the craft.

"You okay?" she asked. "You don't look so well."

I didn't want to explain to her, so I just shook my head. Now I knew that I would help Tyler: now I knew that I *had* to remove Kellerman. I had justification for lethal force. He was an enemy agent, and anyone with him was just as bad.

"I'll do what you're asking, Tyler," I said. "I'll take Kellerman down. But I need the star-data, and we'll need weapons. How many civvies have sided with you?"

"Maybe four."

"We'll need to think this through. We need to plan our escape off-world. My people are soldiers, not pilots. I'm not sure that we could get this starship airborne, let alone off-world. Do you know anyone with flight experience?"

"I'm a trained aerospace pilot," Tyler said, proudly. "Got a Class Eleven flight licence. I learnt at the academy – I've flown commercial tugs."

I nodded and pointed to the engines – a quad of oversized thrusters. "Tugs are different to military ships. She's a T-89 Interceptor. Made for short cross-system jumps, and close ship-to-ship fighting. She has a quantum-space drive, but she'll be slow flying faster than light."

"I just know what buttons to push. And I'm pretty sure that I can fly it off-world."

I raised an eyebrow at her. "Pretty sure, or *sure*?"

"Sure enough." She waved at a bank of missiles racked under one of the stubby wings. "I can take care of the flight, but you and your people will need to do the rest. The weapon systems will be down to you."

I laughed out loud. "They don't make them like this in the Alliance. Those are plasma warheads – twelve of them. That gun under the nose is an H-28 laser cannon."

"Which means?"

"That this ship could take out most of Helios." That was an exaggeration, but the warheads were serious military hardware. "We're talking multi-kilotonne detonations. Real heavy ordnance. The chin gun is an anti-infantry laser – it'll cut men, or Krell, to ribbons."

"Oh, right," Tyler said absently. She obviously wasn't into guns.

"Why does Kellerman need a ship like this?"

"Maybe to get off the planet if things got really bad? Maybe to make sure that the Directorate gets their pound of flesh out of him? It has probably been here since Helios Station was established. I found it a few months ago, but there hasn't been any air traffic like this since we arrived here."

"If Kellerman is so damned obsessed with the Artefact, then why doesn't he just fly over to it and activate the thing? Surely he'd try."

"Kellerman might be mad but he isn't stupid. He has a strong sense of self-preservation. The Artefact is the great unknown. If he uses his own ship to get there, and he's on the away party, then it's his neck on the line. If he sends another party over there, and he stays on Helios Station, he's risking his ride off Helios."

"I suppose so." I took a final lap around the

ship. There was a large crew hatch on the starboard side of the Interceptor, made for ground troops to deploy directly from the belly. "Have you been inside?"

"Once, when I first found it. There are hypersleep capsules, and berths for about twenty crew."

"Then it's definitely our ticket off Helios. There won't be any need to send a signal from Operations – we can use this to escape."

I patted the wing. The metallic compound used in the construction of the ship had a low profile and had been treated with stealth tech. The body of the ship felt reassuringly solid. I was sure that this was the right thing to do, and part of me even longed to confront Kellerman. Was this Martinez's righteous vengeance, filling me? Polluting my blood, making me firm in the face of adversity?

Tyler grimaced. "But you'll still need to take out Kellerman. He has the sky covered. He could shoot us down, as soon as we clear station airspace."

I rounded the curve of the hull. "I promise that I will take care of him—"

"*Shut the fuck up and get down on your knees!*"

The words were shouted with extreme hostility, echoing all around us.

The lights overhead fizzled.

I vaulted towards the lab area – moving before I had properly registered what had happened. *Tyler has set me up*, I instantly decided. *She's double-crossed me.* But then Tyler was screaming, and I heard a punch connect from somewhere behind me. She fell silent.

Security troops were flooding the lab.

"Show me your hands or I will shoot!"

It was Deacon, a shock-rifle jammed into my chest. I brought my gun up, trying to get clearance for a shot.

Deacon was a faster shot than me. He fired his rifle. White lightning lit the room and I collapsed to the floor, juddering and wailing. The rifle had only been set to stun but that was bad enough – 55,00 volts coursed through me. I was paralysed, convulsing uncontrollably. Shock-rifles were security-issue weapons, largely designed to cause non-lethal incapacitation, but that didn't mean being hit by one was a pleasant experience. My pistol dropped from my hand and clattered away from me. I tried to reach for it, tried to override my body's natural reaction to the discharge of the shock-rifle.

"Make sure that he stays down!" someone else barked. Kellerman. Just his voice infuriated me, gave me a new surge of strength—

Deacon was over me again, rifle raised. He snarled – a look of pure determination on his face. I willed my limbs to move, but my pistol was still just out of reach. Deacon lifted his rifle up, and slammed the butt into my temple.

In the space of ten minutes, so much had been promised to me, and yet it had been taken away just as quickly.

CHAPTER TWENTY-TWO

YOU KILLED BLAKE

The dark receded.

I wasn't grateful when it did, because consciousness and pain returned together. Great waves, all over my body.

Then came the questioning, always the questioning.

"How do we activate the simulants?"

"How long before Command sends a response team?"

It was Deacon. I couldn't see anything except vague shapes but I could sense him well enough. His face burning and full of anger, right in front of mine. I smelt his hot breath.

"My name is Captain Conrad Harris, of the Alliance Simulant Operations Programme, Alliance Army," I said. "Serial code 93778."

"Give us answers!"

I repeated my identification information again and again. The words became a mantra; sometimes mingled with shouted denials and screamed protestations. I was fully trained in counter-torture technique. They would not have the pleasure of breaking me. I was a prisoner of war now.

Then the beating started again and pain exploded across my ribs, back and limbs. Hard enough to hurt, but not hard enough to kill. They could have killed me immediately and easily, but I guessed that they wanted me alive.

I spat blood on more than one occasion. My injured leg had developed a deep numbness, beyond pain. *Damn you all. I can take this for ever. I've felt worse.* More ribs were cracked.

"This isn't a military base and you aren't subject to military law. The Doctor can do what he wants with you."

I was dimly aware that others were screaming as well – probably from chambers nearby. I thought that I recognised Jenkins shouting something, although it could've been Martinez. I definitely heard Tyler: screaming so loud that the cries echoed off the walls. She was pleading for the pain to stop. I wished that I could help her.

For a moment, her voice sounded like Elena's. Begging for help, for me to listen. Demanding that I stop her from going into the Maelstrom. I wished that I could help her too.

Blackness came again, and the cycle repeated.

One minute I was in a chair, buckled down by wrist and ankle restraints. The next I was sprawled across a cell floor. The detail might've just been in my head, maybe created by my subconscious to fill in the blanks. I couldn't tell whether the torture lasted for hours or days: time became an irrelevance.

"*Stop it!*" someone finally called out. "*I told you – I want him alive!*"

Kellerman again. Sitting in his chair, at the cell door; a perfect rectangle of white light framing him, piercing the dark of the torture chamber.

Everything stopped when he arrived. Now I could make out Deacon's sweaty face. There were two security men with him, stripped to the waist, bloated with anger and hate. Bare chests all scarred and pocked by their time on Helios.

I laughed but the noise ended with a wet, painful choking that wracked my body. *I'm so cold.* Wetness on my forehead, over my chest. *It's blood. Just blood.*

"He's had enough. Get him cleaned up and restrained. Bring him to my chambers."

I wore a fabric hood over my head, fastened tightly at the neck. Not so harshly that I would suffocate, but tight enough for me to understand my captors meant business. The fabric carried an overpowering stink of fetid blood and dried sweat. The hood had been used lots of times before – others, maybe equally as disloyal to Kellerman, had been in this same position.

Perhaps Tyler got something wrong. Maybe not everyone who went into the tunnels did so of their own free will.

"Take off the hood."

Someone roughly removed the item, and I shook my head free.

We were in Kellerman's room. He sat behind his desk and I sat in front of it – a perverse reconstruction of our meeting just days earlier, with Deacon at my back. This time my wrists were clamped to the arms of the chair. I tried to twist myself free, but cold metal bit into my flesh, and it didn't do any good. One of my eyes was swollen, almost shut, and the other felt bruised. My vision wavered a little – I needed proper medical attention.

"You killed him, Kellerman," I erupted. "You killed Blake!"

Kellerman regarded me coolly, and locked his gnarled fingers. His lack of reaction infuriated me. I growled across the room, tried again to free myself. The chair legs clattered on the floor. Kellerman watched on.

"You killed Blake!" I roared again.

I spat across the room. *See how you like that.* A gobbet of blood-tinged phlegm landed on Kellerman's cheek. Finally, his façade broke, and his face crumpled into a frown. He wiped the spittle away, shaking his dirtied hand disdainfully. Behind me, I heard Deacon jumping into action, the rattle of his shock-rifle coming to aim.

"No need for concern," Kellerman said, holding up a hand. "Captain Harris is angry. Tensions are running high."

"Fuck you! You're a traitor, Kellerman. A Christo-damned Directorate spy!"

"The Directorate presented me with an opportunity."

"You lured us to Helios!"

"Not you specifically. I stopped reporting to Command in the hope that they would send a rescue team. I couldn't afford to lose any more staff, although I still needed bodies – to go into the Artefact. I had no way of knowing that Command would send a simulant team."

"Fuck you!" I raged again. I knew that I was losing what little energy I had left, but I couldn't sit across from this shadow of a man – this traitor – without acting against him. "Blake was only a kid. He didn't deserve to die. Neither did Sara, or any of the others—"

Or Elena, or our child—

"I had hoped to persuade you to help me. It was my intention to scare you with the encounter in the desert. The Krell we faced were experiments, and they were loose in that region at my request – their bio-tech communicators surgically removed. Private Blake's death was unanticipated. Even so, I thought that it would solidify your animosity towards the Krell. Miss Tyler ruined all of that. She forced me to adopt a more direct approach."

I knew, then, that when I next had the opportunity I would kill Kellerman.

"You're mad. You don't know what the Artefact is, or what it is capable of."

"I suppose that was conveyed to you by Miss Tyler?" he said, smoothly. "I've already told you that the Artefact is a beacon, and that the Alliance has known about the Shard for a long time. Both of those things are true. If the Artefact is activated, it will yield access to an untold alien empire – stretched across the Maelstrom. With access to Q-jump points throughout the region, imagine the alien technology that could be salvaged. That is what the Directorate wants, and that is what I am giving them."

"I'm going to fucking kill you! I'm going to take the star-data—"

"The main approach to the Artefact is guarded by an enormous Krell presence," Kellerman said, ignoring my outburst. "I don't think that even your simulants would be able to deal with that level of resistance. Thanks to Miss Tyler, you already know of the tunnels beneath the desert. I have been able to identify a possible path to the Artefact through those tunnels. The simulant team will be ideal to undertake this mission. You will, on my command, follow the identified route and activate the Artefact with the Key."

"You're a fool!" I shot back, grinning at him. "My squad would never help you. You don't even know how to use the simulant technology."

Kellerman's mask of tranquillity did not drop at all. "You and your troopers might be difficult to crack, but Mr Olsen was less so. You are trained soldiers; he is not."

Kellerman turned to a bank of monitors, switching several of them on. My smile faded as images appeared on the tri-D viewers. They showed cells, like that in which I had been held. My squad was detained in one cell, sprawled on the floor, battered and beaten. The images were monotone and grainy, but there were dark pools on the ground – those could only be bloodstains. I felt a burst of relief on seeing them. The team was in bad shape, but they were all alive at least.

The last holo showed Olsen, wringing his

hands nervously, pacing like a caged animal. He looked up at the camera, with bloodshot eyes.

"Mr Olsen will be assisting me. He will ensure that your team makes transition."

Damn Olsen! He was a coward. I'd always known that. His life was a bargaining chip, and he'd sold the rest of us out. His choice didn't surprise me. He was just a different breed to me: he would rather roll over than stand up and fight.

"You stupid fuck, Kellerman! Whatever Olsen told you, the team can't make transition. My simulants were destroyed in the crash! You asked me about that yourself. I can't do what you want me to do, no matter how much you torture or bully—"

Kellerman held up a finger for silence.

"I know that you cannot make transition," he said, whisper-quiet. "But you are still going into the Artefact."

I sat for a moment, considering the suggestion. Not suggestion: order. There was a man with a gun in his hands behind me, and the only authority in light-years of space in front of me.

"You will accompany your team into the Artefact. They will use their simulants, you will not. I will observe from Operations. Despite the close proximity to the Artefact, I anticipate that the simulants will be immune to its transmission. You will be a test subject. You will be escorted into the Artefact itself, by your squad, and you will activate it. We will see how it affects you."

"And what if my team turns on you? What if I refuse to go?" I said, defiantly.

"The real bodies of your squad will remain on

Helios Station. I can execute them from here if necessary. If I understand the simulant technology correctly, this will lead to the loss of the reciprocal simulant. That would be one less simulant to protect you, Captain Harris, as you make your way through Krell-occupied territory."

He swivelled his hover-chair again, turning to the bank of monitors.

"Miss Tyler will also remain in my custody. It won't take much for me to kill her."

A holo showed Tyler sprawled across another cell floor. She had been beaten badly. Bruises had already started to appear on her exposed arms. She was still, silent. At the very least unconscious, maybe dead. I looked from Tyler to Kellerman, and back again.

Just one more person I've let down – not just on Helios, but in life.

No. I wasn't going to let anyone down. Not any more.

"Damn you, Kellerman!" I screamed. "I want that star-data *now*! And if you won't give it to me, I'll damned well take it from you."

Kellerman's face was still. He was a husk of a man. Obsession had taken everything away from him. His half-lidded eyes were dark; like Krell eyes. He cheeks were sullen and hollow. He was nothing but an idea, and his fixation with that idea had become so overwhelming that it had stripped away his national allegiance, his personality, his soul.

"Why do you want the star-data? What is it that drives you?"

Elena's memory burnt bright. At least he didn't know about her. At least she was still *mine. I'm not telling you anything.*

I twisted in my restraints again. This time, the chair turned over and I pitched to the floor with it, hitting my right shoulder. I thrashed, riding out the pain all across my body. Blood filled one eye, but I didn't care.

Kellerman leant over me, completely unimpressed by my display. There was no hint of fear or concern in his eyes.

"If you won't tell me, then I can't help you," he concluded. "That is your choice, but we have more in common than you might think. We can both hear the Artefact's signal. We're both idealists, in our own way." Kellerman righted himself in his chair: now the colonel addressing his troops, the priest attending his flock. "And so I will give you what you want."

I paused in the midst of my rage, of my fury. What did he mean? A fleeting – impossible – hope filled me again. *Elena! I'm so sorry – but I can save you. I can follow you.*

"You will have the honour of carrying the Key. It will activate the Artefact, and it contains the star-data from the Shard wreck."

I breathed hard – fighting to contain my emotions, trying to think of some rational way out of this mess. Was this supposed to make me feel better about doing his dirty work? Encourage me in some way to go through with this?

Kellerman ignored my indecision. "I understand from Mr Olsen that you have a nickname, among your peers: Lazarus. Maybe you will come back from this; perhaps you will be resurrected. Let us hope. I am sure that you are the man for this task." He set his jaw and nodded over at Deacon. "Get him ready for insertion into the sand-crawler."

Deacon pulled the hood back over my head.

CHAPTER TWENTY-THREE

IT CAN'T BE DONE

Three years ago

She had been gone for two years.

A weaselly-eyed bartender sat at one end of the sticky serving counter, and I sat alone at the other. The lights were dimmed and most of the tables empty – awaiting the end of the mining shift. I reckoned that it would be rowdy in here once the time came; it wasn't a place where military folk were welcome. Called "Yankee's Rest", it was a dive, real worn out, frequented by asteroid miners and civilian hauliers. The North American Union flag was draped above the optics on the bar. Seemed like no one had bothered to tell the proprietor that the Union was long gone.

I'd taken a civilian shuttle run from the *Point* to the next inhabited outpost – an asteroid mining station with the catchy title of XV-78. It was such an unpopular destination that no one had bothered to give it a proper name. Maybe no one stayed long enough to name the place: they either went Corewards, back to Alliance space, or took the next Q-jump to the *Point*. I hadn't been here before, and I didn't plan on returning. But O'Neil had suggested that we meet here, and that was enough for me.

Not just O'Neil – Colonel O'Neil. I had to remind myself that he was a colonel now. Head of the entire Sim Ops Programme, second only to Old Man Cole himself. It had taken all of my favours, all of our history together to arrange this meeting.

An old holo-viewer sat above the bar, playing a fresh newscast – the words DIRECT FROM LIB-ERTY POINT FOB scrolled across the flickering screen. The *Point* was close enough that there was barely any time delay on the broadcast.

A civilian newscaster presented a segment on the nightly feed.

"*It has been almost eighteen months since the agreement of the Treaty with the Krell Empire. In what President Francis is calling the most momentous achievement in human history, the Krell Empire is finally at peace with the Alliance.*"

Of course, that wasn't quite true: the peace wasn't complete. There had been the occasional border-skirmish between simulant teams and Krell raiders, but all-out war seemed to have been suspended. I buckled down and did my duty; going where I was told, when I was told.

"*Although Alliance Command has declared the mission a success, it also remains a tremendous human tragedy that the crew of the expedition have not been recovered. Viewers will no doubt recall that there were sixteen starships involved in the extensive operation, including the flagship UAS* Endeavour. *That ship, along with a crew of over five hundred personnel, continued to transmit for a year following arrival within the Maelstrom, but since then nothing has been heard from that fated vessel. The search for the* Endeavour *has officially, as of today, been called off. The crew will be declared MIA – missing in action."*

None of the crew came back. No one knew why, or at least Command weren't willing to explain the disappearance. I had my own, personal theory: that Elena and her crew were expendable and that the Alliance had simply sold them out to the Krell.

I hunkered down at the bar, taking a mouthful of foul-tasting beer from a dirty bottle. I had dressed as inconspicuously as I could – for the first time in months, not in military fatigues, but civilian clothes.

"You like drinking alone?" came a voice from behind me. At the same time, a meaty hand slammed onto my back.

I slowly roused and looked around. My instant reaction was to salute, but O'Neil shot me a glare that told me not to bother.

"Glad that you made it," he said solemnly.

Colonel Patrick O'Neil sat down beside me. He was bigger than me, a few years older too. His face was cratered with scars from decades of active service, and his short greying hair was receding.

He too was dressed in a civilian outfit – a worn leather flight jacket and denim slacks. He looked far more comfortable in civvies than I did; almost like he had a life outside of the military. O'Neil waved at the bartender, flashing a bank note and ordering a beer. The disinterested barman slid a bottle across the bar.

"Tastes like shit, doesn't it?" O'Neil said to me. "You know, the further out from Earth that you get, the worse the beer tastes."

"That a fact? Then I guess that *Liberty Point* has the worst beer of all."

"And XV-78 is a close second," he replied. "How have you been, Conrad?"

"Could be better," I said. I waved up at the holo. "You picked one hell of a day to meet me. Was it deliberate?"

"With all the fanfare at the *Point*, it seemed as good a time as any to get away. Some anonymity, you know? Go somewhere where nobody knows your name."

"I guess you'll be busy, or whatever, with all the interviews and shit. How is the new job working out?"

O'Neil swigged his beer, unwilling to take the bait. He had been in command of Simulant Operations, responsible for sending a dedicated team into the Maelstrom as an escort.

"I know that you authorised the *Endeavour*'s mission," I said. "I imagine Command wants the public onside, after all, and your maverick approach to striking peace with the Krell has paid off."

For everyone, except me.

"Listen," he started, exhaling through his nose, "I provided a military presence."

"And I know that without such a presence, there was no way that Command would've sanctioned the op."

"It wasn't – isn't – that simple."

I nodded. "Never is." I had to rein in my resentment, try not to wear it so blatantly. I didn't want to alienate O'Neil completely. "Thanks for agreeing to see me."

"Christo, you pestered me enough times. How many transitions have you made now?"

I shrugged. "I don't know. Hundred and fifty?"

He guzzled down some more of the beer. "That's more than anyone else on Sim Ops. You're starting to get quite the reputation, Conrad."

"I don't want a reputation," I said, as finally as I could. "I want a favour."

"That so?"

"You know what I want."

O'Neil smiled and laughed, but neither action held any humour. He shook his head and slouched onto the bar, like he was playing the part of an exhausted asteroid miner – back from a long day in the shafts – rather than a colonel in the Alliance Army.

"I know what you want," he said. "I've seen your request for an operation. I've seen your *repeated* mission projections. Your petitions to not just the Army, but the Navy as well."

"I want to go after the UAS *Endeavour*. I want to go after her."

"Dr Elena Marceau was a good woman. A damned good woman. But she fully knew what she was getting herself into when she signed up for that mission."

"Did she? And what did she get herself into, then?" I said, my voice rising involuntarily. Anger made my face flush, and I turned to bore my eyes into O'Neil.

"Dr Elena Marceau will be declared MIA as of this evening. You've seen the broadcasts. Nothing you say or do is going to change that."

"Then why did you agree to meet me?" I asked, standing now, jabbing my finger into his shoulder.

"Because, hard as it may be to accept, I care about you as a friend and as a military colleague. You've been part of Sim Ops from the start, and I value your contribution. But you need to move on. She's gone."

"You could authorise another mission – allow me to insert into the Maelstrom, to properly search for her!"

"I could do no such thing. Old Man Cole himself doesn't have that sort of authority. I know that you won't stop until you have the answer that you want, but it isn't going to happen. Even if we wanted to go after her, we can't."

"What do you mean, we can't? There has to be a way. Those people gave their lives to achieve peace with the Krell, and all Command has done is sell them out."

"Command has done nothing of the sort. Elena knew the risks when she signed up. We have no star-data. Even if we had something reliable, the

Q-jump points are a mystery to us. Her ship went further than any other human vessel has ever gone—"

"We can just follow the *Endeavour* to the rendezvous coordinates," I insisted.

"The *Endeavour* isn't there any more," he countered. "I'm telling you more than I should, but if it will get you off my back then it's worth it. *Endeavour* has gone off the grid. It went somewhere else inside the Maelstrom, but we don't know where."

"Then the crew might still be alive! You know as well as I do that the Krell take prisoners."

"The answer is *no*," O'Neil said. "She's gone. We don't have the ability to track the *Endeavour*. If we had star-data, proper astrocartography, of the Maelstrom, then things might be different. But, quite frankly, I don't see that happening in your lifetime."

"Thanks for nothing, O'Neil."

"You knew my response before you even attended this meeting."

"I'll resign."

"We both know that won't happen. You won't do that, because you can't do that. You're addicted."

I shrank back onto the barstool. O'Neil was right. Elena had been right as well, and now she was gone for ever.

"Go see a psychosurgeon," O'Neil muttered. "I can recommend a good one, non-military, if it helps. Maybe get a mind-wipe – they can do wonders these days, remove selective memories, whatever works. She's ex-Directorate, but helped me out a couple of years back after Sandra left me. Now drink your beer, and we'll catch the next shuttle to the *Point*."

"Fuck that. I'm sure as shit not going to see any Directorate headshrink, and I'm not going anywhere. I don't want to forget!"

"All right, have it your way." He fumbled with something inside his worn leather jacket. "Maybe this will ease your pain." He removed a crumpled envelope and gave it to me, without opening it. "I shouldn't be doing this. But, like I say, you're a friend and a colleague. Maybe this will give you some closure, some peace, for what it's worth."

Then he finished his beer, patted me on the back like we were old buddies, and left the bar.

I stared down at the envelope for a long time before I finally gathered the mental strength to open it. My fingers trembled as I peeled back the plastic sheath.

There was a single sheet inside. It had a military transmission heading, printed with numerous security warnings, restrictions and non-disclosure cautions.

I turned the sheet over in my hands.

Three words, printed. A communication from the UAS *Endeavour*. Now months old, sent from the original coordinates of the ship – the original rendezvous site.

DON'T FORGET ME

The message had been keyed with Elena's biometric imprint. I had no doubt that it was genuine.

It was addressed specifically to me, although she must've known that the communication wasn't private.

I sat there for hours afterwards, and read the message again and again.

CHAPTER TWENTY-FOUR

I AM EXPENDABLE

I imagined what I couldn't see.

A jury-rigged laboratory, crammed with simulator-tanks and other tech salvaged from the med-bay of the *Oregon*. Maybe the same lab that Tyler had shown me: those darkened walls, scrawled with an ancient language no human tongue could ever speak, with knowledge that no human mind should ever possess.

Jenkins was forced into her simulator-tank, thrashing and screaming obscenities at the security team.

Kaminski shouted to Jenkins that it'd be okay, then again to the bastards making them do this that he would be back for them.

Martinez, stoic and calm, biding his time – mumbling a prayer under his breath as he was forced into his tank.

There was no compassion or sympathy for their situation. The security team laughed and jeered as my people were loaded into their tanks. There was the centre of this attention – Dr Kellerman. He grasped the armrests of his hover-chair so tightly that his old knuckles had gone white with the pressure.

"Get them all into the simulators," he barked. "No time to waste. I want those tanks online and the neural-link established."

Olsen anxiously followed instructions. This was not what he was used to; being expected to do things yesterday, being expected to do things with old and used equipment. But the fear of death – what greater motivation is there? – drove him on. His medical smock was filthy and torn, smeared with blood at the neck and shoulder.

The simulators waited patiently. Eventually all operators were sealed inside. None of Kellerman's people paid any attention to the empty simulators – to my simulator, to Blake's simulator. Both tanks sat unused and abandoned, a testament to my failure.

View-screens allowed a visual connection with Operations. The station staff watched on in silent anticipation.

"Good luck," Kellerman said.

"Are all operators ready for connection?" Olsen asked hesitantly.

"All operators are engaged," reported a technician.

"Establishing remote link with the sand-crawler," another said. "Link is good, repeat link is good."

"Are the operators ready for uplink?" asked the chief technician.

Jenkins punched the interior of her tank, giving

Kellerman the finger. He ignored her wasted gesture. Olsen checked each of the tanks in turn, then raised a hand and spoke into his communicator.

"All operators confirm readiness. Commence uplink when you are ready."

"We are good to go, repeat good to go. Commencing uplink in T-minus ten seconds."

I awoke with a start.

I sat in the crew compartment of a sand-crawler, strapped into a seat. A glass-globe helmet on my lap. Inside a battered H-suit, with oversized gloves and another breather tank on my back – the same suit that I had worn into the desert, only a couple of days ago. I flexed my arms and legs, and found that I was no longer restrained. An ugly headache spewed behind my eyes as soon as I moved. Gingerly, I reached up to my brow and found that my injuries had been treated – a medi-pack was taped over my forehead.

Am I alone out here? I suddenly panicked.

But I realised that I wasn't. Two enormous armoured bodies sat opposite me in the passenger cabin, frozen in place. A third sat in the driver's section up front. They too were strapped into seats, but their bodies were far too big for them. These things were not human – these things were beyond human: they were simulants. There was something beautiful and monstrous about them, in equal measure. Skin an alabaster white, almost marble in clarity. Human beings rendered beyond perfect. Impressions of their operators – of Jenkins, Martinez and Kaminski. Seven foot tall, with a musculature that a human body could never support. Perfect for only one purpose, made for war.

I watched as each came to life. In all of my years as a sim operator, I'd never seen simulants coming online like this. Power lights flickered on the interior of shielded face-plates, illuminating the human parodies inside each combat-suit. Those suits were unadorned, undecorated. No one had labelled them, marked them with honour badges or designations.

First there was Jenkins, her arms thrashing as she carried over activity from her real body. Then Kaminski, eyes flickering open as he made transition. Then Martinez, head shaking inside his helmet as he awoke.

I want to be like them, I thought. *I want to escape this tortured body.*

"Sound off!" I said, simply through routine.

I had a personal communicator around my neck and a bead in my ear. Every member of the squad called in, and there were other voices in the background.

"*Confirming transition. We have affirmative on Corporal Jenkins.*"

"*Confirmation on Private Kaminski.*"

"*That's an affirmative on Private Martinez. Transition successful.*"

Jenkins and Kaminski conducted the same ritualistic rundown of their new bodies – stomping feet, lifting limbs. In the driver cab Martinez had already mastered his body, and was over the crawler controls. Kaminski popped his helmet, revealing a caricature of his actual face.

"What the fuck is going on?" he demanded, his voice a mellow sonic boom. He scanned the cabin, his eyes widening as he saw me. "What's happened?"

"I'll live," I groaned back. "We're on a crawler. Kellerman – he wants us to go to the Artefact, and activate it."

"There's no way that we're going through with this," Jenkins screamed. She followed Kaminski's example and removed her helmet, throwing it hard against the cabin wall. "Martinez, turn the crawler around and let's get this over with."

"Jenkins, calm it—!" I started.

The crawler PA system chimed.

"Captain Harris, this is Dr Kellerman. I am speaking on the general squad channel, through the sand-crawler," he said. His voice was crystal-clear; whatever tech his boys had installed in the crawler antenna, it was good enough to filter out the background chatter. "Please do keep your squad in check."

"Go fuck yourself, Kellerman!" Jenkins declared, pushing her face into Kaminski's camera. Each suit was equipped with one, including mine.

"This mission is being recorded, via your combat-suit camera equipment," he went on. "We are receiving real-time video and audio data at Helios Station. Everything is being relayed to me via the sand-crawler comms antenna. The crawler is appropriately equipped for the mission. You will find your weapons in the storage compartments."

"And what's to stop us rolling back to the station and taking you and your security team out?"

Jenkins snarled. "You've obviously never seen what a sim is capable of."

"Captain Harris, please remind your squad that I have their real bodies here. I can execute them."

Jenkins' mask of confidence slipped a little. She looked to me, then back to the camera, suddenly unsure of what she should do. I motioned her to sit down.

"As I have already told you, your survival depends on that of the rest of your squad," Kellerman said. "The Artefact *will* be activated. You will find the Key in the crawler."

A secure storage box sat on the cabin floor; the same box from the expedition to the Shard starship. Without looking, I knew that the Key was inside.

"Fuck this!" Jenkins shouted again.

Her anger was hot and volatile. Mine had cooled. Kellerman probably thought that made me despondent, that my miserable situation made it more likely that I would do as he wished. He was wrong about that: my anger was malleable, and I was going to use it. I glared down at the metal storage box again, thought of what the Key represented: *the star-data*. I was already scheming, considering the limits of Kellerman's surveillance capabilities.

"We have successful transition," I muttered.

"That's more like it," came Kellerman's voice. "We are reading you loud and clear. Your signal indicates that you are leaving the vicinity of the outpost. Be advised that you should have a clear route cross-country for the next few kilometres. Atmospherics projected as optimal between here and the entrance to the tunnels. It looks like the gods are smiling on you."

So I am expendable, I thought.

I reached over to my wrist-computer and cut the two-way connection. In the passenger cabin, I exchanged a meaningful and sombre look with Jenkins and Kaminski. Now the connection to Kellerman and Operations was cut, Jenkins' presentation softened. An impossible sadness crossed her simulated features as she looked down at me. The bodies weren't meant for such depth of emotion; they were sharp instruments, tools of war, and nothing more.

"It's all right. This is just another mission."

"I'm so sorry, Harris," she said. "I really mean it."

I shook my head. "We'll get through this. No more casualties. I promise you that."

Kaminski sighed deeply. "We'll do whatever we can, Cap. We'll protect you."

"That's exactly what Kellerman is counting on." I swallowed involuntarily. "Doesn't look like we have much of a choice. We can't go back to the station – he'll just execute your real bodies."

"And if we do as he wants, and go into the Artefact, then…" Jenkins said, her words trailing off. She didn't need to complete the sentence with *"you're dead."*

"We'll find a way through it. I might not be in a simulant, but I'm still your commanding officer. I want the three of you to stay frosty."

Jenkins and Kaminski nodded unenthusiastically. Martinez looked back from the driver cabin and did the same.

"Now, what have we got on this crawler?" I
asked Martinez.

He flashed an empty smile. "Looks like Kellerman's people have been busy. This thing handles
like a cow, but it has a kick." He slammed a palm
against the ceiling above him. "There are gun-
turrets on the roof. Must've stripped some of those
gun-bots they had on base."

Kaminski motioned to the view-ports on the
flanks of the crawler. "Shielded vision-slits as well.
There's some real heavy-duty metal grilling on the
view-ports. It's more like an armoured personnel
carrier than a crawler."

Will it be enough? I wondered. Whatever shit
Kellerman had stapled to the sand-crawler, it was
still a civvie transport. We were expected to drive
it through Krell-occupied territory. My squad was
dressing it up, trying to make my situation sound
better than it was.

"Are we really going to do as he's asking?"
Martinez said.

I very deliberately nodded. We were still being
watched. "This'll be fine, people. We can just drive
the crawler into the Artefact, activate it, and pull
out. Just keep the chatter to a minimum."

I want him to hear everything I've just said,
I thought. *And I want him to believe it.* I just
needed time to think of a plan. Already, the pieces
were beginning to fall into place. I was going to
make sure that Kellerman paid for everything he
had done out here.

I made conscious eye contact with each of my
squad, and they nodded in turn: they understood

exactly what I was doing. I needed to tell them about the Directorate ship, but not while Kellerman was listening. I was going to make it through this, but not as Kellerman expected. I might be the one going into the tunnels, but he was already dead. He just didn't know it yet.

"We're staying with you all the way," said Kaminski.

"We're lean, mean killing machines," Jenkins added, flashing a destructive grin. "And we're the best damned bodyguards you're ever going to find."

"What's our status, Martinez?" I asked.

"Weapons systems are operational. No targets to track just yet," he called back. "Looks like the crawler navigation system has been loaded with maps for above and below ground."

"How long until we reach the entrance to the cave network?"

"A few hours, tops," Martinez said. "I've just got to follow Kellerman's route."

"Constant scanner sweeps," I ordered. "Weapons prepped and loaded for operation at short notice."

There were grunts of recognition from the squad.

Through the swirling dust, in the empty light of Helios' suns, we made our progress towards the underground caverns.

CHAPTER TWENTY-FIVE

POINT OF NO RETURN

Once we were out of the mountainous region surrounding Helios Station, the barren plains were easily traversed. Despite the squad's constant vigilance, we didn't encounter Krell resistance.

I wandered the cabin, watching the scanner diagnostics and monitoring bio-sensor sweeps. The landscape outside was relentlessly monotonous. The desert was empty. Our only companion was the howl of the angry wind.

That, and the Artefact's song.

"You think this wind could drive a man mad?" Kaminski asked.

"Only if you let it."

Kaminski nodded in agreement. He cradled his M95 rifle across his lap, like a small child. Kellerman had equipped the crawler with a sizeable armoury – all of the salvaged sim-class weaponry. The squad had broken out rifles, handguns, grenades. I looked down at my own hands, felt them trembling inside my gloves. The plasma rifles were far too big for me to carry on a protracted operation, so I'd selected a PPG-13 pistol.

"It never stops though, does it," Kaminski went on. "Think of being out here for ever. The staff here must be sick of the noise."

"It's like screaming," Jenkins pitched in. "Like women and children screaming. Maybe this is the noise of everyone who has died here. Maybe Blake's voice has joined the wind."

Kaminski's face crinkled in disapproval.

"No chance. Blake will be somewhere warm and wet. Just how he likes his women."

Martinez hooted in approval.

"I'm not sure why I put up with this shit," Jenkins said. "Maybe when we get back to the *Point*, I'll apply for a transfer."

The comment wasn't meant seriously, but I immediately thought of Blake's transfer request. *What if his resignation had been accepted before this operation?* He would be well on his way back to the Core Systems, planning the rest of his life. I suppressed the thought, and knew not to raise it with the rest of the squad.

"So the hatchet is buried now?" I asked Kaminski and Jenkins. "Between you two?"

"What hatchet?" Kaminski answered. "I only see guns here."

"Right on, brother," Jenkins said. They fist-bumped with armoured gauntlets, producing a loud thunderclap in the enclosed cabin.

"Glad to see it."

The wind picked up again, and the conversation

was over. I felt an awkward weight from one of the pouches on my suit belt, and opened it.

Inside was my father's pistol, cleaned and ready to use. Ammo clips had been taped to my suit webbing.

"What a thoughtful bastard…" I mused to myself.

Kaminski went up front to monitor progress with Martinez, and I overheard them discussing the route ahead. Jenkins sat opposite me, her sim-body still. She gave me a tired smile, flashing new teeth.

"For what it's worth," said Jenkins, voice barely audible above the churn of the crawler engine, "I know that it wasn't your fault. About Blake, I mean."

"Thanks, Jenkins."

"He was just – you know – so young," she said, fumbling with her words. "I had a brother, once."

"I never get the impression that you want to talk about your family." Other than the occasional mention between operations, Jenkins didn't seem to want to share much about her background with me or the rest of the squad.

She shrugged her enormous armoured shoulders. "Nothing to tell. He died."

"You don't have to tell me."

"It's all right. I don't mind any more. He wasn't much older than Blake. He was in San Angeles, when it got nuked. Damned Directorate. I guess I always thought of Michael – Blake – as my brother."

I wanted to tell her about the Directorate

Interceptor so badly. I wanted to tell her that Kellerman was a traitor, to stir her honest hatred of the Directorate. But now wasn't the time, not while Kellerman could still be listening and watching. The camera on Jenkins' shoulder stared down at me, unblinking.

"And what does that make me?" I asked, smiling.

"It makes you an asshole," she said. "I'm going to check on Martinez. You need anything, just holler."

Jenkins wandered into the driver cab, and I watched her go. The effortless stride with which she moved suddenly made me feel uncontrollably envious. She was made for war: I was a spent force.

Behind my eyes, so deep in my head that it felt as though it had always been there, I felt the ringing. I shook my head and tried to ride out a wave of nausea.

It was the Artefact, calling out to me.

Daylight eventually failed. Both suns still bore down from far above, but their light grew faded and old. I watched with a mixture of anticipation and resignation. With each passing minute, the sky darkened. Cloud cover became denser and denser. Eventually Martinez was driving using his infrared sights and suit scanners.

"You'll be okay, *jefe*," Martinez reassured me. "I'll keep you safe."

I fumbled through the cabin, flinching with every step. I felt like a fever was breaking. Maybe I had an infection. I reached down to my leg, patting the injury. I couldn't remove the H-suit, so couldn't see inside, but it felt wet even through the protective fabric.

The crawler PA chimed.

"This is Dr Kellerman. I'm sorry to inform you that a storm front is developing just beyond your sector. We are unable to predict its development or movement pattern."

This time, my squad remained silent. There was no point in arguing with Kellerman, no point in crossing him further. They understood that it was better to wait.

I sighed in acceptance. *Got to play the part.* "We will proceed as planned. Keep us updated on the storm's progress. We need to know if it reaches the Artefact, or moves in the direction of Helios Station."

"I will do so. Godspeed. Dr Kellerman out."

"Harris out."

As I ended the communication, I saw that the sky had now turned black. Streaks of brilliant red lightning coursed the horizon. So completely alien, that the display was almost beautiful.

"This is going to be one hell of a storm," Kaminski muttered.

I couldn't have put it better myself. The suddenness with which it had materialised felt unnatural, but perhaps this was the way of Helios.

"Do you believe what Kellerman is feeding us on this?" Jenkins asked. "Because I certainly don't. A storm develops as soon as we crash-land on Helios. Now another storm is mounting as we make our way to the Artefact. Feels like more than a coincidence."

The thunderheads above twisted and swirled in response, blotting all light.

"Maybe you have a point."

"Eyes on the prize," Martinez interrupted, holding up a hand.

He activated the crawler headlights. A rack of strong lamps had been attached to the roof and prow, and they seared through the miasma of dust and grit to illuminate a pathway ahead: the entrance to the underground tunnels. There was a huge boulder beside the cave, sprayed with a colourful skull-and-crossbones motif. An arrow pointed down into the darkness. *Point of no return.*

"Take us in, Martinez."

The crawler gently shifted gears and began the descent into the unknown.

CHAPTER TWENTY-SIX

SEE YOU ON THE OTHER SIDE

After my father died, Carrie and I were passed between a series of aunts and uncles – usually well-meaning, often misguided, always transient. With my mother gone as well, there was no one else left to care for us. We never moved far – always within the Detroit Metro, shifting from one tower block to the next.

We probably spent the longest time with Aunt Ritha, or my memory of her is certainly the brightest. I was never quite sure how we ended up in Ritha's care, but oaths sworn in poverty are hard to break and Ritha had promised my mother she would see to us if it ever became necessary. Ritha was an enormous black woman, over six foot tall, and her height gave her an awkward hunch. She always wore an apron – the same apron, tarred with brown and yellowed stains – but I had never seen her cook food. Ritha had migrated to the Metro from Haiti, or so she said, and her convoluted backstory of illegal immigration into the United Americas created a vaguely exotic appeal to the local gangs. That, and the fact that Ritha was addicted to scolometh – a chemical derivative of scopolamine. She spent most of her days on the couch in the tiny one-bed apartment, watching the tri-D viewer in a stupor. Occasionally shuffling to the door in her years-old slippers to meet another dealer, then shuffling back to the indentation on the equally ancient couch.

All that said, Ritha was a good woman. She wasn't a blood relative, obviously – none of those aunts or uncles were, I don't think – but she tried her best. She sold a few drugs on the side and always made sure that we had ration vouchers for food on the table.

I liked Ritha.

The problem was her partner: a rat-faced bastard called Leeroy.

He was a much smaller man, Detroit born and bred, so pale that he looked transparent. Hair shaven, scalp a tapestry of gang tattoos, nose razor-sharp. As with Ritha, my memory of him is a single outfit of clothing: a DETROIT WHISTLERS vest, the neck line pulled down so that it exposed most of his chest, and a pair of too-large combat trousers stolen from an Alliance soldier on shore-leave. Leeroy never touched scolometh – was somewhat proud of that – but his drug of choice was just as easy to obtain. He'd drink whenever and whatever he could.

Leeroy and I didn't see eye to eye, and when he drank our differences seemed to expand until there was a gulf between us. *Everything* about Carrie and me he hated. Couldn't see why Ritha had to care for us. Couldn't see why she would want to. Ritha wasn't one for arguing; she would just let him rumble on, rant, the reflection of the tri-D playing on the thick lenses of her antique glasses.

The shouting I could take. The shouting didn't hurt.

The beatings hurt.

Those started almost immediately on our arrival at Ritha's. For literally any reason, Leeroy would find an object and hit me with it. His preferred tool was a baseball bat: kept beneath his bed for protection, stained dark with the blood of prior use, the faded words AMERICA'S FINEST printed on the handle. He'd usually aim for my legs or across my back. I remember that the face hurt, most of all.

As I got older, I would flee the apartment. Ritha never really showed much interest in what Leeroy was doing, if she even noticed, but she would sometimes have the mercy to give me small jobs to do. Deliver some money to a neighbouring block, take a package to meet one of her dealers. I was grateful for the opportunity to be away from the stifling atmosphere of the tiny apartment.

Leeroy would often follow me, and we would be involved in an hour-long game of cat-and-mouse. I got good at it, in the end. The best hiding places were in the abandoned or bombed-out tenements: those empty black shells, full of winding narrow corridors, full of hiding places. I'd crouch among the debris of the old world, listening for Leeroy as he stalked behind me.

"Come out, you miserable piece of shit!" he would yell, voice strangely high pitched, quivering with rage. "I told Ritha not to give you and that dumb-shit sister of yours any more ration vouchers. We're on a budget, you piece of shit, and that money is mine."

I would run from him. And, like I say, I got good at hiding. Watching him from gantries or collapsed stairwells; that haggard white figure, stalking through the blackened corridors. The quickening of my heart-rate as I misplaced a foot: then the flight would start again. His yelled pro-testations as I fled, took up a better hiding place.

He never caught me. I think if he had, out of the apartment and away from Ritha's gaze, Leeroy would've killed me. That fear drove me on, made me better – the best – at hiding and running.

I hadn't thought about Ritha and Leeroy for a long time. I rarely revisited that part of my his-tory, and for good reason, but right now – in the tunnels beneath the desert – it sprang to mind.

The sensation was exactly the same: *being chased through the dark by something malicious, through narrow and twisting corridors.*

I only wished that it was Leeroy following me, now, and not the Krell. But that feeling of being watched was impossible to shake.

The crawler was descending. Progress became slow and arduous. Following Kellerman's specu-lative maps, we encountered dead-ends or rock falls where there should have been open paths, and Martinez was forced to backtrack twice.

"This place is massive," he commented, as we drove onwards.

"I'm trying to plot possible enemy movements through the network," Kaminski said. "So many hiding places."

"This is supposed to be the easy part," I said. "These tunnels are apparently well-explored."

Martinez navigated the crawler through a passageway, narrower than many we had encountered so far. A vast cavern unfolded ahead. It reached into darkness far above. The crawler prowled, cat-like, around stalagmites the size of ten men. Ahead, even larger stalactites dripped from the ceiling. Water flowed from some, gradually pooling in the lower recesses of the cave. Great insects flitted among the life-giving fluid. As they stooped to drink from the pools, they flashed brilliantly with internal light.

"It's raining up there," I said. "The water has started pouring into the caverns below. If the storm has broken, then the Krell will be loose above."

"Then this is where the Krell will be," Jenkins said, pensively.

We all sat in silence for a moment. Of course, she was right. The Krell liked water, liked humid environments. The desert above was anathema to them – they occupied the sector around the Artefact because of the effect it had on them. The dark, watery, and rank tunnel network below: this was their preferred habitat.

So why haven't we seen them yet?

I rubbed my eyes. I was tired from the constant observations.

"How far underground are we?"

Kaminski sucked his teeth in indecision. "Can't tell, but there's a lot of rock above us. The sensor-suite can't penetrate it."

The crawler sensors projected a holo of the immediate area, and I studied it carefully. Heavy rock strata. That would be dense, likely capable of blocking radio transmissions or at least heavily disrupting them. I didn't need a chemical analysis to tell me that this was our best chance to break communication with Kellerman.

"Martinez, run a check on our signal back to Helios Station."

There was a pause as Martinez did as ordered. "We're still broadcasting, but the signal has degraded. Not sure whether we will be able to keep airing as we go further underground."

That was good enough for me. Now was the best time to act on my plan. I didn't know the precise transmission capabilities of the crawler, or of the individual suit-cameras. But the storm and the rocks above us would interfere with comms, as would the Artefact the nearer we got to it.

I theatrically rubbed my chin, leant over the control console. *Got to make a show of this.*

"So, we need to follow this path?" I asked, pointing out the route on the holo-map. "If the Krell try to follow us down here, they'll probably use the same access point as us. All-stop, Martinez. We're going to seal that tunnel."

The crawler came to an immediate standstill.

"But you'll need to get out," Kaminski said. The logistics of our situation dawned on him. "We can extract, but you'll be trapped down here."

"I'll have to think of another way out of here if that happens," I said, again precisely and clearly. *All for show.* "We don't have long before the Krell get wise to our position. Kaminski, Jenkins – button up. I want you to go outside."

Jenkins hauled one of the demo-charges from the passenger cab. "I'm up, Cap."

Kaminski was less convinced, frowning at me – on the cusp of refusing the order for my good. *Don't blow this, 'Ski – don't argue with me.*

"Execute that order, Kaminski."

Just as I had expected, the communicator suddenly broke with static.

"Captain Harris, this is Dr Kellerman. I do hope that you don't intend to use that demolition charge. Those are *nuclear* charges."

"That's exactly what we're doing. Anything wants to chase us into the caves with that storm acting up, it's going to come in the same way we did."

"Captain, that is the primary route to the Artefact! What if a later expedition needs to use the same path?"

"Then they will have to find another way in. We have to seal that shaft. It's the best chance we have of making it to the Artefact."

"Do not seal those tunnels, Captain," Kellerman said, definitively.

"Try to understand this: if these tunnels are flooded, then the Krell will be rampant down here. We're only a four-man team."

Kellerman didn't answer immediately, as though he was considering my answer. Did he believe me?

How much did he really know about the tunnels, about the presence of the Krell down here? He had sent expeditions into the dark before, but nothing like this.

"Try to keep comms to a minimum, Keller-man – every broadcast we make out here could be attracting Krell," I said, before he had responded. "Kaminski, Jenkins – you're up."

I cut the connection. Swallowed hard. Kept my eyes on Kaminski and Jenkins, prayed that they wouldn't collapse from a bullet in the head back at Helios Station. They were unsuspecting of what I planned, unsuspecting that I was taking an enor-mous gamble. But seconds passed, and no one made extraction. The scheme was too risky for me to feel any relief – not just yet, at least.

Jenkins sealed up her combat-suit and strapped a demo-charge to her back. She holstered a pistol on her thigh. With obvious relish, she armed her M95 plasma rifle and flamethrower. The pilot-light on the muzzle of the flamer lit immediately.

"Martinez, I want both crawler guns primed and ready to fire. Kill the engine."

"Affirmative, sir."

"I'll man the hatch," I said. "Constant scanner sweeps when they're outside – covering fire if they need it."

"We know what we're doing," Kaminski said. Both he and Jenkins slammed helmets into place, hiding their faces behind reflective face-shields, making them look anonymous.

"All good," Jenkins declared.

"Keep it swift and keep it clean," I ordered.

I hauled open the crawler hatch and was immediately glad it wasn't me going out there. The cave was enormous, probably hundreds of metres across, and made me feel insignificant. Without the aid of the crawler sensor-suite, it was also utterly pitch-black. My ears prickled with the change in atmospherics and I was overwhelmed by the stink of damp and death that filled the cabin. I grappled with my respirator and sucked down cold oxygen.

I immediately recalled the Alliance operation on Torus Seigel IV. That was the last time I'd been fighting in my own body, while I was with Spec Forces. The conditions there had been similar: an endless night above ground, a rat's nest of endless tunnels below. Ten years ago now; a different life that I was suddenly revisiting.

Jenkins and Kaminski jumped down from the crawler. They flashed on their suit-lamps, casting bright light over the muted greens and greys of the cavern interior. With a regular supply of water down here, the wildlife was more obvious than on the surface. Alongside the alien insects, colourful and bio-luminescent fungi polluted the rock pools. Weird, needle-covered shell creatures scurried about. There was a loud *drip-drip-drip* of water falling from above, a gushing in the distance.

This is definitely where they will be, I thought. *And yet the place is empty.*

Jenkins scanned the nearby area with her rifle, looking for signs of hostile activity. With the ceiling so far above, it was impossible to determine what might be up there.

"Get back inside, Captain," she said, over the comm. "Better you watch with Martinez."

"Affirmative."

She had a point. I slid the hatch shut, and wandered up front with Martinez. He was still hunched over the control console, watching the scanner-feeds and external cameras. We were an island of light amid the dark; the crawler head-lights disappearing somewhere before the cavern perimeter.

"Kill the lights," I said. "We're too exposed out here. There could be anything watching us."

"Affirmative, Cap."

The lights went dark. Kaminski and Jenkins had full sensory awareness inside their suits – the light would only serve to make us an easy target, make us vulnerable.

I looked down at the chronometer. The team had been outside for less than a minute, but it felt like an eternity. Time seemed to stretch, become elastic.

Jenkins jogged back the way that the crawler had come. She aimed her flamethrower into the tunnel. Kaminski stalked behind her, weapon panning back and forth.

My pulse raced unnaturally. There was extreme risk in my plan. I needed to cut comms between the station and my squad. Closing the tunnel would stop the Krell from following us under-ground, but would also disrupt our signal back to the station. Kellerman had certainly foreseen the former consequence, but maybe not the latter. Although he might react by executing one of my team, I didn't think that he would do that. He had no qualms about expending their lives, but I still had the Key; executing one of the team meant one less bodyguard for me and reduced my prospects of making it to the Artefact. I desperately wanted to explain all of this to my squad. Would the others be angry with me for taking the gamble? Maybe, but I couldn't discuss it with them: right now, we were still broadcasting. This was a risk that I – *we* – were going to have to take.

"Patch us into the combat-suit camera feeds," I said.

The direct feeds from Jenkins and Kaminski appeared on the crawler console. Martinez manipulated the controls and activated night-vision mode, improving the visual quality. This was exactly what Kellerman would be viewing back at Helios Station.

"Approaching tunnel entrance," Kaminski said, his communicator channel open to the crawler.

The tunnel mouth was fifty metres ahead of them. Jenkins waved Kaminski up, and she dashed through rock pools to cover another few metres. Her footfalls echoed off into the distance. So loud: the noise made me flinch.

"Spooky as hell down here," Jenkins panted.

"I'm getting possible movement," Martinez said. "Maybe just water though. There's a lot of it coming through this section. *Mucho movimiento*."

Jenkins reached the tunnel mouth and unstrapped the charge from her back, holding her flamer one-handed. It was a big, clumsy weapon, but she handled it expertly. Kaminski came up behind her and hunkered down beside the rocky wall. The situation was impossibly tense. My eyes kept flitting to the crawler view-screens, to the deep darkness that surrounded us.

"Best place to seal the tunnel will be a few metres in," Jenkins said. "If I set the charge for three minutes, we can roll out in the crawler before it hits. You sure that you want me to do this?"

I had a moment of indecision. I didn't know about the structural viability of the caves, and I doubted that any expedition had ever performed a demo test. Kellerman would never have allowed it.

"Orders, Cap?" Jenkins asked again.

"Do it – ten metres inside, three-minute delay," I decided.

Jenkins knelt down to ready the charge. Kaminski motioned her on, his rifle up to cover her.

There was a distant, high-pitched keening noise. Like a banshee howl, loud enough to be detected by suit receivers and relayed back to the crawler.

"Wait!" I called.

Jenkins paused.

"You hear that? Turn up your external audio receptors."

I watched through Kaminski's suit-camera: Jenkins frowned behind her face-plate.

"Sounds like the wind," she said. "Maybe coming down through the rocks."

It's the Artefact. Not in my head, but sounding through the tunnels. Get a Christo-damned grip; these people depend on you.

"Ignore it. Execute the order," I said to Jenkins.

But that confirmed it: none of the others could
hear the signal like me.

Jenkins attached the charge to the tunnel wall.
The rock was slick with water and algae. The
charge slipped free the first time. She attached it
again. The display panel illuminated.

"Done. Nuke is placed."

"I'm getting readings all around us," Martinez
interrupted. "I don't like this at all. Scanner is
showing definite motion."

"Get back inside the crawler," I ordered. "Move
now."

They moved on at a brisk jog.

I stared down at the scanner. It showed a certain, solid build-up of hostiles. Flashing blips,
moving swiftly all around the cavern.

"Clearing tunnel mouth!" Kaminski whispered.

He turned back towards the crawler – so distant
on his camera-feed, rendered throbbing green by
his helmet visuals.

In front of Kaminski, head so close that it almost
touched his face-plate, was an enormous Krell
primary-form. It was poised on a rock, powerful
legs coiled underneath it; massive razor-claws raised
and ready to strike. Maybe the image froze for a
second, or perhaps it really was that still: like some
twisted alien sculpture. Its mouth was open wide,
exposing rows of teeth, and it screamed right into
Kaminski's face – spittle showering him, enough of
it landing on the camera lens to cloud my view.

I visualised myself *there*, in the death-grip of
the Krell primary-form: I instantly recognised the
poise of the xeno, knew what it was about to do.

"Kaminski!" I roared.

My reactions were slow, human.

Kaminski's were improved, superhuman.

He was already reacting. His rifle was up, firing. The Krell was caught off-guard, and two
plasma pulses impacted its torso just under the
ribcage. In a brilliant flash of light – bright enough
to momentarily blind the vid-feed – the creature
collapsed backwards. It thrashed violently, sending water and alien flora spraying into the air.

"I'm moving!" Kaminski called. "I'm moving!"

"They're all around us!" Jenkins said, following Kaminski.

The cave was abruptly filled with the tell-tale
squawking of Krell primary-forms. They were
dropping from the ceiling, I realised, and using
the stalactites to guide their descent.

"Tracking multiple targets," Martinez shouted.

Something heavy *thump-thumped* on the roof.
I unconsciously grabbed for my pistol, cycling the
safety off, even though I knew that it wouldn't do
me any good against these odds.

"Get ready to move out, Martinez," I ordered.
"Power up the engine. Soon as they are onboard,
we're gone. Activate the guns!"

The sand-crawler turrets sprang to life. There was
a pair of guns on the roof – multi-barrelled, solid-
shot assault cannons. Automated, they selected the
most viable targets and opened fire. Equipped with
camera-mounts as well; I watched as the muzzles of
each gun glowed white-hot, churned through the
attackers. More bodies collapsed from above, in various states of injury.

The noise was tremendous: the chatter of the guns, the screaming of the descending Krell, echoing off the vast cave walls. Overwhelming, even inside the crawler.

I feverishly looked back to Jenkins' vid-feed. There was too much happening at once for me to keep track of, and once again I cursed my fallible body. She fired from the hip with her flamethrower. Kaminski was in front of her, blasting through bodies. Two huge xenos landed beside him, in another explosion of water. They advanced. With lightning reactions, he armed a grenade and threw it.

A fraction of a second later, the grenade exploded. Shards of alien blood and body tissue showered Kaminski and Jenkins. Everywhere, jagged shadows were cast by approaching Krell and weapons-fire.

In that instant of perfect light, I saw that the ceiling was lined with Krell. There were hundreds of them roosting above. Even as they made their way towards the transport, more were emerging from their hibernation.

"Flamethrower on the left," Kaminski called.

Jenkins swung about-face, charging her flamer. A jet of combustible chemical fluid sprayed the area, ignited almost instantly. Another group of aliens descended and squawked commands to those above. I watched in morbid fascination as Jenkins activated her flamer again and again, as white-orange flame poured over the massed bodies.

Kaminski and Jenkins were finally at the hatch.

"Open up!" Jenkins said. She pounded her hand against the metal framework.

I dashed for the door controls, tripping over my increasingly-pained leg. The cavern rumbled with the weapons-discharge all around. I willed myself onwards, grabbing for the hatch and wrenching it open with all of my bodily strength. Another wave of stench hit me, but this was different: the tang of roasting alien flesh, the acrid burn of plastic from the damaged combat-suits. My eyes stung with the heavy smoke from Jenkins' flamer, and I choked as I tried to breathe.

Jenkins tumbled into the crawler. She was covered in xeno blood, still firing her flamer into the mass of aliens that had gathered at the hatch.

Eyes streaming, I looked at the chaos outside. *Something* emerged from the burning napalm laid down by Jenkins' flamer – a ragged shadow, still aflame. It was already dead, but momentum kept the thing moving. Kaminski stumbled on another body—

I imagined what he was seeing inside his faceplate: painted with so many targets that his auto-sighting probably couldn't even decide which needed to be killed first—

The burning xeno-form lurched forwards, raptorial forearms raised. It was a scarecrow of a thing; flesh melted by flamer-fuel, blackened and desiccated. Only then did Kaminski see it – the open mouth, the impossibly dangerous knife-tipped arms.

The alien was on top of him, and he stopped firing. One forearm pierced his torso, clean through the combat-suit. Four layers of reinforced, ablative plastic-steel compound – like it wasn't even there. Another punctured the plastic of his face-plate. Kaminski instantly went limp, his simulated body held firm in the alien's grip. His rifle clattered to the ground, trampled underfoot by the enormous attacker.

"He's gone," Jenkins stated flatly.

I stumbled backwards, in denial and horror. Such human reactions, such undermining emotions: strangers to me for so many years, now returned in force.

No sim to hide in out here. I'll end up the same.

Just like that, Kaminski was snubbed out. With his neural-link severed, he would awaken back at Helios Station – probably screaming in pain. I knew that experience too well. There was no time to grieve for him now.

"Get back!" Jenkins yelled at me, without turning.

I scrambled from the lock, and she laid down another carpet of flame. The xeno and Kaminski disappeared beneath it. Even then, two more Krell leapt from hiding places, charging through the flames to reach the crawler. One grappled with the doorframe, claws screeching against the metal. The other scrambled up into the crawler. I fumbled with my pistol.

Jenkins pushed me back into the crawler, hauling shut the hatch. She slammed the alien bodies aside. The xenos were left outside, pounding against the hatch in frustration.

"Move, move!" Jenkins called to Martinez. "Thirty seconds until that charge goes off!"

Jenkins had full battlefield intelligence. She

knew exactly how long until the charge detonated, in real-time.

Overhead the turrets fired continuously, shaking the vehicle. Two, three, maybe more, xenos were on the roof now. The crawler rocked side to side violently.

"They're trying to overturn the crawler. Get us out of here," I said, grappling with an overhead support rail to steady myself.

"My pleasure," said Martinez.

The crawler roared into action. The headlights doused the area in brilliant light. Everywhere, in impossible numbers, the aliens descended. The scanner trilled continuously.

I counted the seconds, erratically, in my head. There was a muted explosion behind us and a moment of uncertainty: the explosion could seal us within the cave with those things, or it could deter them from pursuit.

There was a second deep rumble of a different tone. The crawler rocked indecisively. Martinez fought with the controls, desperately trying to keep us upright.

"What's happening?" I yelled.

"Looks like part of the ceiling is coming down," Martinez said, consulting a tri-D topographic map of the area on the control console. "These tunnels aren't going to hold—"

Something big hit the side of the crawler. Whether it was the Krell, or just rock, I couldn't tell. Then something else hit us from above. The crawler roof deformed with the impact.

I fell sideways as the crawler lurched, hitting

my head on a locker. As I went down, I stole a glance at the view-screen. There was no path any more, no visible route. Only a wall of falling rock, water and dust.

I was thrown sideways again, but this time Jenkins caught me. She held me tight against her huge armoured body, grappled with another locker to keep us both upright.

We were falling, falling—

"It's all right," she whispered to me as we went. "It's going to be all right."

If there were Krell outside, they were being buried just like us. The cave-in seemed to be all around, so loud that it blotted out all other sound. I couldn't even tell if the gun-turrets were firing any more. Death by Krell, or crushed in a cave-in: it was all the same to me, and in my real body it could happen so quickly.

A fractured skull, a shattered spine.

I closed my eyes.

I woke with a start, taking in my surroundings.

"There was a war in heaven. It was centuries ago, perhaps millennia. So long ago that it doesn't matter any more. Time is difficult to express in human fractions when the stars glow for ever."

The voice was so clouded by static that it was impossible to identify the speaker.

Martinez had stripped off much of his combat-armour. Wet, fresh sweat glistened on his back. From where I sat – propped up in a passenger seat – I heard his ragged, panting breath. Like a dog; feral, barely contained.

When he spoke, his voice was hoarse and ragged. "How do you know this? What are these things?"

The speaker, who could only have been Kellerman, continued with the monologue as though no question had been asked.

"The Krell and the Shard are all that is left of the war. The organic versus the mechanical. The war tore apart the galaxy, with those species strong enough to survive, scrabbling for what little resources remained. The Shard have a long memory, even if all they have left is wreckage and dust."

"Is that why they insist on staying here?" Martinez asked, his tone bordering on aggressive insistence. "Answer me, *padre*!"

Kellerman laughed. "Perhaps what is left of the Shard is only a tiny fraction of the whole. A ghost of what the species once was, if you will. The Krell seem to be in much better shape. They must have won the war, I suppose."

Martinez's hands twisted into fists, and he pounded the control panel. The whole crawler rocked with each blow. I frowned, struggling to stand. I was pinned beneath a support strut, across the legs and torso.

Then I realised the inside of the crawler was in utter disarray. Equipment lay smashed on the floor. Crates were battered and dented. I struggled harder to get free.

—*at the back of the med-bay, among shattered storage tubes and twisted metal, sprawled parodies of my real body*—

Jenkins lay opposite me, her body in an odd

position – legs buckled backwards, arms crushed beneath her torso. Her head was at an awkward and unusual angle, hair draped over her pale face. Blood dripped from the corner of her mouth in thick strands. Her chest had been pierced by a piece of wreckage – a beam emerging from her back.

—twisted metal spars above me. Blackened by the intensity of the explosion. Difficult to discern what those were; whether they had once been part of the window structure or whether the diamond-tread pattern meant that they had been part of the floor—

I shouted, calling to Martinez. The crawler continued rocking. My voice sounded alien, distorted by static.

"Martinez! Get back here and turn off the antenna!"

—a voice rang out, loud and clear, from somewhere outside of the wreckage: "A curfew is in effect. Please return to your homes. A curfew is in effect. Alliance Army soldiers are inbound for your protection"—

Martinez shifted in his seat, turning his enormously muscled neck to look at me. His face was covered in cuneiform tattoos, dripping from his eyes like the blood from Jenkins' mouth.

"Martinez, get that communicator turned off!"

"When you're here, all you want is to be back out there!"

CHAPTER TWENTY-SEVEN

BORN DEAD

I jolted awake, screaming Martinez's name. The whine of the Artefact's call still touched my mind, reluctantly receding as I woke up.

The crawler had hit solid ground. It kept moving, continued forwards, but very slowly. A regular crunching sounded from somewhere below – the grind of metal on metal.

Martinez was howling – either in frustration or elation. But the scene inside the crawler wasn't from my vision: the interior cabins were intact. I was pressed up against Jenkins' armoured body. She peeled me off her, and slowly evaluated me. She stared at the middle-distance of her face-plate; considering my bio-signs on her HUD. Her face was painted with holo-projections from inside her helmet.

"I – I blacked out," I stammered.

"You'll survive," Jenkins declared. "No internal damage. Or nothing new, anyway."

I stumbled back from her. "And you?"

She grinned. "I was born dead."

A trio of stingers protruded from her left thigh, already streaming ugly black fluid. The ammo had punctured her combat-suit, polluting her bloodstream with whatever toxins this Krell Collective used. She brusquely plucked the stingers from her leg. It didn't seem to hurt Jenkins, but it made me squirm. She must've suffered the injuries back in the cavern, had simply fought on through them.

"Thanks for the save."

"Anytime," Jenkins said.

"The crawler is wasted," Martinez said. "Trans-axle is blown." That crunching noise became louder, unhealthier. "These maps are sketchy, but we're pretty deep underground now. No way I can repair the crawler in these conditions." The transport ground to an abrupt stop. Something mechanical hissed outside – hydraulics or maybe steering, it didn't matter what. "But the Krell have let up. The scanner is clear."

This was the moment of truth. I listened for the chime of an incoming comm message. Then I expectantly looked over the faces of Martinez and Jenkins. If Kellerman executed them, they'd drop dead in the crawler – the neural-link between sim and operator immediately severed. A few seconds passed: nothing. Jenkins looked back at me, frowning, confused by my behaviour.

"It's all right, Jenkins," I said. "I have a plan, or as close to a plan as I can get. Martinez, what's the comms mast status?"

He ran a check on the crawler systems. "Non-operational. No contact with Helios Station. The radio mast was also damaged during the attack."

"Good. What about suit relays back to the station?"

"Also negative. They were set up to relay through the crawler antenna. Without the mast, they can't broadcast."

"So we're out of contact with Helios Station?"

"Far as I can tell."

Jenkins crossed her arms over her chest. She had every right to be suspicious. "What's this all about?"

"I needed to be sure that we were out of communication with the station. I wish that I could've told you earlier, but I have important intel. Kellerman and Deacon are Directorate. And Kellerman has a starship."

Jenkins' eyes widened.

"It's a Directorate Interceptor. High-end, black ops stuff."

"That asshole," Martinez said, pounding a fist into the empty navigator's seat.

I gestured with my hand for Martinez to calm. "Easy, Martinez. He has the ship stowed in the lab module. Looks almost brand new, with a full complement of air-to-ground warheads."

"Does it have a Q-drive?" Jenkins asked.

"It does. Tyler showed it to me."

"Does she know how to fly it? Is the ship working?" Jenkins went on. "Can we use it to get off this rock?"

"Affirmative on all counts."

"Fucking A!" Martinez said.

"You've got to get to that starship."

"What about you?" Jenkins asked. "The tunnels

are sealed. There's no way that we can follow you down here."

"I took a risk, Jenkins. There was no other way to break comms with Helios Station. Right now, Kellerman probably thinks that we're on our way to the Artefact – that I'm executing his orders. So long as he thinks that, we're safe, and I hope that Kaminski and Tyler are too.

"I won't be leaving Helios without the Key. On the Shard ship, Kellerman showed me a star-map. The Shard, whatever they were, knew the Maelstrom well. They had plotted stable Q-jump points. They knew how to avoid the solar storms. The Key contains the star-data.

"We're going to get off Helios. So here's what we're going to do. Sooner or later, you're both going to have to make extraction. These tunnels are going to be swarming with Krell, once that storm develops. After you make extraction, overwhelm security, evac Helios Station and pick me up."

Martinez gave a bitter laugh. "You make it sound simple. But where are we going to evac you from, Cap? The tunnels are blown. There's no way we could fight our way through these caves skinless."

"Use the ship. Pick me up from high ground, somewhere you can find me easily."

Martinez and Jenkins traded looks. They had guessed exactly what I was suggesting, and from the expressions on their faces, they didn't think much of the idea. Martinez punched some keys on the crawler control console, casting up a wire-frame holo in pale green light.

"I don't think that you will want to be going anywhere near the high ground, Captain," he said sombrely. "I think that you'll want to avoid that completely."

The holo rotated, showing the Artefact and the surrounding sectors. If Kellerman was right about the tunnel network, it would lead us – me – directly to the foot of the Artefact, on high ground overlooking the desert.

A desert swarming with Krell of every conceivable type...

I nodded. "Maybe in other circumstances, but now it's the perfect cover. Local comms will likely be obliterated in nearby regions. I'll have the Key, and you can use the Artefact as a beacon for navigation."

I tried to make it sound nice and easy, as though it was a simple rescue operation. I left aside that there were an impossible series of variables: such as whether the team would be killed on extraction, whether they would be able to overpower the guards at Helios Station, whether they would actually be able to pilot the Directorate ship cross-country, in a storm, to the foot of the Artefact—

"If all else fails, retrieve the Key. Take it back to Command and make sure that they send a rescue party – for Elena."

"Not necessary. You're going to be fine," Jenkins said. She just couldn't accept the finality of it all.

I shook my head. "This might not be about me any more."

"What about Kellerman?" Martinez said. "You really think that he will leave you alone down here? He might send troops after you."

"Fine; the more personnel he has out in the desert looking for me, the less he has on-station guarding you when you extract. You've seen how few people he has left. Ten or so security troops? I don't think that he will send anybody. He won't want to risk his own skin, and for all he knows I'm doing just what he ordered. Let's hope that Kaminski has made extraction safely."

"I can't believe we've lost him," Jenkins said, shaking her head. "But there were so many of them out there."

No post-extraction debrief, this time.

Martinez slammed a fist across his heart, the heavy gauntlet thumping against his ablative chest armour. "Christo watch over him. We'll have a full prayer later."

"See you on the other side, 'Ski," Jenkins added.

I didn't have that luxury, but I hoped that she was right. *With Kaminski dead, I'm a step closer to having to fight through this thing on my own, in my own skin.* Eventually, every simulant operator developed the same dread: of being forced to fight in their own imperfect, natural body. Right now, Kaminski might be doing just that – back on Helios Station. And I was too, but in the darkened tunnels beneath Helios' desert.

"So what do we do now?" Jenkins asked.

"We just keep going. What's our distance to the Artefact?"

Martinez consulted the crawler controls. "A kilometre, I guess. But these tunnels – they aren't properly mapped."

The idea of traversing a kilometre through the

caves filled me with anxiety. Self-belief, and the lack of any viable alternative strategy, was all that kept me going.

"There's no other way," I said, trying to explain myself to my team. "If I stay in the tunnels, the Krell will come sooner or later. At least if I make it through, I'll be in a better position for evac. Don't get me wrong, Martinez. I don't want this to happen. I know there are no guarantees out there."

They fell silent for a long moment. I just couldn't see any other way through this, and whatever happened I knew I couldn't leave the Key. I craved for the information that it carried, wanted it even more than the next transition. Any risk, any gamble, had to be worth taking if there was even the slightest chance that I'd make it off Helios with the star-data.

"Are you absolutely solid that you want to go through with this?" Jenkins asked. "There has to be something else that we can do—"

"There isn't. If this works, I can escape with the Key – with the star-data. If it doesn't, then you can escape with the star-data. That's all that matters now."

"All right, Cap," Jenkins said with a solemn nod. "Whatever you want."

Martinez sighed and nodded in agreement too.

"Then stock up on ammo," I said. "Gather all the supplies we can carry. We'll cover the distance on foot. That cavern back there isn't going to stay sealed for ever. We've got to move fast."

I unsealed an ammo crate and strapped spare power cells onto my H-suit, for the PPG-13 pistol.

The others followed my example. Jenkins shouldered the remaining demo-charges and flamer cells. Martinez loaded up on grenades.

I did a final check on our supplies, and then turned to the team. They were hyped-up, a curious mixture of anticipation and reluctance.

Jenkins did a motherly check over my environment suit, making sure I had my oxygen tank and water supply. I was too tired to argue with her. I bit my lip as she patted down the leg panels. Just the touch of her hand through the fabric against my injury was enough to send a jolt of pain through me. Then she checked on the connecting piping for my respirator mask. Away from the airborne dust particles of the desert, the atmosphere was an easier breathe, but there was a danger of atmospheric toxicity from the weaponry we carried. Jenkins' flamer could contaminate a whole cavern with burning material.

"Everything looks sound," she said. "Wear your helmet for extra protection. You need some more painkillers before we go?"

"I've finished everything that Kellerman left for me," I said, jerking a thumb at the empty lockers.

All that was left was the Key. I grasped the box in which it was housed, and flipped open the catches. I took it out, turning it over in my hands. It felt unusually heavy, unnaturally cold. I slipped it into a tool holster on my suit belt.

Martinez unsealed the hatch. He took point, with me next and Jenkins at the rear.

The crawler was thoroughly wasted. Exposed metalwork was twisted and decayed; huge acid-drenched holes bored into the armour plating. Stinger-spines pierced the roof. The gun-turrets poured thick, black smoke.

"I'll miss the old bitch," Martinez said.

We moved as quickly as possible through a series of narrower passes. Always in single file, with weapons panning every shadow and crevice. It was utterly dark, save for the occasional flash of some alien insect scuttling around on the floor. Martinez and Jenkins acted as my eyes. I considered what they saw: using the full sensory suite of the combat-suit, the assistance of an onboard AI. They had been forced to deactivate their suit camouflage systems, because otherwise they would have been effectively invisible to me. My H-suit carried a small and ineffectual shoulder-lamp – mounted just below the camera – but it was weak, and didn't illuminate any more than a few feet ahead of me. I prayed for an HUD, for some proper tactical information.

I checked the clock, set into the rim of my helmet so that I could see it from inside the suit. Fourteen hours had elapsed since I had awoken in the sand-crawler. In different circumstances, that would be the mission timeline. Now, it felt like every passing second was living on borrowed time. Something squirmed in my gut – either fear, or perhaps hunger. I hadn't eaten since we had left Helios Station. I hadn't felt like it, but Kellerman hadn't stocked the crawler with rations anyway.

You don't have a plan, a voice whispered in my

ear. *You have nothing. Just give up now – there's no point in carrying on like this.*

I scrambled over rocks as Martinez and Jenkins effortlessly stalked alongside me. They didn't experience hunger and they didn't tire.

"Terrain opening up," Martinez declared. "Another big cave."

I tuned up the amplification on my audio sensors and used them to guess the size of the chamber by the *drip-dripping* of water in the distance; moisture trickling from above. I had to rely on my ears over my eyes now.

Martinez held up a hand – a blurred shape ahead of me. He fell into a crouched bracing position. Something had changed; the tone of the dripping had shifted, become harsher.

"Cap, you'll want to see this," he muttered.

"Defensive positions. Jenkins, cover our retreat."

"Affirmative, Captain," Jenkins replied. Unspoken: "*like it will do us any good.*"

I staggered ahead to Martinez's location. He fell back to meet me, guiding me by the elbow. I wanted to shrug him off, to quarrel with him that I wasn't an invalid, but one look out into the darkness made me think twice about that.

I'm becoming Kellerman. We're both broken.

I sniggered to myself. Back at Helios Station, he had warned me that he and I had more in common than I might think. I was reacting just as he would.

"Leave me, Martinez. I can do this."

"All right. I'll light us up."

Martinez took some flares from his armour

webbing. He activated them one at a time, and tossed them into the cavern. They fizzled bright red and green, illuminating a large area in fitful multi-coloured light. The experience was strangely disorienting: I could suddenly see again, although the cave was so vast that I couldn't tell where it ended. I blinked against the bright light.

"Thanks, Martinez. What am I meant to be seeing?"

"Over there," Martinez pointed.

I scanned the site, maybe a hundred metres away from us. The floor was littered with destroyed sand-crawlers. Not like the transport we had driven down here; these were unmodified civilian models, now just burnt-out wrecks.

"I've run a bio-scan," Martinez said. "No reads."

"These must have been Kellerman's pioneers," I said to myself. "Form up on that nearest crawler. I want to check it out."

"Why?" Martinez asked. "This is a bad place. Full of *espíritu malign*. We need to move on – make the most of our lead-time. The Krell will be on our tail—"

"Are you questioning my orders, Martinez?" Suddenly, for whatever reason, it was very important that I investigated the crawler.

Martinez shrugged his enormous shoulders.

Both of them followed me down to the crawler. It was extensively blackened, probably by boomer-fire. Unlike many of the crawlers, at least this one was still the right way up.

"Looks dead to me," Martinez said. "They must have taken a longer route down here."

Mapping the tunnels, just like Tyler said.

A noise – scratching, like clawing from an animal seeking release – came from inside the crawler. The entry hatch had been sealed shut by fire, but the noise was loud enough to be audible from outside. I clambered towards the crawler, over rocks and through fetid water pools. The flares were still burning brightly, and threw dancing shadows across the shattered hull.

"I'm going inside."

"Negative, Cap," Jenkins said. "Let me go first…"

I had to get inside the crawler, although I didn't know why. I easily yanked open the hatch, the metal frame creaking as it gave. It was hardly necessary to use the hatch – there were holes in the crawler outer plating, big enough for me to squirm through, and every view-port had been blown out.

"At least let me come in with you," Jenkins said, following me. She activated her suit-lamps to inspect the interior. "Christo…"

The scene was horrifying and yet strangely calming.

Death comes to us all, a voice whispered in my ear. *Even those who would deny it.*

There were six still figures in the passenger compartment, eternally harnessed. They wore hostile-environment suits, like mine, with helmets covering their faces. Instead of bodies in the midst of flight – desperate to escape the crawler – the dead were inexplicably tranquil. Like they had known what was coming when their crawler ignited, greeting death without a fight.

"They've been dead for a long time," Jenkins muttered.

"The crawler burnt out," I said. "They probably suffocated from the smoke—"

"*I miss you.*"

I turned to Jenkins, although it didn't sound like her voice. She had braced herself in the hatch, unwilling to completely enter. She scowled behind her face-plate.

"You said something."

"I didn't," she said, shaking her head. "Must be hearing things, Cap."

I placed my pistol on the lap of the nearest corpse. It was propped upright in the seat, poised as though resting rather than dead. Gloved hands sat on the knees. The helmet had completely fogged during the fire, and the originally off-white H-suit had become a dirty, smoky black.

"They strapped in even though they knew they were going to die," I muttered.

"This is some bad shit," Jenkins insisted. "We should move out."

Just then, her lamps illuminated a scrawled message on the crawler cabin wall. I motioned for her to keep the area lit.

Three simple words.

Three familiar words:

DON'T FORGET ME

I swallowed and recoiled from the wall.
Am I going mad? This can't be happening.

"You see that?" I asked Jenkins. She had to be my touchstone, my litmus test against insanity.

"Affirmative. Doesn't mean anything to me."

Of course it didn't, but it meant something to me. Something that Kellerman hadn't known about. *This isn't happening*, I insisted.

"Someone wrote that before they died," I said to Jenkins.

"Looks that way." Jenkins looked on impassively, unimpressed. "It's really better if we keep moving – the Krell could be here at any moment—"

But I couldn't listen to her. This place was something special. Had to be: no one knew of those words, no one but Elena. I had to examine the crawler, whether Martinez and Jenkins wanted me to or not. With irrational determination, I reached over and lifted the helmet of the nearest corpse—

Elena's face stared back. Big, dead eyes. Mouth open in a scream. She had been dead for years. Face contorted, withered; charred to blackened bone by the extreme temperature. Hair plastered to her head.

Fuck no – please don't tell me that she died like this! She was never on Helios—

I shuddered and withdrew from the body.

It wasn't Elena's face. I rubbed the H-suit chestplate clean, looking for some means of identifying the body. A name was printed on a stitched ID tag: S TYLER.

"Tyler's sister. So she made it this far."

With a determination that I couldn't explain, I tore off the ID tag. Jenkins watched on with an uneasy grimace, but I ignored her. I stuffed the tag into another pouch on my belt.

You'll go mad just like Sara and her people. Just a matter of time.

"Cap, we should go," Jenkins implored.

"It didn't do her any good," I said, taking a final look around the cabin. "We need to remove the body, do something to consecrate her passing."

But there was nothing I could do, in the circumstances. *I'll come back here*, I thought to myself, *and see that she is properly sanctified. She should have a proper burial.* Even as the thought formed, I knew that it wouldn't happen.

"No time. We need to move."

"Double-time it in there," Martinez said over the comm. "I'm getting some ghost signals on the scanner."

Martinez's voice brought me crashing back to reality. We were in enemy territory, surrounded by potential hostiles. He and Jenkins were right – we needed to keep moving. I was being irrational, and I couldn't explain it.

"Affirmative on the withdraw," I finally said, nodding to Jenkins. She looked relieved at my command. "Let's get moving."

We backed out of the crawler. Jenkins jumped down first, and her boots cast up plumes of dust. Her head bobbed as she covered the nearby rock formations and natural permutations of the cavern floor, searching for targets. Content that the area was clear, I clambered down from the transport, and followed Jenkins. Martinez had deployed away from the crawler. He had thrown out some more flares, creating a lighting perimeter hundreds of metres around the destroyed vehicles.

"Holy Christo," I muttered.

There were bodies, just like those inside the crawler, in every direction. Many were sprawled out on the floor, face down, and all were crawling away from something. In the same direction, I realised: back the way that we had come.

"The suits are from Helios Station," Martinez said, crouching to examine one of the bodies.

All of the H-suits were emblazoned with crew and station badges from the outpost. There were hundreds of them down there, but it didn't look like they had all died at the same time. Some were crumbling, ancient corpses, while others were still old, but fresher.

"It goes on like this for some way," Martinez said, motioning out into the darkness beyond the flare light. "They must've put up a good fight. They were probably running from something."

"But they didn't stand a chance," I said. "Look at the injuries."

There had been multiple causes of death. Some of the corpses were torn to shreds by Krell weaponry – puckered with stinger-spines, swollen by exposure to bio-toxins and boomer-fire, torched by Krell flamers. Jenkins prodded at one of the more desiccated corpses, bone and fabric crumbling on contact.

"Mostly Krell weapons, but some of them died from standard-issue tech," she said, rising up to full height. Her face looked pale. "The impact wounds look like shots from a carbine or pistol."

"They shot each other." Among the tangle of bodies, there were even human weapons; all civilian-issue, the sort of gear we had seen back at Helios Station. "They either went mad, or decided it was better to die down here than go on."

Martinez crossed himself. The action looked bizarre in his combat-suit. "*La misericordia de Dios.*"

Then I saw something else. I scraped the floor with my glove, brushing aside an age of dust and small debris. The floor underneath was smooth, machined. Even in the twitchy light of the flares, I could see that it was a dark metallic compound.

"These caves aren't natural."

"Gets worse up ahead," Martinez declared, pointing into the dark. "No rock at all."

I paced over to Martinez, stepping through the minefield of corpses. Careful to avoid touching their outstretched arms, careful not to look on their terror-filled faces.

He was right. The tunnels became much narrower, and the rock-hewn walls gave way to the same metal.

"So something made these tunnels," I muttered, cautiously eyeing our route through the cavern.

"What are your orders?" Martinez asked. He was just ahead of Jenkins and me, caught in the jumpy light of the flares: red on one side, green on the other. "I'm just going to say this once: I think that you should go back, *compadre*. We can get the ship, fly to the Artefact, and you can sit tight down here – maybe track back to the crawler—"

"We go on through the tunnels," I said. "Nothing else that we can do."

I knew that there was danger out there in the

dark, and I knew that there was sense to what Martinez was suggesting. But *something* drove me on: something indescribable, beyond human terminology.

"Move out."

CHAPTER TWENTY-EIGHT

AT PEACE

Mission timeline: fifteen hours.

The tunnels became narrower. There was no way that we would have fitted a crawler through them. *The Artefact is a rotten tooth*, I considered. *Beneath the gumline, the root is immense and infected*. We were in that root, now somewhere below the rotted structure.

My head felt like it was going to explode, and I had to focus on what Jenkins and Martinez were saying to me, or my mind was quickly dominated by the Artefact's signal. The impossibility of my plan – the idea of making it all the way to the Artefact – dawned on me during the trek.

Can't give up. Got to keep it together.

So many dead bodies. Not enough to account for the two thousand missing staff, but enough to demonstrate that the tunnels had been the site of an unmitigated massacre. We didn't even stop to inspect them.

"I hate this place," I whispered. "It offered me so much, but has taken everything."

"What do you mean?" Jenkins asked, panning the area behind us with her rifle. When she turned away from me, I immediately panicked, desperately looking ahead to make sure that Martinez was still with me.

"Elena. It offered me Elena."

"Don't worry about that now," Jenkins said. There was pity in her voice. It made me angry; not just with her, but with Kellerman, with the whole damned cosmos. I was so drained from being angry.

"A long time ago, I tried to follow her," I went on. Easier to just recite past glories, to remember what had come before, than to think about what was going to happen next. "Command wouldn't authorise the mission. Too expensive, too risky. Not without star-data."

I wanted to keep talking. Jenkins' voice was a comfort in the darkness, something real in the midst of this nightmare.

"That was where I went wrong. I let Elena go. I should have tried to stop her, should have told her that I loved her."

"We all have to make choices," Jenkins said. "But it isn't the good choices, the easy ones, that define us. It's the bad choices, the hard decisions."

"Hindsight is a wonderful thing."

"I suppose so. Sometimes a bad decision isn't obvious until it's too late."

Now, I was paying for that decision, that choice. Elena had gone out into the cold, hungry stars. I had let her go. She had been alone, desperate and separated from the rest of the human race. And now I was too.

"It's ironic," I said. "Elena always wanted me to live a *real* life, to enjoy *unsimulated* reality. All those years ago, I couldn't do that."

Maybe she blamed herself for inducting me into the Sim Ops Programme. Maybe she felt that was her bad choice. She was wrong about that; she might've inducted me, but I was the one who became addicted. I kept going back out into space for more, simply because I craved it.

The anticipation of making transition.

The rush of inhabiting a new simulant body.

The gratification of doing things that no natural human being was capable of.

And yes, even the horror of extraction. Even the pain of dying, again and again, became like a drug to me eventually.

"Elena knew that none of it was real," I said, shaking my head. "She tried to warn me against becoming addicted. Tried to warn me that I was losing touch with reality, losing her."

"Just remember who you are, Harris," Jenkins said. "*Lazarus*. You always come back. We're all going to get through this."

She didn't sound convinced at all.

The tunnels became wrinkled, scarred with ancient cuneiform. Consoles of black obsidian lined the walls. I approached one of them, and the controls glowed green in reaction. Martinez and Jenkins tried to do the same, but they couldn't reproduce the effect.

My head ached worse than ever before. Even

death by vacuum had been more pleasant than this. Whatever Kellerman had fed me to overcome the pain caused by the beating I'd suffered back at Helios Station, it had now completely worn off. I was in the throes of a chemical comedown. I limped on. My data-ports burnt. I'd never felt this sort of hurt in a simulant, let alone my own skin.

Something flashed red on my wrist-comp display. I stared down at it for a long time. TRANSPONDER TRACKING ACTIVE. *So Kellerman still has his talons in me, even now.*

I didn't bother telling the others.

Martinez's bio-scanner chirped a regular warning, letting us know that there were hostiles out in the dark.

It had been making the same noise for hours.

The Krell were following us.

Mission timeline: twenty hours.

"The floor is rising," I said to the others.

Martinez and Jenkins nodded in agreement. The incline was almost imperceptible, but the tunnels were coiling back, taking us to the surface.

To the site of the infection.

"How far do you think we have to go?" I asked. Forming the words took such immense effort.

"Maybe a few hundred metres," Martinez declared. "But it's difficult to say—"

Suddenly, Martinez's bio-scanner began an urgent trilling. I could envisage his sensor-feed: a mass of fast-moving hostiles converging on our position. An amorphous signal-blob, indistinct, impossible to quantify. Behind me, Jenkins fell to one knee, rifle up. I clutched my plasma pistol.

In the dark, Martinez spun about-face, rifle up, searching for targets. I felt the prickle of fear on my spine: the Krell were here, even if we couldn't see them yet.

"Keep all approaches covered," I yelled, my voice echoing down the tunnels. "Watch the six!"

"Conta—" Martinez managed.

Something enormous swooped from the ceiling, accompanied by a claws-on-metal squeal. It came from a shaft above Martinez, and had been hidden until it chose to reveal itself. The primary-form sank its forearms into Martinez's torso. Both blades pierced his combat-suit, lifting him off his feet. All happening so damned fast, too quick for my unaided senses to properly digest, let alone react. The xeno dropped from the shaft, hitting the ground with an enormous boom.

"Help me!" Martinez howled.

"Jenkins!" I shouted. "It has Martinez!"

I'm going to be next—

I started firing. Unguided, incensed. Plasma pulses tore into the xeno's body, sent boiling alien blood over the walls and floor. The thing screamed, scrabbling around on the smooth floor for purchase, forearms still in Martinez's twitching body. It wasn't going to let him go, no matter what I did.

Jenkins immediately joined my fire. It took a couple of shots from her M95 to put the thing down – one to the body, another to the head. Guts and brain matter slid from the cauterised wounds, and the two corpses collapsed to the floor.

Martinez was gone. His body crumpled, huge wounds slewing his internal organs. His face-plate had smashed. No prospect of revival: extraction complete.

"Good journey, *compadre*," I muttered.

I just hoped that he had safely made extraction, back at Helios Station. And as with Kaminski, there was no telling whether his extraction made his real death any more or less likely.

"Oh shit!" I yelled.

Another xeno came out of the shaft. I stumbled backwards, away from the attacker. This one landed on its feet, immediately launching at Jenkins.

Then two more slid from the ceiling. Back the way we had come, I saw the flash of wet bodies in the dark. Boomers and stingers wildly stitched the metal walls and floor.

"Get down!" Jenkins yelled. Behind her face-plate, she was a picture of sheer determination: mouth set, eyes wide.

She pumped the grenade launcher on her rifle. I lowered my head, covered my face. Even slammed my hands to my ears, although I was already wearing my helmet and it would do me no good.

An incendiary grenade sailed down the corridor. It exploded almost immediately – star-bright, scattering Krell body-parts. That wasn't good enough for Jenkins. She pumped the rifle again, fired another grenade. That exploded too. The sound was so loud, amplified by metal walls and floor.

Fuck, fuck! This is really happening.

I was shaking inside my suit. Even using the respirator atmosphere-supply, I tasted the reek of sweat and fear in the back of my throat.

"Press on down the corridor," Jenkins barked at me. "Now! Stay back."

I sheltered behind her. I was in no position to argue; she had the authority now. She fired again and again. Despite her enormous agility and strength, she cleared each sector carefully and cautiously.

They kept coming, and this time there were more of them. Again from the shafts above, from sub-corridors with no apparent use. Every shadow spawned them.

A primary xeno-form hurled itself at her.

Then: a ball of teeth and claws and talons and muscle.

Now: a blazing wreck of dead tissue.

I almost crawled after her. I fired when I could – both hands wrapped around the grip of my pistol. The pain in my head was overwhelming. The Artefact's song was so clear that it was crippling me.

"Stay with me, Harris!" Jenkins called. Her helmet had been torn off, thrown into the mass of invading bodies.

The tunnels became tighter still. The walls were covered in scripture, the characters running like melted wax over metal, dripping and flowing. I brushed a hand against the wall, and icons suddenly flared to life.

But there was also a light at the end of the tunnel, I realised. At first, I only saw it in the afterglow of Jenkins' rifle muzzle, still flaring brightly from the firefight.

Jenkins fell to a knee again, and fired another grenade. The corridor shook violently. I stole a glance back the way we had come.

I didn't dare think about how many Krell were packed into that space. Clawing and shrieking, desperate to break open Jenkins' armoured body and rip her insides out.

And once Jenkins is gone – me too.

Stinger-spines sailed overhead, impacting the walls and leaving studded reminders.

One hit Jenkins hard in the chest. It cleanly spiked through her combat-armour.

"Oh *fuck*!" she said, letting out a surprised grunt. She half turned to me: "Just run! Just fucking get out of here!"

She managed to stay upright; no doubt her combat-suit was compensating for the toxins entering her bloodstream. Just one of those envenomed fragments would be enough to kill me – to drain my body of all life, to wither the *real* heart in my chest.

Jenkins grasped her grenade harness, enormous hands fumbling for an explosive—

Every possible sub-tunnel and shaft was rammed with aliens, and they had already choked the corridor from which we'd come. They were encircling us – now so close they were pressing in. No way back: the only possible route out of this mess was the light at the end of the tunnel.

A primary-form separated from the Collective, and leapt towards Jenkins. Unfurled to full height, it struck mantis-quick: knife-tipped forearms piercing her shoulders, right through her.

"Jenkins!" I shouted, paralysed.

Two or three further attackers descended on her, excited by the scent of blood, sharks following the kill. In such close confines, she couldn't bring the rifle up to fire, and futilely struggled to pull herself free from the talons.

She's already finished, I told myself. *Nothing that I can do.*

"Go!" she managed. Her voice was wet and broken, like Blake's before he had died out in the desert.

I watched in hypnotic terror, detached from the scene. I'd seen this so many times before, seen the Krell kill Blake, Martinez, Kaminski. Even my own death, on vid-feed recordings. Yet this was different: now the Krell had a new purpose. Something almost ceremonial.

Like frenzied piranhas at feeding time, the Krell took Jenkins *apart*. With an inhuman shriek, earsplittingly loud in the enclosed tunnels, the main attacker ripped through her combat-suit. Her body was split in two. The other primary-forms tore at her torso, pulled limb from limb. Artificial blood splashed the walls, coated alien carapaces. The remains of Jenkins' simulated body disappeared beneath the tide of Krell.

The carnage was over in a fraction of a second. Then the Krell lost interest in Jenkins, and moved to surround me. Every xeno-form, every possible mutant strain. I felt their hot, wet alien breath through my helmet, impossible as that was. I was completely encircled.

Is this how it ends, this time? I asked myself.

A big xeno-form loomed over me. Strands of alien mucous, acting with a life of their own, darkened my vision. Simple motions like lifting my gun required so much mental strength that I could barely focus—

Lazarus, they called me. Except that there won't be any resurrection from this.

—and the singing: so glorious and terrible in my head, so strong that I clenched my teeth to ride it out – every static-squeal making the bones of my skull vibrate—

The explosion on the train. That same lost frequency.

"Fuck you!" I screamed at the universe in general.

I was lifted off the floor, caught in the scything talons of a leader-form. It was an ancient and scarred Krell, coated heavily with dust. Eyes burning like dark coals: so alien. Did this thing recognise – through a collective, racial memory shared with the rest of the Krell species – that I had been responsible for executing so many of its kind? I think that it did – in some way that I couldn't fathom and the human race could never understand.

I fumbled with my pistol, eager to fight until the last. There was no way that I was going down without a fight. I aimed it under the leader-form's ribcage, fingers probing the trigger stud, and I ground my teeth. I pulled the trigger, again and again.

Nothing happened. There was no response

from the weapon, no physical feedback as to why it wasn't operating.

Please no!

The power cell was already empty, and the LED display flashed in warning. When had that happened? I hurled the pistol at the leader and it bounced, harmlessly, off the creature's carapace. Both of my arms were free, and I patted my suit down – searching for something, *anything* – to use as a weapon.

There's nothing to help me out here. There never was, and now this is the end.

I closed my eyes. I drew into myself. I imagined Elena's face. The colour of her hair. The smell of her skin. I awaited the killing blow – that final and deadly act from the Krell leader-form.

But the attack never came.

After long seconds, I opened my eyes, still held in the clutches of the xeno bastard, feet nearly a metre off the ground. The leader was frozen. All of the Krell had stopped. Some of the nearer xenos backed away. They formed a wide circle around me, and slowly and surely withdrew.

This was not the same as the planned and purposeful retreat on the *Oregon*. The Krell recoiled from me. They knew *fear*.

I realised that in my struggle to find a weapon, I *had* found something. *The Key.* I clutched it like a knife. Unconsciously, I had lifted it, displaying the ancient device to the gathered Krell.

With grace and delicacy that I had never seen from the species, the leader-form placed me back on the ground. I immediately fell into a combat-stance, baring the Shard device.

The leader looked on with undisguised curiosity. It tilted its massive, armoured head to watch me. There was something almost mournful in its features.

My whole body shook. I tore free my helmet, gasping in lungfuls of poisoned atmosphere. My skin bristled with damp sweat.

We faced off against each other: the xeno leader and I.

A deep sonorous drone filled the air. Something around me was coming online, coming to life.

The xeno bowed its head.

For just a moment, we were at peace: captured in time, both species in awe of this ancient alien technology – whatever the Shard Key really was.

Then the harsh report of gunfire – of human gunfire – snapped me out of it, and the leader-form exploded.

CHAPTER TWENTY-NINE

NO ONE HAS EVER MADE IT THIS FAR

A part of my brain that I had forgotten existed suddenly kicked in.

Wessler-Heslake carbine. Standard civilian security forces issue. 9 mm armour-piercing rounds.

The gunfire was ferocious and intense. Many of the Krell were shredded. Rounds ricocheted off the metal walls and floor. Xeno corpses piled in front of me.

I slammed my body to the concave wall. Through pure chance, I hadn't been hit. In shaking hands, I unholstered my remaining weapon – my father's old revolver – and raised it, unsure of who or what to fire on.

"Captain Harris!" an all-too-familiar voice called above the noise. *Kellerman.* "Surrender!"

Just the sound of his voice made my bile rise, caused the flood of memories to almost envelop me. The Artefact's song rose with my anger: encouraged me to take him on, to take him apart.

In my mind's eye, I saw his bones breaking like matchsticks, his blood flooding the tunnel floor—

Get a grip!

The gunfire stopped. With eel-like fluidity the Krell fled into the walls and ceiling shafts.

Kellerman approached through the smoke, wading through the dead and dying. *Is he really here, or is this some trick of my damaged mind?* But phantoms didn't usually wear exo-suits, and Kellerman was strapped into his. He was equipped for battle: the exo had been extensively modified, using parts from a cannibalised simulant combat-suit. Armour plates lined the torso and limbs, and new servos extended across his legs, feet and hands.

Deacon was at his shoulder, carbine panning the dark. Whatever was left of Helios Station was in tow; researchers with the hard eyes of religious fanatics, dour-faced security personnel. Ten or so of them.

Kellerman held out one hand, but in his other he carried a sidearm. A Klashov-45 – a semi-automatic, Directorate-issue pistol. He attempted a smile in the half-light of the Shard tunnels, but the best he could muster was a corpselike rictus.

"Doesn't suit you, Kellerman," I shouted.

"When we lost contact with the sand-crawler, we assumed the worst," he said. "It took a fusion-borer to get through the cave-in. Thankfully, I equipped your suits with transponders – once we were in the tunnels, it wasn't so hard to find you."

The tracker in my wrist-comp; such a simple thing.

Kellerman's words gave me reassurance, in a

way that he had not intended. He had followed me down here, leaving the base unoccupied. *Has he already executed Kaminski?* Jenkins had just died – her consciousness would have travelled across the surface of Helios almost immediately, back into her real body – and allowing for time to find me, Kellerman must've already left the station by the time she made it back. He'd used a fusion-borer to reach me, not the Directorate Interceptor.

"We've come to assist," Kellerman said. "Hand over the Key."

"Stay there!" I shouted. Pistol still raised: a single shot at this range would put a hole in Kellerman, end his desperate obsession.

Deacon noisily armed his carbine; the *click* of the safety catch a marker in the sand. The sound echoed twenty-fold and impacted me like a gunshot. The message was simple: *You shoot him, I shoot you.*

"Who's faster, Deacon?" I asked.

The security chief shrugged. "Why don't we see? Y'all injured, and slow. I reckon that I could take you. And I'm damned sure that I want to."

Deacon wore an arm-band over his left bicep. Just a piece of black rag, covering the Helios Expedition and Alliance badging. Replacing it with the sword-and-hydra insignia of Directorate Spec Ops. All Kellerman's people wore the same badge. Fresh recruits, malleable to his twisted sense of scientific idealism.

"No army, then?" I asked. "No Directorate troops on Helios? Just sleeper agents for the cause – traitors."

"You don't know shit," Deacon barked back at me.

"Who'd they get to first? You or Deacon?"

Kellerman shuffled onwards, that dead grin still dominating his face.

"We lost people on the way down, but you did a good job of clearing out the tunnels," he said. His tone was controlled, calming.

"Stay the fuck back!" I shouted through gritted teeth. "What happened to my squad? Are they alive?"

Light reflected off something above Deacon's head. Two wet eyes, staring down. The Krell hadn't gone far; they were waiting for the chance to strike. I wondered whether there were xenos lurking behind me as well, whether I would die from a gunshot wound or the claws of a Krell.

"They are well. They're being cared for."

"And Tyler?"

Kellerman's gun was rigid at his side. He hadn't fired it before, I decided. He held the matte-black pistol against his leg, kept his forearm fixed. *Not a trained weapons operator. Probably won't be able to account for the recoil if he has to fire it.*

"I'd say she deserved what she got," Deacon said, grinning idiotically. "Bitch."

"She's alive," Kellerman added.

He fixed me with his eyes. That smile was gone from his face. He took another small step forward. Twenty or so metres away, now. His boot crunched a Krell skull underfoot. Smoke still poured from the alien bodies, acting as a barrier between us.

Another flash of light in the shaft above Deacon: two, three pairs of eyes. I sensed the Krell's barely restrained bloodlust.

"I said, *stay the fuck back!*" I yelled.

"I don't have time for this!" Kellerman snarled, striding onwards – through the remains of Jenkins' simulant. "I want that Key now! Deacon – shoot him but don't damage the Key—"

Several things happened within the blink of an eye, microseconds apart. To my unaugmented human senses, they appeared to all intents to happen simultaneously.

I fired my pistol at Kellerman.

The ceiling exploded with activity.

My shot went wide, and glanced over Kellerman's shoulder. The revolver had a nasty kick, so unlike an energy weapon. The kinetic round hit Deacon in the chest – punched cleanly through his flak jacket. The heavy-calibre slug knocked him backwards.

But even as he was hit, he was firing.

And even as he was firing, he was finished.

My eyes darted to the ceiling, for just a heartbeat, and Deacon knew what was coming. His expression was horrified.

A primary-form lurched out of a ceiling cavity, upside down, and eviscerated him cleanly with its razor-claws. The gunshot wound became an irrelevance. Deacon didn't even have time to evade the attack; just stood there, rifle braced in his hands.

But he managed to open fire, the action carried over in the throes of death.

Deacon's spent corpse collapsed to the floor,

finger still depressed on the weapon trigger. He indiscriminately sprayed the corridor with gunfire. Carbine rounds raked the walls, bullets ricocheting all about.

Kellerman reacted a second later – in battlefield terms, a lifetime too late – and began shooting at me as well.

The traitors rushed on, yelling Directorate battle cries: hack Chinese from Americans grown up on the Outer Colonies.

That was all the invitation the Krell needed. They renewed their attack, streaming from every shadow. Kellerman's men fought back, but they were not simulants. Screams echoed down the tunnels as the massed primary-forms assaulted. These were amateurs, despite their dedication, and there was an awkward moment of indecision – some of them erratically firing in my direction, others trying to hold back the Krell.

Their demise was inevitable, and I knew if I stuck around I would face the same fate. This fight could only go one way – and under cover of the chaos I could escape. I squeezed off another few shots into the melee, hoping to hit Kellerman, but the effort was token. Then I turned and ran as fast as my damaged body would carry me.

The corridors were suddenly aflame with alien cuneiform. Patterns ignited – blues, whites, incredible star-fields – as I ran. Spiral galaxies beyond our own. Worlds within worlds.

No one has ever made it this far.

The Artefact's signal pulled me onwards, as though I was possessed by the spirits of the long-dead architects of this structure. The transmission resonated off the walls and floors. The structure was humming; the metalwork reverberant. An immense power was building around me. Not the predictable, muted power of human technology: there was something self-aware, something malignant about this presence.

The tunnel became rock again. Stumbling over broken ground, I made it to a simple break in the cavern wall, marked by a pile of rocks. I just followed the light. Dust and grit filtered into the network from the opening. Despite my exhaustion, I fervently tore at the loose rocks. It didn't take long, and soon the opening was big enough to pull myself through.

Ahead, like an angry testament to gods long forgotten, the Artefact loomed in all its terrible majesty.

CHAPTER THIRTY

DEAD MAN WALKING

A storm raged around me.

Not just a storm: the storm to end all storms.

I was immediately exposed to the full fury of the wind. The rain was unearthly hard, coming down in great sleeting sheets, a thunderous deluge. Huge droplets hit my naked head, splattered noisily against the padding of my suit. The sky was dark, lit only by the crackle of luminescent lightning, and storm clouds eddied overhead – black, prophetic. As though Helios was venting all of its pent-up elemental power in one go. The place didn't feel natural, didn't feel real. Even the atmosphere was changed: heavy with ozone, cloying to the extent that it was barely breathable.

Assailed by the intense wind, I desperately clutched the Key in one hand and my father's pistol in the other.

"Where are you!" I bellowed into the storm. "Jenkins! Kaminski! Martinez!"

But the sky was empty, and there was no sign

of the Interceptor or my squad. *Time to face it: they're all dead. Kellerman has executed them.* I went to wipe rainwater from my eyes, with the back of my right hand. When my arm didn't respond – or rather did, but with frozen sluggishness – I realised what had happened. A dark bloom appeared at my shoulder, right through the collarbone: blood oozed through an open wound.

I'd been shot. A solid round; probably from Kellerman or Deacon.

"This isn't fair!" I shouted. My arm sagged, and I wrapped my fingers around the Key to hold on to it. My strength was fading fast. "I want to live!"

The Artefact's song overwhelmed me. I pitched forward, struggled to stay on my feet, and retched into the rain. It was a painful dry heave and nothing came up.

I was in the centre of an alien ruin. Shard structures peppered the desert floor, miniature artefacts. Aeons-old slabs of obsidian, slick with rain, draining the light. There were other, more ominous structures as well: wicked-looking spires, sharp and brutal, lined the route ahead.

The Artefact lay at the end of the path, rising out of the desert like the blade of an upturned knife, so big that it touched the sky. I couldn't concentrate on the Artefact – couldn't make out the detail of the vast design. It came into sharp focus, but then rapidly dissolved.

It doesn't want to be seen. It doesn't want to be remembered.

—hurts so bad, throbbing, thrumming behind my eyes—

A *click-click-clicking* noise rose above the wind.

I whirled around, tightening the grip on my pistol.

Kellerman suddenly broke free of the tunnel exit, smashing aside rocks and debris with wild abandon. This was a reborn Kellerman: empowered, renewed. He effortlessly rolled a boulder out of his way and his exo crackled with energy – it had been overcharged, the maniac operator's strength increased ten-fold. He'd lost his pistol somewhere in the tunnels, but that made him no less lethal.

"You can't escape," he shouted. "You're a dead man walking."

"Are you all that is left?" I called back, my pistol raised to fire at him. My arm – my good arm – trembled.

Kellerman appeared in double vision. The lank remains of his hair were plastered to his head, rain dripping from the craggy features of his face. Another lightning fork split the sky, illuminating him from behind. Inside his exo, he was a skeleton within a skeleton: a ragged mass of bones.

"None of them matter," Kellerman answered.

No one followed him out of the tunnel mouth, but there was movement all around us. The Krell were everywhere: skulking between the Shard ruins, hanging upside down from blasted structures. Relishing the rain, flashes of light winking off wetted carapaces. A gun-graft materialised out of my peripheral vision. The Key seemed to repel them – but for how long?

The ammo read-out on my revolver flashed, mocking me.

One round left.

One fucking round left.

A terrible despair descended on me: *I am going to die out here.* Whatever happened, I was finished. I was going to die like Sara Tyler, like the other explorers condemned by Kellerman's obsession. Like Elena, like Blake, like my father. I considered shooting myself. Take my father's way out of the problem, the easy way out. *What's one more death to a man who has experienced so many?* As if reading my thoughts, as if unhappy with that suggestion, I saw a primary-form leap between structures – moving nearer.

I scanned the horizon – momentarily – *please let them be here!*

With preternatural speed, using his exo-suit leg servos, Kellerman *leapt* towards me. My reactions were blunted, and the sudden speed with which he was moving caught me off-guard.

I fired.

The shot missed him completely, whistling off into the wind.

Kellerman body-slammed me with all of his mass. His armoured shoulder connected with my sternum, forced the breath from my lungs. We fell backwards, joined, and collapsed into the dirt. Water splashed all around us.

Kellerman followed up the attack immediately, and I had no time to react. He balled a fist, hammered it into my good arm. The blow sent a shockwave through me, and I dropped my pistol.

Kellerman was on top of me now, rising up with both powered fists over his head – ready to strike again. His body was so wide, twice as big as he was before.

"I'm sorry, Elena," I whispered. I wasn't sure whether I had actually vocalised the thought.

Kellerman paused, held off the assault. Sitting astride my battered body, he grabbed the collar of my suit. He pulled me close to his face.

"Is that who you hear, when the Artefact calls out to you?" Kellerman asked. "Is that who you hear? Elena – that was the name. Who is she? Some fifty-credit whore back at *Liberty Point*?"

His skin was a ghostly white. A tracery of blue veins popped up all over his skull.

Leeroy, chasing me through the tenement with that damned bat—

"You have no Christo-damned right to even say her name!" I shouted back. My H-suit was soaking wet – absorbing water and blood, becoming heavier. I was losing my edge from the gunshot wound.

Kellerman gave me a slow, informed nod, like he understood exactly what I was saying. *Can he see the Krell all around us?* I asked myself. *Are they really here?* A whole Collective had assembled, spectators to our confrontation. I still held the Key, and it was growing warmer and warmer: hot enough now that I could feel it through my padded gloves.

I swiped at Kellerman with my good arm – a sidelong punch to his head. He pulled back, evading the blow. Then he hauled me to my feet, exo-assisted fingers tearing at the fabric of my H-suit.

He shook me, and although I struggled to fight back against him I just couldn't. He had expanded to fill the universe. His face split into a demonic leer: eyes burning hot embers, filled with red light. More alive than he had ever been before.

"Isn't it wonderful?" Kellerman asked. Not of me, but of the universe at large; indicating towards the Artefact, dwarfing us both now.

"Fuck you, Kellerman!"

He flung me into a nearby ruin. My injured shoulder impacted the solid structure – I felt something else breaking in my back or arm. Hard to say. I could still feel my legs, so it wasn't my spine.

So damn cold. Numb inside and out.

I shook my head; needed to concentrate. The Artefact's transmission had settled into an unbearable thrumming. All around me, the atmosphere pressed uncomfortably.

Kellerman appeared over me.

"Let me tell you what I hear," he said. "I was on Epsilon Ultris in an official capacity, as part of a Sci-Div expedition, in a sector that the Alliance Army had *approved* I visit. The UAS *Santiago* fired a barrage on my position. Sixteen of my best people, blasted away in the press of a button, because some idiot technician didn't check whether there were allied forces in the area. Command called it friendly fire. *Friendly fire!* I ask you, as a military man, what is friendly about a plasma ordnance barrage?"

My heart began a slower, staccato beat. *It will be a release*, I decided. My thoughts were jumbled, disconnected. I struggled to decide which pain was worse. Despite being wounded by a gunshot and severely beaten, my head was winning the competition. I blinked blood from my eyes – not even sure where I was bleeding from any more.

"That's the noise I hear: the humming, in the second before the plasma barrage reached us. The sky was on fire, Harris – the damned sky! I've never heard anything like it, before or since. The sound of death, the sound of annihilation. The end of all things. I survived by pure chance. But, I ask you, what kind of a survival is *this*? The Alliance: they did this to me. When they took my legs, I thought that my life was over. That I would never again set foot on an alien world, never again experience the thrill of a new finding. And you are just the same: you could never do what you do inside your body. Injured or otherwise."

For an instant, I could hear the same noise as Kellerman: the electric hum caused by the atmosphere igniting. I imagined the air crackling all around us, the retina-destroying flare of light as the barrage claimed the horizon—

"I'm nothing like you," I managed, taking slow breaths. *Fuck – my ribs hurt so bad*. "And I never will be."

"We are both trapped in these fallible bodies. Both doomed to live out existence in mortal frames that we have outgrown."

"Never."

I struggled to my feet, went to punch Kellerman – only overstretched, left myself open to a counter. Kellerman was no fighter but he had strength on his side. He dodged the blow. Launched a powerful elbow strike, right into my face. Bone and steel connected: something popped in my face. Bright red blood spewed from my nose.

With monumental effort I tried to scramble to my feet again. The thrumming sound had increased in pitch, become all-enveloping. It felt like the universe was collapsing in on itself.

"The Directorate wants what I have," Kellerman snarled.

"This is madness," I slurred. "You don't know what will happen if you activate the Artefact. You can feel what it is doing to us now. You don't know what you are dealing with. Once the Artefact is activated, the Directorate won't give a shit about your research."

"I don't care about the Directorate, but I hate the Alliance. Knowledge is all that matters. I will call the Shard here. Can you imagine the advances that a race like that can offer us? The Directorate is a means to an end. They helped me, and I helped them."

Kellerman raised a booted foot and kicked me hard in the gut. Broken, spent, I collapsed to the ground.

"It's over. This is how it ends. Give me the Key."

I shook my head. Couldn't talk any more: breathing was too much effort.

Kellerman kicked me again and again. Every blow was a ball of iron into my stomach. I doubled over in pain. Something else inside me ruptured.

The Key fell from my hand. I was too weak to hold it any more.

Kellerman strode past me. He was a force of nature now, elevated beyond a man. His footfalls were slow and heavy, and he confidently scooped up the alien relic.

I lay on the floor, in the dirt, rain falling all around me. So cold. Fading so fast.

The Krell poured out of the tunnel, amassing an army, encircling us. They had finished the rest of Kellerman's away team, and now we were completely alone out here.

My vision splintered. Debilitating, crippling pain kept me down on the floor. I prayed for the starship – for Jenkins and my squad to make their appearance. But even as I managed to scan the sky, there was no sign of them.

More alien devices and structures were rising out of the sand. The consoles started to glow, pulsating with new life. One of them – sitting at the very foot of the Artefact – blazed especially bright. I recognised the cuneiform: the same as the scripture on the Key. Kellerman lurched over to the Artefact control console.

The ringing in my head was so strong that I couldn't think straight. I wanted to live so badly – and I wanted the Key. I searched the area for my pistol – for a rock, for a gun, for anything. But my head ached so fucking badly—

Got.
    To.
    Stay.

Awake.

Somewhere a child was crying. A high, new-born's cry. A baby that I had never known.

—*the explosion*—

—*the UAS* Santiago *acquired the firing solution*—

—*that noise: high pitched – so loud that my head split*—

—*Blake's face as the stinger hit*—

—*Elena as she turned to leave*—

Old Death lurked nearby. Come to claim his dues, after so long. The Dark Angel himself – beating enormous black wings, hovering in the rain. Casting a long and shifting shadow across both Kellerman and me.

Breathing hurts so bad.

Stay.

Awake.

My father in the rain, part of his head missing – jaw working to shout something into the wind: words lost to eternity, just like Elena.

Blake – uninjured, as I wanted to remember him – yelling at me.

Elena, in that black dress she had worn on the train – her long hair swept back by the rain, but her face full of dignity. She was shouting something too.

"I'm sorry!" I yelled. "I let you all down."

Kellerman had his back to me, manipulating the alien console. It flared with new light – bright, inviting whites and blues, haloed by the rain. Framed by the Artefact, Kellerman held up the Key in both hands: the high priest offering a sacrifice to the gods, the console his altar.

I retched some more. Kellerman was being sick

as well – great bloody strands pouring from his rotten mouth.

I only wished I could hear what Elena was saying. I listened so hard, pulled myself back from that yawning abyss from which there could be no return.

And then, abruptly, I could hear exactly what she was saying:

"You always come back."

Lazarus, they called me.

In impossible agony, I hauled myself to my knees. My vision was cast red, blood weeping from wounds all over my face. Every breath, every heartbeat, was a war.

Through teary eyes, my vision shaking – my *reality* destabilising – I looked up at the sky.

Not Death.

Something else.

Something less familiar.

There were lights. Not lightning, but electric lights. Bright, angelic lights – scanning the area. Two searchlights, mounted in unison.

The lights abruptly focused on me. A black shadow appeared overhead. That noise – the thrumming – was nothing more than a propulsion engine. As the shape came nearer, I saw the flare of starship thrusters – firing a bright blue as the craft hovered. Through the miasma of dust and rain, it took me a moment to realise what I was looking at.

The angular matte-black armour plating.

The distinctive nose shape.

Those bulbous engines.

The Directorate Interceptor *Pride of Ultris* hovered beside the Artefact.

She had been concealed by the storm. But now, using her VTOL capability, the ship was impossible to ignore.

Here comes the motherfucking cavalry.

CHAPTER THIRTY-ONE

EASY WAY OUT

Kellerman was so absorbed in the activation of the alien machine, that he had not even seen the ship arrive. The Krell were more observant: as one, the Collective raised their heads to the invader.

The *Pride* circled the Artefact, engine pitch shifting as she manoeuvred. The operation wasn't perfect and she tilted hazardously as she began another sweep. The delicate anti-gravitic engine struggled with the conditions.

One hand to my knee, pulling my injured leg up next, I stood. Braced against the wind and the rain, seething with anger – alive, driven. Cold vengeance filled me.

Kellerman faltered, suddenly realising what was happening. He glared up at the ship – his ship – with hair whipping about his face, caught in the backdraft of the Interceptor's engines.

The weapon pods deployed smoothly under her wings.

The wasp is about to sting.

"What the fuck?" he managed

The *Pride of Ultris* opened fire.

There was a loud whistle, ultrasonic, caused by the launching of the plasma ordnance.

The entire mountain range became a sea of fire. The *Pride* launched missiles into the massed Krell, scattering them. Her chin-mounted cannon pulsed continuously, clearing the area around Kellerman and me. The Krell shrieked and clamoured, scattering to avoid the slaughter.

A searing heat washed over me, burning my head and neck. I flinched as structures exploded, toppled into the desert. Red-hot embers dispersed in the air, smoke pouring from the surrounding area.

And for the first time since I had met Kellerman, I saw something new in his eyes.

Fear.

His mouth hung open, strands of blood and spittle and vomit weeping into the wind. He was back on Epsilon Ultris – watching as the world around him ignited.

I took my chance.

I launched into him – gaining strength with every stride, intent on stopping him. This was what I was born to do: in this body or another. I wanted the Key, wanted Elena.

Kellerman turned at the last moment. Our bodies connected – my shoulder to the small of his back, between armoured plates. I bowled him into the console. The jittery searchlight panned over us – dowsing us in bright light one second, plunging us into darkness the next.

I pounded Kellerman with my fists again and again. To the face, the chest, the stomach – anywhere.

"Get – off – me!" Kellerman stammered.

The control console pulsed, so bitterly disappointed that the promise of activation had not been realised. The Artefact's scream echoed in my mind, made that nausea well up within me again. But this time I fought it down, held it inside.

We struggled over the Key – Kellerman grasping it, recoiling with every new blow. Our hands locked over the relic – now burning hot.

Its edge looked so much like a knife.

Slowly, surely, I turned the blade towards Kellerman. I knew exactly what I had to do.

I brought the Key down, with every possible reserve of strength left in my body.

I planted it into Kellerman's stomach. Into the meat of the gut; past the armour plating of his exo-suit. Whatever material the Key was composed of, it was hard enough to slice through the exposed workings of the exo. Pushed the Key in further, one hand on the hilt, the other on his shoulder. Through tissue and organs until it hit bone.

"For Blake," I whispered, drawing his head up to my mouth. "For Elena."

Then I let him go, with a gentle push. My hands were wet with his blood.

For a long beat, he just stood there: staring at me with defeated eyes. Then he reeled back, crumpling to the floor. Caught in the orange light of the exploding mountain range, rendered immediately human and fallible again. Where the Key had been lodged was an expanding hole – full of blood and intestines. Kellerman futilely clutched at it, tried to hold everything in.

Above us, the ship wobbled and one of the side airlock hatches opened. A welcome face appeared – Jenkins, aiming from the moving platform with a plasma rifle. I'd never been more pleased to see her. Beside her, Kaminski tossed a winch out of the hatch. The heavy rappel cable landed beside me. It was really them; not simulants, not echoes.

"Grab hold of this!" Jenkins yelled.

Another flash of motion in the storm: another Krell primary-form, swiftly moving through the fire and smoke. They were recovering fast from the plasma strike.

The ship tilted precariously again, the engines whining in protest.

"Get in!" Jenkins shouted.

I stooped in front of Kellerman, grabbed the Key from his weakening hands. He lay in a pool of blood; almost too much for one man to hold inside. There was something metallic on the floor nearby – my father's revolver.

"Good luck," I shouted, kicking it a little nearer to Kellerman's position. I tossed him an ammo cartridge. Both just out of his reach – he was going to have to work for them.

"I'm ordering you to get back here!" Kellerman said. "I am supervisor of Helios Station, and have authority over the armed forces posted on this world!"

Death was already on his shoulder. *Will he take the easy way out?* I wondered. It was more than he deserved, more than he was worth.

"Ten shots, Kellerman. Make them count."

The cable whipped around before me. Hand over hand, every motion agonising, I hauled myself up. When I reached the hatch, friendly hands dragged me inside. Gasping for breath, aching all over, I collapsed onto the deck. It vibrated softly beneath me.

"He's in," shouted Jenkins, to the command module. "Medical assist – now! Prime the auto-doc!"

"Christo, Jenkins! That was damned close."

"We had to thin the Krell numbers to get down to you," she said. She grinned, a real shit-eating smile. "There were too many of them. We knew that we wouldn't hit you."

"We *hoped* that we wouldn't hit you," Kaminski corrected.

"I'm okay," I mumbled. Talking was too much effort. "I'm okay. Just get us out of here."

"Closing the hatch!" Jenkins hauled the lock shut. "Ready for evac."

The Interceptor was small, and from where I sat I saw right through to the nose of the ship. Tyler was up front, strapped into the bridge command seat. She looked back at me – her face a mess of bruises and lacerations, grimacing nervously.

"The controls are going crazy," she shouted. "Might be the storm, or maybe something else. Keeping us airborne is going to be difficult. Something is pulling us back."

Just then, the Interceptor banked dangerously. I struggled to my feet, Jenkins hauling me up, and we all converged on the command module.

The Artefact was so close that it dominated

the viewers. It crackled with lightning, and with every new discharge I felt static erupt in my head. Beyond the Artefact, the storm claimed the desert for kilometres in every direction. As the Interceptor listed unsteadily, I saw a glimpse of the huge Krell force building in the mountains.

"We're losing altitude," Tyler shouted.

The ship engines whined again.

"Sweet Christo," Kaminski muttered. "We go down out here, it's all over."

"It's the Artefact," I roared. Only adrenaline and determination kept me standing. "Destroy it. Use the warheads."

Jenkins and Kaminski activated the weapons systems again.

The Interceptor performed a pinhead turn. Something responded on the control panel and warning bulbs illuminated. A sighting grid appeared on the view-screen ahead. Cross-hairs closed on the Artefact.

"Let's hope this works," I shouted.

Warheads screamed out from under the wings of the Interceptor, covering the distance to the Artefact almost immediately. Several of them hit home – at this range, it was almost impossible to miss. The view-screen flashed with icons and messages, confirming impacts. Bright explosions coursed over the Artefact, each causing a chain reaction of further detonations.

Gradually, the enormous structure collapsed in on itself, toppling away from the *Pride*. It sent up an enormous plume of dust. With each new detonation, the ache in my head diminished, until eventually it was gone altogether. For the first time since we had arrived on Helios, despite my catalogue of injuries, my head was clear.

Instantaneously, the *Pride of Ultris* righted itself. Tyler breathed a long sigh of relief.

"We've destroyed it," she said. "Ship scans confirm that the signal is dead. It's gone!"

"Hell yeah!" Kaminski hollered.

I manipulated the ship sensor-suite. I could see the area below us in precise detail.

There was Kellerman, and he wasn't alone. The Collective advanced through the remains of the Artefact, through the clouds of dust caused by the explosion. Kellerman was still alive: firing the pistol again and again into the oncoming horde. Even from this distance, it was obvious that he was fighting a losing battle.

He looked up at the camera, for just a second. *How many rounds does he have left?* He aimed the pistol at the Interceptor, and fired twice. The gesture was nothing more than futile, given the ship's armour plating, and I didn't even feel the rounds impact.

"You want us to go back for him?" Tyler asked, turning in the flight chair. She paused uncertainly, frozen over the controls.

"Let him take his chances," I said, without even thinking. I switched off the monitor.

Tyler nodded. "Good decision, Captain."

The *Pride* abruptly started to gain altitude and banked away from the mountain range. The engine tone became smooth. Bulbs across the control panel illuminated green. We were gaining velocity and pulling away from Helios' planetary gravity, now. It wouldn't be long before we broke the atmosphere completely.

It was over.

I dropped to the deck, closing my eyes and breathing long mouthfuls of processed air. It had never tasted so good. Kaminski and Martinez noisily chestbumped, yelling in triumph. For once, the noise sounded good: to hear happy human voices. They were dirt-stained and carried minor injuries – Kaminski a swollen jawline, and Martinez a bleeding cut on his head – but they were alive, and that was all that mattered.

"Jenkins!" I slurred. "I think that you could be right about the medical assist."

EPILOGUE

THE LONG WAY HOME

We had been in space for three long days.

Helios was a distant memory – another life.

I spent most of my time in the observation deck. There were very few private areas on the *Pride of Ultris*, and the ship felt cramped even with a skeleton crew of five. The deck was cluttered with emergency evac gear – space suits, spare oxygen canisters – but as nobody came up here it was my place, where I could go to properly collect my thoughts.

And there was so much to think about. Some of it good, some not. Dreams and nightmares; hope and despair. Such a mixture of emotion that it was almost overwhelming. I wasn't one for introspection, or at least I tried not to be, but I felt changed by the experience.

I sat on the bare metal deck, watching the distant stars and planets above me through the observation dome. To call it a deck was an over-statement; it was really nothing more than a glass bubble on the back of the ship, affording a view into the deep of space.

I had a new collection of death-trophies, reminders of the world we had left behind, assembled in front of me.

Blake's dog-tags. I was going to make good his wish – that at least something would be returned to his family, to remember him by.

Sara Tyler's tattered name-tag. That was for Tyler, and I had been meaning to give it to her since we left Helios' orbit.

The Key. The only surviving record of the star-data.

Battered and worn, imprinted with alien circuitry. Ingrained with Kellerman's blood. I hoped beyond hope that it was still operational. In the darker hours since we had left Helios, I agonised that it might be damaged. The data could have been erased, corrupted. Would Science Division even be able to interpret the star-data?

Just the thought of the device gave me a glimmer of hope, and I had to fight to quell it.

"You need some company, Cap?"

Jenkins clambered up the metal access ladder and into the observation area. There was barely room for two of us up there. She crawled into the opposite corner to me, between two crates.

"Yeah, sure."

"How's the leg?"

I patted down my injured leg. It still hurt to touch, but having some proper medical attention from the onboard auto-doc had helped. The bone-ache that had accompanied the original injury had now subsided: a medi-nanite injection meant that I had avoided any lasting damage.

"I'll live."

"And the ribs?" she said, grinning now. "And the shoulder…?"

"The same as the last time you asked." I returned the smile.

"Glad to hear it. You can get some decent medical care when we get back to the *Point*."

Time heals all wounds. The auto-doc had removed the bullet from my shoulder – that also sat on the deck, beside the other collected artefacts.

"Tyler tells me that's where we're headed," said Jenkins, "but she's no pilot."

I laughed. "We're taking the long way home, I guess. Thanks for coming back for me. I really thought that I was finished. Go through it with me again – what happened on Helios Station?"

Jenkins had told this story ten times already. I had the feeling that it would be repeated when we got back to the *Point* – both in the bars of the District, and to Alliance Command. On our return, at best we would face a protracted enquiry; at worst a court-martial. I allowed the death of a senior science officer. *Who also happened to be a Directorate defector.* I was quite sure that Military Intelligence would be very interested in our story.

Jenkins sucked her teeth and began. "Helios Station was overrun with Krell. When he extracted, Kaminski was detained by Kellerman. Your plan with the demo-charge – it sent him berserk, and he followed us into the tunnels." This was her favourite part of the story. "He left only a small security force for cover, and took the rest of his people with him. When Martinez and I extracted, we overpowered the guards. We went for the Directorate ship, and we came after you."

"Good job." I was still incredulous that the strategy had worked.

"We broke out Tyler. By then, there wasn't anyone else left alive on the station. Kellerman wasted Olsen before we extracted. The rest is history."

Not everything had worked to plan. We were still out of comms with *Liberty Point*. Neither Kaminski nor Tyler could operate the *Pride*'s FTL communicator. Combined with the fact that Helios Station had been overrun, no one knew that we were coming home.

Jenkins' smile faded a little, when she looked over the collected objects arranged in front of me on the deck.

"Do you think that Command will be able to use the Key?"

I sighed. "I hope so. Maybe I can follow her. Follow Elena."

Jenkins paused for a long moment, then added: "I'm sure that Command will be very interested in the star-data, but it'll be for different reasons. It could change everything. Command will want to go back into the Maelstrom."

"I'll be ready."

"I have the feeling that this isn't over," Jenkins said. "Not by a long way." Then she laughed, breaking the tension. "We've all been thinking."

"All of you? Even Kaminski?"

"*Even* Kaminski," Jenkins said. "We were thinking that it's about time the squad had a proper name. When we get back to the *Point*, we're going to be legends."

If we get back, I noted.

"We need something catchy. Maybe named after you?"

"What did you have in mind?" I knew Jenkins too well; it was obvious that she already had something.

She smirked. "What about the Lazarus Legion?"

I shook my head. "Maybe. I'll think on it. How is flight prep going?"

"Martinez is setting the freezers. We're approaching a possible Q-jump point; time to sleep soon."

She climbed back down the access ladder, leaving me to my thoughts.

I glanced outside, into space, and traced a thin line of stars across the viewer. Out there was the Maelstrom, beyond the grasp of human understanding or logic. Helios was nothing more than a pinprick of light in the blackness.

extras

orbit

meet the author

Jamie Sawyer

JAMIE SAWYER was born in 1979 in Newbury, Berkshire. He studied Law at the University of East Anglia, Norwich, acquiring a master's degree in human rights and surveillance law. Jamie is a full-time barrister, practising in criminal law. When he isn't working in law or writing, Jamie enjoys spending time with his family in Essex. He is an enthusiastic reader of all types of SF, especially classic authors such as Heinlein and Haldeman.

Find out more about Jamie Sawyer and other Orbit authors by registering for the free monthly newsletter at www.orbitbooks.net.

interview

What was the inspiration behind Artefact?
The idea really developed from piloted drone warfare –
these US warfare systems that are used in Afghanistan
and Iraq, but operated by pilots back in Nevada. I got to
thinking about how the operators live their lives: fighting wars by day in countries that they have probably
never visited, then returning to their homes by night to
lead a normal life. The simulant technology is really
just an extension of drone warfare. As the technology
is extrapolated so too is the psychological stress on the
operator. Harris is an example of someone who becomes
increasingly dependent on this destructive cycle, becoming – as one character puts it – a war junky.

**Does fighting a war remotely make him any less of a
soldier?**
That's an interesting question, which is hopefully
addressed at the end of the story. Harris ultimately finds
that he doesn't need to fight remotely, and that revelation
is in some ways liberating. It also almost kills him!

**What about the Artefact itself – how did you come up
with the idea?**
This is something of an SF trope, born out of an interest
in works of authors like Arthur C. Clarke. I've always
enjoyed the sense of wonder that these classic authors
created – the notion that the universe is so much bigger

than we could ever understand. The idea of an alien
machine of unknown purpose – that offers such potential to those who understand it, but equally corrupts
them at the same time – was something that engaged
me. Because physical proximity to the Artefact causes
that corruption, I thought that it connected well with the
principles of simulant warfare.

What was the most challenging thing about writing this novel?

The writing is the easy part! As with any working
author, balancing my day job and writing is the real
challenge. There never seem to be enough hours in the
day. Thankfully, I have a very understanding family – I
usually write during the evening and at weekends.

How much research went into the novel?

I read up a lot on the Vietnam War and the US–Soviet
Cold War, but most of the future history is my own cre-
ation. There are also echoes of a subverted Space Race
in the book; I researched the early space missions extensively. Time dilation also plays an important part in
the book, and I read a lot about theories on that topic.
Despite the research, I was grateful to have the assistance of a scientific edit!

Which was your favourite character to write?

This is a tough one! I liked writing all of the Simulant
Operations squad. They came alive for me as I wrote;
when bad things happen to them (and, rest assured,
some *very bad* things happen!) I really felt for them.
My favourite character was probably Captain Conrad
Harris. He is the point-of-view character for the novel,
and I had plenty of opportunity to explore his origins
and motivations. He has a very blunt and directed world
vision; acting first then thinking about it afterwards. But

I also liked writing Corporal Jenkins: she's far fiercer than the rest of the squad and often has instant emotional reactions that the others don't.

What can we expect from the next Lazarus War novel, Legion?

More action. More explosions. More suspense. Captain Harris is not going to let this rest – he wants to act on the information that he uncovers in *Artefact*, and he finally has hope. Unfortunately for him, in the Lazarus War universe hope can be a terrible thing. There is also a war brewing with the Krell – though they might not be the biggest threat in the galaxy any more. Harris and the Lazarus Legion will push the simulant technology to the very limits, expanding its employment beyond the realms of *Artefact*...

On that topic, how does the simulant technology actually work?

That's classified.

What else do you read and watch in your spare time?

I am a big SF fan and an enthusiastic reader – especially classic SF such as Heinlein and Haldeman. But I'm equally inspired by video games and cinema. I'm an avid fan of the *Alien* and *Predator* universes, in all media, and those have heavily influenced me. I'd love to write a novel set in those universes one day.

introducing

If you enjoyed
THE LAZARUS WAR: ARTEFACT,
look out for

LEGION

The Lazarus War: Book 2
by Jamie Sawyer

1

Hard-drop

Two years after Helios

I made transition in orbit around Maru Prime; a burning hellhole of a planet somewhere in the Quarantine Zone. Or, at least, what was left of the Zone.

I was inside a Wildcat armoured personnel shuttle. My first act in the new body was to activate the holo-photo inside my helmet: Elena on Azure. The tiny icon was tacked to the bottom right of my face-plate. Reminded of who I was fighting for, I moved on to the mission.

"Squad, sound off!"

Four simulant faces stared back at me through the dark: underlit by green safety bulbs inside tactical helmets.

"Affirmative!" Jenkins bellowed back. Callsign CALIFORNIA; the name stencilled onto the chest-plate of her combat-suit.

"Copy," Kaminski said. Callsign BROOKLYN.

"Confirmed," Martinez said. Callsign CRUSADER. He clutched a cheap plastic rosary, the beads woven between armoured fingers.

"Affirmative," came the last, and newest, member of the unit: Private Dejah Mason. The name NEW GIRL had been printed onto her chest but she had no other battle honours, rank badges or insignia.

"We have another successful transition, Major," Jenkins said, nodding enthusiastically inside her helmet.

I was still getting used to the new rank and I wasn't entirely comfortable with being addressed as major. I'd been a captain for so long that being called by a different title felt wrong.

"I have eyes on the other squads," Jenkins added. "All five are inbound per mission plan. All on the timeline. Uploaded to your suit."

"Copy that, Sergeant."

Jenkins' grin broadened so that it filled her face. While my new rank felt unnatural, Jenkins had adopted hers without hesitation.

Uplinks from the commanding officers of the other teams scrolled across my HUD: each confirming successful transition, chirping intel on the approach. A full platoon. Each unit was being transported in a Wildcat APS, like us, and was approaching the designated landing zone.

I flexed my arms and legs. Felt the renewed vigour of transition into a simulant body. It was bigger, stronger, just better than my real body. That lay preserved in a simulator-tank, safely ensconced in the operations centre aboard the UAS *Mallard*.

"What's the op?" Kaminski said. He was chewing gum inside his helmet; I wasn't sure how he'd managed to smuggle food into the dormant sim before we'd made transition. I let it slide.

"Didn't you read the briefing?" Mason asked in disbelief. Voice heavily accented with the Martian burr that Standard seemed to have developed on the red world.

"Baby, I never read the briefing."

Kaminski spoke with practised indifference but I knew that it was only skin deep. His vitals danced across my HUD: his autonomics told of a professional. Kaminski worked hard to maintain his false image – ever the wiseass.

Mason hadn't been a soldier for long, let alone a simulant operator, and she didn't know better. Barely twenty, with the body and face of a college cheerleader. Not the sort of trooper Alliance Command used on propaganda recruitment vids: the idea of one of America's finest getting shredded by Krell stinger fire wouldn't sit well with the folks back home. Mason had some big boots to fill and she was already the sixth replacement that I'd taken on – the other five having failed miserably to meet my expectations. I thought, briefly, of Michael Blake – Mason's distant predecessor – but buried the memory as quickly as it surfaced.

"We're approaching Maru Prime," I said, activating a condensed holo-briefing on my wrist-comp.

Maru Prime was an angry red planet composed entirely of molten lava – star-bright, palpably hot, even at this distance. It had no surface, instead being held together by the dynamics of gravitational and tidal forces far too complex for a grunt like me to understand.

A structure came into view in orbit around Maru, gliding above the roiling lava seas.

"This is Far Eye Observatory."

The facility was a painfully delicate lattice-work construction, a collection of bubble-domes, solar vanes and spherical crew modules. A series of huge radar dishes sat on the station's spine: all pointed into deep-space. Many components had taken obvious damage, with large chunks of the rigging punctured and the whole structure leaning at a precarious angle.

"Two days ago," I explained, "Far Eye began to slide from its orbital position."

"It's being sucked off," said Kaminski, sniggering. "Or sucked down, depending on how you see it."

I ignored Kaminski; doing otherwise would only encourage him.

"The station suffered a malfunction in the primary grav-shunt," I said. "As a result, its orbit is in rapid decline. Command wants us to retrieve the personnel. In particular, they want this man."

The image of a thin-faced Sci-Div officer appeared on all five face-plates. Tanned skin; Persian stock. By Earth-standard years he was in his early fifties. He had dark eyes and hair. A beard, rough-grown, peppered grey.

"Our HVT is Professor Ashan Saul."

HVT: high-value target. I'd already researched Saul – who he was, where he had served. It made for interesting reading. Despite his Iranian heritage, his bloodline was long-retired to the Core Worlds. He was a xenolinguist by profession – specialising in the interpretation of alien language. That particular detail had instantly grabbed my attention. There were also huge empty periods in Saul's scientific career: blocks of time when he was inexplicably absent from recorded duty. Nothing stunk of covert ops involvement quite like an unexplained black line through your last posting.

"So they send six Sim Ops teams out into the Quarantine Zone to rescue one man?" Martinez asked. "Seems like overkill."

"I said we're supposed to bring all personnel back. And it's made more complex by this."

I adjusted the external camera controls, so that a wider graphic of space surrounding Maru Prime became visible. The sector was literally full of activity. Flocks of fighters wove between larger vessels, Alliance ships chasing down Krell bio-fighters.

There were three Alliance warships anchored in high orbit: the *Mallard*, the *Washington's Paragon*, and the *Peace of Seattle*. Assault cruisers with enough onboard firepower to level a small planet. They faced off against six advancing Krell starships of unknown designation, ranging in threat category. The alien vessels were variations on an aquatic theme – black as space, shaped like mutant molluscs.

Both groups were on full offensive: firing torpedoes, railguns, flak cannons. The battlespace within a few thousand klicks was alight with plasma, the immediate and empty explosions of ships dying in vacuum. Tracer fire slid overhead: Alliance tech met with Krell organic equivalents. I picked out the *Mallard* somewhere in the fray – null-shields flaring, laser batteries bristling. Our real bodies, in the *Mallard*'s Simulant Operations Centre, were our vulnerability. One stray missile to the *Mallard*, one missed point-defence reaction, and we'd be open to vacuum.

Our Wildcat was in the thick of the fighting, plummeting to the station below.

"With this much shit going on above our heads," I said, "Command thinks that we will be able to achieve retrieval of Professor Saul without attracting significant enemy attention."

Martinez sucked his teeth. "How long we got?"

I shrugged. "Until Far Eye Station gets eaten by the planet below? Twenty-seven minutes. But we'll be long gone by then. We're going to breach, evac the civvies, then pull out."

"This all sounds a little too easy," Jenkins added. Sarcasm was never her strong point. "What's the complication...?"

On cue, something hit the APS.

A warning chimed in my helmet. Direct from the shuttle: CRITICAL DAMAGE DETECTED!

We were hit, hard enough to slam the boat off course.

The APS swung about, throwing me back into my seat. Reflexively, I grabbed the restraints. The shuttle engines started a throaty, unpleasant roaring: the deck underfoot buckling with each new turn.

I checked my heads-up display; the stream of data projected onto the interior of my combat-suit helmet. I was hardwired into my armoured suit – fully powered, sealed, battle-ready – and what data couldn't be relayed onto the HUD was ported directly into my neural-link. *Shit.* Significant structural damage. The main propulsion unit was compromised. I absorbed the information immediately; was already planning how we could stay combat-effective.

"We'll have to do this the hard way. Looks like you get your complication, Jenkins."

"Great."

There wouldn't be time to correct our approach vector. We would miss our landing window. I patched through to Naval command, aboard the UAS *Mallard*.

"Command, this is Lazarus Actual. Do you read me?"

I'd learnt to embrace the callsign; if everyone was going to call me it, then why resist? Since Helios, it was hard to argue with the suggestion that I always came back.

"Copy, Lazarus Actual, but only just," the anonymous voice of Command replied. "Your bird has suffered a hit."

"I know. I guess we just got unlucky."

"There's a first time for everything, Lazarus. It's a glancing bio-plasma impact. You're losing fuel fast. You want to extract?"

"That's a negative. We're going to make a hard-drop to the outpost."

The officer whistled. "Sure you want to risk it?"

"Not like we have a choice."

"That wasn't what I asked. There are five other teams inbound on the same objective."

"So I'm supposed to let some other simulant outfit claim the prize? We're operational and we're proceeding with the mission."

"Your call, Lazarus. Gaia's luck. Be aware that the drop window is closing fast."

"Affirmative."

"You have your orders. Command out."

"Lazarus Actual out."

The cabin lights flickered, signalling radio silence with the *Mallard*. The craft was now descending at entirely the wrong angle; slamming me against the wall of the passenger cabin.

I turned to my squad. "We're hard-dropping to Maru Prime – straight down the pipe."

"You cannot be serious," Kaminski said. When he was anxious, his Brooklyn accent became thick: like he'd just left New York City. Right now, it was the thickest I'd heard it in a long time. "New Girl ain't up to this."

"My name is Mason. And of course I'm up to this. I'm a trained soldier just like the rest of you."

"Whatever, New Girl. Six transitions ain't the same." Kaminski tapped the numeric badge on his shoulder: one hundred and eighteen deaths so far. "Just looking out for you is all. Once you get your Legion badge, then we can talk some more."

"Quit the chatter," Jenkins ordered. "On the major's mark!"

I unstrapped my safety harness, standing as steadily as I could. That was no easy task: the APS was shaking apart now, caught on a drift in the upper atmosphere of Maru. The mags in my boots automatically kicked in: held me to the deck underfoot. I checked everything I needed was strapped down, locked the plasma rifle to my back-plate. Grenades, power cells, sidearm – anything loose was going to be lost in the descent to the station below.

"Suits sealed!" Jenkins yelled. "On the order, people!"

Martinez and Kaminski were up and out of their harnesses, strapping equipment onto their combat-suits.

We were approaching the station fast. The ugly domed structures spun beneath us as the APS tumbled through the sky. The view was heat-blurred and hazy. *It's going to be hot out there. I hope that the combat-suits can take it.* There would be no way that real skins, even in full EVA gear, could operate in those temperatures. My onboard AI informed me that I could withstand six minutes, thirteen seconds before the heat caused catastrophic damage. *That will have to be long enough,* I decided.

"Let's do this."

The rear access hatch of the APS cycled open and I was immediately accosted by a wave of super-heated atmosphere – nearly strong enough to pull me out of the shuttle. I grappled the overhead safety webbing with one hand and fought the urge to cover my face with the other. That was the natural reaction, because Maru Prime's surface was blindingly bright and exuded heat.

"Fall in!"

We assembled at the rear lock of the APS. The craft circled the base one more time, altitude only a few thousand metres now.

"Don't forget who we are," Jenkins roared over the comm. "Lazarus Legion: prepare for drop."

*   *   *

I took a running jump out of the airlock.

The rest of the squad did the same. Maru Prime had a strong gravitational field – over a gee, according to Science Division's analysis – and I felt it as I launched into the upper atmosphere. The tug of planetary forces was enough to pump the air temporarily from my lungs. My onboard medi-suite issued me with combat-drugs; a mixture of endorphins, analgesics and smart-drugs hit my bloodstream.

My body was like an aerodynamic dart – armoured arms and legs held together to decrease drag. I heard nothing but saw everything. The blinding, furious world beneath me: bubbling, constantly spewing and churning. The prickle of heat on my face, the immediate damp of sweat forming on my brow and my back. The combat-suit attempted to remedy that, atmospheric conditioning working overtime to keep me at optimum combat temperature.

All five of us, in perfect formation, were freefalling to the station below. The actual structure seemed to come up to meet us almost right away, the bare plains of landing bays and storage depots listing precariously.

People, civilians mainly, paid good money for this sort of experience. The serenity of the drop was absolute but it was an acquired taste. One false move, and I'd either be crushed by Maru's gravity, or would fly drastically off course and burn up in the atmosphere.

The trick was riding the momentum of the planet's gravity well *just so*.

"Thrusters!" I yelled.

The Trident Class V was a premium combat-suit, made for battle in space. A full EVA suit but so much more. Of interest to me right now was the onboard manoeuvring system: thrusters incorporated into the backpack unit.

I fired the manoeuvring jets and immediately changed direction. I moved into an upright position, kicked out with both feet and braced to hit the station landing pad. There was a muted hiss as the thrusters fired again, then the wrench of external forces competing with Maru's gravity.

The distance counter inside my helmet began to slow. I held up a hand, watched the armoured glove glow red with heat from the descent. Maru Prime's atmosphere was thin and vapid, so the drop hadn't caused as much frictional heat as it could've done.

"I ... I'm having some trouble out here!" Mason suddenly broke in over the comm.

Shit. With supreme effort, I twisted my head in her direction. Every muscle in my neck felt locked, every bone fused by the opposing forces pulling at me. Because the Legion had done this so many times before I'd been concentrating on my own drop-technique.

Private Mason had never hard-dropped. She spiralled alongside me, maybe a hundred metres off course. Her thruster pack fired – bright blue against the glaring red of the landscape below – and she spun head over heels.

The combat-suits carried an active camouflage suite, made to mimic the surrounding conditions. Her suit flashed an angry red – mirroring the planet below – then, as her body spun, shifted to copy the black starfield above. The armour eventually gave up completely: the onboard AI must've decided that it was impossible to imitate the constantly shifting environment.

"Told you she wasn't ready," Kaminski tutted.

"You want me to fetch her?" Martinez asked. He panted heavily over the comm; even he was finding this taxing.

"I'm the nearest," I said. This was my problem. "Adopt primary drop formation and secure the LZ."

"Affirmative."

I fired my thruster. My descent was slowing, but I was still moving fast, and that made the lateral shift difficult. I pulled alongside the twisting figure.

Up close, I saw the damage that Mason's uncontrolled descent had caused. Her armour plating was blackened, glowing an incandescent white in places, angry blood-red and orange in others. Inside her helmet, her face was a mask of horror – eyes wide and pallor an absolute white.

"I . . . I can't get . . . angle!" she stammered.

"Breathe deep. Focus."

I issued the orders verbally. In my head, I requested that her suit administer a dose of combat-drugs. Almost immediately, her rhythms flattened. It wouldn't be enough to put her out, or even stop her from panicking, but I hoped that it was enough to keep her alive.

"Help me! Please!"

"Fire the thruster in three short bursts." I was becoming increasingly hot; I realised suddenly how far off course Mason had actually drifted. "Just stay with it."

The thrusters were all thought-activated, and a panicked mind implicitly carried delay. She spiralled again and again, armour glowing hotter with every turn: every exposed angle blistering. Streamers of smoke had started rising from the damaged exterior. Unless I helped her, she was going to roast inside the armour.

"Fire the thruster! Now!"

Mason fired and her descent wobbled.

"Oh shit, oh shit, oh shit . . ." she babbled.

"Keep quiet and keep the comms channel clear. Give me your hand."

Mason reached out to me, her gloved fingers spread. I fired my thruster again, edging nearer to her – I could almost feel the heat coming from her frazzled body, more powerful than that emanating from Maru Prime below.

"I can't reach—"

She wobbled some more, spinning again. An alarm sounded in my helmet: SQUAD MEMBER IN CRITICAL CONDITION. *Thanks, I hadn't noticed.*

I reached for her, the tip of my forefinger brushing her arm.

Distance: two hundred metres.

"Reach again!" I shouted.

Then suddenly Mason was upright, her thruster pack firing pure blue. She ground her teeth. Reached with splayed fingers. I grappled with her hand, locking around her wrist.

Distance: one hundred metres.

"Come on, Private. You can do this!"

She nodded firmly, thruster firing in a steady rhythm.

The distance counter slowed even further and suddenly we were over the LZ. The thruster pack gave one last, monumental fire – allowing me almost to hover above the landing pad. My feet touched down on the deck, absorbed the impact through the rest of my body. I stood for a second, breathing deep, enjoying the fact that I was on solid ground.

"You okay?"

Mason's combat-suit had temporarily locked. She sagged inside the armour, sweated forehead touching her inner face-plate.

"Christo," she whispered. "That was a ride. Thanks."

I didn't answer her, just scanned the landing pad. The rest of my squad watched on with something approaching disbelief. They were assembled outside the station's primary airlock with weapons drawn.

"Maybe Kaminski was right when he said that she wasn't ready," Jenkins said.

"She's alive," I answered, using the restricted channel between Jenkins and me. I didn't want Mason's confidence any more bruised than it already was.

"You really want a ride, maybe I can show you sometime," Kaminski said.

Mason didn't bother with a reply.

"Stow that shit," I ordered, back on the general channel. "Get us inside the station and conduct a sweep."

introducing

If you enjoyed
THE LAZARUS WAR: ARTEFACT,
look out for

TRACER

by Rob Boffard

*A huge space station orbits the Earth, holding the last
of humanity. It's broken, rusted, falling apart. We've
wrecked our planet, and now we have to live with the
consequences: a new home that's dirty, overcrowded,
and inescapable.*

*What's more, there's a madman hiding on the station.
He's about to unleash chaos. And when he does, there'll
be nowhere left to run.*

Seven years ago

The ship is breaking up around them.

The hull is twisting and creaking, like it's trying to
tear away from the heat of re-entry. The outer panels are
snapping off, hurtling past the cockpit viewports, black
blurs against a dull orange glow.

The ship's second-in-command, Singh, is tearing at her seat straps, as if getting loose will be enough to save her. She's yelling at the captain, seated beside her, but he pays her no attention. The flight deck below them is a sea of flashing red, the crew spinning in their chairs, hunting for something, anything they can use.

They have checklists for these situations. But there's no checklist for when a ship, plunging belly-down through Earth's atmosphere to maximise the drag, gets flipped over by an explosion deep in the guts of the engine, sending it first into a spin and then into a screaming nosedive. Now it's spearing through the atmosphere, the friction tearing it to pieces.

The captain doesn't raise his voice. "We have to eject the rear module," he says.

Singh's eyes go wide. "Captain—"

He ignores her, reaching up to touch the communicator in his ear. "Officer Yamamoto," he says, speaking as clearly as he can. "Cut the rear module loose."

Koji Yamamoto stares up at him. His eyes are huge, his mouth slightly open. He's the youngest crew member, barely eighteen. The captain has to say his name again before he turns and hammers on the touch-screens.

The loudest bang of all shudders through the ship as its entire rear third explodes away. Now the ship and its crew are tumbling end over end, the movement forcing them back in their seats. The captain's stomach feels like it's broken free of its moorings. He waits for the tumbling to stop, for the ship to right itself. Three seconds. Five.

He sees his wife's face, his daughter's. No, don't think about them. Think about the ship.

"Guidance systems are gone," McCallister shouts, her voice distorting over the comms. "The core's down. I got nothing."

"Command's heard our mayday," Dominguez says. "They—"

McCallister's straps snap. She's hurled out of her chair, thudding off the control panel, leaving a dark red spatter of blood across a screen. Yamamoto reaches for her, forgetting that he's still strapped in. Singh is screaming.

"Dominguez," says the captain. "Patch me through."

Dominguez tears his eyes away from the injured McCallister. A second later, his hands are flying across the controls. A burst of static sounds in the captain's comms unit, followed by two quick beeps.

He doesn't bother with radio protocol. "Ship is on a collision path. We're going to try to crash-land. If we—"

"John."

Foster doesn't have to identify himself. His voice is etched into the captain's memory from dozens of flight briefings and planning sessions and quiet conversations in the pilots' bar.

The captain doesn't know if the rest of flight command are listening in, and he doesn't care. "Marshall," he says. "I think I can bring the ship down. We'll activate our emergency beacon; sit tight until you can get to us."

"I'm sorry, John. There's nothing I can do."

"What are you talking about?"

There's another bang, and then a roar, as if the ship is caught in the jaws of an enormous beast. The captain turns to look at Singh, but she's gone. So is the side of the ship. There's nothing but a jagged gash, the edges a mess of torn metal and sputtering wires. The awful orange glow is coming in, its fingers reaching for him, and he can feel the heat baking on his skin.

"Marshall, listen to me," the captain says, but Marshall is gone too. The captain can see the sky beyond the ship, beyond the flames. It's blue, clearer than he could have ever imagined. It fades to black where it reaches the upper atmosphere, and the space beyond that is pinpricked with stars.

One of those stars is Outer Earth.

Maybe I can find it, the captain thinks, if I look hard enough. He can feel the anger, the disbelief at Marshall's words, but he refuses to let it take hold. He tells himself that Outer Earth will send help. They have to. He tries to picture the faces of his family, tries to hold them uppermost in his mind, but the roaring and the heat are everywhere and he can't—

1

Riley

My name is Riley Hale, and when I run, the world disappears.

Feet pounding. Heart thudding. Steel plates thundering under my feet as I run, high up on Level 6, keeping a good momentum as I move through the darkened corridors. I focus on the next step, on the in–out, push–pull of my breathing. Stride, land, cushion, spring, repeat. The station is a tight warren of crawl-spaces and vents around me, every surface metal etched with ancient graffiti.

"She's over there!"

The shout comes from behind me, down the other end of the corridor. The skittering footsteps that follow it echo off the walls. I thought I'd lost these idiots back at the sector border – now I have to outrun them all over again. I got lost in the rhythm of running – always dangerous when someone's trying to jack your cargo. I refuse to waste a breath on cursing, but one of my exhales turns into a growl of frustration.

The Lieren might not be as fast as I am, but they obviously don't give up.

I go from a jog to a sprint, my pack juddering on my spine as I pump my arms even harder. A tiny bead of sweat touches my eye, sizzling and stinging. I ignore it. No tracer in my crew has ever failed to deliver their cargo, and I am not going to be the first.

I round the corner – and nearly slam into a crush of people. There are five of them, sauntering down the corridor, talking among themselves. But I'm already reacting, pushing off with my right foot, springing in the direction of the wall. I bring my other foot up to meet it, flattening it against the metal and tucking my left knee up to my chest. The momentum keeps me going forwards even as I'm pushing off, exhaling with a whoop as I squeeze through the space between the people and the wall. My right foot comes down, and I'm instantly in motion again. Full momentum. A perfect tic-tac.

The Lieren are close behind, colliding with the group, bowling them over in a mess of confused shouts. But I've got the edge now. Their cries fade into the distance.

There's not a lot you can move between sectors without paying off the gangs. Not unless you know where and how to cross. Tracers do. And that's why we exist. If you need to get something to someone, or if you've got a little package you don't want any gangs knowing about, you come find us. We'll get it there – for a price, of course – and if you come to my crew, the Devil Dancers, we'll get it there *fast*.

The corridor exit looms, and then I'm out, into the gallery. After the corridors, the giant lights illuminating the massive open area are blinding. Corridor becomes catwalk, bordered with rusted metal railings, and the sound of my footfalls fades away, whirling off into the open space.

I catch a glimpse of the diagram on the far wall, still legible a hundred years after it was painted. A scale picture of the station. The Core at the centre, a giant sphere which houses the main fusion reactor. Shooting out from it on either side, two spokes, connected to an enormous ring, the main body. And under it, faded to almost nothing after over a century: Outer Earth Orbit Preservation Module, Founded AD 2234.

Ahead of me, more people emerge from the far entrance to the catwalk. A group of teenage girls, packed tight, talking loudly among themselves. I count ten, fifteen – *no*. They haven't seen me. I'm heading full tilt towards them.

Without breaking stride, I grab the right-hand railing of the catwalk and launch myself up and over, into space.

For a second, there's no noise but the air rushing past me. The sound of the girls' conversation vanishes, like someone turned down a volume knob. I can see all the way down to the bottom of the gallery, a hundred feet below, picking out details snatched from the gaps in the web of criss-crossing catwalks.

The floor is a mess of broken benches and circular flowerbeds with nothing in them. There are two young girls, skipping back and forth over a line they've drawn on the floor. One is wearing a faded smock. I can just make out the word Astro on the back as it twirls around her. A light above them is flickering off–on–off, and their shadows flit in and out on the wall behind them, dancing off metal plates. My own shadow is spread out before me, split by the catwalks; a black shape broken on rusted railings. On one of the catwalks lower down, two men are arguing, pushing each other. One man throws a punch, his target dodging back as the group around them scream dull threats.

I jumped off the catwalk without checking my landing zone. I don't even want to think what Amira would do if she found out. Explode, probably. Because if there's someone under me and I hit them from above, it's not just a broken ankle I'm looking at.

Time seems frozen. I flick my eyes towards the Level 5 catwalk rushing towards me.

It's empty. Not a person in sight, not even further along. I pull my legs up, lift my arms and brace for the landing.

Contact. The noise returns, a bang that snaps my head back even as I'm rolling forwards. On instinct, I twist sideways, so the impact can travel across, rather than up, my spine. My right hand hits the ground, the sharp edges of the steel bevelling scraping my palm, and I push upwards, arching my back so my pack can fit into the roll.

Then I'm up and running, heading for the dark catwalk exit on the far side. I can hear the Lieren reach the catwalk above. They've spotted me, but I can tell by their angry howls that it's too late. There's no way they're making that jump. To get to where I am, they'll have to fight their way through the stairwells on the far side. By then, I'll be long gone.

"Never try outrun a Devil Dancer, boys," I mutter between breaths.